BRENDA JOYCE

A Rose in the Storm

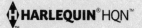

Recycling programs
for this product may
not exist in your area.

ISBN-13: 978-0-373-77770-9

A ROSE IN THE STORM

Printed in U.S.A.

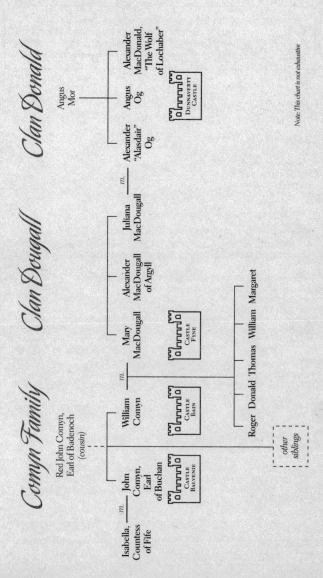

Comyn Family

Isabella, Countess of Fife — *m.* — Red John Comyn, Earl of Badenoch *(cousin)*

John Comyn, Earl of Buchan

CASTLE BALVENIE

William Comyn — *m.* —

CASTLE BAIN

Roger   Donald   Thomas   William   Margaret

other siblings

Clan Dougall

Mary MacDougall   Alexander MacDougall of Argyll   Juliana MacDougall

CASTLE FYNE

— *m.* —

Clan Donald

Angus Mor

Alexander "Alasdair" Og   Angus Og   Alexander MacDonald, "The Wolf of Lochaber"

DUNNAVERTY CASTLE

Note: This chart is not exhaustive

A Rose
in the Storm

CHAPTER ONE

Loch Fyne, the Highlands—February 14, 1306

"IT IS TOO damned quiet."

Will's voice cut through the silence of the Highland afternoon, but Margaret did not hear him. Mounted beside him at the head of a column of knights, soldiers and servants, surrounded by the thick Argyll forest, she stared straight ahead.

Castle Fyne rose out of the ragged cliffs and snow-patched hills above them so abruptly that when one rode out of the forest, as they had just done, one had to blink and wonder at the sight, momentarily mistaking it for soaring black rock. But it was a centuries-old stronghold, precariously perched above the frozen loch below, its lower walls stout and thick, its northern towers and battlements jutting into the pale, winter-gray sky. The forest surrounding the loch and the castle was dusted white, and the mountains in the northwest were snowcapped.

Margaret inhaled. She was overcome with emotion—with pride.

And she thought, *Castle Fyne is mine.*

Once, it had belonged to her mother. Mary MacDougall had been born at Castle Fyne, which had been her dowry in her marriage to William Comyn, which had filled her with great pride. For Castle Fyne was a tremendous prize. Placed on the most western reaches of Argyll, providing a gateway from the Solway Firth, surrounded by lands belonging to Clan Donald and Clan Ruari, the castle had been fought over throughout the centuries. It had been attacked many times, yet it had never once slipped from MacDougall hands.

Margaret trembled, more pride surging within her, for she had adored her mother, and now, the great keep was her dowry, and she would bring it with her in her upcoming marriage. But the anxiety that had afflicted her for the past few weeks, and during this journey, remained. Since the death of her father, she had become the ward of her powerful uncle, John Comyn, the Earl of Buchan. He had recently concluded a union for her. She was betrothed to a renowned knight whom she had never met—Sir Guy de Valence—and he was an Englishman.

"'Tis such a godforsaken place," her brother said, interrupting her thoughts. But he was glancing warily around. "I don't like this. It's too quiet. There are no birds."

She sat her mare beside Will, her only living brother. Suddenly she wondered at the silence, realizing he was right. There was no rustling of underbrush, either, made by chipmunks and squirrels, or the occasional fox or deer—there was no sound other than the jangle of bridles on their horses, and the occasional snort.

Her tension escalated. "Why is it so quiet?"

"Something has chased the game away," Will said.

Their gazes met. Her brother was eighteen—a year older than she was—and blond like their father, whom he had been named after. Margaret had been told she resembled Mary—she was petite, her hair more red than gold, her face heart-shaped.

"We should go," Will said abruptly, gathering up his reins. "Just in case there is more in the hills than wolves."

Margaret followed suit quickly, glancing up at the castle perched high above them. They would be within the safety of its walls in minutes. But before she could urge her mare forward, she recalled the castle in the springtime, with blue and purple wildflowers blooming beneath its walls. And she remembered skipping about the flowers, where a brook bubbled and deer grazed. She smiled, recalling her mother's soft voice as she called her inside. And her handsome father striding into the hall, his mantle sweeping about him, spurs jangling, her four brothers behind him, everyone exhilarated and speaking at once....

She blinked back tears. How she missed her father, her brothers and her beloved mother. How she cherished her legacy now. And how pleased Mary would be, to know that her daughter had returned to Loch Fyne.

But her mother had despised and feared the English. Her family had been at war with the English all her life, only recently coming to a truce. What would Mary think of Margaret's arranged marriage to an Englishman?

She turned to face William, discomfited by her emotions, and in so doing, glanced back at the sixty men and women in the cavalcade behind them. It had been a difficult journey, due mostly to the cold winter and the snow, and she knew that the soldiers and servants were eager to reach the castle. She had not visited the stronghold in a good ten years, and she was eager to reach its warm halls, too. But not just to revisit her few memories. She was worried about her people. Several servants had already complained of frozen fingers and toes.

She would tend them immediately, once they reached the great keep, just as she had seen her mother do.

But the anxiety that had afflicted her for the past few weeks would not go away. She could not pretend that she was not worried about her impending marriage. She meant to be grateful. She knew she was fortunate. Her uncle controlled most of the north of Scotland, his affairs were vast, and he could have simply ignored her circumstances once both her parents had passed. He could have kept her at his home, Balvenie, in some remote tower, and established his own steward at Castle Fyne. He could have sent her to Castle Bain, which William had inherited from their father. Instead, he had decided upon an advantageous political union—one that would elevate her status, as well as serve the great Comyn family.

But another pang went through her as she walked her mare forward on the narrow path leading up to the castle. Her uncle Buchan also despised the English—until this truce, he had warred against them for years. The sudden allegiance made her uneasy.

"I think Castle Fyne is beautiful," she said, hoping she sounded calm and sensible. "Even if it has come to some neglect since Mother's death." She would repair every rotten timber, every chipped stone.

"You would." William grimaced and shook his head. "You are so much like our mother."

Margaret considered that high flattery, indeed. "Mother always loved this place. If she could have resided here, and not at Bain with Father, she would have."

"Mother was a MacDougall when she married our father, and she was a MacDougall when she died," William said, somewhat impatiently. "She had a natural affinity for this land, much like you. Still, you are a Comyn first, and Bain suits you far more than this pile of rock and stone—even if we need it to defend our borders." He studied her seriously. "I still cannot fathom why you wished to come here. Buchan could have sent anyone. I could have come without you."

"When our uncle decided upon this union, I felt the need to come here. Perhaps just to see it for myself, through a woman's eyes, not a child's." She did not add that she had wanted to return to Castle Fyne ever since their mother had died a year and a half ago.

Margaret had grown up in a time of constant war. She could not even count the times the English King Edward had invaded Scotland during her lifetime, or the number of rebellions and revolts waged by men like Andrew Moray, William Wallace and Robert Bruce. Three of her brothers had died fighting the English—Roger at Falkirk, Thomas at the battle of River Cree and Donald in the massacre at Stirling Castle.

Their mother had taken a silly cold after Donald's death. The cough had gotten worse and worse, a fever had joined it, and she had never recovered. That summer, she had simply passed on.

Margaret knew their mother had lost her will to live after the death of three of her sons. And her husband had loved her so much that he had not been able to go on without her. Six weeks later, on a red- and-gold autumn day, their father had gone hunting. He had broken his neck falling from his horse while chasing a stag. Margaret believed he had been deliberately reckless—that he had not cared whether he lived or died.

"At least we are at peace now," she said into the strained silence.

"Are we?" Will asked, almost rudely. "There was no choice but to sue for peace, after the massacre at Stirling Castle. As Buchan said, we must prove our loyalty to King Edward now." His eyes blazed. "And so he has tossed you off to an Englishman."

"It is a good alliance," Margaret pointed out. It was true her uncle Buchan had warred against King Edward for years, but during this time of truce, he wished to protect the family by forging such an allegiance.

"Oh, yes, it is an excellent alliance! You will become a part of a great English family! Sir Guy is Aymer de Valence's bastard brother, and Aymer not only has the ear of the king, he will probably be the next Lord Lieutenant of Scotland. How clever Buchan is."

"Why are you doing this, now?" she cried, shaken. "I have a duty to our family, Will, and I am Buchan's ward! Surely, you do not wish for me to object?"

"Yes, I want you to object! English soldiers killed our brothers."

Will had always had a temper. He was not the most rational of young men. "If I can serve our family in this time of peace, I intend to do so," she said. "I will hardly be the first woman to marry a rival for political reasons."

"Ah, so you finally admit that Sir Guy is a rival?"

"I am trying to do my duty, Will. There is peace in the land, now. And Sir Guy will be able to fortify and defend Castle Fyne—we will be able to keep our position here in Argyll."

He snorted. "And if you were ordered to the gallows? Would you meekly go?"

Her tension increased. Of course she would not meekly go to the gallows—and initially, she had actually considered approaching her uncle and attempting to dissuade him from this course. But no woman in her position would ever do such a thing. The notion was insane. Buchan would not care for her opinion, and he would be furious with her.

Besides, so many Scots had lost their titles and lands in the years before the recent peace, forfeited to the Crown, to be given to King Edward's allies. Buchan had not lost a single keep. Instead, he was marrying his niece to a great English knight. If a bargain had been made, it was a good one—for everyone, including herself.

"So, Meg—what will you do if after you are married, Sir Guy thinks to keep you at his estate in Liddesdale?"

Margaret felt her heart lurch. She had been born at Castle Bain in the midst of Buchan territory. Nestled amidst the great forests there, Castle Bain was her father's birthright and her home. Their family had also spent a great deal of time at Balvenie, the magnificent stronghold just to the east where Buchan so often resided.

Both of those Comyn castles were very different from Castle Fyne, but they were all as Scottish as the Highland air she was now breathing. The forests were thick and impenetrable. The mountains were craggy, peaks soaring. The lochs below were stunning in their serenity. The skies were vividly blue, and no matter the time of year, the winds were brisk and chilling.

Liddesdale was in the borderlands—it was practically the north of England. It was a flat land filled with villages, farms and pastures. Upon being knighted, Sir Guy had been awarded a manor there.

She could not imagine residing in England. She did not even wish to consider it. "I would attempt to join him when he visited Castle Fyne. In time, he will be awarded other estates, I think. Mayhap I will be allowed to attend all of his lands."

William gave her a penetrating look. "You may be a woman, Meg, and you may pretend to be dutiful, but we both know you are exactly like Mother in one single way—you are stubborn, when so moved. You will never settle in England."

Margaret flushed. She did not consider herself stubborn. She considered herself gentle and kind. "I will cross that bridge when I come to it. I have great hopes for this union."

"I think you are as angry about it as I am, and as afraid. I also think you are pretending to be pleased."

"I am pleased," she said, a bit sharply. "Why are you pressing me this way, now? June is but a few months away! I have come here to restore the keep, so it is somewhat pleasing when Sir Guy first sees it. Do you hope to dismay me?"

"No—I do not want to distress you. But I have tried to discuss this handfast several times—and you change the subject or run away. Damn it. I have many doubts about this union, and knowing you as well as I do, I know you are afraid, too." He said softly, "And we only have each other now."

He was right. If she dared be entirely honest with herself, she was worried, dismayed and afraid. But she then looked away.

"He may be English but he is a good man, and he has been knighted for his service to the king." She was echoing her uncle now. "I was told he is handsome, too." She could not smile, although she wished to. "He is eager for this union, Will, and surely that is a good sign." When he simply stared, she added, "My marriage will not change our relationship."

"Of course it will," William said flatly. "What will you do when this *peace* fails?"

Margaret tried not to allow any dread to arise. "Our uncle does not think this peace will fail," she finally said. "To make such a marriage, he must surely believe it will endure."

"No one thinks it will endure!" William cursed. "You are a pawn, Meg, so he can keep his lands, when so many of us have had our lands and titles forfeited for our so-called treason! Father would never have allowed this marriage!"

Again, William was right. "Buchan is our lord now. I do not want him to lose his lands, Will."

"Nor do I! Didn't you overhear our uncle and Red John last week, when they spent an hour cursing Edward, swearing to overthrow the English—vowing revenge for William Wallace!"

Margaret felt ill. She had been seated in a corner of the hall with Isabella, Buchan's pretty young wife, sewing. She had deliberately eavesdropped—and she had heard their every word.

How she wished she had not. The great barons of Scotland were furious with the humiliation King Edward had delivered upon them by stripping all her powers—she would now be ruled by an Englishman, an appointee of King Edward's. There were fines and taxes being levied upon every yeoman, farmer and noble. She would now be taxed to pay for England's wars with France and the other foreign powers he battled with. He would even force the Scots to serve in his armies.

But the coup de grâce had been the brutal execution of William Wallace. He had been dragged by horse, hanged, cut down while still alive, disemboweled and beheaded.

Every Scot, whether Highlander or lowlander, prince or pauper, baron or farmer, was stricken by the barbaric execution of the brave Scottish rebel. Every Scot wanted revenge.

"Of course my marriage was made for politics," she said, aware that her voice sounded strained. "No one marries for affection. I expected a political alliance. We are allies of the Crown now."

"I did not say you should have a love match. But our

uncle is hardly an ally of King Edward's! This is beyond politics. He is throwing you away."

Margaret would never admit to him that if she dared think about it, she might feel just that way—as if she had been thoughtlessly and carelessly used by her uncle for his own ends—as if she had been casually tossed away, to serve him in this singular moment before his loyalties changed again. "I wish to do my part, Will. I want to keep the family strong and safe."

William moved his horse close, lowering his voice. "He hardly has a claim, but I think Red John will seek the throne, if not for himself, then perhaps for King Balliol's son."

Margaret's eyes widened. Red John Comyn, the Lord of Badenoch, was chief of the entire Comyn family, and lord even over Buchan. He was like another uncle to her—but truly he was a very distant cousin. Her brother's words did not surprise her—she had overheard such speculation before—but now she realized that if Red John sought the throne, or attempted to put the former Scottish King John Balliol's boy Edward upon it, Buchan would support him, leaving her married to an Englishman and on the other side of the great war that would surely ensue.

"Those are rumors," she said.

"Yes, they are. And everyone knows that Robert Bruce still has his eye upon the Scottish throne," William said with some bitterness. The Comyns hated Robert Bruce, just as they had hated his father, Annandale.

Margaret was becoming frightened. If Red John sought the throne—if Robert Bruce did—there would be another war, she felt certain. And she would be on the opposite side as an Englishman's wife. "We must pray for this peace to hold."

"It will never hold. I am going to lose you, too."

She was taken aback. "I am getting married, not going to the Tower or the gallows. You will not lose me."

"So tell me, Meg, when there is war, if you become loyal to him—to Sir Guy and Aymer de Valence—how will you be loyal to me?" His expression one of revulsion and anger, William spurred his gelding ahead of her.

Margaret felt as if he had struck her in the chest. She kicked her mare forward, hurrying after him, aware that he wasn't as angry as he was afraid.

But she was afraid, too. If there was another war, her loyalty was going to be put to a terrible test. And sooner or later, there would be another war—she simply knew it. Peace never lasted, not in Scotland.

Dismay overcame her. Could she be loyal to her family and her new husband? And if so, how? Wouldn't she have to put her new husband first?

Her gaze had become moist. She lifted her chin and squared her shoulders, reminding herself that she was a grown woman, a Comyn and a MacDougall, and she had a duty to her family now—and to herself. "We will never be enemies, Will."

He glanced back at her grimly. "We had better pray that something arises to disrupt your marriage, Meg."

Suddenly Sir Ranald, one of Buchan's young knights— a handsome freckled Scot of about twenty-five—rode up to them. "William! Sir Neil thinks he has seen a watch in the trees atop the hill!"

Margaret's heart lurched with a new fear as William paled and cursed. "I knew it was too damn quiet! Is he certain?"

"He is almost certain—and a watch would scare the wildlife away."

Sir Ranald had ridden in front of them, blocking their

way, and they had stopped on the narrow path. Margaret now realized that the forest surrounding them wasn't just quiet, it was unnaturally silent—unnervingly so.

"Who would be watching us?" Margaret whispered harshly. But she did not have to ask—she knew.

MacDonald land was just beyond the ridge they rode below.

Margaret looked at Sir Ranald, who returned her gaze, his grim. "Who else but a MacDonald?"

Margaret shivered. The enmity between her mother's family and the MacDonald clan went back hundreds of years. The son of Angus Mor, Alexander Og—known as Alasdair—was Lord of Islay, and his brother Angus Og was Lord of Kintyre. The bastard brother, Alexander MacDonald, was known as the Wolf of Lochaber. The MacDougalls had been warring against the MacDonalds over lands in Argyll for years.

She looked up at the forest-clad hillside. She saw nothing and no one in the snowy firs above.

"We only have a force of fifty men," Will said grimly. "But there are four dozen men garrisoned at the castle— or so we think."

"Let's hope that Sir Neil saw a hunter from a hunting party," Sir Ranald said. "Master William, you and your sister need to be behind the castle walls as soon as possible."

William nodded, glancing at Margaret. "We should ride immediately for the keep."

They were in danger, for if the MacDonald brothers meant to attack, they would do so with far more than fifty men. Margaret glanced fearfully around. Not even a branch was moving on the hillside. "Let us go," she agreed.

Sir Ranald stood in his stirrups, half turning to face

the riders and wagons below. He held up his hand and flagged the cavalcade forward.

Will spurred his bay stallion into a trot, and Margaret followed.

IT REMAINED ABSOLUTELY silent as their cavalcade passed through the barbican, approaching the raised drawbridge before the entry tower. Margaret was afraid to speak, wondering at the continuing silence, for word had been sent ahead by messenger, declaring their intention to arrive. Of course, messages could be intercepted, and messengers could be waylaid—even though the land was supposedly at "peace." But then heads began popping up on the ramparts of the castle walls, adjacent the gatehouse. And then murmurs and whispers could be heard.

"'Tis Buchan's nephew and niece…."

"'Tis Lady Margaret and Master William Comyn…."

Their cavalcade had halted, most of it wedged into the barbican. Sir Ranald cupped his hands and shouted up at the tower, to whomever was on watch there. "I am Sir Ranald of Kilfinnan, and I have in my keeping Lady Margaret Comyn and her brother, Master William. Lower the bridge for your mistress."

Whispers sounded from the ramparts. The great drawbridge groaned as it was lowered. Margaret saw some children appear on the battlements above, as she gazed around, suddenly making eye contact with an older woman close to the entry tower. The woman's eyes widened; instinctively, Margaret smiled.

"'Tis Lady Mary's daughter!" the old woman cried.

"'Tis Mary MacDougall's daughter!" another man cried, with more excitement.

"Mary MacDougall's daughter!" others cried.

Margaret felt her heart skid wildly when she realized

what was happening—these good folk remembered her mother, their mistress, whom they had revered and loved, and she was being welcomed by them all now. Her vision blurred.

These were her kin. These were her people, just as Castle Fyne was hers. They were welcoming her, and in return, she must see to their welfare and safety, for she was their lady now.

She smiled again, blinking back the tears. From the ramparts, someone cheered. More cheers followed.

Sir Ranald grinned at her. "Welcome to Castle Fyne, Lady," he teased.

She quickly wiped her eyes and recovered her composure. "I had forgotten how much they adored my mother. Now I remember that they greeted her this way, with a great fanfare, when I was a child, when she returned here."

"She was a great lady, so I am not surprised," Sir Ranald said. "Everyone loved Lady Mary."

William touched her elbow. "Wave," he said softly.

She was startled, but she lifted her hand tentatively and the crowd on the ramparts and battlements and in the entry tower roared with approval. Margaret was taken aback. She felt herself flush. "I am hardly a queen."

"No, but this is your dowry and you are their mistress." William smiled at her. "And they have not had a lady of the manor in years."

He gestured, indicating that she should precede him, and lead the way over the drawbridge into the courtyard. Margaret was surprised, and she looked at Sir Ranald, expecting him to lead the way. He grinned again, with a dimple, and then deferentially bowed his head. "After you, Lady Margaret," he said.

Margaret nudged her mare forward, the crowd cheer-

ing again as she crossed the drawbridge and entered the
courtyard. She felt her heart turn over hard. She halted
her mare and dismounted before the wooden steps leading up to the great hall's front entrance. As she did, the
door opened and several men hurried out, a tall, gray-
haired Scot leading the way.

"Lady Margaret, we have been expecting ye," he said,
beaming. "I am Malcolm MacDougall, yer mother's
cousin many times removed, and steward of this keep."

He was clad only in the traditional linen leine most
Highlanders wore, with knee-high boots and a sword
hanging from his belt. Although bare-legged, and without
a plaid, he clearly did not mind the cold as he came down
the steps and dropped to one knee before her. "My lady,"
he said with deference. "I hereby vow my allegiance and
my loyalty to you above all others."

She took a deep breath, trembling. "Thank you for
your oath of fealty."

He stood, his gaze now on her face. "Ye look so much
like yer mother!" He then turned to introduce her to his
two sons, both young, handsome men just a bit older than
she was. Both young men swore their loyalty, as well.

William and Sir Ranald had come forward, and more
greetings were exchanged. Sir Ranald then excused himself to help Sir Neil garrison their men. William stepped
aside with him, and Margaret was distracted, instantly
wanting to know what they were discussing, as they were
deliberately out of her earshot.

"Ye must be tired," Malcolm said to her. "Can I show
ye to yer chamber?"

Margaret glanced at William—still in a serious and
hushed conversation. She felt certain they were discussing the possibility of an enemy scout having been on the
hillside above them, watching their movements. "I am

tired, but I do not want to go to my chamber just yet. Malcolm, has there been any sign of discord around Loch Fyne lately?"

His eyes widened. "If ye mean have we skirmished with our neighbors, of course we have. One of the Mac-Ruari lads raided our cattle last week—we lost three cows. They are as bold as pirates, using the high seas to come and go as they please! And the day after, my sons found a MacDonald scout just to the east, spying on us. It has been some time, months, truly, since we have seen any MacDonald here."

She felt herself stiffen. "How do you know that it was a scout from clan Donald?"

Malcolm smiled grimly. "We questioned him rather thoroughly before we let him go."

She did not like the sound of that, and she shivered.

He touched her arm. "Let me take ye inside, lady, it's far too cold fer ye to be standing here on such a day, when we have so little sun."

Margaret nodded, as William returned to her side. She gave him a questioning look but he ignored her, gesturing that she follow Malcolm up the stairs. Disappointed, she complied.

The great hall at the top of the stairs was a large stone chamber with high, raftered ceiling, a huge fireplace on one wall. A few arrow slits let in some scant light. Two large trestle tables were centered in the room, benches on their sides, and three carved chairs with cushioned seats sat before the hearth. Pallets for sleeping were stacked up against the far walls. A large tapestry of a battle scene completed the room, hanging on the center wall.

Margaret sniffed appreciatively. The rushes were fresh and scented with lavender oil. And suddenly she smiled—remembering that the hall had smelled of lavender when she had last been present as a child.

Malcolm smiled. "Lady Mary insisted upon fresh rushes every third day, and she especially liked the lavender. We hoped you would like it, too."

"Thank you," Margaret said, moved. "I do."

The servants they had brought with them were now busy bringing their personal belongings, which filled several large chests, into the hall. Margaret espied her lady's maid, Peg, who was three years older than she was and married to one of Buchan's archers. She had known Peg for most of her life, and they were good friends. Margaret excused herself and hurried over to her. "Are you freezing?" she asked, taking her cold hands in hers. "How are your blisters?" She was concerned.

"Ye know how I hate the cold!" Peg exclaimed, shivering. She was as tall and voluptuous as Margaret was slender and petite, with dark auburn hair. She wore a heavy wool plaid over her ankle-length leine, but she was shivering anyway. "Of course I am freezing, and it has been a very long journey, too long, if ye ask me!"

"But we have arrived, and safely—no easy feat," Margaret pointed out.

"Of course we arrived safely—there is no one at war now," Peg scoffed. Then, "Margaret, yer hands are ice cold! I knew we should have made camp earlier! Yer frozen to the bone, just as I am!"

"I was cold earlier, but I am not frozen to the bone, and I am so pleased to be here." Margaret looked around the hall again. She almost expected her mother to appear from an empty doorway, smiling at her as she entered the room.

She then shook herself free of such a fanciful thought. But she had never missed her more.

"I am going to light a fire in yer room," Peg said firmly. "We cannot have ye catching an ague before ye marry yer English knight."

Margaret met her steadfast gaze grimly. From her tone, she knew that Peg hoped she would catch a cold and be incapable of attending her own June wedding.

She did not fault her. Peg was a true Scotswoman. She hated the MacDonalds and several other rival clans, but she also hated the English bitterly. She had been aghast when she had learned of Margaret's betrothal. Being outspoken, she had ranted and raved for some time, until Margaret had had to command her to keep her tongue.

While they were in some agreement on the subject of her wedding, Peg's opinions simply did not help.

"I believe my mother's chamber is directly atop the stairwell," Margaret said. "I think that is a good idea. Why don't you make a fire and prepare the room. And then see to supper."

Margaret wasn't hungry, but she wanted to wander about her mother's home with some privacy. She watched Peg hurry away to harangue a young lad who was in charge of her chest. As they started for the stairwell leading to the north tower where her chamber was, Margaret followed.

Because the keep was so old, the ceiling was low, so low most men had to go up the stairwell hunched over. Margaret did not have to duck her head, and she went past the second landing, where her chamber was. She glanced inside as she did so, noticing the open shutters on a single window, the heavy wooden bed, and her chest, brought with them from Balvenie. Peg was already inspecting the hearth. Margaret quickly continued up the stairs, before her maid might object. The third level opened onto the ramparts.

Margaret left the tower, walking over to the crenellated wall. It was frigidly cold now, as the afternoon was late, the sun dull in an already cloudy sky. She pulled her dark red mantle closer.

The views were magnificent from where she now stood. The loch below the castle was crusted with thick ice near the shore, but the center was not frozen, and she knew that the bravest sailors might still attempt to traverse it, and often did, even in the midst of winter. The far shore seemed to be nothing but heavy forest.

She glanced south, at the path they had taken up to the keep. It was narrow and steep, winding up the hillside, the loch below it. From where she stood, she could see the adjacent glen. A wind was shifting the huge trees in the forest there.

It was breathtaking, beautiful. She wrapped her arms around herself, suddenly fiercely glad that she had come to Castle Fyne, even if it was on the eve of her marriage to an Englishman.

Then she stared at the glen below more sharply— it was as if the forest were moving, a solid phalanx of trees marching, up the hill, toward the castle.

A bell above her began to toll. Margaret stiffened. There was no mistaking the shrill warning sound. And suddenly there were racing footsteps behind her, going past her. Men began rushing from the tower she had just left, bows over their shoulders, slings filled with arrows. They ran to take up defensive positions upon the castle's walls!

Margaret cried out, leaning over the ramparts, staring at the thickly forested glen—and at the army moving through it.

"Margaret! Lady Margaret!"

Someone was shouting for her from within. She could

not move or respond. She was in disbelief, and the bells were shrieking madly above her.

Her heart lurched with sickening force. The forest wasn't marching toward her—it was hundreds of men, an army, carrying huge, dark banners....

The archers were now upon the walls, taking up positions clearly meant to defend the castle from the invaders. Margaret rushed inside and down the steep, narrow stone staircase, slipping on the slick stone, but clutching the wall to prevent herself from falling.

William was in the hall, one hand on the hilt of his sword, his face pale. "We are under attack. There was a damned scout, Meg, watching us as we rode in! Were you on the ramparts? Did you see who is marching on us?"

Her heart was thundering. "I could not see their colors. But the banners are dark—very dark!"

They exchanged intense looks. The MacDonald colors were blue, black and a piping of red.

"Is it Clan Donald?" she cried.

"I would imagine so," Will said harshly, two bright spots of color now on his cheeks.

"Will!" She seized his arm, and realized how badly she was shaking. "I hardly counted, but by God, I think there are hundreds of men approaching! They are so deep in rank and file, they could not fit upon the path we followed—they are coming up the glen below the ridge!"

He cursed terribly. "I am leaving my five best knights with you."

It was so hard to think clearly now—as she had never been in a battle before, or in a castle about to be attacked. "What do you mean?"

"We will fight them off, Meg—we have no choice!"

She could not think at all now! "You cannot go to battle! You cannot fight off hundreds of men with our dozen knights and our few foot soldiers! And you cannot leave five knights with me! You would need every single one of them."

"Since when do you know anything about battle?" he cried in frustration. "And our Comyn knights are worth ten times what any MacDonald brings."

Oh, how she hoped he was right. Peg came racing into the chamber, her face so white it was ghostly. Margaret held out her hand and her lady's maid rushed to her side, clasping her hand tightly. "It will be all right," Margaret heard herself say.

Peg looked at her with wide, terrified eyes. "Everyone is saying it is Alexander MacDonald—the mighty Wolf of Lochaber."

Margaret just looked at her, hoping she had misheard.

Sir Ranald rushed into the hall with Malcolm. "We will have to hurry, William, and try to entrap their army in the ravine. They cannot traverse the glen for much longer—they will have to take a smaller path that joins the one we came on. If we can get our men positioned above the ravine, there is a chance that we can pick them off, one by one and two by two—and they will not be able to get out of it alive."

Was there hope, then? "Peg just said that it is the bastard brother."

William became paler. Even Sir Ranald, the most courageous of their men, was still, his eyes wide and affixed to her.

One of Malcolm's sons rushed inside, breaking the tension but confirming their fears. "It's the Wolf," he said grimly, eyes ablaze. "It's Angus Mor's bastard, the Wolf of Lochaber, and he has five or six hundred men."

Margaret was deafened by her own thundering heartbeat. The Wolf of Lochaber was a legend in his own time. Everyone knew of Alexander MacDonald. It was said that no Highlander was as ruthless. It was said that he had never lost a battle. And it was said that he had never let his enemy live.

Dread consumed her. Margaret thought about the legend she had heard, gripping Peg's hand more tightly.

Just a few years ago, Alexander had wished to marry his lover, the widowed daughter of Lord MacDuff, but he had been refused. So he had besieged the castle at Glen Carron in Lochaber. And when it finally surrendered, he had taken the laird prisoner, forced him to his knees, and made him watch as he coldly and ruthlessly executed those who had fought against him. He then burned Glen Carron to the ground. He had been about to hang Lord MacDuff, but his lover had begged for mercy. The Wolf had spared his future father-in-law's life, but only after forcing him to swear fealty to him—and then he had kept him prisoner for several years. As for his lover, they were immediately married, but she died in childbirth a few months later.

If Alexander MacDonald was marching upon them, with hundreds of men, he would take Castle Fyne and he might destroy it before he was done.

"What should we do?" She did not know if she had ever been as afraid. But even as she spoke, a fierce comprehension began. Her question was foolish. They must defend the keep. Didn't they have the combined force of about a hundred men with which to do so?

Sir Ranald was grim. "There are two choices, Lady Margaret. Surrender or fight."

She inhaled. No Comyn and no MacDougall would consider surrender without a fight first.

"We will surprise him with an ambush at the ravine and stop him," William said. He looked at Sir Ranald and Sir Neil, who had joined them, and Malcolm and his son. "Can such an ambush succeed?"

There was a hesitation—Sir Ranald exchanged glances with Sir Neil. "It is our only hope," Sir Neil said.

Margaret felt her heart lurch with more dread. Peg seemed to moan at her side. Maybe the stories weren't true, maybe God would help them—maybe, this one time, the Wolf would suffer defeat.

"We will ambush them at the ravine, then," William said. "But Margaret—I want you to return to Bain, immediately."

"You want me to *flee?*"

"You will do so with Sir Ranald and Sir Neil. If you leave now, you will be well out of any danger."

Her mind was spinning—as if she was being whirled about while upside down. She could not leave! She glanced around at the women and children who had crowded into the hall. The menfolk, even the most elderly, were on the ramparts, preparing for battle.

Sir Ranald took her elbow. "He is right. You must be taken out of harm's way. This castle belongs to you, which makes you a valuable bride—and a valuable prisoner."

A chill swept over her. But she shrugged free. "I am not a coward—and I am not about to become anyone's prisoner. I am lady of this keep! I can hardly flee like a coward, leaving you here, alone, to defend it. And what of the men, women and children here? Who welcomed me so warmly?"

"Damn it, Margaret, that is why you must go— because the castle is a part of your dowry. It makes you too damned valuable!" William shouted at her now.

She wanted to shout back. Somehow, she did not. "You go and you turn Alexander MacDonald back. In fact, do your best to make certain he never returns here! Ambush him in the ravine. Kill him, if you can!"

Peg gasped.

But Margaret's mind was clear now. William would ride out with their men to fight the notorious Wolf of Lochaber. And if they could kill him, so be it. He was the enemy!

Sir Ranald turned. "Malcolm, send someone to the Earl of Argyll and another man to Red John Comyn."

The Earl of Argyll—Alexander MacDougall—was her mother's brother and he and Red John would surely come to their rescue. But both men were a day's ride away, at least. And neither might be in residence; word might have to be sent farther afield.

Margaret stared as Malcolm rushed off, her mind racing. Sir Ranald said grimly to her, "If our ambush does not succeed, you will need help to defend the keep."

It was hard to comprehend him now, and just as hard to breathe. "What are you saying?"

William spoke to Sir Ranald. "Should we prepare the ambush with the men we came with? And leave the castle garrison here?"

Margaret tried to think—why would they leave fifty men at the keep? And just as it dawned on her, Sir Ranald turned to face her. "You must prepare the castle for a siege."

Her fear confirmed, she choked. She knew nothing of battles, and less of sieges. She was a woman—one of seventeen! "You will not fail!"

His smile was odd—almost sad, as if he expected the worst, not the best. "We do not intend to fail. And I hate leaving you, Lady Margaret, but we are undermanned— your brother needs me."

She was shaking now. She prayed William and Sir

Ranald would succeed in turning back Alexander Mac-Donald. "Of course you must go with William."

William laid his hand on Sir Neil's shoulder. "Stay with my sister and defend her, with your life, if need be."

Sir Neil's mouth hardened. Margaret knew he wanted to fight with William and Sir Ranald, but he nodded. "I will keep her safe and out of all harm," he said harshly.

Margaret had the urge to weep. How could this be happening?

Malcolm rushed back into the hall. "I have sent Seoc Macleod and his brother. No one knows these forests the way they do."

Suddenly Margaret thought about how bad the roads were—how thick with snow. Both men—Argyll and Red John—might be close, but reaching them would not be easy, not in the dead of winter.

"If we succeed in the ambush, we will not need Argyll or Red John," Will said. He looked to Margaret. "If we fail, and he besieges this keep, it will be up to you to hold him off until our uncle or our cousin arrive."

Their gazes had locked. She could only think of her utter lack of battle experience. William, who had been fighting the English since he was twelve, smiled at her. "Sir Neil will be at your side—and so will Malcolm."

She managed to nod, fearfully. Then, wetting her lips, she said, "You will not fail, William. I have faith in you. God will see to our triumph. You will destroy MacDonald in the ravine."

William suddenly kissed her cheek, turned and strode from the room, his huge sword swinging against his thigh. The other Buchan knights followed him, but Sir Ranald did not move, looking at her.

Margaret hugged herself. "Godspeed, Sir Ranald."

"God keep you safe, Lady Margaret." He hesitated, as if he wished to say more.

Margaret waited, but he only nodded at Sir Neil and Malcolm, then he ran after William and the others.

Margaret heard the heavy door slam closed and felt her knees buckle as they left. She was about to sink onto the closest bench, just for a moment, when she realized that every woman and child in the room was staring at her. The great hall was absolutely silent. Slowly, she turned around, scanning the faces of everyone present—noting each fearful and expectant expression.

She had to reassure them.

Yet what could she say, when she was so frightened? When their lives might well rest in her clumsy hands?

Margaret straightened her spine, squared her shoulders. She smiled, firmly. "My brother will succeed in driving the Wolf back," she said. "But we will prepare for a siege. Start every fire. Bring up the casks of oil from the cellars. Begin boiling oil and water." Peg stared at her, her mouth hanging open, and Margaret realized her tone had been oddly firm, so strangely commanding and decisive.

Margaret lifted her chin and added, "Bring up the stockpiles of rocks and stones. Prepare the catapults. And as soon as William has left, raise the drawbridge and lock it and set up the barricade."

Murmurs of acquiescence greeted her. And as everyone left to do her bidding, Margaret prayed William would chase the Wolf of Lochaber away.

CHAPTER TWO

MARGARET STARED ACROSS the castle's ramparts, feeling as if she had been transported to a different place and an earlier, frightening time. The battlements she had walked earlier no longer resembled any castle she had ever visited in her lifetime. Trembling, she hugged her mantle to her cold body.

The ramparts were crowded with casks of oil, piles of rock and stone, slings and catapults of various sizes, and a dozen pits for fires. All the women of the keep were present, as were a great deal of children—they had sorted through the rocks and stones, assembling the various piles by size and weight, while preparing the pits for the fires they might later light, some still coming and going with armloads of wood. Although the drawbridge was closed, a small side entrance in the north tower was being used now. Margaret had quickly realized that they could not run out of wood for the fires, or oil, or stones. Not if they were besieged.

Her archers remained at the walls. Perhaps fortunately—for so she was thinking—they only had two walls to defend. Because the keep was on the cliff overlooking the loch, two of its sides were insurmountable. They had three dozen archers on the vulnerable walls, and quivers of spare arrows were lined up behind each man. Another dozen warriors stood beside the archers, armed with swords, maces and daggers.

Margaret did not have to ask about the extra dozen soldiers. Although she had never been in a siege, she took one look at them and knew what their use might be: if the walls were successfully scaled, the archers would become useless. The battle for control of the castle would turn into hand-to-hand combat.

Margaret stared down at the glen, where the huge MacDonald army was gathered. It had not moved for the past three hours.

How she prayed that meant that William and Sir Ranald were picking off each and every enemy soldier as the Wolf attempted to traverse the ravine.

She felt a movement behind her and half turned. Malcolm smiled at her. If he was afraid, he had given no sign, but then, everyone seemed terribly brave. Margaret was so impressed with the courage of her people. She hoped that no one knew how her heart thudded, how lightheaded she felt—how frightened and nervous she was.

"Has there been any word?" she whispered. Malcolm had sent two scouts out earlier to report on the ambush.

"Our watch has not returned," he said. "But it is a good sign that the Wolf cannot move his men forward."

She shivered. Hadn't she also heard that the Wolf had a terrible temper? He would be furious at being thwarted. Unless, of course, he was dead.

How she prayed that was the case!

"Ye should go down, my lady," Malcolm said kindly. "I ken ye wish to hearten the men and women, but it is growing very cold out, and if ye sicken, ye will dishearten them all."

Margaret remarked Sir Neil, on the other side of the ramparts, as he and an elderly Highlander attempted to fix one of the catapults. Peg was with them, apparently telling them how she thought it best repaired. Had the situation not been so dire, Margaret would have been amused, for Peg was so nosy all of the time. And she was also a bit of a tease, and Sir Neil was terribly handsome with his fair complexion and dark hair.

He had been indefatigable. She did not know him well, but she was impressed with his tireless efforts on behalf of the keep—on her behalf.

Of course, if they were besieged and defeated, they would all die.

She looked at Malcolm. "Is it true?" She kept her voice low, so no one would overhear her. "That the Wolf slays all of his enemies—that he never allows the enemy to live?"

Malcolm hesitated, and she had her answer. "I dinna ken," he said, with a shrug meant to convey ignorance.

How could such barbarism be possible? "Have you met him?"

Malcolm started. "Aye, my lady, I have."

"Is he a monster, as claimed?"

Malcolm's eyes widened. "Are such claims made? He is a powerful soldier—a man of great courage—and great ambition. 'Tis a shame he is our enemy and not our friend."

"I hope he is dead."

"He will not die in an ambush, he is far too clever," Malcolm said flatly. And then his gaze veered past her and he paled.

Margaret whirled to stare down into the glen and she choked. The army was moving, a slow rippling forward, like a huge wave made of men. "What does that mean?" she cried.

Before Malcolm could answer, Sir Neil came running across the ramparts with a red-haired Highlander, Peg following them both. "Lady Margaret," Sir Neil said.

"One of our watch has returned and he wishes a word with you!"

Margaret took one look at the watchman's frozen face and knew the news was not what she wished for it to be. And while she wanted to shout at him to declare the tidings, she held up her hand. "You are?"

"Coinneach MacDougall, my lady."

"Please, step aside with me. Malcolm, Sir Neil, you may join us." Her heart was thundering, aware that everyone upon the battlements was gazing at them. She led the three men down the narrow stairwell and into the great hall, where she turned to face them. "What happened?" She kept her tone quiet and calm.

"The ambush has failed, my lady. The Wolf and his army are passing through the ravine now. Within an hour, they will be at our front gates," Coinneach said, his expression was one of dismay.

She knew she must not allow her knees to give way—not now. "Are you certain?"

"Yes. Some dozen of his knights are in the pass, even now."

Margaret stared at him, unseeingly. "My brother? Sir Ranald?"

"I dinna ken, my lady."

She supposed no news was better than the news of their deaths. Please God, she thought, let William and Sir Ranald be alive—please!

She did not think she could bear it if she lost her brother.

"Do you know if any of our men are alive?" she asked.

"I saw a handful of yer knights, my lady, fleeing into the forest."

She breathed hard. "They will return here, if they can." She had no doubt.

"It might be better if they rode hard and fast for Red John or Argyll," Sir Neil said. "We will soon be under siege, and they could attack MacDonald from the rear."

Maybe her men were not returning, after all. She squashed her instant dismay, turning back to Coinneach. "Is the Wolf—is Alexander MacDonald—alive?"

"Aye—he is at the very front of his men," Coinneach said, his blue eyes now reflecting fear.

She felt sick.

Footsteps pounded down the stairwell, and they all turned toward the sound. Peg skidded into the hall, her eyes wide. "A man is below, outside the barbican—with a white flag!"

Margaret was confused. She turned to Malcolm, who said quickly, "The Wolf has sent a messenger ahead, my lady, I have little doubt."

She felt her eyes widen. "What could he possibly want?"

"Yer surrender."

MARGARET PACED FOR the next half an hour, as she waited for Sir Neil and Malcolm to disarm the messenger—verifying that was what he was—and then bring him safely and securely to her. Peg sat on one of the benches at one of the trestle tables, staring at her, her expression aghast. Margaret was accustomed to her friend's wit and humor, not to her silence and abject fear.

She turned as they entered through the front door, having used the narrow side entrance in the north tower. A tall Highlander in the blue, black and red plaid walked inside, between Sir Neil and Malcolm. He was middle-aged, bearded and lean. He had been disarmed—his scabbard was empty, as was the sheath on his belt where a dagger should hang.

When he saw her he smiled, but not pleasantly. Margaret shivered.

"Margaret of Bain?" he asked.

She nodded. "Do you come from the Wolf?"

"Aye, I do. I am Padraig MacDonald. He wishes to parley, Lady Margaret, and I am instructed to tell you as much. If you agree, he will bring three men, and you may bring three men, as well. He will keep his army below the barbican, and you can meet just outside its walls."

Margaret stared, incredulous. Then she glanced at Malcolm and Sir Neil. "Is this a trap?"

"Parleys are not uncommon," Malcolm said. "But the Wolf is canny—he doesn't keep his word."

"It is a trap," Sir Neil said firmly. "You cannot go!"

Margaret could not even swallow now. She faced the messenger. "Why does he wish to parley? What does he want?" As she spoke, Peg came to stand beside her, as if protectively.

"I was told to offer you a parley, lady, that is all. I dinna ken what he will speak of."

Parleys might not be uncommon amongst warriors, but she was not a warrior, she was a woman—and her every instinct was to refuse.

"You cannot go," Sir Neil said again, blue eyes flashing. "He will take you hostage, lady, faster than you can blink an eye!"

It was so hard to think! She stared at Sir Neil. Then she looked at the messenger, Padraig. "Please stand aside."

Malcolm took him by the arm and moved him out of earshot. Margaret stepped closer to Sir Neil, with Peg. Breathing hard, she said, "Is there any way I could meet him and we could take *him* prisoner?"

From the look in Sir Neil's eyes, Margaret knew he thought she had gone mad.

Peg said, "Margaret! He is the Wolf! Ye will never ambush him! He will take ye prisoner, and then what?"

"Dinna even think of turning the tables on him, lady," Malcolm said, having returned.

Margaret glanced briefly at the messenger, who was staring—and almost smirking—at them. What did he know that they did not? "Is there any way we could parley without my being in danger of being taken captive?"

"It is too dangerous," Sir Neil said swiftly. "I swore to Sir Ranald that I would keep you safe. I cannot let you meet the Wolf!"

"Margaret, please! I am but a woman, and even I know this is a trap!" Peg cried.

"Even if it is not a trap, too much can go wrong," Malcolm said, sounding calm in comparison to the rest of them.

He was right. And Margaret was afraid to step outside the castle walls. Besides, she would never convince the damned Wolf to retreat. She squared her shoulders and left the group, walking over to the waiting Highlander. As she approached, his eyes narrowed.

Margaret smiled coldly at him. "Tell the great Wolf of Lochaber that Lady Comyn has refused. She will not parley."

"He will be displeased."

She refrained from shivering. "But I wish to know what he wants. Therefore, you may return to convey his message to me."

"I dinna think he will wish for me to speak with ye again."

What did that mean? Would the Wolf now attack? Her gaze had locked with Padraig's. His was chilling.

A moment later, Sir Neil and Malcolm were escorting him out. The moment he was gone, Margaret collapsed upon the bench. Peg rushed to sit beside her, taking her hands. "Oh, what are we going to do?"

Margaret couldn't speak. Was the Wolf now preparing to attack her? He certainly hadn't come this far to turn around and go away! And what of William and Sir Ranald? If only they were all right! "Maybe I should have met him," she heard herself say hoarsely.

"I would never let ye meet with him!" Peg cried, now close to tears. "He is an awful man, and all of Scotland knows it!"

"If you cry now, I will slap you silly," Margaret almost shouted, meaning her every word.

Peg sat up abruptly. The tears that had seemed imminent did not fall.

"I need you, Peg," Margaret added.

Peg stared and attempted to compose herself. "Can I bring ye wine?"

Margaret wasn't thirsty, but she smiled. "Thank you." The moment Peg had left, she stood up and inhaled.

Oh, God, what would happen next? Could she possibly defend the castle—at least until help arrived? And what if help did not arrive?

Surely, eventually, her maternal uncle, Alexander MacDougall of Argyll, would come. He despised every MacDonald on this earth. He would wish to defend the keep; he would want to battle with them.

Red John Comyn would also come to her aid if he knew what was happening. He was her uncle's closest ally and his cousin. But time was of the essence. They had to receive word of her plight *now*. They had to assemble and move their armies *now!*

Her head ached terribly. There were so many decisions

to make. The weight of such responsibility was crushing. And to think that in the past, she had never made a decision greater than what she wished to wear or what to serve for the supper meal!

Booted steps sounded, and with dread—she now recognized the urgency in Sir Neil's stride—she turned as he stormed into the hall. "He is at the bridge, below your walls—and he wishes to speak with you."

She froze. "Who?" But oh, she knew!

"MacDonald," he said, eyes blazing.

Her stomach churned and her heart turned over hard. Only a quarter of an hour had passed since Padraig had left. If the Wolf of Lochaber was outside her gates, clearly he had been there all along.

And suddenly, like a small, frightened child, she felt like refusing the request. She wanted to go to her chamber and hide.

"I can take you up to the ramparts," Sir Neil said bluntly.

It crossed her dazed mind that Sir Neil would only suggest such a course of action if it was safe, and of course, if the Wolf wished to parley now, she must go. She fought to breathe. It was safe for her to be high up on the ramparts, surrounded by her knights and archers, as they spoke. She felt herself nod at Sir Neil.

But as they started for the stairwell, comprehension seized her. She halted abruptly. How could it be safe for him to come to her castle walls?

He would be exposed to her archers and knights.

She looked at Sir Neil with sudden hope. "Can our archers strike him while we speak?"

Sir Neil started. "They are waving a flag of truce."

What she had suggested was dishonorable, and she knew Sir Neil thought so. "But is it possible?"

"He will undoubtedly be carrying a shield, and he will be surrounded by his men. The shot would not be an easy one. Will you violate the truce?"

She wondered if she was dreaming. She was actually considering breaking a truce and murdering a man. But she knew she must not stoop to such a level.

She had been raised to be a noble woman—a woman of her word, a woman of honor, a woman gentle and kind, a woman who would always do her duty. She could not murder the Wolf during a truce.

Finding it difficult to breathe evenly, Margaret went up the narrow stairwell, Sir Neil behind her. As she stepped outside onto the ramparts, it was at once frigidly cold and uncannily silent. There was light, but no sun. Her archers remained, as did her dozen soldiers and the women and children who had been present earlier. But it almost seemed as if no one moved or breathed.

Sir Neil touched her elbow and she crossed the stone battlements, still feeling as if she were in the midst of a terrible dream, trying to find her composure and her wits before she spoke with her worst enemy. Standing just a hand-span from the edge of the crenellated wall, she looked down.

Several hundred men were assembled between the barbican and the forest. In the very front they stood on foot, holding shields, but behind them the soldiers were mounted on horseback. Above the first columns a white flag waved, and beside it, so did a huge black- and-navy-blue banner, a fiery red dragon in its center.

And then Margaret saw him.

The rest of the army vanished from her sight. Frozen, she saw only one man—the Highlander called the Wolf of Lochaber.

Alexander MacDonald was the tallest, biggest, darkest one of all, standing in the front row of his army, in its very center. And he was staring up at her.

Black hair touched his huge shoulders, blood stained his leine and swords, a shield was strapped to one brawny forearm, and he was smiling at her.

"Lady Comyn," he called to her. "Yer as fair as is claimed."

She trembled. He was exactly as one would have expected—taller than most, broader of shoulder, a mass of muscle from years spent wielding swords and axes, his hair as black as the devil's. His smile was chilling, a mere curling of his mouth. She stared down at him, almost transfixed.

And when he did not speak again, when he only stared—and when she realized she was speechlessly staring back—she flushed and found her tongue. "I have no use for your flattery."

The cool smile reappeared. "Are ye prepared to surrender to me?"

Her mind raced wildly—how could she navigate this subject? "You will never take this keep. My uncle is on his way, even as we speak. So is the great Lord Badenoch."

"If ye mean yer uncle of Argyll, I canna wait. I look forward to taking off his head!" he exclaimed, with such relish, she knew he meant his every word. "And I dinna think the mighty Lord of Badenoch will come."

What did that mean? She shuddered. "Where is my brother?"

"He is safely in my keeping, Lady Comyn, although he has suffered some wounds."

She was so relieved she had to grip the wall to remain standing upright. "He is your prisoner?"

"Aye, he is my prisoner."

"How badly is he hurt?"

"He will live." He added, more softly, "I would never let such a valuable prisoner die."

"I wish to see him," she cried.

He shook his head. "Yer in no position to wish fer anything, Lady Comyn. I am here to negotiate yer surrender."

She trembled. She wanted to know how badly William was hurt. She wanted to see him. And hadn't Malcolm said that the Wolf was a liar? "I will not discuss surrender, not until you have proven to me that my brother is alive."

"Ye dinna take my word?"

She clutched the edge of the wall. "No, I do not accept your word."

"So ye think me a liar," he said, softly, and it was a challenge.

Margaret felt Sir Neil step up behind her. "Show me my brother, prove to me he is alive," she said.

"Ye tread dangerously," he finally said. "I will show ye Will, after ye surrender."

She breathed hard.

He slowly smiled. "I have six hundred men—ye have dozens. I am the greatest warrior in the land—yer a woman, a very young one. Yet I am offering ye terms."

"I haven't heard terms," she managed to say.

That terrible smile returned. "Surrender now, and ye will be free to leave with an escort. Surrender now, and yer people will be as free to leave. Refuse, and ye will be attacked. In defeat, no one will be spared."

Margaret managed not to cry out. How could she respond—when she did not plan to surrender?

If only she knew for certain that Argyll and Red John were on their way with their own huge armies! But even if they were, for how long could she withstand the Wolf's attack? Could they manage until help arrived?

For if they did not, if he breached her walls, he meant to spare no one—and he had just said so.

"Delay," Sir Neil whispered.

Instantly Margaret understood. "You are right," she called down. "You are known as the greatest warrior in the land, and I am a woman of seventeen." How wary and watchful he had become. "I cannot decide what to do. If I were your prisoner and my brother were here in my stead, he would not surrender, of that I am certain."

"Are ye truly thinking to outwit me?" he demanded.

"I am only a woman. I would not be so foolish as to think I could outwit the mighty Wolf of Lochaber."

"So now ye mock me?"

She trembled, wishing she hadn't inflected upon the word *mighty*.

"Yer answer, Lady Margaret," he warned.

She choked. "I need time! I will give you an answer in the morning!" By morning, maybe help would have arrived.

"Ye call me a liar and think me a fool? Lady Margaret, the land is at war. Robert Bruce has seized Dumfries Castle—and Red John Comyn is dead."

She cried out, her world suddenly spinning. "Now you lie!" What he claimed was impossible!

"Yer great Lord of Badenoch died in the Greyfriars Church at Dumfries, four days ago."

She turned in disbelief. Sir Neil looked as stunned as she was. Could the patriarch of their family be dead? If so, Red John was not coming to her aid! "What do you mean—Red John died? He was in good health!"

Slowly, the Wolf smiled. "So ye want the facts? Ye'll

hear soon enough. He was murdered, Lady Comyn, by Bruce, although he did not deliver the final, fatal blows."

Margaret's shock knew no bounds. Had Robert Bruce murdered Red John Comyn?

If so, the land would most definitely be at war!

"Bruce is on the march, Lady Comyn, and yer uncle, the MacDougall, is on the march, as well—in Galloway." He stared coldly up at her. "And do ye not wish to know where yer beloved Sir Guy is?"

Sir Neil had taken her arm, as if to hold her upright.

"He was also at Dumfries, sent there to defend the king."

She had not given her betrothed a thought since that morning. Had Sir Guy fought Bruce at Dumfries? If so, he was but two days away. She did not know what the Highlander was implying, but Sir Guy would surely come to her rescue. "This castle is a part of my dowry. Sir Guy will not let it fall."

"Sir Guy fights Bruce, still. Argyll is in battle in Galloway. The Lord of Badenoch is dead. Ye have no hope."

Now she truly needed time to think—and attempt to discover if his claims were true. For if they were, she was alone, and Castle Fyne would fall.

"He could be lying," Sir Neil said, but there was doubt in his tone.

She met his gaze and realized he was frightened after all. But then, so was she. She turned back to the Highlander standing below her walls. "I need a few hours in which to decide," she said hoarsely.

"Yer time is done. I demand an answer, lady."

She began shaking her head. "I don't want to defy you."

"Then accept my generous terms and surrender."

She bit her lip and tasted her own blood. And she felt

hundreds of pairs of eyes upon her—every man in his army stared at her—as did every man, woman and child upon the ramparts. She thought she heard Peg whisper her name. And she knew that Sir Neil wanted to speak to her. But she stared unwaveringly at the Wolf of Lochaber. As she did, she thought of her mother—the most courageous woman she had ever known. "I cannot surrender Castle Fyne."

He stared up at her, a terrible silence falling.

No one moved now—not on the ramparts, not in his army.

Only Margaret moved, her chest rising and falling unnaturally, tension making it impossible to breathe normally.

And then a hawk wheeled over their heads, soaring up high into the winter sky, breaking the moment. And disgust covered the Wolf's face. Behind him, there were murmurs, men shifting. More whispers sounded behind her. The sounds were hushed, even awed, from behind and below.

Finally, he spoke, coldly. "Yer a fool."

She did not think she had the strength to respond. Sir Neil flinched, his hand moving to his sword. She had to touch him, warning him not to attempt to defend her. She then faced the dark Highlander below her again. "This castle is mine. I will not—I cannot—surrender it."

She thought that his eyes now blazed. "Even if ye fight alone?"

"Someone will come."

"No one will come. If Argyll comes, it will be after the castle has fallen."

She swallowed, terrified that he was right.

It was a moment before he spoke again, and anger roughened his tone. "Lady Margaret, I admire yer courage—but I dinna admire defiance, not even in a beautiful woman."

Margaret simply stared. She had given him her answer, there was nothing more to say.

And he knew it. The light in his eyes was frightening, even from this distance. "I take no pleasure in what I must do." He then lifted his hand, but he never removed his eyes from her. "Prepare the rams. Prepare the siege engines. Prepare the catapults. We will besiege the castle at dawn." And he turned and disappeared amongst his men, into his army.

Margaret collapsed in Sir Neil's arms.

PEG SHOVED A cup of wine at her. Margaret took it, desperately needing sustenance. They were seated at one of the trestle tables, in the great hall. Night was falling quickly.

And at dawn, the siege would begin.

Sir Neil sat down beside her, not even asking permission. Malcolm took the opposite bench. Peg cried, "Ye should have surrendered, and it isn't too late to do so!"

Margaret tensed, aware that Peg was terrified. When she had left the ramparts, she had gazed at some of the soldiers and women there—everyone was frightened. And how could they not be?

Alexander MacDonald had been forthright. If they did not surrender, he would defeat the castle and spare no one.

She hugged herself, chilled to the bone. Should she have surrendered? And dear God, why was such a decision hers to make?

She inhaled and set the cup down. "Is it possible he is telling the truth? Is it possible that Red John is dead—and that Robert Bruce has seized the royal castle at Dumfries?"

Sir Neil was pale and stricken. "Bruce has always claimed the throne, but I know nothing of this plot!"

"Even the Wolf would not make up such a wild tale," Malcolm said. "I believe him."

She could barely comprehend what might be happening. "Is Bruce seeking the throne of Scotland? Is that why he attacked Dumfries?" And did that mean that Sir Guy was there with his men? Sir Guy was in service to King Edward. He was often dispatched to do battle for the king. Was that why MacDonald had claimed no one would come—because Sir Guy would be occupied with his own battles for King Edward?

Sir Neil shook his head. "Bruce is a man of ambition, but to murder Red John? On holy ground?"

"If the damned Wolf is telling us the truth," she said, "if Red John has been murdered, Buchan will be furious." The Comyns and Bruces had been rivals for years. They had fought over the crown before—and the Comyns had won the last battle, when their kin, John Balliol, had become Scotland's king. "A great war will ensue." She was sickened in every fiber of her being—these events were too much to bear.

"Lady Margaret—what matters is that if this is true, Red John will not be coming to our aid. Nor will Sir Guy."

Margaret stared at Malcolm as Peg cried, "We can still surrender!"

She ignored her maid. "But Argyll will come to our aid if he can."

"If the land is at war, he might not be able to come," Sir Neil said grimly. "And MacDonald claims he has the means to stop him."

She looked at Sir Neil and then Malcolm. "I am frightened. I am unsure. So tell me, truly, what you think I should do?"

Malcolm said, "Your mother would die defending Castle Fyne."

Sir Neil stood. "And I would die to defend you, my lady."

God, these were not reassuring answers!

"But, my lady, if you decide you wish to surrender, I will support you," Malcolm said.

Sir Neil nodded in agreement. "As would I. And no matter what MacDonald has said, you can decide to surrender at any time—and sue him for the terms he has already said he would give you."

But that did not mean the Wolf would give her such terms. He had been very angry when they had last parted company.

Margaret closed her eyes, trying to shut out the fear gnawing at her. She tried to imagine summoning MacDonald and handing him the great key to the keep. And the moment she did so, she knew she could not do such a thing, and she opened her eyes. They all stared at her.

"We must fight, and pray that Argyll comes to our aid," Margaret said, standing. If they were going to fight, she must appear strong, no matter how terrified.

The men nodded grimly while Peg started to cry.

MARGARET DID NOT sleep all night, knowing what would begin at dawn. And because Peg kept telling her that she must surrender, and that she was a madwoman to think to fight the Wolf of Lochaber, she had finally banned the maid from her chamber. Now, she stood at her chamber's single window, the shutters wide. The black sky was turning blue-gray. Smoke filled the coming dawn. The sounds of the soldiers and women above her on the ramparts, speaking in hushed tones as they stoked the fires and burned pots of oil, drifted down to her.

She could not bear the waiting, and she had never been as apprehensive. She heard footsteps in the hall on the landing, and she picked up her mantle, threw it on and hurried out. Sir Neil stood there, holding a torch.

"Are we ready?" she asked.

"As ready as we can be. If they think to scale our walls, they will be badly burned, at the least."

And that was when she heard a terrible sound—a huge and crushing sound—accompanied by the deep groaning of wood.

"It has begun," Sir Neil said. "They are battering the first gates on the barbican."

"Will they break?"

"Eventually," he said.

Margaret hurried past him, heading for the stairwell that went up to the crenellations. He seized her arm from behind. "You do not need to go up!" he exclaimed.

"Of course I do!" She shook him off and raced upstairs, stepping out into the gray dawn.

Smoke filled the air from the dozen fire pits, as did the stench of burning oil. The sky was rapidly lightening, and Margaret saw men and women at the walls, but no one was moving. "What's happening?" she asked.

Malcolm stepped forward and said, "They are just moving their ladders to our walls."

Margaret had to see for herself, and she walked past him.

She stared grimly down. Dozens of men were removing ladders from carts drawn by horses and oxen, pushing them toward her walls. She could not tell what the hundreds of men behind them were doing, and she glanced south, toward the barbican. Several dozen men were pushing a huge battering ram forward. She held her breath as the wheeled wooden machine moved closer and closer to the gates, finally ramming into it.

The crash sounded. Wood groaned.

In dismay, she realized the gates of the barbican would not hold for very long. A slew of arrows flew from her archers upon the entry tower, toward those men attacking her barbican. Two of the Wolf's soldiers dropped abruptly from their places by the battering ram.

Instantly, other soldiers ran forward, some to drag the injured away, others to replace them.

"It isn't safe for you to remain up here," Sir Neil said, and the words weren't even out of his mouth before she saw more arrows flying—some toward the men below, who were erecting the ladders upon her walls, and others coming up toward her archers and the women on her ramparts. Sir Neil pulled her down to her knees, arrows flying over them and landing on the stone at their backs.

"You are the mistress of this castle," Sir Neil said, their faces inches apart. "You cannot be up here. If you are hurt, or God forbid, if you die, there will be no one to lead us in this battle."

"If I am hurt, if I die, you must lead them." Just then, the arrows had not hit their targets, but she was not a fool. When the Wolf's archers were better positioned, they would strike some of her soldiers, and perhaps some of the women now preparing to throw oil on the invaders. And as she thought that, she heard a strange and frightening whistling sound approaching them.

Instinctively, Margaret covered her head and Sir Neil covered her body with his. A missile landed near the tower they had come from, exploding into fire as it did. More whistles sounded, screaming by them, rocks raining down upon the ramparts now, some wrapped in explosives, others bare. Two men rushed to douse the flames.

Margaret got onto her hands and knees, meeting Sir Neil's vivid blue gaze. "You must tell me what is happening—when you can."

THE SOUNDS OF the Wolf's siege became worse, and did not cease. The battering of the front gate, the screams of missiles and explosives, the locustlike whirring of arrows. But other screams accompanied these sounds— the frightened whinnies of horses, the cries of the men who were shot, and worse, the screams of those in agony as boiling oil scorched their heads, shoulders and arms.

Margaret now stood in the south tower, not far from the entry tower and the barbican. From her position at the uppermost window on the third floor, she could watch the battle. Thus far, no MacDonald soldier had made it over her walls, and the gates of the barbican were holding. Her archers were great bowmen, she now knew, and a great many of the Wolf's men had been shot by them, both as they climbed the ladders and as they wielded the ram.

But his men were not the only casualties. His archers were causing damage, too.

She had seen three of her men struck by their arrows and missiles on the wall adjacent to the south tower. He had hundreds of men in this battle, while she had less than fifty. She could not afford to lose even three of her archers.

And he commanded his army by riding back and forth amongst his men. He was never alone, and he rarely rode out of the column of his knights and foot soldiers. Still, she had espied him the moment she had come to stand at the tower window. He was an unmistakable figure, powerful and commanding, even from a distance.

She had never hated and feared anyone more.

And she refused to admire his courage as her archers were continually firing upon him.

"How can ye watch?" Peg asked.

Margaret did not face her. "I do not have a choice."

"There is always a choice," Peg said bitterly.

Margaret turned. "You have been very clear, Peg, and while I have valued your opinions in the past, they are not helpful now."

"We will all die here," Peg said, bursting into tears.

Margaret grimaced, finally leaving the window. "We will not die," she said, taking her into her arms. "Not if my uncle Argyll comes to our rescue."

Peg sniffed. "You are as brave as your mother, and now, the whole world will know it."

Margaret knew she wasn't brave—she was sick with fear, but she would never tell her maid that.

She began to worry that the tides of battle were changing. The cadence of the striking battering ram quickened—more men had been added to its service. Fewer men were being struck by her archers—she did not see wounded soldiers dropping to the ground as she had at the start of the battle, and more were climbing up. Fewer arrows flew from her walls at the Wolf's army while the hail of arrows and missiles from below had become a constant barrage.

She saw one of her archers fall from her walls, very close by the window where she stood, an arrow protruding from his chest. She could not stand it. She ran from the tower, and as she did she heard a great crash from outside, from the barbican, and the huge sound of splintering wood.

Margaret rushed onto the ramparts and paused, trying to adjust to the chaos around her. MacDonald soldiers were literally atop the crenellations now. Dozens of women stood throwing oil at them. Arrows and stones were a constant hail, raining down upon them. Explosives intermittently landed, detonating.

"They have breached the barbican!" someone shouted.

A woman her own age was heaving a pot of burning oil at a soldier who was now standing on her ramparts. As she threw the cauldron at him, he thrust out his arm, knocking the pot aside. Hot oil spilled, but he only grunted. Then he seized the woman by the hair.

A dagger flashed in his hand.

Margaret did not think twice. From behind, she stabbed him in the back.

He roared, turning, enraged. Before she could strike again—now to defend herself—Sir Neil struck him through with his sword from behind. His eyes widened in shock, and then he fell, clutching his bleeding midsection.

"You cannot be here," Sir Neil said to her.

She ignored him, seizing the pot the woman had thrown and rushing to the fire pit with it. For an instant she paused, uncertain of how to put the hot oil into her pot.

The young blonde woman, whose life she had saved, now held a ladle and she scooped the boiling oil into her cauldron. Their eyes met.

Margaret smiled grimly, turned and found herself flinging oil onto another soldier climbing across her walls. From the corner of her eye, she saw Sir Neil wielding his sword against an enemy soldier, the two men exchanging frightening blows.

Her oil struck the man on his face, neck and shoulders. He screamed, falling off her walls.

But another man was behind her. Margaret whirled, throwing the contents at the next man. As he fell, she thought, *This is impossible. We will never keep this up.*

But for the next few minutes, or perhaps the next few hours, that is exactly what she and the blonde woman did. Even as the invaders fell from the ladders and the walls, others succeeded in landing upon the ramparts, where Sir Neil, Malcolm and his men engaged them with their swords, maces and daggers.

"Lady," she heard Sir Neil call.

Margaret had just thrown oil over the side of the ramparts, at a very young boy, whom she had missed. He now hung to his ladder, grinning at her, a dagger clenched in his teeth. Arrows rained past him, over her.

She had become accustomed to the barrage and she did not flinch or even duck. She glanced at Sir Neil, who was bleeding from his shoulder. "They are about to scale the walls below the first tower, and once they are within, they will lower the drawbridge," he panted.

For an instant, she simply stared at him.

"It is over, we have lost—you must flee."

Their gazes were locked. Then Sir Neil took his sword, raising it threateningly. The boy she had been fighting ducked, and then raced back down his ladder.

Margaret tried to comprehend him. Dying men littered the floor of the ramparts, alongside the already dead. Some were MacDonald soldiers, others were her own archers and men. Two women, one elderly, also lay as corpses.

Margaret had never known such despair—or such desperation. "Is there any chance we could hold them off below?"

"We have lost most of our archers. No."

She inhaled, hard.

"It is a matter of hours, or even less, Lady Margaret, and they will have breached our walls entirely. We do not have enough men to fight them now. Your horse is ready. I will take you to safety."

Sir Neil was in earnest now—he meant to rush her away. They had lost.

She knew she must not fall into the Wolf's hands. But she stared across her ramparts. The women continued to boil oil and throw it at the enemy, but they were so clearly exhausted. The blonde stared at her now, her mouth pursed. Had she heard? Did she know that Sir Neil wished for her to flee? A few of her soldiers were fighting the enemy with daggers, not far from her. And she had only four archers left, but they were not even firing their arrows now. Instead, they were staring at her, too, as was Malcolm.

How could she leave them now? When the Wolf intended to execute them all?

"I am not abandoning my people," she heard herself say.

Sir Neil choked.

She had no will to explain. But the men and women who had survived were her responsibility.

She must beg for the Wolf's mercy, she thought.

"It is time to surrender," she said tersely.

"Lady Margaret," said Sir Neil, "he will not accept your surrender now, when victory is but hours away!"

God, was he right? She knew nothing of warfare! "If we try to surrender now, maybe he will show mercy later."

Sir Neil was aghast. "You will be his captive, Lady

Margaret, and you're too valuable to be taken hostage. We must go! I swore to keep you safe!"

He was right—she would be taken prisoner. In that moment, Margaret knew she would rather be a hostage for the rest of her life than flee her people, leaving them to be slain by the Wolf of Lochaber. She must fight him tooth and nail, she thought, until he showed them mercy.

One battle had ended, now, another had begun.

"Raise the white flag," she said.

CHAPTER THREE

MARGARET STARED UP at the gray sky, watching the white flag of surrender as it was hoisted high above the south tower. It slowly unfurled.

Tears blurred her vision as the hail of arrows lessened, as the barrage of missiles and stones ceased. The clang of swords was silenced, as were the whistling screams from the projectiles, the whirring from the arrows, the shouts of men being burned and falling to their deaths.

Castle Fyne was lost. The Wolf had won.

Pain stabbed through her chest. It was over.

She glanced around carefully. A great many women had survived the battle for the keep, but only four archers, three soldiers, Malcolm and Sir Neil remained from amongst her men. Dismay sickened her.

She did not want to count the dead, which littered the ramparts. But there were dozens of wounded who needed care.

But no one moved. The women simply held their pots; her four archers their bows. Malcolm had come to stand beside her with Sir Neil. The enemy hung on to their ladders, while the other MacDonald soldiers, already atop the ramparts, remained unmoving.

It had become silent and still below, too. The sounds of the battle in the barbican were gone. She glanced across the army below her, which was still, and she heard a bird chirp. She scanned his hundreds of men, looking for him. Then she heard another bird, and another one.

"Where is he?" she spoke in a terse whisper.

"There," Sir Neil said.

Margaret looked back down at the assembled army, but still, she did not see him. "Sir Neil, it is time for you to go. You must tell Buchan what has happened."

Sir Neil hesitated; she knew he did not wish to leave her.

"You must go, I am commanding you to do so!" She did not know if the MacDougalls would attempt to take the castle back from MacDonald, but Buchan would be furious, and he would assemble an army. Or would he?

"Very well," Sir Neil said. He ran into the north tower.

And then she heard Alexander MacDonald. "Lady of Fyne!" It was a harsh, unfriendly shout.

Her gaze veered to the sound as he now rode his gray stallion forward, appearing alone in front of his hordes of men. Margaret gripped the edge of the wall and leaned over it. Revulsion began.

It was laced with anger, replacing the fear, and for that she was grateful.

He halted the steed. A wind whipped his long dark hair as he stared up at her. A lengthy, terrible moment passed.

Margaret could not see his expression, but she knew he was angry—she felt it.

"So ye surrender now," he said to her.

Their gazes had locked, even from this small distance. "Yes." She trembled, realizing that she clutched her dagger still. Aware of how close he was, and that her archer stood just above him, she stared.

"Ye should have surrendered last night."

She looked at his hard face. He had high cheekbones, a strong jaw. Most women probably thought him attractive.

She looked at his broad shoulders. His leine was bloodstained. Had he been wounded? How she hoped so! He wore two swords, both sheathed. Another dagger was in his belt. A shield remained strapped to his left forearm. His thighs were bare, his boots muddy and wet.

She lifted her gaze back to his. "I am a woman, not a warrior. I made a choice, and it was the wrong one." She realized she clutched her dagger. She lifted it, showing it to him, and then, symbolically, she dropped it over the wall.

It twirled as it fell down to the ground, not far from him.

"No, Lady Comyn, yer a warrior, and ye have proven it this day." His eyes blazed. "Have yer men open the front gates."

She thought about Sir Neil, who was probably just slipping out of the side entrance in the north tower, which could accommodate a single man and a single horse. She hoped to give him as much time as possible to escape. "I will come down and open it for you, myself," she said.

His gaze narrowed.

"My lord." She looked quickly away.

THE CASTLE WAS shockingly silent as Margaret descended to the courtyard. Only an infant could be heard mewling, and some horses snorted outside, amidst Alexander's army. Malcolm walked with her, past the elderly men, women and children who had gathered, to the raised drawbridge beneath the entry tower. Great bolts locked it into place, and everyone had come to watch her open it and admit their conqueror.

Margaret was using all of her strength to appear calm and dignified—and unafraid.

"Ye may not be able to draw the bolts back by yerself," Malcolm said.

Good, she thought. For she wished for Sir Neil to be long gone by the time she let the damned Wolf in.

Margaret strained to pull one bolt back. In the end, she could not manage, and Malcolm had to help her. Then they went to the winch, which she would never be able to move. They exchanged glances. Margaret pulled on the lever with all of her weight. When it did not move, she tried for a few more minutes, until she had no choice but to signal her few remaining men. They leapt forward, and slowly, the great bridge began to come down.

Margaret stepped back from the tower with Malcolm, her hands at her sides, fists clenched. The courtyard remained eerily silent, except for the groaning of the bridge as it was lowered.

She heard his horse's hooves first. Then the gray steed appeared, the Wolf astride, his face hard, a dozen Highland knights behind him. The sound of their chargers echoed, and it was deafening.

He crossed the bridge and emerged from the entry tower. He halted the charger before her, leaping from it and striding over to her.

Margaret did not move as he approached, their stares locking. How she hoped to appear brave and defiant—yet how frightened she actually was.

He looked exactly as she had imagined the Wolf of Lochaber to be—he appeared a mighty, indomitable warrior—a legend among men.

There was hostility burning in his blue eyes, and it was chilling. His gaze skimmed over her, from head to toe, and then he held out his hand.

She reached down to her girdle. Her hand trembled. She could not still it so she ignored the obvious sign of her agitation. She detached and then handed him the castle's great key ring. As she did, their gazes met again, and this time, they held.

"All of Scotland will speak of this day."

She squared her shoulders, instantly furious. For the first time in its history, Castle Fyne had fallen. For the first time in a hundred years, it was no longer a Mac-Dougall stronghold.

"All of Scotland will speak of the Lady of Fyne and the Wolf of Lochaber and the battle waged betwixt them," he said.

She trembled. What was he trying to say?

His gaze never moved from her face. "Few men would dare to fight me. The bards will sing of your courage, Lady Margaret." And grimly, he inclined his head.

Was he showing her respect? She was incredulous. "I have no care for what you think," she said, hoping she did not spit the words out. "But I have a great care for the men, women and children here—and the wounded, who need immediate attention."

His gaze narrowed as he studied her. "Yer hatred shows." Then, "Come with me." His black-and-blue plaid swinging about his shoulders, he started across the courtyard. The crowd remained silent.

Margaret hesitated, even though the command had been sharply uttered. Then she saw several women bow to him as he passed. He nodded curtly at them.

Margaret realized she must wage a careful game now, to gain his mercy. She hated him, but she must hide it. She walked after him, slowly.

He was already within the great hall, flinging off his plaid. Peg and two other women were hovering nervously there. Fires were burning. "I am hungry," he said, pacing. "As are my men. Bring food and wine."

Margaret stood very still, having just entered the hall, as a dozen huge Highlanders came inside. Alexander turned to several of them. "Remove all prisoners to the dungeons, including the wounded," he said.

"Aye," Padraig, the messenger, said.

"And inspect every room. Make certain no one is in hiding, and that no weapons are hidden, to be used against us."

Margaret wished she had thought to hide some weapons to use against him. Padraig and four other Highlanders left.

Then she saw that he had turned his attention to her. "Stay here," he said. Alexander jerked his head at two men, and went to the north stairwell. He gestured at three more men and vanished up it with them.

Margaret looked across the room at Peg, aware that three other huge enemy Highlanders remained—to guard her. But then, she would hardly be left alone, even if there was no means of escape. Ignoring her guards, she said, "Bring them sustenance. And do your best to keep him pleased." Peg nodded and rushed off to obey.

MacDonald returned, clearly having gone up to the ramparts to assess it. He spoke with his men, and she heard him ordering a watch, then arranging his garrison within the castle. She hugged herself, trying to overhear him. So many of his men would sleep within the castle walls, but hundreds would be camped outside. As for the excessive watch, was he expecting an attack—perhaps from her uncle Argyll, or Red John, if he had lied about his death?

"Ye fought bravely—ye have the courage of a man—but ye should have surrendered last night."

She stiffened. "I could not surrender. Castle Fyne was my mother's, and it was mine."

"Did ye truly think to best me?"

"I hoped to hold you back until my uncle arrived. This is MacDougall land!"

"'Twas MacDougall land," he stated, pointing at her. "'Tis MacDonald land now."

She inhaled, the sound sharp. She now hated the Mac-Donalds as much as her mother had. "The Lord of Argyll will never let you take this keep from me," she said, when she could speak. "And my uncle Buchan will be furious. The one or the other, or together, they will take Castle Fyne back."

"If they attack, I will destroy them."

She tensed, because it was hard not to believe him. When he made a statement, it was as if he could move a mountain with his bare hands. But he was human; he was *not* a hero in a legend, even if a legend had been made about him.

"Why?" she asked. "Why did you attack now?" She wanted to know what moved him. "Your brothers are Alasdair Og and Angus Og! You have islands aplenty throughout the high seas! You have lands aplenty, here in Argyll. Castle Fyne has been on your borders for years."

He folded his massive forearms and said, his gaze chilling, his tone soft, "I have always wanted Castle Fyne. Whoever commands the castle controls the route into Argyll from the sea."

"You will cause a war."

He laughed. "Will I? We have been at war for as long as I can recall, you and I—MacDougall against Mac-Donald."

"Is this about routes from the sea—or revenge?"

"Yer clever, Lady Margaret. Of course we lust fer revenge."

She felt ill. "So you seek vengeance now, against my uncle? For the massacre of Clan Donald? Even after all these years—even when my aunt Juliana married your brother?" She heard how high and tight her tone was, hoping to appeal to him with the reference to the marriage between their rival clans.

His chilling smile vanished. "There is more here than vengeance, lady—a kingdom is at stake."

He was referring to Bruce, but every Highlander she knew cared more for revenge than anything else. "You told me you looked forward to fighting my uncle."

"I do. Did I not tell ye that a great war rages in the land? That Robert Bruce is in rebellion against King Edward? Castle Fyne is even more important now."

Her heart slammed. For years, the damned MacDonald lords of the isles had been agents of King Edward, upholding his rule. Could they have suddenly changed their allegiance? "You rebel against King Edward? You favor Bruce, all of a sudden?"

"We ride with Bruce, Lady Margaret. We war for Bruce. Bruce is Scotland's next lawful king. King Edward will rule us no more."

Had she seen pride in his eyes? God, what did this mean, for her, for her family? "Is my cousin, Red John Comyn, truly dead, then?"

"Aye, he is truly dead."

Margaret's heart thundered. "Did Bruce *murder* him?"

Staring relentlessly, he nodded.

"Why?" she cried. "Why would Robert Bruce kill the Lord of Badenoch—enraging half of Scotland?"

"He did not mean to kill him. They argued," Alexander said, watching her closely. "Christopher Seton stepped into the fray, defending Bruce. In truth, Roger de Kirkpatrick delivered him to God."

Margaret had to sit down. Suddenly it felt as if her entire world had been turned upside down. The patriarch of her family had been murdered, and his bitter rival was on the march, seeking the throne, intending to win it by war. Dear God, Robert Bruce was in open rebellion against England.

And, apparently, Alexander MacDonald and his clan were his allies.

And Bruce surely approved of the attack on Castle Fyne. The great Comyn family had always been his enemy. He would be seizing what castles and garrisons he could. He would want MacDonald, his ally, to control a major route into Argyll from the south and the islands.

Margaret walked past him and sat down at the table, shaken. What did all of this mean? How did this affect her, her family and Castle Fyne? Especially now that she was his hostage?

In one fell swoop, all the alliances and allegiances of the past decade had changed. As for rescue, he had said her uncle Argyll would not come now. Was it possible? He had always hated the English. But he would never ally himself and his kin with his blood enemy—Clan Donald. Was her family truly on England's side, as well?

She considered Buchan now—her uncle would be furious over his cousin's murder. He had always despised Robert Bruce—he had despised his father. Her powerful guardian would be plotting revenge against him. Of that she had no doubt. He would never stand idly by and allow Bruce to become Scotland's king. Saving her would be the last thing on the Earl of Buchan's mind.

She shivered. William's words from the day before echoed. *He is throwing you away!*

Her heart lurched as she thought of Sir Guy—her only ally.

They had never met. They had exchanged two letters. In them, he had been a courteous suitor, but that meant nothing now. What did this war mean for their marriage? Sir Guy was in King Edward's service, that could not change, not when his brother Aymer de Valence was commander of Berwick. So Sir Guy would be summoned to fight Bruce.

Would Sir Guy still wish to marry her? If so, he would attempt to take Castle Fyne back!

Suddenly Alexander MacDonald settled on the bench opposite her.

She tensed, acutely aware of his proximity. "What happens now?"

He sipped from his wine and said, "Bruce will march on his enemies. He will seek to gather up allies."

"Will you join him?"

He met her gaze. "I will join him, lady, when I am certain Castle Fyne is secure."

She refrained from telling him that the castle would never be secure in his possession—not as long as she lived. "Where is Bruce now?" Sir Guy would probably be with the king's men, battling against him.

"When I left Dumfries, he was riding for Castle Ayr, while others riding with him were attacking Tibbers, Rothesay and Inverskip."

She felt more despair. With Bruce on the march, she could not count on rescue from Sir Guy, either.

"Ye have not asked about yer future husband, lady. Surely ye wonder if he will come to rescue ye?"

She knew this was a trap. And she did not like his guessing her thoughts. "How can he come? He fights for the king. He must be at Castle Ayr now."

"Have you no care for his welfare? Do ye wish to ask if he is hurt or unharmed?"

She tensed. "How would you know if he has been wounded?"

"I fought him at Dumfries. Ye will be pleased—he rode away with nary a scratch." His gaze was steady upon her face.

She was acutely aware of the fact that she had not given a single thought to her betrothed's welfare. "I am pleased," she finally said. She suddenly blinked back hot tears, as much from frustration as despair. There was another reason Sir Guy might not come to her rescue—without Castle Fyne, she had no dowry, and she had no value as a bride.

She felt a moment of panic; she forced it aside. Buchan would pay her ransom, sooner or later. "When will you seek to ransom me and William?"

He leaned against the wall. "I haven't decided what I wish to do with ye."

She gasped. She had assumed he would ransom her—it was the most common course of action, in such an instance. "I am a valuable hostage."

He could have refuted her claim. Instead, he said, "Yer a very valuable prize, lady. I have yet to decide what will be best for me."

She was reeling. If he did not ransom her, she could be his prisoner for months—for years! "Am I now to be your pawn, in the years of war that will come?"

"Perhaps," he said.

She was so distraught that more tears were arising. She fought them, aware of how exhausted she was. She had already fought this man once that day, in real battle, and it had been the longest day of her life. Yet now, she fought him again. "And what of the other prisoners? What of my brother?"

"What of them?" He shifted in his seat, signaling Peg for more wine.

Peg hurried over. As she poured the wine, Margaret said, "When can I see William? I would like to tend his wounds."

"Tend his wounds? Or plot and plan against me?"

She tensed. "I do not even know how badly he was hurt. Where is he?"

"I am having him moved to a chamber in the entry tower," Alexander said. "He will remain there, under guard."

She hadn't expected him to be removed to the dungeons with the other prisoners, as he was a nobleman. "When will he be moved?"

He slowly smiled the smile she had come to hate. It was so cold. "Ye cannot see him, Lady Margaret. I will not allow it."

She was in disbelief. "You would deny me the chance to attend my brother—when he has been wounded?"

He stared at her. "Aye, I would."

She gasped. "I have lost three brothers, as well as both my parents. He is my only brother, and I beg you to reconsider. I do not even know how badly he was hurt!"

"Then ye need ask and I will tell ye. He suffered a gash from a sword on his leg, lady, as well as a blow to his head. And he has been properly attended."

"But I am accustomed to taking care of the wounded! Please—let me attend him!"

"So will ye give me yer word that ye will not plot against me? That ye will not plan on how best to overthrow me?"

She tensed. Of course they would discuss how to best overthrow him, damn him!

"I dinna think so."

Margaret could not move, still stunned by his refusal. "And if I beg?"

"Yer pleas will not be heard." He was final. "Sit down, Lady Margaret, before ye fall down."

Margaret was so angry she shook, but she knew she must hold her tongue now—when she wished to accuse him of cruelty, when she wished to curse him for all he had done. "And what of the rest of your prisoners? What of my archers and soldiers and Malcolm? What of Buchan's knights whom you captured in the ravine?"

He now stood up. "They hang tomorrow at noon."

She did not cry out. She had expected such an answer. In war, the enemy was often executed. And he had told her, point-blank, that if she did not surrender, he would spare no one. "And if I beg you for mercy for them? If I beg you to spare their lives?"

"Mercy," he said softly, "makes a warrior weak."

She inhaled, staring; he stared back. "I cannot allow you to execute my people."

"You cannot allow or forbid me anything. I am lord and master here."

She needed to control her temper. She needed to overcome her fear. She needed to persuade this man to have mercy on her kin. Margaret looked down at the table, which she clasped so tightly her knuckles were white. How could she get him to change his mind?

She somehow softened and glanced up. "My lord, forgive me. I am but a woman, and a weary woman, at that. I have never had to defend a castle before. I have never had to engage in battle, and I have never been in the midst of a siege. And I have never had to make so many decisions, decisions that should have been made by men." Tears filled her eyes. She welcomed them. "I have never been so frightened! The last thing I would ever wish is to command a keep against a siege, much less against the Wolf of Lochaber!"

"Ye refused to surrender," he said softly, a potent reminder of her sins.

"I was foolish, but then, I am a woman."

He slowly shook his head. "Dinna think to outwit me, lady, when we both ken yer no fool."

"My choice was a foolish one!"

"And ye will pay the price for the choice ye made. Only a fool would allow his enemy to live to fight another day—they hang tomorrow at noon."

She had lost. His mind was made up. She began to shake, her fury erupting. "Damn you!"

"Have a care," he warned.

"No," she said, tears falling. "I will not have a care, you have stolen *my* castle from me, *mine,* and now, you will execute *my* people, *mine!*"

"I have defeated ye, Lady Margaret, fairly, in battle. The spoils are *mine.*"

"There is nothing fair about my having been attacked so rudely, by the mighty Wolf of Lochaber!" She knew she should not be shouting at him, but she could not stop now. "You may have won the day, Wolf. But this is my castle. This is MacDougall land. No matter what happened today, this will always be MacDougall land!"

"War changes everything."

"I will never let you keep this place!"

His eyes widened. "What do ye say?"

She knew she should become quiet. She knew she must control her rage. She must not cry in front of him. But could not stop herself from doing any of those things.

"If no one comes to fight you, MacDonald, then I will fight you!"

"But ye have already fought—and lost."

"Yes, I have fought—and I have lost. But I have learned a great deal. The next time, I will be prepared. And there will be a next time."

"Ye dare to threaten me?"

"I make a vow—to defeat you!" And she was so exhausted and so overcome, that shouting at him now caused her knees to buckle. And then the floor tilted wildly, the hall spun...

And then there was only darkness.

CHAPTER FOUR

THE FIRST THING Margaret saw when she opened her eyes was Peg, who sat by her hip on the bed, holding her hand tightly. The next thing she saw was Alexander MacDonald, who stood in the doorway of the chamber, staring at her, his face hard and set. As she blinked, realizing she had fainted and been carried into a bedchamber, he turned and strode away.

She trembled, so exhausted she sank back down into the pillows, instead of attempting to get up.

"Ye swooned! Ye never swoon," Peg cried. "Ye have fought a war today, as if ye were a man, but yer a lady!"

Margaret felt tears of exhaustion and despair arise. He was gone, so she did not need to hide them. "Oh, Peg, what are we going to do? He will hang Malcolm and the others at noon tomorrow!" And their deaths would be her fault.

Peg, who was so loquacious, now simply sat there. Her face remained pale with distress.

Margaret realized that something of great significance was on her mind, and she sat up. "What is it?"

Peg shook her head, as if in denial. "Ye fought him earlier with arrows and swords, but just now, ye fought him with words, Margaret, and that will not serve yer cause."

"He has attacked and taken my castle. Many of my

men have died. I could hardly sing him songs and serve him sweetmeats."

Peg rolled her eyes. "Fer such a clever lady, yer such a fool!"

"What does that mean?"

"It means that he has been looking at ye all night long as if yer a tasty morsel and he's truly a wolf. He wants ye."

Margaret stared, shocked. "What are you trying to say?"

"If ye pleased him, lady, he would probably go to London and back for ye—or even Rome!"

Her heart raced. "Are you suggesting…a liaison?" She could barely get the word out.

But wasn't seduction a ploy used by women since the beginning of time?

Margaret stared as Peg got up. "I am going to bring you soup and bread," she said, as if she hadn't heard the question.

"No, wait," Margaret said uneasily. "Do you really think I could change his mind if I…slept with him?"

"Aye, I do—as long as ye kiss and caress him wildly." She gave her a look. "If ye spit at him, he'll hardly wish to please *ye* tomorrow!"

Margaret shuddered. She had to save her men's lives. But could she use her body in such a manner? Would she even be able to tolerate his touch? But now, his proud image flashed in her mind, as she had seen him standing before her castle walls. Most women would find him attractive. She might even think him handsome, if they were not mortal enemies. "I am supposed to marry Sir Guy in June," she managed to say.

Peg shrugged. "So? Ye hate having to marry an Englishman anyway."

She grimaced. Peg was so brutally honest! "Yes, I dread having to marry an Englishman. But that is not hatred." She added, "If there is a man whom I hate, it is Alexander MacDonald."

"I think it's the same. And have ye noticed that he's handsome?"

Margaret gave her an incredulous look. "No," she lied. She pulled a cover up, as it was cold. She now realized she was in a small chamber adjacent to the one she had claimed as her own upon her return to Castle Fyne. MacDonald must have taken the other chamber. "Buchan will be equally furious," she said slowly. Was Peg right? Could she seduce the mighty Wolf to her will? Would he be so pleased with her tomorrow that he would change his mind about executing her men?

"Aye, he will be angry—mayhap more than Sir Guy! But if ye want to save Malcolm and the others, what other hope is there?"

She imagined her powerful guardian in a rage. She had seen it before, and she shuddered. She wasn't sure what he would do, but he would consider her behavior treachery.

"What will ye do?" Peg asked.

"I don't know—but I do not have much time to think about it." But even as she spoke, she knew there was no decision to make. Doing nothing was not a choice. She had to make another attempt to persuade her captor not to execute her men.

Margaret slid from the bed. "Peg, one more thing. Can you go to the entry tower and attempt to see William?"

Peg nodded. "I will set a soup to boil first."

Margaret watched her leave. Then she walked to the door, and glanced into the narrow hall outside. It was lit by rushes set on sconces, against the walls. A big Highlander sat there on a stool, and he smiled at her politely when she saw him.

She had a guard.

Then she glanced at the adjacent chamber—her room. Alexander wasn't within—he was downstairs still, in the great hall—but she stared at the bed in the center of the room, trying to imagine going to him that night.

She couldn't.

IT WAS A good hour before Peg returned, and when she did, she held a platter in her hand, a bowl steaming in its midst. Although sick with worry and lacking any appetite, the moment Margaret smelled the savory aromas of the mutton soup, she felt a hunger pang.

Peg used her hip to push the door closed; outside, Margaret's Scot guard was staring at them. Then she came and set the tray down on the bed.

"Thank you," Margaret said, taking up a piece of bread and dipping it in the soup. There was no knife on the tray, but she couldn't be surprised at that. "Is he still downstairs?"

"They have finished eating and drinking, most of his men are going to bed for the night. He will probably be up shortly," Peg said. Her regard was questioning.

Margaret felt an immediate tension as she lifted the bowl to drink the soup. Then she set it down. "There is no decision to make. I cannot stand by and simply wait for tomorrow to come, and hope that God will bring some great cataclysm upon us, interfering with the executions."

Peg nodded. "I think ye should go to him. Maybe ye'll enjoy being in his arms, even if he is the enemy."

Margaret did not want to even consider such a possibility, which was unlikely, in any case. She dipped another piece of bread in the soup. "Did you see William?"

Peg hesitated, and Margaret was instantly alarmed. She set aside her food. "Peg!"

"I saw him, Margaret, but we did not speak. They were bringing him food and water, so the door to his chamber was open."

"What is it?" Margaret tried to hold her anxiety in check.

"He was badly hurt! His head is bandaged—the linens are red—and so is the bandage on his shoulder. He is as white as a corpse, and he was lying so still, I dinna ken if he was even conscious."

Margaret leapt up from the bed, pacing wildly. "Damn that Wolf of Lochaber! He said they had tended my brother! I must attend him!"

Peg seized her arm. "If ye seduce him tonight, he will let ye do anything ye want tomorrow—I am certain of it!"

How could she make love to Alexander, when he was keeping her brother prisoner, and denying him care? Oh, she was so angry!

"Ye canna let him see how much ye hate him," Peg warned.

Peg was right. She had to control her emotions, as rampant as they were.

Peg walked to her and clasped her arm. "I ken yer nervous and worried. I have more news, and some of it is good—I overheard William's guards speaking. Sir Ranald was one of our knights who escaped after the battle in the ravine."

"Thank God for that!" Margaret cried. "He must be a day's riding ahead of Sir Neil!" And she did not think Sir Ranald would try to reach Argyll or Red John—he had known she was sending word to them already. But he would never think to ride all the way to Buchan for rescue. He would probably ride for Fowliss; one of her aunts was married to the Earl of Strathearn.

"Do ye want to hear the rest of it?" Peg asked.

She flinched, for she did not like Peg's tone—or her distraught look.

Peg barreled grimly on. "Sir Ranald will not be a day ahead of Sir Neil."

"What are you telling me?" Sir Neil could not be dead!

"Sir Neil is in the dungeons below—he was captured shortly after he tried to flee here."

Margaret walked to the bed and sank down on it. He wasn't dead, and she thanked God for that, but he would die tomorrow with the others—if her plan failed.

Peg came and sat down beside her. They hugged. Peg said softly, "Ye canna let Sir Neil hang. He is so young, so handsome, and so loyal to ye."

"No, I can't." And as they stared at one another, it truly struck her—she must seduce her enemy, in order to save her men. She heard the door open adjacent her room.

Alexander had gone to his chamber. Apprehension filled her.

She strained to hear—they both strained to hear—his quiet tones as he spoke with the guard. His voice sounded calm as he spoke.

Margaret remained unmoving, thinking about how cold and ruthless Alexander MacDonald was. She thought about the battle they had waged against one another, and she thought about the legends about him.

Would she really beguile, play and outwit the Wolf of Lochaber? Could she really go up against such a warrior and win?

Hadn't women seduced men for their own ends, throughout the course of time?

And then she had the oddest recollection—of how

dearly her parents had loved one another, and how they were so open about stealing off to make love.

But their marriage had been an unusual one. Few married couples cared for one another. Although most were deeply bonded for political and familial reasons, love was a different matter. Love affairs abounded, and so often defied not just politics and family, but common sense.

This love affair would be entirely political—a seduction meant to save the lives of the men of Castle Fyne.

Margaret stood. "Wish me well."

Peg seized her hand. "Forget he is the enemy. He is big and handsome—think about that!"

Margaret wished she could, but she could not. As she walked to the door she thought about her uncle Buchan. After what she meant to do, she would probably be sent to a nunnery for the rest of her life. But she had to save her people.

Margaret opened her door and the guard leapt to his feet. "I wish a word with Alexander," she said with what dignity she could muster. And ignoring any response he might mean to make, as well as his surprise, she walked over to the Wolf's open door.

He was standing in the center of the chamber, and he had just shed his boots and sword belt. The latter hung on the back of the room's single chair; the boots were on the floor. He stood barefoot on a fur rug—the stone floors were freezing cold in winter—and he turned to face her, his hands on his waist belt.

Margaret had paused in the doorway. As their eyes met, his gaze did not even flicker, he was so still—and so watchful.

She knew she flushed—her cheeks felt warm. Did he know what she intended?

The bedchamber was strikingly silent now. She stepped

inside, aware that he was watching her with the kind of care one reserved for the enemy, and that he hadn't said a word in response to her appearance.

Margaret closed the door. Then she turned back to the Wolf. "Are you well fed, my lord? Have you had enough to drink?"

He began to smile, now unfastening his belt and tossing it aside, onto the bed. As he did, Margaret stared at the sheathed dagger on it.

"Do ye really wish to play this game?" he asked softly. But his gaze had slipped to her mouth.

He did want her, she thought, stunned. Peg had been right. "It is time for me to accept the fact that I am your prisoner, and in your care. We should not be rivals." She thought she sounded calm—an amazing feat.

His smile remained, and even as cynical as it was, it changed his hard face. Even she had to admit that he was a striking man. "And now ye wish fer my company?"

"I wish to do what I must do to make my stay with you as pleasant as possible," Margaret said tersely. There was no point in playing him for a fool—he was hardly that. But he might believe she had decided to make the best of their situation—and seek opportunity in her captivity, through a relationship with him.

His smile vanished. "I despise liars, Lady Margaret."

His warning was clear. "I have never been a liar," she said, and that was true—but she was certainly lying now. "I have had a few hours in which to think. I am your prisoner and entirely dependent upon you for my welfare. Only a very foolish woman would continue to fight you, my lord."

"So instead of fighting, ye come to my bed?"

"Why is it so strange? You are master here, I was once the lady."

His stare had intensified. Margaret remained in front of the closed door, unmoving. Her heart was thundering so loudly that she thought he could hear it. He surely knew of the game she played; he surely knew how desperate and afraid she was.

For a long moment, he did not speak. Then, "Yer no bawd."

How right he was. "I'm no bawdy woman, but I'm afraid, my lord," Margaret said softly. "My uncle will be furious with me for losing the keep. So will Sir Guy. I need a protector."

"They will be more furious if they learn ye have slept in my bed."

He was so very right. But why was he making objections? Did he think to resist her? "They do not have to know."

He eyed her. "If ye stay here, everyone will know."

Margaret hadn't thought this would be easy, but she had not expected him to object, nor could she fathom why he did not simply seize her, as most men would. She smiled tightly and walked past him to the bed.

As she did, he turned, so he continued to face her, his gaze still wary and watchful.

"I need a protector," she said, her back to him. She untied her girdle, hoping he did not note how her hands trembled, placing it on the bed beside his waist belt and dagger. The latter winked up at her.

It was in easy reach.

"Yer uncle will disavow ye as his blood if ye sleep here tonight. Then ye will need a champion."

She shook her head, pulling up her gown—a surcote— and removing it over her head. She heard him inhale. She did not turn, clad now in a thin cote and her chemise. "You do not know Buchan. I will be blamed for the loss of the castle, for allowing you in, for the deaths of every-one—I am afraid." She was lying now—Buchan would not blame her for attempting to fight the great Wolf off.

He did not answer her.

What should she do next? she wondered. Continue to disrobe? If she removed her undergown, she would be wearing nothing but her shoes and her thigh-length chemise.

"I willna spare the prisoners, Lady Margaret," he said softly, from directly behind her. "If that is the reason ye have come."

She jumped, as he was so close now his breath feathered her ear—and he had taken a hold of her left wrist—but the movement caused her shoulders to hit his chest. His grasp on her wrist tightened, while he clasped her waist with his other hand.

Her heart somersaulted wildly. What was he doing? She was in his arms. Yet wasn't this what she wanted of him?

Had he really just said that he would not spare her men? The intimate position they were in was making serious reflection impossible. Margaret could only feel his breath on her ear, his hard chest, rising and falling against her back, and the heat of his pelvis and loins.

Her heart was pounding. Every nerve ending she had was taut. "Am I asking you to spare them?" she gasped hoarsely. "I am coming freely, my lord."

"Ye do not come freely. Ye despise me with yer every breath." But he spoke in a harsh murmur, and his mouth now brushed her ear.

She gasped, because a fire was racing along her arms, and up and down her legs. Did she desire the Wolf of Lochaber? For his arms were around her, and she could not think clearly, except to note how strong and mus-

cular he was, and how warm she was becoming. "No,"
she managed to answer. "I have come freely, my lord."

His hand on her waist tightened. "Ye think to ask me
on the morrow for mercy for yer men. That is why ye
seek me in my bed—not for any other reason. If ye stay
with me, my answer willna change," he warned. And
his mouth was so close to her earlobe, she could feel
his lips brushing her there as he spoke. It was almost a
feathering kiss.

She couldn't breathe, much less move. An explosion
of sparks accompanied his words, his breath. It was as if
he had set her on fire, and that fire was racing through
her entire body. She was aware of how aroused he was.
There was no mistaking his condition. His body was
hard and heated.

What should she do? she wondered, with both panic
and breathlessness.

Alexander clasped her shoulders, pulling her back
even more closely against him, and he kissed the side of
her neck. Margaret felt the rush of deeper desire then. It
was as if her abdomen had been hollowed out, and she
felt faint with the expectation of pleasure.

His hand slid from her shoulder to her breast and over
it entirely, causing her erect nipples to tighten painfully.
"So ye will stay, anyway?"

She almost wanted to say yes! But how could she
stay with him? What was she thinking? She was Lady
Margaret Comyn, the great Earl of Buchan's niece and
ward—she was Mary MacDougall's daughter! They were
the worst of enemies! And he would hang her men tomorrow anyway.

"I want to stay—I want to save my men," she somehow breathed.

"Ye canna save them." He turned her around abruptly,

so she was no longer in his embrace, and their gazes collided. His blue eyes smoldered with lust. She wondered what her own eyes looked like. "I wish ye were a bawd."

She hugged herself and stepped back breathlessly. What had just happened? She began to shake, still feeling feverishly hot. "I'm not a bawd," she admitted hoarsely. "I thought I could seduce you."

"Ye could seduce me—if ye truly wished to."

He sounded odd, as if rueful. Margaret trembled as he paced away, and glanced again at his belt and dagger on the bed. The blade winked up at her, but she did not have the courage to seize it. She was no more a murderess than she was a seductress.

She realized he was watching her. But he knew she would never grab that knife and use it, just as he had known she was incapable of a casual lover's tryst, no matter how much desire had just arisen between them.

"Ye should leave matters of war alone, Lady Margaret. And the prisoners are a matter of war. Buchan will forgive ye the loss of the keep, he will expect his men to be hanged, but he would never forgive ye for lying with the enemy—on the eve of yer marriage to Sir Guy."

She suddenly wondered if he was trying to protect her. But they were enemies. Why would he do that? "I care more for my men than I do for my uncle's approval. But it doesn't matter now. I can't go forward with a seduction, my men will hang even if I do, and I doubt there will be a marriage now," she finally said, thickly.

"Why would ye think that? Buchan needs Sir Guy now more than ever. Sir Guy will wish to have Castle Fyne now more than ever."

"You have stolen Castle Fyne," she cried, "leaving me with nothing."

"Sir Guy is a man of great ambition, like his brother, Aymer. I am certain he will come to take this castle back, and with it, his bride."

Margaret wanted to believe him. The only problem was, if Sir Guy attacked Castle Fyne, how would he ever best such an opponent? And that would not help her men—they would already be dead. The implications of her failure to seduce him—and dissuade him from the executions—were settling in. She was ill.

"Ye need to leave matters of war to the men," Alexander said again. "And ye should leave my chamber. Good night."

She had achieved nothing. And she would never understand MacDonald. Why hadn't he taken what she offered? Most men would have leapt at such an opportunity, especially as it would drive a wedge between her and Sir Guy, which was to his advantage. She did not want to think of him as an honorable man, so she refused to do so. But while she knew she should leave—she should flee—she did not. "Most men would not have refused my advances."

"I'm not like most men."

"Why? Why did you dissuade me from my folly? What have you gained tonight?"

His stare was unwavering. "Ye'd hate me more tomorrow."

He was right, she thought, but why would that matter to him? Margaret realized that Alexander MacDonald was no simple, single-minded, bloodthirsty warrior. He was a canny man—a worthy opponent. She remained uncertain of his ambitions, outside of his desire to command Castle Fyne.

Only one fact was clear. She now had the knowledge that he lusted for her. Worse, Peg had been right—a part of her had enjoyed being in his arms. How could she use the attraction they seemed to share to her advantage? Without truly compromising herself?

Margaret walked to the bed and retrieved her clothes. She shivered, facing him. "I did not expect to enjoy being in your arms." She was grim.

His eyes widened, filling with wariness.

"We are enemies, and you have stolen my castle and tomorrow you will hang my men. Yet we shared an embrace, one we both enjoyed."

He stared for another moment. "Yer young, Lady Margaret, and untried. Life is filled with surprises. Especially during times of war." He paused and then added, "But I am pleased ye want to be with me. Ye can be sure there will be more surprises for us both."

How certain he was, she thought, her heart lurching. "No. We will never be together again, if that is what you are suggesting."

His stare changed, becoming sharp, even speculative. "Never? That is an arbitrary word, one I rarely use."

She did not want to debate him now, not when they remained alone together in his chamber, in the dead of the night, when her blood still raced. "You are a MacDonald. You are already my worst enemy. But if you hang the men I am responsible for, you will become my blood enemy."

"Yer a woman," he said swiftly, his face hardening. "Ye dinna need make blood enemies, ye dinna need to seek vengeance fer anything."

"How wrong you are."

"Ye amaze me, Lady Margaret, with yer boldness." He wasn't smiling. He didn't appear pleased, either. Had she moved him, just a bit?

"I am not trying to amaze you, Alexander, but I am my mother's daughter."

"Yes, ye are," he said grimly.

Margaret wondered then if he had known her mother. "It doesn't have to be this way. We do not have to be the worst of enemies." It was, perhaps, her last plea.

"Ye have decided this day that we are already the worst of enemies," he said grimly. "They hang on the morrow."

She turned abruptly, about to walk to the door. Then she halted. "I was on the ramparts with them. I fought you, too."

He crossed his muscular arms and stared coldly at her.

"You should hang me tomorrow, too."

"I am not hanging ye."

He was furious, now. She trembled, incapable of looking away from him. "Because I am such a valuable hostage? Dowry and all?"

"Because yer such a valuable hostage—and yer a woman."

"How can you be so ruthless?"

"I am fond of living."

She hugged her clothes more tightly to her chest. Oddly, comprehension flashed just then, and for one instant, she did not hate him. In that instant, she understood—he was fighting just as she was for his life and the lives of his men. He was a feared and respected warrior, and rightly so. And then the moment was gone.

"Ye need to leave, Lady Margaret," he warned.

She shook her head in refusal. "My brother is hurt. He is my only living family. I must attend him—*please*."

"You can tend his wounds tomorrow." He walked to the door and opened it and then stepped aside.

She was stunned by his acquiescence. "You will let me see him?"

"I will allow you to see him—this one time."

Margaret nodded, tears falling, and she ran past him, escaping.

MARGARET HUDDLED UNDER the fur covers, staring out of her chamber's window as dawn stained the sky with fingers of mauve. She had slept fitfully and uneasily all night when she was exhausted—when she had needed the kind of deep sleep that would refresh her, so she could battle another day. But every time she had dozed she had dreamed of the hangings to take place that day and had instantly awoken.

Because it was so cold and they were prisoners, Peg had shared her bed. But Margaret's restlessness had caused her to finally make a pallet on the floor. Peg now sat up, yawning.

Margaret began to greet her when she heard a movement in the chamber next to hers. Alexander had arisen. She was careful not to allow her thoughts to revisit their encounter of the previous night. She did not want to recall the sparks of desire she had felt while in his arms.

But he had said she could see her brother. As Peg began to braid her long hair, Margaret leapt from the bed, slid on her shoes, seized her mantle and hurried to her door. As she opened it Alexander came out of the adjacent chamber and their gazes collided.

"Good morn," he said, unsmiling. His eyes moved over her as he gestured to the guard, "Alan will take ye to William when ye wish."

"I am ready now, thank you," she cried. "Can Peg come to help me?"

He looked away. "Aye." He said to Alan, "She may

tend her brother's wounds, but do not leave them alone together." With that, he nodded at her and went downstairs.

A moment later, both women were following Alan
through the keep and into the courtyard. The guard carried a small chest for Margaret, one in which she kept
her herbs and potions. It was freezing cold out, and they
could not cross the bailey fast enough. The horses garrisoned in the stables there were just being given fodder,
the men tending them the only others present. They entered the tower's door and hurried up its narrow winding staircase to the second floor.

A Highlander sat on a barrel outside William's closed
chamber door. Alan spoke briefly with him, and he
opened the door for Peg and Margaret.

William lay upon the narrow pallet inside, and Margaret choked back a gasp of horror.

He seemed asleep—he might have been unconscious.
He had clearly bled heavily, as both his head bandage
and the one on his chest were entirely red. Having lost
so much blood, he was as white as a corpse. Her worry
knew no bounds.

"Will!" Margaret rushed inside to kneel beside him,
taking his hands.

Peg said, "I will get warm water and lye soap."

"Bring clean linens," Margaret said, not looking away
from her brother.

His lashes fluttered and she called out to him again,
now holding his hand and stroking his face. "Dear
brother, it is I, Margaret. Wake up!"

William moaned and looked blearily at her. "Meg?"

"You are awake! I am here to take care of you now."
She was so afraid that when she removed the bandages,
she would find an infection. She could not bear it if
Will died.

"Where am I? What happened?" he asked hoarsely.

"The Wolf has taken Castle Fyne. We are his prisoners."

His eyes flew wide now. "Are you all right?"

"He hasn't hurt me, nor will he—I am his hostage. But I lost, Will, I lost this place, and it is now in Mac-Donald hands." She did not want to tell him about the impending executions. He was ill, and she wanted him to use his strength to heal, not worry.

"We will retake it. Buchan will come, or maybe, Sir Guy." His lashes fluttered, as if he did not have the strength to keep his eyes open. "He did not hurt you?"

"Don't worry about me—I am under guard, but otherwise, I have been treated with the utmost respect." That was actually the truth, she thought.

"I know you—stubborn, and now defiant." He opened his eyes again and stared. "Don't defy him, Meg. Wait for Buchan to come."

She managed a smile and it felt ghastly. She would not tell him about the death of their cousin Red John Comyn, either, or the rebellion of Robert Bruce. He needed not worry about those things. "I am not defying him," she said. And that was the truth, too—now.

He seemed doubtful. "You are probably plotting an escape…don't. Wait for rescue, Meg." His voice had become so weak that she had to lean close to hear him. Eyes closed, he said, "Did we get a messenger out before the castle fell?"

She was aware now of Alan, hovering some small distance behind her and listening to their every word. "Malcolm sent two young Scots, just before the siege."

"Good!" His eyes opened and his words were hard with satisfaction as he spoke. "Argyll and Buchan will come, sooner, not later."

Margaret managed to smile, still holding his hand. "You shouldn't speak, you should rest." Peg finally returned, rushing into the room with soap, a bowl of water and linens. "I am going to clean your wounds and change the bandages."

William did not respond, and Margaret set to work.

TWO HOURS LATER, Margaret hurried into the great hall, where she found Alexander. Both tables were entirely occupied by his men; they were finishing breakfast. The tables were littered with plates piled with unfinished crusts, fish carcasses and meat bones. Conversation was rampant. As she rushed in, every man present turned her way and the room silenced.

She slowed her urgent stride, aware of thirty or more pairs of eyes upon her—the gazes of his men, her foes. From the head of one table, Alexander regarded her also, his expression impassive and impossible to read.

She approached him and curtsied.

"How fares your brother?"

"Not well." She met his gaze, unsmiling. "He lost far too much blood. I cleaned both wounds, and I am very concerned. He is weak, my lord, and while there is no infection yet, we both know that one could set in shortly. The next few days are crucial."

"I am sorry he was wounded."

She tensed, because she was fairly certain he did not care about her brother, except as another useful hostage. "I am excellent with herbs and potions. I learned how to attend a great many maladies and war wounds from my mother. Now I must hope that the salves I have used were not used too late."

He studied her. "Is that an accusation? My own man

tended him yesterday, Lady Margaret, and as ye have said, he has no infection."

She had been accusatory, but that would not get her anywhere. "I am grateful you had someone clean his wounds and bandage them. I am grateful you did not leave him to die."

"Ye remain the worst liar. Yer not grateful, and yer sick with fear."

She felt that fear then, as if a huge sob were about to choke her. "I have lost three brothers, brothers I dearly admired, brothers I loved. I cannot lose William, too!"

"And I hope ye do not. Will ye sit down, Lady Margaret?"

She had no appetite, but that wasn't why she did not want to sit down at his table. A remembrance flashed in her mind, of being in his arms last night. It was a terrible recollection. "I was hoping to see my men today—before you hang them."

He smiled grimly at her. "I will allow ye to see them, but if ye think to mount an insurrection at the last moment, be forewarned. They'll die by my sword and it willna matter to me."

"A rebellion at the last moment is not on my mind," she cried. "Although I wish I was capable of mounting one."

He studied her, his scrutiny so intense it was unnerving. "I thought we had come to some terms—last night."

She trembled again. Last night she had glimpsed him as a powerful, sexual and handsome man. Last night, she had felt a moment of admiration and respect for him, but that moment was gone.

"We did not come to any terms. You are my captor, I am your prisoner, my brother might die in your care—and you are about to execute my good soldiers."

He stood up abruptly. "I will take you to the dungeons." He gestured at four men, who instantly arose, their swords clattering against the table's edge as they did. He then pointed at Alan, too.

He led the way down to the dungeons, Margaret directly behind him, his five men behind her. Her heart raced madly now. She estimated it was half past eight in the morning. In four hours or less, Sir Neil, Malcolm and the others would die.

Little daylight came into the dungeons. One wall had two small, barred windows, set high above the prisoners' heads. Otherwise, there was no possibility of natural light entering the cell, so burning torches had been set into the ground, which was dirt. Two of Alexander's men had remained below, outside the single large cell where the prisoners huddled. Margaret remained directly behind Alexander now, aware of the temperature dropping dramatically. It was terribly cold belowground.

He came to an abrupt halt, and she stumbled not to crash into him from behind. Peeking past him, she saw the two guards leap to attention now.

"Open the door," Alexander said to them.

Margaret had never been inside a dungeon before—although she had been inside the cellars at Castle Bain and Balvenie. Those cellars had had stone floors, and they had been dank and dark, too—but this was so much worse. The dungeons stank of urine and feces. She thought she could smell blood, too, and she felt so much despair.

This was all her fault.

Margaret peered past Alexander; Sir Neil, Malcolm and the others were all standing now, and staring at them. Or were they staring at her? With accusation in their eyes? Accusation she so rightly deserved?

She heard the key turning in the lock, a rusty groan. Alexander shifted to face her. "Ye may go inside."

She met his gaze, realizing she was filled with trepidation now. How could she face her men, now? Did they even know they would soon die?

Alexander suddenly said, "Margaret, ye need not do this."

She stiffened, condemning herself for her cowardice—when she was hardly going to hang that day. And she did not like the way he had addressed her—so intimately. But she would not dispute him now. She stepped past him.

Instantly, her gaze turned to Sir Neil and Malcolm as she entered the cell. "Are you all right?"

"Lady Margaret, you should not be here," Sir Neil gasped.

She rushed to him and seized his hands—he had been wounded, she saw, in his shoulder, but it had been bandaged and there was not that much blood. "What happened? You were hurt!"

"Lady—I failed you!" He gripped her hands tightly. "And I beg yer forgiveness, I was to keep you safe, I failed. I was to ride for rescue, and I was captured!" Tears filled his dark blue eyes.

"Sir Neil, you could never fail me," she cried, meaning it. "You are the bravest knight I know. You fought tirelessly for me. I want to see your wound!"

"It is a scratch," he said. "Lady Margaret, are ye all right? Have ye been hurt?" Eyes blazing, he looked past her at Alexander with fury.

She hadn't realized that Alexander stood behind them, openly observing them and listening to their every word. Now Sir Neil was murderous, and if looks could kill, Alexander would be dead. "I have been treated well, Sir Neil, and you must not worry about me."

He studied her, clearly assessing if she spoke the truth. When he was reassured, he said, "I will always worry about you. I am your vassal. And you are my lady!"

She wanted to hug him, but that would be entirely inappropriate. Instead, she clung to his hands and he kissed each one. "I beg your forgiveness, Lady Margaret. I must know that I am forgiven my failures, before I die."

"There is nothing to forgive." She released him now, glancing at Malcolm. "Are you unhurt?"

He nodded. "Ye should not be here, Lady Margaret. The dungeons are no place for a lady."

She looked past him at the soldiers and archers in the cell. No one was hurt, and for that, she was thankful. "Of course I came to see you. I must speak with you all."

She took a deep breath. "I have failed you all. I refused to surrender to the mighty Wolf of Lochaber, when I am but a young, untried woman. My pride as a Mac-Dougall knew no bounds. Pride led me to believe we could achieve the impossible—that we could defeat a superior force, that we could defeat the great Wolf." She fought rising tears.

"Lady, we all wished to fight," Malcolm said grimly.

"We would do so again, if we had such a choice," Sir Neil cried.

"Aye," the others agreed in a chorus.

She shook her head and said hoarsely, "Had I surrendered, you would all be free now. Instead, you are the Wolf's prisoners."

No one tried to speak now. Everyone was intent, awaiting her next words, her direction. And it amazed her that they would follow her still.

"I am not worthy of you, and certainly, I was not worthy to lead you. The Wolf said he would spare no one if I did not surrender. I should have considered that far more carefully when I chose to fight him. But I did not." She paused, but not for effect. She hated what she must now divulge.

"I have begged him to change his mind. He will not do so."

No one moved, and no one seemed surprised. Sir Neil said, "You were the most worthy leader a knight could have, lady, and I would follow you into battle another time."

"Aye, I would follow ye again," Malcolm said. "Yer the great lady of Fyne!"

"I would follow ye, lady," one of her archers said. "We would all follow ye, a great lady like yer mother, into battle—or anywhere ye might lead!"

Everyone murmured in agreement.

Margaret could not believe the extent of their loyalty. She had never been as moved, as shaken. She whirled to face Alexander.

He stood as still as a stone statue, an arm's length from her, his expression impossible to read.

"I cannot bear this burden, this fault of mine! If you hang them, you must hang me, too, MacDonald!" she cried. And she had never meant anything more.

Behind her, several men gasped. Alexander said, unsmiling, "Ye will not hang, Lady Margaret. I said so last night and I am saying so, now." He was final.

Before she could argue with him, Sir Neil said, "Lady Margaret, do not prostrate yourself before him. Do not submit, do not bend. This is war. Men die in war. I am prepared to die. We are all prepared to die for you."

Margaret hugged herself, tears now falling. She could not let them die…they would follow her into battle again…they would follow her anywhere….

She stiffened, seized with a terrible comprehension—

she thought she knew how to commute their death sentences.

"You would follow me anywhere?" she asked.

"Aye," everyone said.

Trembling, she turned to face her captor again. His gaze instantly narrowed. "You lost a great many men, yesterday," she said.

With suspicion, he said, "Aye, I did."

"My men have proven their loyalty—and their courage in battle."

He waited.

"They will get down on bent knee before you, my lord, and swear their oath of loyalty to you now—if you will spare their lives."

He stared and she felt his mind racing. After a long pause, she said, "They will be loyal in battle, my lord, and this is war. You need every soldier you can get."

His stare had sharpened. "And ye, Lady Margaret? Will ye get down on your knee before me, will ye make an oath of fealty, too?"

She inhaled, their gazes locked. She did not dare look away now—not that she had the power to do so. It was as if time had stopped.

This was, beyond any doubt, a defining moment. She must save the lives of her men. But she was a Comyn and a MacDougall. Could she swear her allegiance to the Wolf of Lochaber—to Clan Donald?

Her mind felt frozen now. And there did not seem to be time to think. She only knew that if she refused, he would probably execute her men; if she accepted, he would spare them.

"Yes," she said.

Sir Neil cried out. "Lady! You cannot do such a thing!"

She blinked back hot tears, thinking of her mother

now. Even as she spoke, she did not look at Sir Neil—she only had eyes for Alexander. "I can, and I will. This is war, Sir Neil, and in war, men change sides all the time. Why can't I change my loyalties, too?" But she felt a tear sliding down her cheek. Her mother would approve. She simply knew it. But she felt ill, because once she performed an act of homage to Alexander MacDonald, her family would be her enemy.

But she must not contemplate that now.

"Bring them up into the courtyard at noon," Alexander ordered his guards, eyes ablaze. "The prisoners will make their vows before me—as will Lady Margaret Comyn." With that, he looked at her.

Margaret was taken aback. Why was he angry?

But Alexander then whirled and strode out of the cell, across the dungeons, and vanished into the stairwell.

Margaret hugged herself, staring after him. And all eyes remained upon her.

CHAPTER FIVE

"YE'LL SWEAR YER loyalty to the Wolf of Lochaber?" Peg had spoken with both disbelief and hostility.

It was noon. Margaret stood on the topmost step of the stairs leading from the great hall into the courtyard. Her men had already assembled there—Malcolm, Sir Neil, the archers and the soldiers. They were under a heavy guard.

The sun was high, amidst blue, cloudless skies, the mountains in the distance snowcapped. But she barely noticed the beauty of the land, for she was ill—very, very ill. In her stomach, in her heart—and in her soul.

She looked at Peg as she came to stand beside her. "He will spare them if I do."

Peg's eyes were on fire. "Yer mother despised the MacDonalds—as we all do!"

Margaret trembled, her stomach churning. What was she about to do? Could she really get down on one knee before Alexander MacDonald, and swear to keep her faith to him and him alone, as her liege lord, for the rest of her time on this earth?

"Mother would do what she had to do, to save her people," Margaret whispered.

"She *hated* the MacDonalds!" Peg cried.

She had hated Clan Donald more than she had hated the English—that was true. But Margaret was certain her mother would have sacrificed her own interests, as

Margaret was doing, to save the lives of the men who had fought so courageously for her.

"How will ye go to war against yer own family? Ye'll have to fight every Comyn now, every MacDougall. What of William? He'd never let ye do this, Margaret, if he were not so ill!"

"Hush! Enough!" Unfortunately, every word Peg had uttered was true. Alexander was at war with all of England and half of Scotland—he was at war with the great Comyn family now. It would not be long before their armies met, the one on Bruce's behalf, the other opposed against him. And what was she to do, then?

Would she be at Castle Fyne, awaiting word of a battle, whilst knowing her kin was fighting her liege lord?

She suddenly tensed, as Alexander emerged from the entry tower. He made a tall, proud figure, the wind whipping his dark hair about his shoulders, his mantle streaming like a cape behind him, both swords riding his thighs. The stiff breeze also buffeted his linen leine against his hard body. He appeared as powerful and as indomitable as when she had first glimpsed him.

She thought of his older brother, the lord of the Islay. Alasdair Og had married her maternal aunt, in spite of the hatred between their clans. She had heard so many tales about the couple, so it was impossible to know the truth—one such legend had it that Alasdair had abducted the lady Juliana from her bed, in the middle of the night, against her furious objections—and they had been married before dawn. Other tales claimed it had been love at first sight, and she had ridden off at midnight to meet him, against the explicit command of her father—risking her life to do so. It was also said that their marriage had been arranged during a brief truce between the clans.

If Juliana had been unwilling at first, then they had

a great deal in common, Margaret thought. But this was not marriage. She was merely swearing to give her loyalty to Alexander in times of both war and peace, for as long as she lived. Juliana had had to marry the enemy; she had had to sleep with him and bear his children.

She realized she was staring at him, and that he was staring back.

"Oh, he makes a fine figure of a man," Peg said angrily. "Is that why ye'll swear fealty now? Betray yer beloved family? Did something happen last night? Do ye yearn for his embrace another time?"

Margaret was so angry, she could not breathe properly. "How dare you! I thought we were friends. I am trying to do what is right! This is hardly an easy decision."

"This isn't right!" Peg cried. "Yer a great lady—a Comyn lady! Ye usually think so hard. But not this time. I think he's turned yer head! What of Buchan? Have ye thought at all about yer uncle now? Buchan will never forgive ye for this!"

He would disown her; of that, Margaret had no doubt, just as Sir Guy would, and she would have no one as a protector, no one except for the mighty Wolf.

"Go see William, then, at least tell him what ye intend," Peg now pleaded.

Margaret wrapped her mantle more closely about her and started down the steps, leaving Peg behind. She approached Alexander, who stood with the guards, not far from her men.

She could not smile as he turned to her. "It is noon," she said. "I will pay you homage first."

"No. You will stand aside, until the end."

She started, meeting his intense blue stare. Why did he wish for her to go last?

He turned away. "Bring me the first soldier."

One of her archers came forward, bareheaded and unarmed. He got down on one knee, clasping his hands in prayer, which he then outstretched. "My lord Alexander, mighty Wolf of Lochaber, I, Duncan MacDougall of Ardvaig, promise on my faith to ye, now and for all time, as I live and breathe, to be yer loyal man, to never cause ye harm, and if I dinna keep the faith, may God strike me down."

Alexander took his hands and clasped them. Solemnly, he said, "I, Alexander of Clan Donald, son of Angus Mor, lord of Glencarron, Coll and now of Castle Fyne, do accept yer pledge of fealty. Ye may rise, Duncan, and take up yer arms and join my men."

Duncan stood, smiling, and Alexander clasped him on the shoulder, smiling back. Then another archer came forward, getting down on one knee, making his oath of fealty.

Margaret stood back, somewhat behind Alexander, watching as he received each of her men in their acts of complete submission. As each man came forward, she thought about her parents, her uncles, her betrothed. She thought about her brothers, all dead, and William, who still lived. She thought about Alasdair Og and Lady Juliana.

Scotland was never at peace. Every lord, whether great or small, had rivals; every clan had friends and enemies. Fathers lost sons and wives lost husbands. Politics changed in a single breath. Widows married rivals. Battles raged daily. Stolen cows might be at stake—or stolen crowns.

The politics of the land frequently changed. Hadn't they just done so? The Comyns hated the English—now, they would surely fight for the English, against Bruce. This great lord, Alexander MacDonald, had once kept

the law for King Edward in the wilds of the western islands. Now he fought against the king, in the hopes of
making a new one.

She blinked back hot tears. Alliances changed, and
now, she would be in a war, and on the side opposed to
her entire MacDougall and Comyn families. Her heart
felt as if it were breaking in two.

Sir Neil had come forward, his gaze on her, not on Alexander. Margaret brushed her falling tears away awkwardly, wishing she hadn't succumbed to such female
weakness. She met Sir Neil's worried gaze again, and
somehow, lifted her chin proudly.

Ignoring Alexander, who stared at them both now,
Sir Neil said, "Lady, are ye certain? 'Tis not too late to
change yer mind!"

If Sir Neil did not perform homage and swear fealty,
he would be hanged. Margaret knew one thing—she
would never let that happen. "I am not changing my
mind, Sir Neil." She spoke as firmly as she could, but
heard the quaver in her own tone. Worse, she felt more
hot tears burning her eyes.

His eyes filled with doubt. Margaret stepped forward
and clasped his arm. "Please. We will fight for the Wolf
now, we will fight for Bruce—we will put a Scot on the
throne."

His eyes flickered. She realized he might not be allied with Bruce, but he thought as she did—any Scot was
better than King Edward.

Sir Neil smiled grimly at her and turned. "I beg your
pardon, my lord," he said.

"Ye have it," Alexander said, and Margaret wondered
at the slight flush mottling his high cheekbones.

Sir Neil knelt, extended his hands, and swore to be
faithful to Alexander for the rest of his life, God strike

him down otherwise. Alexander took his hands and accepted the pledge. When Sir Neil had arisen to his full height, Alexander dropped his hands. He did not clasp his shoulder, as he had thus far done to the previous men. For one moment, the two men stared at one another—as if antagonists, not friends.

"I will treat ye well, as long as ye remain faithful," the Wolf said.

"I dinna care how ye treat me. She is my lady, ye must treat her well," Sir Neil said.

"Go and receive your weapons and join my men," Alexander returned evenly. But he glanced at Margaret, as did Sir Neil.

Margaret nodded at the knight, and he left. One of the MacDonald soldiers greeted him, grinning and clasping his arm. They walked off together, across the courtyard, to the weapons store in the north tower.

"He is very loyal to ye."

She met Alexander's gaze. "I do not know why. He only came into my uncle's service six months ago. I do not know him well, although after these past few days, I can say he is strong, faithful and brave."

"It is good, to have a loyal knight," he said. Then he turned, gesturing impatiently; only Malcolm and Margaret were left.

She wondered at his words, though. It had seemed as if he meant that it was fortunate for her, that Sir Neil was so loyal. But he was not her knight now.

Her stomach churned. Soon it would be her turn. Could she really betray her family? But there was no choice. She had promised to do just that, and Alexander was fulfilling his end of the bargain.

Malcolm had paused before Alexander, and before he even spoke, Margaret knew a crisis was at hand. His shoulders were stiffly set, his head tilted with defiance. His gray eyes blazed.

Alexander's calm demeanor changed; his hand went to the hilt of one sword. "Ye will not make homage today?"

"I will never swear an oath of fealty to ye, MacDonald," Malcolm spat.

Margaret gasped as Alexander said, "Hang him."

She rushed forward. "Malcolm, you will die this day if you do not make your vows!"

He faced her, eyes blazing. "I am a MacDougall, Lady Margaret, and I gladly die—a MacDougall!"

She cringed. He would never change his mind. "Oh, Malcolm! This is my fault! I should have surrendered the castle to him!"

"No, lady, ye were brave, and I am proud to have served ye, even in defeat. And I will not judge ye for what you have decided to do this day. I ken, ye wish to save the lives of yer men. But I canna go against my brothers, my uncles, my cousins…not even for ye."

She started to cry.

Two of Alexander's men now seized Malcolm, one of them shackling his wrists behind his back. They marched him across the courtyard, past the great hall. A scaffold was at the far end of the bailey.

Margaret watched the three men, Malcolm walking proudly between the MacDonald soldiers, until she simply couldn't see. Her tears entirely blurred her vision.

"Ye have only lost one man today—and the choice was his, not yours, to make."

She faced Alexander furiously. "You could still spare him!"

He studied her. "I cannot spare him."

She actually understood why Malcolm could not be spared, but she hated Alexander anyway.

And she hated herself for crying. For failing to surrender when given the chance, and for what she must now do. Margaret dropped to both knees. She wiped her wet face on her sleeves, and joined her hands as if in prayer, then held them out. She could not breathe properly now. More sobs threatened, from deep within her chest.

He seized her hands. "Get up," he said. As he spoke, he dragged her dead weight upward, until she was standing.

"What are you doing?" She tore her palms from his. "I haven't made my pledge yet!"

"I will not accept yer vows."

She was so distraught, so desperate, so angry, at first, she did not understand him and she stared through her tears. And as he stared back, his face hard, she realized what was happening. "You deceived me? Is this treachery? You said you would spare them, if I swore my oath of fealty, too."

"I am not accepting yer oath, Lady Margaret," he said, in that tone she hated, that tone that was as final as the word of God.

She screamed at him. "This is trickery! You have tricked my men! They were following me!"

He looked past her. "Get her maid. Take her away," he said.

Her men were loyal to her. They had only pledged their faith to Alexander, because they were following her—because they expected her to do so, too! She could not allow her men to pledge to him, and then fail to do so, herself.

Margaret sank back down to her knees. She held out her hands, but gazed up at Alexander. "I, Lady Margaret Comyn, of Castle Fyne, daughter of Mary MacDougall, niece of the Earl of Buchan, do swear to you, Alexander

MacDonald, lord of Castle Fyne, son of the lord of the isles, my faith, here and now, for as long as I live—God help me and strike me down if I lie!"

"Get up," he snapped at her. "I dinna accept!"

She shoved her hands upward, at him. "Bastard!"

Flushing, he said fiercely, "Get her on her feet, and get her gone."

Margaret was seized from behind. "Let me be," she screamed at the men, struggling to become free of them as they held her arms from behind. But as she struggled viciously against them, she stared at Alexander, hoping he knew just how much she hated him. He had tricked her, and she had never hated anyone more.

He stared coldly back at her.

A loud thump sounded.

Margaret went still. Slowly, she turned her head, and saw Malcolm hanging from the scaffold, his hands on the noose at his throat as he frantically attempted to loosen it.

She choked on the horror, turning her head away. As she did, someone seized her and pulled her forward, and she was enclosed in a powerful embrace.

Margaret realized Alexander was shielding her from watching Malcolm die. But all the same, she cried.

MARGARET KNELT BY William, who was unconscious, holding his hands. She could not stop weeping. Her heart was entirely broken. All was lost.

Castle Fyne was lost, her men were lost, and Malcolm had been hanged. And the damned Wolf of Lochaber had tricked her and her men.

But of course he had. Someone had said, from the beginning, that he was clever and shrewd and not to be trusted. She would never trust him again.

Why had he refused her oath of fealty? She was so

distraught she could not think of a single reason for him to have done so.

Holding her brother's hands, she laid her cheek on the pallet, tempted to crawl into bed with him. But he was hurt and the pallet was narrow and she did not want to disturb him. God, she was so alone! She needed comfort from someone, anyone, but there was no one to offer it to her.

When her tears finally ceased, she curled up on the floor beside William's bed, exhausted. There were no rugs in his chamber, and the stones were freezing, but she almost welcomed the chilling cold. She did not care if she lived or died.

And when strong hands grasped her, and she was lifted into powerful arms, she was too exhausted to fight him another time.

Alexander carried her to her chamber, and left her there in her bed.

MARGARET AWOKE AND was surprised, because a bright, strong light was shining through her chamber's single window, indicating it was midafternoon. For one moment, she was confused, as she attempted to sit up. She was so oddly weak—as if she had been ill. And then there was total recollection.

She sank back down onto her bed, recalling the siege, her captor, her men performing homage to him, and the hanging of Malcolm. And for one moment, she lay very still.

Why had Alexander carried her from the entry tower to her own chamber? And why had he refused her oath of fealty?

She was so weak—and so hungry—that she could not think clearly. She could not recall when she had last been as ravenous. Margaret attempted to sit up again, and this time, she felt dizzy.

She took her time, now concerned—she must not become ill. Castle Fyne had fallen, and she had lost her men, but the country was at war—Robert Bruce was fighting the English, and seeking Scotland's throne. Castle Fyne could be retaken—it had to be retaken. Now, she thought about the first messengers, sent by Malcolm before the siege. Had the one headed for her mother's brother ever reached him?

And where was Sir Ranald? Would he return with help? He would never abandon her!

Margaret managed to shove her feet to the floor, trembling from the exertion. Someone had removed her shoes, and they were on the floor, but she ignored them. She stood, her balance so precarious that she staggered to the door and fell upon it, sinking to her knees on the floor.

The door was opened immediately. "Yer awake!" Alan cried, sounding relieved. He stooped over her, extending his hand. "Let me help ye."

"Don't touch me," she warned. She seized the door handle and stood up. How could she be so weak, when she needed to be so strong?

Alan met her gaze, his wide, and he turned and rushed off.

Margaret paused, gathering up her strength, hoping Peg might appear, to help her sort through the facts—and plot the future. As she did so, she heard *his* determined strides, on the stone stairwell, and she tensed.

Alexander appeared on the stairs, Peg behind him. His gaze locked instantly with hers.

She found it difficult to breathe. "Why am I so weak? What has happened?"

"Ye slept for three entire days, and Peg says ye haven't eaten since the siege."

She felt her stomach contract with pain. "How is William?"

"He is weak, but he is healing. There is no infection," Alexander said. "Do ye have a death wish, now? To stand barefoot on the stone in the midst of winter?"

"I have no plan to die." As if he cared—but then, of course he did—she had a great value to him as his hostage.

"How pleased I am to hear that." He faced Peg. "Get her shoes."

Peg fled past him into the chamber, seizing Margaret's shoes. She stepped into them, never removing her gaze from his. "Why did you deceive me? Why did you refuse my act of homage? I could be your vassal now."

"Do ye wish to come down and dine?" he asked flatly, indicating he had no wish to answer her.

She said, very coldly, "I would rather starve than dine with you."

"I am not foolish enough to invite ye to dine with me. Ye hate me. I ken. But ye must eat."

"I am your hostage so you want me alive. I am tempted to starve myself just to deny you." How she meant it. Thwarting him in any way would give her a great satisfaction.

Behind him, Peg gasped. His eyes were chilling now. "Yer defiance will not serve ye well, and yer clever enough to comprehend that." He turned. "Feed her." He strode back down the stairs.

Margaret held out her hand and Peg rushed to her, seizing it. "How can ye defy him? He is our master now!"

"I can and I will—and he will never be my master," Margaret said. Then, "Is William truly getting better?"

"He is awake, and there is no infection. But he remains weak, having lost so much blood. Still, he is asking about ye. Oh, I have been so worried about ye, Margaret!"

Margaret smiled grimly at her. At least her brother was on the mend, and she thanked God for that. She ignored Alan, who remained at attention, not far from his stool. "And Sir Neil? How is he?"

Peg started. "He has been terribly worried about ye, Lady Margaret. We all have."

She absorbed that. "And what of the fact that Mac-Donald would not let me swear fealty to him? Are they furious?"

Peg hesitated. "I dinna think so. I think they're relieved."

Margaret grimaced, imagining that Peg was right.

"And they are occupied with the tasks being given them," Peg added. "Every man has been set to repairing the fortifications. Our soldiers are getting on with the Wolf's men. They do not seem to mind being his men, either."

She wondered at that. "Has there been any news? Any news of this war between Bruce and the English, any word of Buchan or even Sir Guy?"

Peg lowered her voice. "I have only heard the Wolf speaking once, to Padraig—that Bruce went directly to Glasgow from Castle Ayr."

She was so weak and so hungry, it was hard to make sense of this fact. "That is all you have heard? What does that mean? Why would Bruce go to that city?"

"To seek absolution for his sins," Peg said. She shrugged. "'Tis what I heard, and he did murder Red John inside a church!"

"He cannot receive absolution," Margaret said. "He will surely be excommunicated by the Pope—if he hasn't

already been. Oh, if only we could learn whether or not
Buchan and Sir Guy know of the fall of Castle Fyne! Peg,
we must have war news!"

"Aye, in time, but right now, his lordship is right,
ye must eat, Lady Margaret, so ye can gain back yer
strength—if ye still wish to fight him."

Peg was right—she needed her strength, and all of
her wits. "Peg, I am a Comyn and my mother's daughter. I will fight him until I take Castle Fyne back—or
until I die."

Peg flushed. "I dinna think ye'd have changed yer
mind. But ye should not speak of dying."

Margaret nodded. She was seventeen, and she did
not want to contemplate dying anytime soon. They went
down the narrow stairwell side by side, Peg supporting her by holding her elbow. The great hall was empty,
and Peg left Margaret alone at the table, rushing off for
a meal.

Margaret stared at the hall. No one had changed the
rushes, and no one had scented them with lavender. She
saw some scraps and bones along the walls on the floor,
where his men's pallets were piled up until the evening.
There were some rotting morsels of meat on the table,
too, not far from where she sat.

Her every instinct was to order the rushes removed,
the floors swept clean, the tables scrubbed, and new
rushes brought in. But this was his keep for the moment,
and she must not lift a finger to improve it.

Peg returned with a platter of bread, cheese and cold
venison. Margaret was starving and for the next ten minutes, she ate ravenously, and in silence. When she was
done, she thanked Peg and got up. "I am going to inspect
the keep," she said. "I want to see what he is doing." She
left Peg clearing the table, and went outside.

She paused in surprise, as the courtyard was a hive of activity, and the ramparts above were as busy. The castle had suffered a great deal of damage during the siege, and Alexander's men were everywhere, some firing anvils, others sawing wood, others with hammers in hand. The walls were being repaired with mud and stone, the stone having clearly been brought in from the countryside. The drawbridge had been damaged somewhat in the siege, and it was down, a dozen men bent over it with hammers, planks of new wood and rope. The gates of the barbican were open and great planks of wood were being used to fortify it after the destruction caused by the Wolf's battering rams.

There was even more. Other men were dragging huge casks from the cellars, and some of those casks were being winched up onto the ramparts. Still others were entering the keep, leading horse-drawn carts filled with rocks and stones or firewood.

Ignoring Peg, who had come outside behind her, Margaret walked down the stairs, realizing that this was why the Wolf was such a mighty warrior. He took nothing for granted. Clearly, these repairs had been underway since she had collapsed, as clearly he was preparing the castle for war.

Images flashed of the siege she had just resisted, of men climbing up the walls of her ramparts, of arrows and missiles flying, of her archers lined up, shooting at them, of her women attempting to stop them with burning oil. She felt sick.

She did not want to be a part of another siege again, yet she desperately needed just such an attack, if the castle were to be freed.

War now frightened her as never before, for it was no longer an abstract concept. Her gaze moved over everyone in the crowded bailey, and then in the barbican. She realized she was trying to locate the Wolf. Not having done so, she looked up at the ramparts.

Her heart lurched. Alexander stood there. He was with a great many men, directing their actions. He had shed his swords and mantle, and the breeze outlined his leine against his powerful body, while his dark hair streamed in the wind.

How mighty he appeared. Was she a madwoman, to think she might ever defeat him?

He glanced down at her.

She instantly turned away.

"Lady Margaret!"

She turned at the sound of Sir Neil's voice. He was hurrying to her, clad only in his leine and boots, a dagger at his waist, a hammer in hand. He was smiling and she smiled back. "I heard you were awake," he exclaimed. "We have been so worried about you."

"I am sorry to have caused alarm," she said, searching his gaze as he paused before her. "How are you, Sir Neil?"

He sobered. "In truth? I didn't care for the Wolf's trickery, lady, but he is a good leader. He is fair and strong. He works us hard, but he feeds us well."

"You swore fealty, so you must be his advocate now." She somehow smiled when she did not feel like smiling at all.

"But I will still protect ye," Sir Neil said. "My one vow cannot change the other."

Margaret decided not to point out the falsity of that. "This is rather impressive," she said, glancing around. "Is he expecting an attack?"

"He has not said so, but I watch him closely, lady, and I believe he is. He has been urging these repairs and preparations, and when we are not mending stone and wood, we are in the fields, practicing with our swords and riding our horses." He touched her sleeve. "Sir Guy is on the march."

Her heart slammed. "Is he marching here?"

"I don't know, my lady. He left Castle Ayr days ago, when it fell to Bruce."

Was Sir Guy marching toward them? If he attacked, could he win? His reputation was an impressive one, but not as impressive as the Wolf's. Would his brother, Aymer de Valence, aid him? If so, perhaps sheer numbers would win the day.

"How many men does Alexander have?" she asked.

"He has five hundred here. But he has the support of his brothers—I have heard that he can summon hundreds more, lady."

"So can the English," she said rather tersely.

Sir Neil started at her tone. Then he flushed, as Alexander said, from behind her, "Be careful of what ye wish for."

She felt an impossible tension, and slowly, she turned. "How could I not wish for your defeat?"

"If I am defeated, Castle Fyne falls—it could easily be destroyed."

Margaret was taken aback. "It is a great stronghold—are you telling me it could be razed to the ground?"

"No castle is indestructible, lady, not in this modern day, when we have siege engines and battering rams."

"Sir Guy would never destroy Castle Fyne, not when we are to be married."

"A razed castle can be rebuilt," he said.

She shuddered. "Will Sir Guy attack?" She realized that, as much as she wished for him to do so, she was afraid. She had just been in a siege, and dear God, how she hoped to never have to endure another one.

"King Edward would wish for him to command this castle," Alexander said. "Just as Bruce wishes for me to command it."

She took comfort in the fact that Alexander expected Sir Guy to attack, sooner or later, while she now feared her home's strategic importance in this war.

The watch from one of the towers shouted in warning. Margaret froze. Fear rose up.

Alexander touched her arm. "We are not being attacked, Margaret. A rider has come."

She whirled to face him with sudden hope. Could the rider be from Buchan? Argyll? Sir Guy? Perhaps someone had come with a demand that she be released!

"It is my scout, returning with war news."

ALEXANDER'S SCOUT WAS about her age, his hair long and blond, his nose freckled. The moment he rode into the courtyard on his blowing mount, he was warmly greeted by Alexander and Padraig. The two men instantly took the lad inside.

Margaret did not think twice, she quickly followed. And now, she wondered at the relationship of Alexander and Padraig. The auburn-haired Highlander was clearly highly trusted by him. This was not the first time she had seen them together, and she thought that Padraig might be second in command.

They had gathered about one of the trestle tables, as the maids within rushed to bring the boy food and wine, while stoking the fires in the hearth even higher. Margaret hesitated by the door, awaiting discovery—awaiting Alexander's command to leave. But he only glanced briefly at her before clasping the young lad's shoulder and guiding him aside. "How goes it, Seoc?"

Seoc grinned. "Well, my lord, and I have war news aplenty."

Margaret could barely hear. She itched to move closer to them, but wasn't certain she dared. The men huddled together, Seoc now speaking, the others listening closely. She could not make out their words, other than the mention of Rothesay and Inverskip.

"Do ye wish to join us?" Alexander asked, glancing at her.

Certain she was red of face, Margaret walked over to them. "Why would you allow me to join you?"

"Because yer the lady of Fyne and the country is at war," he said simply, his gaze steady upon her.

She could not comprehend his motives. Did he mean that she should be apprised of the war? It seemed incredible.

Alexander turned back to the boy. "What else?"

"Bruce took Dalswinton easily," Seoc said, "and Christopher Seton has taken Castle Tibbers."

Margaret refrained from making a sound. But Dalswinton was a Comyn stronghold, one belonging to the deceased Red John.

Padraig smiled, handing Seoc a mug of wine, which he downed. "Boyd is a good man, as is Seton." He looked at Alexander. "Dumfries, Ayr, Tibbers, Rothesay, Inverskip, and Dalswinton. A pleasing start."

Alexander glanced at Margaret. "Ye've forgotten Castle Fyne."

Padraig glanced at her, as well. "I was being polite."

Margaret remained unmoving. Robert Bruce was on the march, she thought, with a sense of panic. Was he now unstoppable?

"There's more," the boy said, his mouth stuffed. "Red John's wife, Joan, is now at Berwick. She is begging her brother for aid—she wishes fer an alliance with him— she wishes fer revenge."

Margaret trembled, feeling for Joan de Valence, whom she knew somewhat. Red John had married Aymer's older sister years ago, when Margaret was a small child. Such unions were commonplace. However, during the reign of King John Balliol, Joan had relinquished most of her ties to her brother, for this was when both the Comyn and MacDougall families had gained so much power in the north of Scotland, and had spent so much time warring against King Edward.

Now, she sought help from her English brother. Now, the Comyn and MacDougall families were united in their ambitions to avenge her husband, Red John, to stop Bruce from stealing the throne, and perhaps even to destroy him.

But what of Sir Guy? Did she dare ask Seoc herself?

"Aymer de Valence will gladly unite with his sister now," Alexander said thoughtfully. "And if he did not, King Edward would order it."

Margaret wondered at his tone. He had sounded as if he knew the English king.

Alexander looked at her and asked Seoc, "What of Sir Guy de Valence, his bastard brother?"

Seoc now looked at Margaret, clearly aware of her betrothal. "He has crossed the Firth of Clyde, my lord, and is at Glen Lean."

Margaret gasped. Sir Guy was but a day or two away!

Alexander was staring at her now. "Have a care, Lady Margaret, yer eagerness to escape my hospitality shows." Before she could answer—not that she had a reply to make—he turned to the boy. "And his force?"

"He has eleven hundred men, my lord, including two hundred mounted knights."

Sir Guy outmanned Alexander, Margaret managed to think.

He looked at her again, and slowly, he began to smile. "So we go to battle, then."

Did he look forward to engaging Sir Guy—when he was outnumbered? Margaret was incredulous.

He turned back to Seoc. "Tomorrow, ye ride to my brother at Dunaverty. Tell Angus all of this news, and that I have taken Castle Fyne. Also tell him to be certain he has provisioned the stronghold for war."

"Aye, my lord," Seoc said, no longer eating.

"And ask him for five hundred men—and as many knights as he can spare."

Seoc nodded again. "If ye wish, I can leave in a moment. I'm not tired, my lord."

Alexander smiled and clapped his shoulder. "It would please me greatly if ye left tonight."

Seoc beamed, clearly basking in the Wolf's approval.

Padraig now approached. "I am proud of ye," he said. "Can I talk to ye for a moment, afore ye go?"

"Aye, Father."

Margaret hadn't realized that they were father and son. Padraig and Seoc stepped aside, moving to the other table, where they sat and began to converse.

"What ails ye, Lady Margaret?"

She stared at Alexander, reminding herself that if she was very fortunate, in a few days Sir Guy would take Castle Fyne, and she would be free of the mighty Wolf of Lochaber. But she remained nervous. "I do not like war, not even when it is for a good cause," she finally said.

"Sir Guy will never defeat me, lady."

She inhaled raggedly. "I have heard you have never

been defeated in battle—but there is always a first time. And this time, you are outmanned. This time, God is on our side, not yours—as you stole what is mine."

"I happen to think God would be very pleased with me, for seeking to put Bruce on the throne," Alexander said.

"Bruce murdered a man on holy ground!"

"He did not deliver the final blows, and he is next in line to be Scotland's lawful king."

"I do not care about the destiny of kings," she cried, meaning it. "I care about this one place, which my mother passed on to me."

"So if ye have yer wishes come true, I will be defeated, Castle Fyne will be yer portion—and ye will wed in June," he said, staring closely.

She wanted Castle Fyne back, but if Sir Guy was victorious, they would soon be married.

He said softly, "I canna see ye as an English wife."

She flinched. "I will never be an English wife—I will be an Englishman's wife."

He laughed, but the sound was mirthless. "'Tis the same. If ye wed Sir Guy, ye will become his wife, and ye'll lose all yer rights—ye'll be as English as he is, fighting his wars, against me, against Bruce."

Margaret did not speak, for he had just verbalized her worst fears.

He then hardened. "Do ye really believe he can defeat me?"

Margaret hugged her mantle closer. A terrible battle loomed—in the midst of a terrible war. She was frightened—but there was more than just her fear of the siege to come. She simply couldn't identify her emotions as she stared at him. "I will pray for your defeat."

"And will ye pray for my death?"

"I pray for no man's death," she said. But hadn't she once wished him dead, before the siege?

She should wish him dead now—but she simply couldn't. Shaken, she whispered, "When will Sir Guy attack?"

"He will not attack. I ride out at dawn, lady."

"What?"

"He will not attack here—I will attack him—at Loch Riddon."

CHAPTER SIX

MARGARET PACED, ALONE in her bedchamber, aware of darkness settling over the hills and forests outside. When Peg slipped into the chamber, she whirled and rushed to her. "Sir Guy is marching on us," she cried. "Clearly, he intends to free Castle Fyne."

Peg paled. "Will there be another siege?"

"Alexander intends to meet him at Loch Riddon—he intends to be the attacker, not the attacked." This was why he was such a mighty warrior, she thought grimly, turning and pacing again. She did not have to know very much about warfare to realize that attacking gave one an advantage.

"I am glad we won't have to suffer another siege," Peg said. "And ye may have yer English husband, after all."

Margaret looked sharply at her—her tone was strange. Peg was opposed to the union, and she had been blunt about it the other day.

So much had happened since she had arrived at Castle Fyne—her entire life had been turned upside down. She was a dutiful woman—a dutiful daughter and niece. Of course she meant to do as her uncle ordered. She knew she was fortunate, that he had arranged a good marriage for her. But she was reluctant to wed Sir Guy, though he might be the one to liberate her.

She suddenly wondered if deep within herself, a tiny part of her wished for his defeat.

There would never be a union, then.

"Does he ride for war at dawn on the morrow?" Peg asked, interrupting her thoughts.

She jerked. "Yes." She shook herself free of such absurd feelings. She wanted Castle Fyne back, even if it meant that she would marry an Englishman. She was the lady of Castle Fyne—and that was more important than anything else.

Margaret picked up her mantle. "Is he in the hall, still?"

Peg hesitated, seeming uncertain. "Yes. Why?"

"I wish to speak with William. If we did not have that guard outside, I would simply wait for him to go to bed, and attempt to steal into Will's chamber. But Alan remains—so I will have to ask him for permission."

"He will deny you," Peg said, taking off her shoes and sitting on the bed. She began to unbraid her long auburn hair.

Margaret was afraid of that, as well. "William needs to know what passes, and I need to see him now that he is better." She also needed to confide in him.

"Maybe ye should just rest, and retire for the night? Ye can speak with Will another time." Peg began finger combing her curls, not looking at her.

Peg's behavior was odd. "Is something amiss?"

The maid flinched. "No." She smiled, but it seemed strained.

Something was bothering her, but Margaret dismissed it. Peg would tell her what was on her mind sooner, not later; she could not keep secrets. Margaret went to the door, opening it, and as she did, she heard Alexander on the stairwell.

She tensed as he appeared on the landing and they both ignored Alan, seated on his stool. "Is there any way you would be kind enough to allow me to see my brother before I retire?"

"No." He walked past her, into his own chamber, where a fire already roared in the hearth.

Her heart sank. Grimly, she followed him to the threshold, but did not enter the room. He was removing his waist belt and dagger. She refused to recall the last time she had seen him doing so. "I wish to see for myself that he is better."

"Ye wish to plan an escape while I am gone." He faced her briefly, before sitting and removing his boots.

"But you will have Alan as my shadow. If we plot anything—he will report it."

"If ye speak French, he will not know the contents of yer plot, Lady Margaret. Nor will I." French was the language spoken amongst the nobility of Scotland, England and France. While Alexander was fairly fluent in French, his men appeared to only speak English and Gaelic. "Yer clever enough to arrange an escape when I am not present, and I have no intention of allowing that."

"How could we escape?" she cried. "William isn't well enough to travel through the forest in the midst of winter."

He eyed her. "I can think of one or two ways—and ye are clever…eventually, ye will, too."

She trembled, wondering if escape might be possible, with him gone. But she could not leave William behind. "I won't leave my brother," she said. "And I can swear to that."

"So I can trust ye for the moment? Tomorrow I go to war, Lady Margaret, and I do not feel like having this battle now. My decision is final."

She knew when she had hit an unmovable rock. Margaret did not even attempt to smile, but their stares locked. She suddenly wondered about his wife—the lover he had married, who had then died in childbirth. Had he ever been kind or considerate toward her? Had he ever given a command, only to later rescind it?

She did not think so.

"Good night, Lady Margaret," he said.

She turned, not replying, going back into her room. Peg was standing in its center, barefoot, but clasping her plaid about her. "I must run downstairs," she said.

Margaret thought that odd, but she nodded, going to each taper and blowing them out. The small fire remained in the hearth for warmth. She crawled into the bed, cuddling under the covers as Peg left.

She wasn't angry, for she had expected him to deny her. She even understood why he had done so.

She hoped she was not becoming soft toward the enemy. First she had been hesitant about wishing for Sir Guy to defeat him, and now, she understood why he would not let her see her brother. But at least William was healing.

Her eyes were closing, and she realized that she would fall asleep easily, in spite of how much she had slept these past few days. She was still overburdened and overtired. So much had happened…and now, there would be another battle…and maybe she would soon be free….

A loud thump awoke her. Margaret clutched the covers, eyes wide, staring into the dark. It took her a moment to calm, as her reaction to being awoken abruptly, in the middle of the night, was one of fear. But no one began a siege in the middle of the night. She had probably been dreaming. Still, her heart continued to race.

She began to relax into the quiet now, and then she realized that other half of the bed was empty. She sat up. "Peg?" she whispered. The embers in the hearth cast a small halo of light. Peg was not on a pallet on the floor, where she sometimes slept when Margaret was too restless and bothersome.

Margaret sank back down, curling up under the covers. Before she could wonder where Peg was, she heard a woman's throaty moans coming from the adjacent chamber.

She felt her cheeks flame. Alexander had a woman in his bed, she managed to think, stunned. But why was she surprised? Most men spent the night with their lovers or their wives. He would hardly be celibate for all of this time.

Margaret clapped her hands over her ears, to block out the disturbing, distressful noises.

The woman seemed quiet now, but Margaret was afraid to unclasp her ears. Slowly, she did so. She was stiff with a tension she could not identify. The one thing she did know was that she was upset.

But why should she care what Alexander did—or who he took to his bed?

She began to worry about where her missing maid might be.

And then she heard a thump, followed by another one and another one, and the rhythmic pounding was unmistakable. Margaret dove under the covers, seizing her pillow, as the woman gasped in pleasure again. She pulled the pillow over her head, but it could not block out the sound of the woman's growing delight. Margaret threw the pillow away, covered her ears with her hands, and gritted her teeth. It was a long time before the adjacent chamber was silent, and even longer before she fell asleep.

MARGARET STOOD BEFORE the fire she had stoked herself, warming her hands. It was at least an hour before dawn.

She had at last fallen asleep when the lovers next door had finally stopped their lovemaking, but she thought she had only slept a few minutes. She was too distressed to sleep any more—and too angry.

The door to her chamber slowly opened, and Peg peeked inside.

Margaret felt a rush of anger, then. "Are you afraid to come into my chamber? Oh, wait, it is the crack of dawn and you are afraid, for you have betrayed me."

Peg stepped inside, eyes wide. "Lady!"

"No, do not 'lady' me!" Margaret admonished. She seized a rush and lit it and held it up, close to Peg, but then wished she hadn't.

Peg was beautiful—radiant. She was flushed, her eyes bright, her hair loose and wild—she looked like she had been well pleased.

"How dare you sleep with him and then come back to me!"

Tears filled Peg's eyes. "I had no choice, my lady!"

"There is always a choice, and we both know he did not rape you!"

"He didn't rape me, but there was no choice, I vow it!"

"I heard how pleased you were to be with him," Margaret choked. "You are my maid! He has stolen my castle! We are his prisoners! What is wrong with you?"

She was crying now. "When ye were ill, he sent for me. I dinna wish to be with him, I swear it, but Margaret, he knows how to please a woman!"

She felt fire exploding in her cheeks. She struck Peg hard across the face, and the sound rang out in the stillness of the night. "He is my enemy!"

"I ken," she wept. "And I'm sorry!"

Margaret trembled in rage. But now, as Peg collapsed on the bed, crying, she could not believe that she had hit her. She clenched her fists. "If you truly loved me, you would not have even considered sleeping with him. Honor would forbid it. If you loved me, you would have been furious when he asked for you."

"I'm only twenty, Margaret. I canna help but notice how handsome some men are! Have ye not noticed just how handsome the Wolf is? He's the mighty Wolf of Lochaber! Every woman wishes for his attention!"

"He's a MacDonald, Peg, or have you forgotten?"

Peg hesitated, but her cheeks were red. "I won't lie to ye. I hated him at first. But this doesn't change anything—I am yer maid."

"It changes everything," Margaret said, incapable of drawing an even breath. "When did this affair begin?"

Redder now, Peg said, "The night ye collapsed."

Margaret was in disbelief, but then she found her voice. "If he summons you again, you will refuse him. *If* you ever wish to return to Bain with me."

Peg cried out.

"You cannot be loyal to us both," Margaret said.

"I am loyal to ye, Lady Margaret, always, and how could ye doubt that? Sharing his bed cannot change that!"

"You did not hear me well. If you share his bed again, you will no longer serve me—and you may stay here, in his service." She was sick now.

Peg did not move. She stared so wide that in the dark room her eyes seemed entirely white.

Margaret heard his door open and close. She clenched her fists.

Peg wet her lips and said, "He willna take no for an answer. He willna let me refuse."

"Then you will stay here, in his service, or go with him to the isles." She was final.

Margaret now turned and entered the hall. A part of

her wanted to cry for the loss of her friend and maid, another part of her refused to do so. Alan must have heard them, for he was on his feet. Margaret ignored him, hurrying downstairs after Alexander, her shoulders now squared.

The great hall was entirely lit. Burning torches had been placed on the wall sconces, and fires roared in both hearths. Three dozen knights slept in the hall, and they were already up and seated at the tables. Castle Fyne's maids were busily bringing them their breakfast.

She faltered. Every Highlander wore his swords, and their shields were piled up close to the door. There was no conversation as everyone consumed their rations for the long day ahead.

She stared past them all. Alexander was not seated. He stood by the head of one table, but he was looking directly at her.

He was going to war. She should wish him dead—both because she wanted Castle Fyne back, and because he had destroyed her relationship with Peg.

But still, she did not wish him dead. As she stared at him, her heart lurched, as if with dread.

Now, she knew firsthand what war was like. He was a great and mighty warrior, but all it took was one true arrow, or one fatal sword, and he would be mighty no more.

She said, very quietly, "I'd like a privy moment."

His eyes flickered as he came forward. "Do ye wish to go upstairs? Or step outside?"

Peg was upstairs. "Outside."

"I thought so." He touched her elbow, as if to guide her. Margaret leapt away instantly.

She hurried ahead of him, her spine stiff, but he opened the heavy door for her. Outside, they paused atop the wood steps leading down to the courtyard. It was freezing and she shivered, noting that the sky was just beginning to pale in the east, but stars winked above them in the blackness of the west.

She faced him. "You have stolen my maid from me."

"That was not my intent."

"But that is what you have done. I cannot have a maid with loyalties to my enemy."

He studied her. It was a moment before he spoke. "I agree. Yer maid must be loyal to ye, not to me. But I dinna steal her. Yer maid has an appetite. She is a bawd. Her character is flawed. She could have refused me. She did not. She is not good enough for ye."

Margaret had not expected such a response. "I have known Peg since we were children. She has been an important friend for most of my life. You knew she was in my service."

"Aye, but I also knew she would rush to my bed, if asked—she is not a true friend, Lady Margaret."

Margaret was taken aback. Was he right? She had always thought of Peg as a true and loyal friend. "And you had to ask her? You could not ask someone else?"

"I dinna think much about it. If ye wish to be angry with me, so be it. But ye should punish her and dismiss her."

She was bewildered. "Why do you take my side? She is your lover!"

His brow lifted. "She warmed my bed for a night or two—she is but a passing amusement, Lady Margaret, not a mistress." He then added, "Ye almost seem jealous."

"I'm hardly jealous." But as she spoke, an odd pang went through her. "I am angry and I am also sad. Because of your need for amusement, I have lost a friend."

He suddenly swept off his mantle and threw it around

her shoulders. "Sometimes, blessings come in disguise. 'Tis good to learn of her weaknesses now, before ye could be truly hurt."

Margaret gazed up at him. Was he *concerned* for her? Did he *care* that her maid was now of questionable loyalty?

And was he right? Was it better to have learned now how easily Peg could betray her, rather than at a later time? Castle Fyne had been besieged and defeated, and Scotland was now in the throes of war. She could have asked Peg for aid in some way related to her predicament, never knowing that she might not be loyal. And what about later, when she meant to use trickery to see William? Would Peg keep her confidence? If Alexander asked her, upon his return from the battle, would she divulge it? "I suppose it is best that I learned of her true character, but I am hardly going to thank you for your part in all of this."

He smiled. "I never thought ye would. Yer a strong, brave woman—ye need strong, brave allies."

The scents hanging to his mantle began to waft over her. She smelled pine, fire, the sea…and man.

His smile vanished. He regarded her closely. "Sir Neil is a better ally. Ye can trust him."

She hugged his mantle closer. Why was he telling her that she could trust Sir Neil? Again, she had the oddest notion that he cared. But she had to be wrong. "Why would you advise me like this?"

He hesitated, no longer smiling. "I admire ye, Lady Margaret, but yer very young and very untried. And ye have no champion now."

"You cannot take that role. You cannot be my champion, not even in this moment—you are my *enemy*."

His stare darkened. "We're on opposing sides of a great war, but yer not my enemy."

She inhaled, their gazes locked. She simply could not comprehend him, but he was fierce. It suddenly occurred to her that, if he hadn't attacked her castle, even though on opposing sides of such a war, they could be friends. But she did not say so.

"And yer in my care. If I can advise ye, I will." He had softened. "I must go, Lady Margaret." He hesitated, his stare piercing. "It would please me greatly if ye dinna wish me dead."

She stiffened. He was going to war. He might be defeated. He might even be killed. And that prospect should thrill her. Instead, she felt nothing but worry and dismay.

She said, very slowly, and choosing her words with great care, "I cannot wish you well, Alexander."

He did not make a sound, but she thought she saw disappointment flaring in his eyes.

She added, "But I do not wish you ill."

MARGARET STOOD ON the bottom steps, gazing out into the great hall. How empty it now was.

Alexander had ridden out of the keep hours ago, astride his gray stallion, followed by his forty mounted knights. Margaret had watched from a window in the south tower as they rode through the entry tower and then the barbican, the MacDonald colors waving high above them. Outside the castle's walls, the rest of his army had fallen into place behind him—first several more columns of mounted knights, and then hundreds upon hundreds of Highland foot soldiers.

She had watched him until he disappeared from view, as the path they traveled vanished into the forest, and then she had watched for another two hours, until his entire army was gone. And only then had she turned away from the window.

She stared into the empty great room. It was almost as if something were amiss with them gone. She almost expected to hear the clatter of spurs and the clank of swords and shields, as Alexander and his men filed in.

But they would not be returning from battle at this early evening hour. Alexander had probably attacked that afternoon—the march to the northernmost tip of the loch was only a few hours—or he might have decided to wait and attack tomorrow in the morning. Margaret wished she had asked. But he probably would not have told her his battle plans, anyway—no matter what he had said, she was his enemy.

Peg came into the hall and glanced at her, carrying a platter. Margaret had banished her to the kitchens before Alexander had even ridden away, so she could spend the day slaving over the hot ovens—so she could repent her sins. Thus far, Margaret had been ignoring the pain of her betrayal all day. It wasn't that easy at this late hour.

They had been close for most of their lifetimes. There were memories now, of the times they had shared as children—of running barefoot through a hillside blooming with wildflowers, or riding double, bareback, and falling off, of skipping over wet stones in a bubbling brook.

And they had grown to womanhood together, through both the trials and triumphs of emerging from adolescence. There had been laughter and tears. Peg had always been there, when her brothers had not come home from war, when Mary had become sick and passed away, when her father had gone out riding, never to return.... When Margaret had received the news that Buchan had arranged a marriage for her to an English knight, Peg had helped her get to her room, for Margaret had been overcome by shock.

The ache in Margaret's chest had been there all day, but it was bubbling up now, more insistently.

"Will ye eat?" Peg asked, her tone and manner subdued.

Margaret glanced at her and nodded. Peg had been reduced from being a great lady's maid to a kitchen maid—a great fall, indeed. Yet Margaret felt no satisfaction. For a part of her hated seeing Peg like this. A part of her wanted for them to embrace, and she would then forgive her, take her back—trust her.

But Margaret knew better. She could not ignore her disloyalty. She could not pretend that it hadn't happened. She had to protect herself from any such future betrayal. Alexander had been right.

"Will ye forgive me, now?" Peg asked. "I am hot, dirty, tired, I have suffered greatly, all day, as ye have wished for me to do."

Margaret looked up and their gazes met. "Even if I forgive you, I cannot take you back."

"How can ye be so cruel?" Peg cried.

"I am not trying to be cruel. You were disloyal to me."

Peg shook her head. "Yer mother would forgive me! She would have understood!"

Margaret set the knife she had picked up aside. She would not let Peg use Mary to manipulate her now. "You betrayed me. I cannot trust you. I cannot allow you to serve me as my maid."

"Maybe, if ye ever wanted a man, ye would not be so noble." Peg turned and rushed out.

She wanted to cry, feeling crushed by heartache and loss. Instead, she sipped her wine. She knew the wine would eventually dull the grief.

Sometime later, another maid came into the hall, a small, dark-haired girl with very fair skin, who was probably close to Margaret in age. Margaret recognized her as one of the kitchen maids and she was asked if the plate could be removed.

"Yes, I am finished."

The maid hesitated. "Lady, ye dinna eat. Ye should eat, to keep up yer strength."

She sounded the way Peg used to sound—as if she were actually concerned. "What is your name?"

"Eilidh, my lady," she said, with a small smile.

Margaret tried to eat a bit more, as the maid cleaned up the rest of the table. Eilidh was industrious, her actions filled with energy. Margaret watched her, very aware that she needed a new maid. "You were on the ramparts during the siege, stoking the fires for the burning oil," she said softly.

Eilidh glanced at her in the midst of wiping down the table. "Yes, my lady, as was my sister, my mother and my nephews. And we saw ye there, too."

Margaret stood up. "I cannot thank you enough for your courage, Eilidh."

"My sister's husband is one of yer archers, my lady— ye saved his life, when ye asked him to swear fealty to the MacDonald. We're all so grateful to ye." She smiled shyly. "We're so pleased to have our lady back."

She clearly meant it. "I am sorry I failed all of you," Margaret said. "I am sorry we lost Castle Fyne."

"Ye dinna fail us, lady. My grandmother served yer mother, until she was handfasted to Master Comyn and she left us. She says yer just like her—brave and kind. How could ye fight off the mighty Wolf? No one blames ye, lady."

Margaret thought, *I blame myself.* But she said, "Eilidh,

would you care to serve me while I am here? I no longer have a lady's maid, but I desperately need one."

Pleasure shone on her small face. "I would love to be yer maid, my lady!"

"Then go upstairs and ready my chamber for the night. Someone else can clean the table." Margaret smiled.

The young maid hurried to obey, and Margaret went to the kitchens, to give the final orders of the night. Peg sat with two other women at the table there, looking defiant and sullen. Margaret ignored her as she asked everyone to finish tidying up.

Upstairs, Eilidh had stoked the fire in the hearth, and was now heating water for a hot bath. Braziers were being warmed for Margaret's bed. She had even brought up a cup of hot wine. Clearly, the maid was eager to serve her. Margaret's every instinct told her she had chosen well. She was about to disrobe, her earlier grief dissipating, when a knock sounded on her chamber door.

Margaret could not imagine why someone was at her door at bedtime. She rushed to answer it, and found Alan outside, a strange look on his face. "My lady, I am sorry to disturb ye, but the Wolf has sent two messengers to us."

"Is there news? Has there been a battle?"

Alan met her gaze. "His lordship attacked this afternoon, not at Loch Riddon, but at Cruach Nan Cuilean," he said. "The English suffered heavy losses, being trapped in a mountain pass, but they managed to flee."

It was over? She was incredulous. "The Wolf has won?"

"No, my lady, their armies will fight again in the morning. Both sides have retreated to their camps for the night, on either side of the mountain."

She became wary. "So he has simply sent us the war

news?" Why would Alexander send two men to her, merely to tell her what had happened? Or, did he have another message of some kind?

Alan flushed and lowered his voice. "His lordship wishes for Eilidh to come to him, tonight."

For one moment, comprehension escaped Margaret.

Alan said quickly, "He would hardly know that ye have asked her to serve ye, Lady Margaret, and I cannot refuse him."

Margaret could not believe it. First he had summoned Peg, now he summoned her new maid? Could he not remain celibate for a single night?

She trembled, torn between dismay and anger. "Excuse me," she said to Alan tartly, then slammed the door in his face.

She turned, and Eilidh burst into tears. "I dinna wish to go, lady! I am not like Peg! I like serving ye, and wish to do so always!"

"Stop," Margaret said. "And let me think." She was of half a mind to send that damned Peg to him—Peg would be eager to go. She began to pace. He was at war! Why did he have to send for a woman? It was unbelievable!

But she needed to confront this problem. "Eilidh— have you already been with Alexander?"

She nodded, seeming ashamed.

Margaret turned away, further dismayed. Did she now care about his affair with Eilidh? She shouldn't care about anything he did, or anyone he did it with! Then she turned back to her. "Did he hurt you?" she asked briskly. She had to know.

"Of course not." She blushed. "He's a frightening master, but he did not hurt me." Then she rushed, "I still dinna wish to go to him again!"

Margaret realized she meant her every word. And she

had to ask, because Eilidh seemed so young. "Eilidh—did he take your virginity?"

She shook her head quickly. "I was no virgin, lady, but before ye think badly, I had a true love. He was killed last year when the MacRuari came rustling here."

Margaret was relieved, though sad for her loss.

There had been a battle that day. It had not gone well for Sir Guy. The armies would meet again tomorrow—and tonight, Alexander wanted a companion.

So many possibilities filled her mind that briefly, she was overwhelmed.

She had never met Sir Guy. What if she went in Eilidh's place? Even if she only had the opportunity to view him from afar?

And she would be close to the battlefield. She would know the outcome immediately.

And if she took Eilidh's place, an opportunity to escape might present itself. She could gather help and return to free William.

Excitement began. Peg was tall and voluptuous. Margaret could never hide under a hood and mantle, pretending to be her. But Eilidh was a petite woman, like herself. It was as if fate had presented Margaret with this moment.

"Give me your clothes," Margaret said. "All of them."

CHAPTER SEVEN

MARGARET COULD NOT stop shivering. She had been astride her mount for about three hours, traveling along a well-used path with Alexander's two men, the way lit by the torch the lead rider held. The night was silent, except for the sound of their horses' hooves on the frozen ground, the jangle of their bridles and their occasional blowing. The men did not talk. Every now and then an owl hooted. Once, in the far distance, she thought she heard a wolf baying.

She had never traveled in the middle of the night before, and she hoped to never do so again. She was just about to ask the men how much farther the camp was, when the path turned abruptly, and they came out of the forest.

Margaret gasped. They had paused their horses on the side of a ridge. Below, the night glowed with light, illuminated by dozens of campfires. Because of the brightness, she could just discern the array of tents formed by the army's encampment. Above the camp, a half moon was hanging, surrounded by winking stars. After the past few hours of traversing nothing but dark, dense and snowy forests, it was a stunning sight.

Her heart began to race.

"Ye'll be warm enough in a few more minutes," one of the men said, somewhat lewdly.

Margaret did not bother to answer. The horses trotted down the ridge now, eager for the end of the journey and the hay they would surely be given. Margaret's heart continued to pound too swiftly. In a few more moments, she would come face-to-face with Alexander.

She was not deluded—he would not be pleased to see her. But he could hardly send her back in the middle of the freezing night.

Their trek through the camp lasted for a few more minutes, and then she saw a tent three times the size of all the rest, a huge banner with a red dragon waving above it.

This time when she shivered, it was not from the cold.

Their horses halted and the two soldiers leapt to the ground. Margaret made certain her hood remained in place, its upper brim hiding her forehead, its cowl hiding her chin and mouth. Only her nose and eyes were exposed.

A soldier helped her alight. She followed both men to the tent's flap door, fighting to remain composed. The first soldier called out, and Margaret heard Alexander reply.

The soldier lifted the flap for her. "Yer to go in, but then, he's expecting ye." He winked at her.

Margaret ignored him and stepped carefully into the tent.

The hide door dropped closed behind her.

Inside, it was warm. The tent was constructed of layers of thick hides, meant to keep the cold out, and several torches burned, at once illuminating the interior and warming it further. A hole atop the tent allowed the smoke to drift outside. Furs covered the floor. A small table and a bench were at one end, a large pallet at the other.

He had been sleeping, she saw. He stood by the pallet, clad only in his leine, which was unbelted and almost reached his knees. His hair was loose and disheveled. The fur covers had clearly just been thrown aside. She was afraid to look him in the eye.

But she looked up, without removing the hood or cowl.

Their regards met.

He would not think that she was not Eilidh, Margaret thought, to reassure herself. He still did not speak, and she could not decipher the look in his eyes. He would probably be furious to learn the truth.

Margaret removed her hood. But his expression never changed—and she realized he was not surprised to see her.

"So ye now wish to become my mistress?"

She inhaled. Had he been mocking? "Can you now see through hoods and cowls?"

"Yer eyes gave ye away, Lady Margaret." And then he moved so swiftly that she had no time to react. She only glimpsed his face for a moment, and his expression was hard. In the next instant, she was in his arms, their faces inches apart.

"Well?" he demanded. "Do ye come freely to me at last?"

His tone was dangerous, but she had expected him to be angry with her. More important, he had been at war that day. He smelled of musk, sweat and even blood. She knew how war could change a man. Her worry increased. "No."

"No? So ye play a new game, instead?"

He was very angry, and sarcasm laced his tone. She wanted to tell him that she had not come to play any kind of game, either, that she needed to meet Sir Guy—and that she had to know what would happen when they battled tomorrow. But his hands still grasped her shoulders. She recalled too well what had happened the last time she had been in his embrace, and she instantly wanted to step away from him.

"Please release me," she began in a harsh whisper.

"Why? We fought today, men died, and ye have come."

He kissed her. His mouth was hard, uncompromising. Margaret went still as he kissed her so deeply that she could not move.

But it was not hurtful or unpleasant. Her heart began to thunder, her blood to rage. That hollow feeling began in her belly. And her every imminent protest died. She reached for his shoulders, almost helplessly. And his kiss changed.

It became hungry.

Suddenly there was so much temptation—to go farther into his embrace, to kiss him back.

And as her skin flamed, as if on fire, as her blood pounded in her veins, as she ached in her belly, she had one very coherent thought. She must stop this terrible kiss, before it became something more—something they could not undo. She unlocked her mouth from his.

"Will ye admit that ye want me?" He breathed hard, his hands clasping her waist.

She could not think, she could only feel the wild urgency burning within. The kiss had been explosive, a harbinger of so much more.

She stiffened, about to pull away. There could not be more!

His hands tightened on her waist, so she could not move. "Why did ye come here, Lady Margaret? We both ken ye dinna come to lie in my bed."

She looked from his hard face and dark eyes to his pallet. Then she realized what she had done, and she jerked her gaze back to his face. She stepped back, and this time, he let her go.

"No. I did not come here to become lovers." She felt dazed.

He was still, except for his hands, which fisted. "'Tis a shame."

She ignored that. "I came here to meet Sir Guy."

His expression hardened.

"We have never met. We have only exchanged letters. I am small like Eilidh. It seemed the perfect opportunity. My future rests in his hands."

"Yer future rests in my hands."

She shivered. "Very well," she said slowly. "I am your prisoner, so you are right."

He now gave her an odd, sidelong look. Slowly, he paced a circle around her. "Ye took a huge risk, to disguise yerself, to travel at night through the forest, in the snow. Why would ye think I'd let ye meet Sir Guy?"

"If there was a parley, I hoped to attend, otherwise, I hoped to glimpse him from a distance."

He halted and crossed his arms. "And what, pray tell, would attending a parley, or seeing Sir Guy from afar, gain ye?"

"I have never seen him!"

"So, ye hope to be reassured that yer English husband is not a toad? Or do ye think to arouse him? So fiercely, that he will forever hold to yer cause?"

She flushed. She knew very well that it would not hurt her cause if Sir Guy found her pleasing. He might become more resolved to have her and Castle Fyne.

"Mayhap," he added, somewhat scathingly, "ye even think to find a moment in which to send him a message—or even to escape."

She knew her cheeks were even warmer, because he

was right. She had wondered if she could bribe a guard to get a message to him, alerting him to the fact that she was there. She had half hoped he would think of a way to help her escape. With great care, she said, "I would escape if I could. It is my duty to escape. You know that."

He gave her an incredulous look. "Ye won't escape, not even from here."

He was so hard that she believed him. Suddenly, there was despair. A silence fell. It was fraught with tension.

He gave her a dark look, walked over to the table and poured two cups of wine. "War is no place for a woman."

"What will happen tomorrow?"

He took up her cup and walked to her. "There will be a battle, and this time, I intend to chase Sir Guy back to England." He handed the cup to her.

He had become savage as he spoke. "My fate is at stake, Alexander."

He stared for a prolonged moment. "I might almost believe that ye came here to make yer fate."

"Staying at Castle Fyne, while my fate swings in the balance between you and Sir Guy, hardly seemed resourceful."

"I dinna think ye truly hope fer Sir Guy's victory."

She was stiff with tension. "I can hardly hope for your victory."

"Ye dinna answer."

"Of course I do. I want Castle Fyne back." She meant her last words.

"But do ye truly wish fer an English husband?" He lifted his cup and drained it.

She did not have a good answer, so she did not speak.

"I dinna think so. Sir Guy will not win." He strode back to the table and poured more wine. Margaret realized he was far more than tense; he was angry.

She took a sip of the wine, trying to hide her dismay. Unfortunately she was afraid that he was right. "Will you let him know that I am here? Is there a reason you cannot do so?"

"Why would I do such a thing? I cannot think of a good reason to flaunt ye before Sir Guy."

She wet her lips. "And if I asked you, as a friend?"

"Ye keep claiming we are enemies. Now, we are friends?"

"You claim we are not enemies."

He gave her a very intent look.

"Ye will never be my enemy." He was final. "But ye should tread with care, Lady Margaret. My mood is foul this night."

"That is exactly what I am trying to do!" she cried. "You know I don't wish you ill, when I should pray for your defeat and downfall!"

He studied her for another moment, then drained his mug. "Ye should have stayed at Castle Fyne."

"Probably—but I am here. For better...or for worse."

She rubbed her arms, thinking of the passion they had just shared. But she must not think about it, not now, not ever. No good could ever come of the desire that could so easily rage between them.

Instead, she must think about tomorrow, for it could bring a new beginning for her—one leading to Castle Fyne's liberation and her freedom—if Sir Guy could defeat Alexander.

"I have to know what happens tomorrow," she said, looking up at him. "If you were in my place, you would feel the same way. Can I watch the battle tomorrow?"

"Ye'll stay here, under guard—far from any fighting, and any chance to escape."

Did he know her so well?

"And Margaret? I will punish my men tomorrow, fer being such fools."

She was instantly alarmed. "Don't punish them. Punish me."

"Ye should have thought about their fates when ye tricked them into thinking ye were Eilidh," he said flatly.

"I could not bear it if you truly hurt them."

"They were ordered to bring me Eilidh. By bringing ye, they risked yer life and limb."

She hugged herself. Had she forgotten how ruthless he could be?

"Are ye still pleased to be here?" he asked bluntly.

"Do you think to teach them a lesson, or me?"

"Ye need a good lesson, lady, because I will not always be present to guard ye. Yer courage is admirable. But it is misplaced. The day will come where it will put ye in jeopardy."

"Why do you care?"

"Ye need a protector, Lady Margaret."

"You almost sound as if you think to be that man."

His gaze held hers. "I want ye to be my mistress."

She gasped. Had he truly just asked her to become his lover?

"Aye, we're at war. Aye, we're blood enemies—a MacDougall and a MacDonald. But my brother married Juliana MacDougall. Ye need a protector, Lady Margaret."

She was stunned. "I cannot become your mistress!"

"Because of the war? Sir Guy? Buchan? Or because yer afraid that ye truly want me?"

She choked. "Yes," she managed to answer. She could not become his mistress because of the war, Sir Guy, her family—and the attraction they shared.

"We could be enjoying this night together. I could be yer protector, in every way. I would protect ye from

Buchan's wrath and Sir Guy's rage. Ye could be mistress of Castle Fyne." His gaze had become searching. "And ye'd never have to become an Englishman's wife."

It was almost as if he was asking for marriage—which he was not. Not that she would consider marriage, which would be far worse than any lover's affair. They were blood enemies; they were at war. She was his prisoner—and she was promised to another.

And even if she were not promised to Sir Guy, she would not sleep with the man who had taken Castle Fyne from her. She could not betray her family that way.

"I will find a pallet for myself—ye can use mine." He picked up his mantle, throwing it over his shoulders. But at the hide door, he paused. "Ye ken I may have to kill him?"

She recoiled. "Why would you have to kill Sir Guy?"

His gaze narrowed. "He stands in my way."

She trembled. Surely he meant that Sir Guy stood between him and Castle Fyne; surely he did not mean that Sir Guy stood between them.

And Alexander vanished into the night.

MARGARET REALIZED THAT she had finally dozed off. Instantly awake, she stared at the ceiling of the tent, as instantly aware that she was huddled up in Alexander's covers upon his bed pallet.

It had been impossible to sleep once he had left. She had slid into his bed, and been consumed with his scent, and perhaps, what lingered of his presence. She had expected him to return with another pallet and share the tent with her, but he hadn't done so. Although exhausted, she could not stop thinking about their conversation, the kiss they had shared and the impending battle.

But she had eventually dozed off. Now she realized

that the camp outside his tent was coming to life; undoubtedly, his army was rousing itself and preparing for the battle to come. Margaret threw aside the covers, used a chamber pot, finger combed her hair and then braided it. A small pitcher of water was on the table, and she used a bit to wash her face and brush her teeth.

All this was done within minutes, as the sounds of horses and men outside the tent escalated. Her heart raced. Today was war.

Margaret threw on her mantle and fur and stepped outside. The dawn was gray and light, the camp a hive of activity, with men coming and going, horses being saddled and wagons being loaded, but she saw Alexander instantly.

He stood beside the huge fire pit outside his tent with three other men. He wore a chain mail tunic and mail leggings, his brat draped and pinned over his shoulders. Padraig and another Highlander stood with him, also clad in mail, furs draped upon their shoulders, and the third man was an armor-clad English soldier.

Her gaze veered across the fire pit to where another English soldier, also clad in armor and mail, held the first knight's horse. Had Sir Guy sent a messenger to Alexander? And if so, why?

As she rushed forward, she wondered if word had gotten out that she was in the camp—and if Sir Guy was demanding her freedom.

Alexander turned before she reached him, either hearing or sensing her approach. His gaze skimmed over her, a habit she was now accustomed to.

"Good morning," he said politely. "Did ye sleep well?"

"I slept perfectly well," she lied. She turned to stare openly at the English knight. His helmet was down, and she met dark eyes set in a craggy and pale face.

"My opponent wishes fer a parley," Alexander said.

Her eyes widened.

"Apparently he fears to engage me in battle a second time." He gave her a significant look and placed his large body between her and the Englishman. "Tell Sir Guy I look forward to our meeting."

The Englishman nodded, not even glancing at Margaret again before he strode to his horse. Her heart sank as he mounted—he did not suspect who she was. Clearly, Sir Guy had not been alerted to her presence, much less demanded her freedom. The pair of riders galloped off.

Alexander was speaking to Padraig very rapidly, in the land's native tongue. Margaret spoke Gael, but his dialect was foreign to her—she could not really discern his words. Padraig nodded and he and the other Highlander hurried off.

Alexander slowly faced her. "I will bring a dozen knights, as he will, and we will meet in an hour in the glen just south of the mountain."

Margaret did not even think about it, she seized his hand. "You must let me come with you!"

"So he can be stirred to undying loyalty by yer wit and beauty?" With sharp scrutiny, he pulled away.

"That would be a boon and I will not deny it, but you already know I do not wish to remain your prisoner," she said. "But surely you wish to avoid further warfare? Surely, you do not want him to attack Castle Fyne. Maybe I can be of some help."

"Ye will be of help, for I have already decided how to use ye, Lady Margaret. As it turns out, I want him to see ye—but for my ends, not yers." He strode past her toward his tent.

He was going to allow her to attend the parley—and she would meet the man she would marry in June! Oh, what did he intend? Concerned, she rushed after him, all elation gone.

Alexander was outside his tent, sharpening one of his huge swords on a stone. She halted, instantly rigid, watching him. The blade screamed as he sawed it back and forth across the stone. She trembled as he straightened, sheathing the sword, finality in the motion. He then unsheathed his right-hand sword and sharpened it in an identical manner.

Watching him prepare for war was frightening. "How will you use me?" She heard how tremulous her tone sounded.

"Ye need to quickly eat, we are leaving shortly," he said, striding past her.

Clearly, he had no intention of answering. She followed him but he was moving so quickly now that she could not keep up. He ordered someone to give her food, and a moment later she found herself with bread and cheese in hand, Alexander gone. A young Scot about her age faced her.

Margaret looked at him, unsmiling. All around them Alexander's men were moving to and fro, most loading wagons and carts with canon, catapults, rocks and missiles.

She shivered, as it began to dawn upon her—she was not just in an army camp, and on the verge of battle, she was about to attend a meeting between the leaders of the two armies—one man her betrothed, the other, her captor. Her tension had risen when she had seen Alexander taking his blades to that stone; now, it became unbearable.

"I'm Dughall," the blond lad said. "Ye had better eat. The Wolf said so."

Margaret ate, not because she was hungry, but because she knew a long day was ahead. Dughall did not speak; he simply stared, very openly, as if she were a great curiosity. She wondered if Dughall had learned of her identity, but she was too preoccupied to ask.

He handed her a flask.

She shook her head. "I prefer water."

"The water here isn't fit for drinking."

Margaret realized that the army had spoiled the water in the river, so she took the flask and drank what she could. The wine had been watered down previously, so it wasn't as strong as she had expected.

She was almost finished when she heard the horses approaching, an unnerving clatter of myriad hooves upon the cold road—and a reminder of what they were about. She tensed and looked past Dughall.

Alexander was astride his gray charger, leading the cavalcade. He paused before her, his blue gaze cold and hard.

Her heart lurched. He was a warrior now, intent upon war and victory. It was hard to believe that last night they had had a sensible conversation—or shared that kiss.

But did she not already know how ruthless he was? How clever? He might be attending a parley, but he had his own ambitions. He would not be easily thwarted. She knew it for a fact.

Yesterday, when Alexander had ridden off to battle, she had not been able to wish him ill. She could not wish him ill now, either. Yet she prayed for Sir Guy's victory.

His regard remained riveted on her. "We're leaving, Lady Margaret. Ye can mount."

She gazed past him. Padraig was astride a red steed just behind him. He was leading a small gray mare, which was apparently her mount. A dozen Highland knights were with them, clad in mail and fur.

Margaret tucked her uneaten portion in the pocket of her mantle, hurrying to her mare. Dughall went with her and helped her up. She took up the reins with both hands, as Padraig released them. The auburn-haired Highlander asked, "Can ye ride?"

Margaret nodded.

Alexander whirled his mount and started forward at a fast trot; everyone followed.

It was two good hours past dawn now, but the day remained gray and bright. Margaret looked from Alexander's broad shoulders to the sky above. It was going to snow, she thought, shivering. Was that good or bad, as far as the impending battle went?

She simply did not know. And as they left the camp behind, the shadow of Cruach Nan Cuilean fell over them, making the morning darker and colder.

Her nerves made her stomach hurt and her head ache. Margaret wondered what Sir Guy wanted. Did he truly wish to negotiate a peace now, after one single battle? Surely, he had not given up on Castle Fyne—on her. Or was this treachery on his part? Perhaps he had laid a trap for Alexander.

She then realized that, if they were riding into a trap, she would be amongst Sir Guy's victims. Of course, he did not know she was present.

Her gaze found Alexander's tall, broad-shouldered form again. He would not be easily tricked and trapped. And she would soon find out just what Sir Guy intended—and what Alexander intended, as well.

Suddenly she saw the blur of the approaching Englishmen. Above them two banners waved. They became more visible, as did the armored knights and their horses, as they came closer. One banner was the red royal banner, the other blue and white, belonging to the great de Valence family.

Her heart thundered now. She could see the men who were approaching, although not well. Their visors were up. All eyes were trained upon them. She wondered which knight was Sir Guy.

When the distance of a great hall separated them, Alexander threw up his hand, abruptly halting them. But Sir Guy and his men had halted, too.

Margaret remained in the midst of the other men as Alexander and Padraig rode slowly forward, at a walk. Two of the Englishmen met them.

Her heart exploded as she stared at the two English knights, for one was heavyset and she instantly identified the other as Sir Guy. His beard was gray. He was of medium height and build, with a swarthy complexion so common amongst the French. He remained at a distance, but she could see he was a fine figure of a man.

She was gazing at her future husband, and he, of course, was unaware of her presence—or even of who she was. She did not know what to think.

"Good morning, Sir Guy," Alexander said, his tone cool. "I am sorry we meet under such circumstances."

"You're sorry?" Sir Guy sounded angry and incredulous. "No one is sorrier than I am!"

Margaret was bewildered. The conversation seemed personal—as if the men knew one another.

"I always laughed when anyone referred to you as the Wolf, Alexander. I would laugh to myself when I would hear the stories of how ruthless you are!" Sir Guy rode his horse in a tight circle now, about Alexander and Padraig, the animal tossing its head. The older knight did not move. "But you are exactly as claimed, damn it. You could have attacked Inverary or Lachlan—but you attacked what is mine!"

They did know one another, Margaret thought in disbelief. And he already called Castle Fyne his?

"Castle Fyne is a very fine castle, Sir Guy. It controls a portion of the sound, most of the loch, and the route into Argyll. And it is on MacDonald borders...I can think of no better place to attack."

"You coldhearted bastard," Sir Guy said.

Margaret flinched, but Alexander seemed amused. "Surely Buchan will give yer intended another portion for her dowry? He has lands throughout the north."

"My lands are in the south and you know it. I will never forgive you for this, Alexander, and neither will Buchan!" Sir Guy jerked hard on his reins in his anger, and his bay stallion reared.

"And I am sorry we are on opposite sides of this war." Alexander was calm—so calm it was hard to decide if he meant his words or not.

"You are a madman, to betray the king and ride with Bruce! When he is caught he will hang, his lands forfeited to King Edward's noblest allies. You will hang beside him, your lands will be forfeit, too."

"Bruce will not be caught, nor will I. King Edward will never take on the lords of the isles—he will always need me and my brothers to rule the seas of the western Hebrides."

"*Never* is an extraordinary word—perhaps you should not use it!"

"If ye have come to rant and rave, then we are wasting the day."

Sir Guy drove his horse up to Alexander's mount, so that their shoulders brushed. "We have fought together, many times. We have supped, shared wine and women.

Once, we were friends. Now, I thought it behooved me to tell you that I will never forgive you for what you have done, and you will pay dearly for your betrayal of me and our liege."

"If ye think I will thank ye for such a warning, think again. But mostly, ye should think long and hard about making threats—when I have yer bride."

Sir Guy stared, and Margaret cried out unthinkingly.

"Do you care about her, at all?" Alexander asked, coldly. "Ye have not asked how she is."

Sir Guy looked past him. Margaret began to tremble as their gazes met.

Sir Guy inhaled, a hissing sound. And he drove his bay steed past Alexander and Padraig, toward her.

Margaret knew she turned red. So this was Alexander's plan—to anger Sir Guy!

And as he came forward, she saw that her uncle had not lied—he was a handsome man. But his gray eyes were filled with disbelief.

The bards who sang about her so often sang about her long, curly red-gold hair. Margaret dropped her hood and released her braid, finger combing her hair into a mane, looking down and away. She wasn't trying to be demure—she was suddenly frightened, terribly so.

This man was going to be her husband. And if she had learned one thing that day, it was that he had a hot temper.

"Lady Margaret?" His tone was as incredulous as his eyes.

She fought for composure and met his regard. Why did she have the terrible inkling that he was neither kind nor compassionate? "Yes, Sir Guy, I am Lady Margaret—your intended."

"My God, he brought you here!"

Margaret bit her lip so hard she tasted blood. She did not want Sir Guy to discover that she had used treachery to slip into Alexander's camp. She glanced at Alexander. He was watching them, and she was instantly relieved—she knew he would not reveal her secret.

"I am so sorry we are meeting this way," she managed to say.

"Has he hurt you?" Sir Guy demanded.

"No."

Sir Guy stared very closely now. "Why do you blush, Lady Margaret?" he asked.

"Because you are staring as if I have two heads!" she cried. But she was thinking of the way Alexander had kissed her last night. She did not have to be well acquainted with Sir Guy to know that he would be furious if he ever found out.

"I am staring because you are even more beautiful than your likeness, or than your uncle described."

She breathed hard. "So you are pleased?"

He began to shake his head. "Of course you please me, Lady Margaret. But I am not pleased that Alexander attacked Castle Fyne—and that he holds you hostage—and he has brought you here."

She wondered if she should reveal that she had taken it upon herself to come to the encampment. But instinct prompted her not to disclose the truth. "I am so sorry Castle Fyne was lost, my lord. But you must know how bravely my people fought to defend it."

His eyes widened. "So it is not a tall tale?"

"What tale, my lord?"

"All of Scotland has been speaking of the lady of Fyne who dared to defend her castle against the mighty Wolf of Lochaber. I did not believe it."

Was he pleased? She could not tell. "I did not think

there was a choice at the time. I did not know of Bruce's rebellion. I thought aid would soon come, and that we could hold the Wolf off until my uncle Buchan or my uncle Argyll came to rescue us."

"You are a woman! You are seventeen! How could you possibly defend a castle under siege?" He was incredulous and angry at once. "Why didn't your brother defend the castle?"

"My lord, my brother left to fight the Wolf in the ravine, hoping to turn him back before he ever could reach our walls! There was no one else left to defend the castle. I am Mary MacDougall's daughter. It was my duty to defend Castle Fyne."

He now stared and she felt terribly uncomfortable. "You should have conceded to one of your knights. No woman can fight a battle. And you should not be here, in his camp." He whirled his mount to face Alexander.

And once his back was to her, she breathed deeply and looked quickly at Alexander. He sent her a glance she could not decipher.

"I want you to release her—now. She need not be a part of this war," Sir Guy said fiercely.

"I cannot release her. She is the lady of Castle Fyne and the Earl of Buchan's niece," Alexander spoke calmly. "She remains a valuable prize, Sir Guy, but that, ye already know."

Margaret trembled, aware that Alexander was being utterly provocative, no matter that his tone was dispassionate.

"We were friends once," Sir Guy exclaimed, pacing his stallion about Alexander and Padraig again. "What if I ask you to release her—because she is a lady, and while you are a wild Scot, I happen to know that you have some small sense of honor!"

Alexander smiled that half smile Margaret now knew so well—the one containing no mirth at all. "And what will I get in return?"

Sir Guy halted.

"Will ye give me Castle Fyne? Will ye turn around and retreat?"

Margaret was shocked. Would Alexander release her if he was given Castle Fyne?

"Never," Sir Guy snarled.

"I dinna think so."

Sir Guy cursed. "What ransom then?"

Alexander sat his gray steed in profile to Margaret. He glanced briefly at her now. "I am not asking for a ransom."

Sir Guy choked, so furious he could not speak.

"She is too valuable to ransom," Alexander said, softly. He did not look at her—his stare was unwavering upon Sir Guy.

"You bastard heathen Scot! She is mine—Castle Fyne is mine! I am going to destroy you, Alexander, or die in the attempt."

"Then ye will likely die."

Sir Guy turned toward Margaret, enraged. She cringed.

"Keep yourself out of harm's way," he said.

She somehow nodded.

But he did not wait to see; he was galloping back to his men. "A de Valence!" he shouted, his war cry. "For King Edward!"

His knights roared the same war chant, "A de Valence! For King Edward!" And as one unit, they wheeled, galloping away.

Margaret held on to her saddle, close to collapse. That was her future husband. She began to feel ill. He had such a hot temper. And he had no care for her—none. He only cared that she brought him Castle Fyne. He only cared that both she and the castle had been taken from him.

A strong hand grasped her arm, steadying her. "Will ye fall off?"

She glanced up at Alexander. She meant to make a jest and make light of the moment, but she could not do so.

"I would be proud if ye ever fought to defend what was mine," he said softly.

Margaret began to shake. She felt even sicker than before.

He raised his voice as he regarded his men. "Take her back to Castle Fyne. Make certain no harm comes to her."

Margaret jerked, realizing that he meant to send her home—and that he was going to battle. "Let me stay! I will even swear not to try to escape!"

He barely glanced at her. "Ye'll return to Castle Fyne." And then he stood in his stirrups, roaring, "A Bruce! A Donald! A Alasdair!"

And his men roared his war cries back at him.

And the ridges and forests of Cruach Nan Cuilean shook.

CHAPTER EIGHT

"WHAT IS WRONG, LADY? Ye've barely spoken since ye came back."

Margaret was seated at the table in the great hall. Young Dughall and another Scot had escorted her back to Castle Fyne two days ago. Eilidh had just set a trencher down before her, and her gaze was concerned. Peg, who was serving the guards at another table, turned.

How she wished for a confidante. The past two days had been interminable. She could not stop recalling her brief stay in Alexander's camp—and the war parley with Sir Guy. She could not cease thinking of her future as Sir Guy's wife, nor of the battle that might still rage near Loch Riddon.

"It has been two days, with no word," she said. "I am anxious to learn what has happened…and to discover if Sir Guy has triumphed."

When she had left, both armies had been preparing to do battle. She was desperate to learn of the outcome.

Sir Guy had vowed to destroy Alexander.

Her heart slammed with worry and fear. She knew she worried about Alexander's welfare—she hoped he would not be hurt in the battle. But she must hope that Sir Guy won. It was her duty to be loyal to him. Her uncle would be supporting Sir Guy in his quest to defeat Alexander and take Castle Fyne back. So would William, so would all her Comyn and MacDougall kinsmen. This wait to learn who had triumphed and who had lost was impossible.

An image flashed, of Sir Guy looking at her, his gray gaze wide with disbelief and disapproval. He did not appreciate what she had done to defend Castle Fyne. She had summoned up every ounce of courage she had to defy the Wolf's demand that she surrender. She knew nothing of sieges, but she had had to quickly learn, and improvise. She had even gone to the ramparts to fight alongside her archers, her soldiers and her women.

He *disapproved.*

She had been aghast. No woman wished to offend her future husband! Every woman hoped to please the man she would eventually wed.

Worse, Sir Guy already considered Castle Fyne his. Yet their union hadn't even been consummated—until they married, Castle Fyne was *hers.* It was her dowry, it had been her mother's—how could Sir Guy speak as if he already possessed it?

But if he triumphed now, if he defeated Alexander, if he took Castle Fyne back, they would marry as planned. He would possess Castle Fyne; he would possess her.

She was trying to remain brave, but she was scared. She kept recalling his hot temper, his lack of respect, his disapproval of her. And she was scared of the man she would marry in June.

She knew she must not compare her future marriage to the union her parents had had. But she could not help herself. Her father had rarely disapproved of her mother. And then she had the treacherous thought: Alexander had not disapproved of her actions, either. To the contrary.

It was so tempting to hope that Alexander was the victor now.

She knew she must not allow her mind to go in such

a direction. Instead, she must concentrate on all the advantages a union with Sir Guy would bring to her and the entire Comyn family.

"The Wolf has never been defeated in battle," Eilidh said, but carefully.

Margaret looked at her, jerked out of her wayward thoughts. "He is outnumbered, Eilidh. He may be defeated this time."

"We will have word as soon as the battle is over," Eilidh said, smiling in a comforting manner. "News flies faster than any bird. We will soon learn who has triumphed, lady."

Eilidh was right on that one point—someone would soon appear at her castle walls, and he would be the victor. But which man would it be?

"And Sir Guy has a great army. He will probably be at our walls at any moment." But now, Eilidh's smile was gone. "And ye'll be a free lady once more."

Margaret knew Eilidh hoped to reassure her. But that was impossible, when her heart was weighing her down, and she was faced with so much uncertainty. "Yes, if Sir Guy triumphs, I will be free."

Eilidh's smile vanished. Peg turned to stare sharply at her.

"I am worried," Margaret said to Eilidh. "That is all." She picked up her knife and used it to push her food around her trencher. She kept recalling how Alexander so often looked at her—with scrutiny and consideration—as he tried to fathom her thoughts. It was as if he cared to know what she was thinking. In his camp, she had wondered if he cared about her welfare.

She did not think Sir Guy would ever care about her thoughts. But she must not compare the two men. No good could come of it.

Eilidh hesitated by her side. "Ye should eat, lady. Yer already like a feather! Ye dinna wish to become ill."

"You're right. I should eat. I should have some wine. Worrying will not solve anything."

Pleased, Eilidh rushed to pour her wine. As she did, Peg stalked out of the hall.

Margaret watched her old friend with a grimace. The pain of her betrayal had already subsided, so perhaps Alexander had been right, and they hadn't really ever been as close as she had thought. But Peg was angry, and that did not bode well.

"Eilidh, I want you to continue to wait on me. In a short time, I have come to depend on you."

"Really?" Eilidh gasped, her surprise obvious.

"Really." Margaret smiled, clasping her hand. She liked the young girl very much. "I will even take you home with me, to the north, if I ever return there."

"Oh, lady, thank ye! Castle Fyne is my home, but I think I wish to serve ye, always! I am so proud to serve the lady of Fyne!"

Before Margaret could respond, she heard pounding footsteps outside the hall. She stiffened, gripping the edge of the table. Dughall burst into the hall.

She took one look at his ecstatic expression, and her heart slammed.

The Wolf had won.

"The Wolf returns, Lady Margaret!" Dughall shouted, confirming her thoughts. "His army is on the road, and his knights are at the barbican, his banner waves proudly, and he is at their head!"

She stood up, stunned. And there was no mistaking the flood of relief within her.

Alexander had defeated Sir Guy.

She was so relieved that she could hardly deny it.

However, she had no intention of analyzing her reaction to Alexander's victory now. He was returning; his army was returning.

She rushed from the table. "Is he hurt?"

"I dinna think so!" Dughall exclaimed, and then he turned and raced back out of the great room.

Her heart thundered now. "We will be feeding a great many men," she said briskly to Eilidh. She took a deep breath. "Have more meat brought up from the cellars, and bring up another barrel of cheese and several barrels of wine. And there will be wounded to attend. Send several maids for linens, as many as they can find. Begin warming water. And my chest—bring it to the hall!" She lifted her skirts and ran out of the great room without waiting for the maid to respond. She hurried up the stairwell and onto the ramparts.

Twilight was upon the land, cool and gray, with a few snowflakes falling. A few of the knights and archers who had been left behind to guard the castle were already present, as were a great many of the castle's women, and they were all leaning over the crenellations, waving and calling out with cheers to the returning army. Her heart was racing madly as she ran along the ramparts, passing her people. She tried to gaze past the crowds, over their heads and shoulders, and over the crenellations. She could just barely see the huge army slowly rippling up the forest road. She could not see the forefront, which had reached her castle walls. She ran faster.

Margaret reached the entry tower and rushed to the closest wall adjacent to it. She seized the rough stone wall and looked down at the barbican.

A pair of fur-clad Highland knights on black steeds led the way, followed by a half a dozen other warriors, one of whom held the Donald banner. The dark-blue-

and-black MacDonald flag whipped in the wind, high above their heads, with its red dragon clawing the blue field in its midst.

Then she saw his gray stallion in the middle of the cavalcade. Her grasp on the wall tightened.

They were inside the barbican now, and approaching the drawbridge, which had been lowered.

Alexander was so tall that even in the middle of his men, his head and shoulders were visible, his dark hair flying in the wind.

She realized tears had arisen. *I am overtired,* she thought. Surely she was not evincing undue concern for the mighty Wolf of Lochaber.

Aware of how disloyal she was being in thinking she might not have to wed Sir Guy now, she stood very still, until Alexander was on the drawbridge and passing beneath the entry tower, almost directly beneath her. She took a long moment to compose herself.

Margaret turned and went back across the ramparts to the north tower, but more slowly. As she went downstairs, she could hear the men in the hall, their conversation loud and raucous—the sounds satisfied and pleased.

She reached the great hall and looked across it. Some three dozen knights were within, a great many bearing bloodstains upon their clothes, some wearing bloody bandages, one being helped onto a pallet. No one seemed unscathed, yet everyone was smiling, mugs were raised, and the women of the castle were in attendance. Laughter was sprinkled throughout the conversations. The women were flirting wildly, the men basking in the attention.

Alexander stood by one of the great hearths with Padraig and Sir Neil, both knights seeming unharmed. So many men stood between them that she could not make him out clearly, but he seemed entirely unharmed, as well.

He suddenly turned and, across the great room, their gazes met.

Margaret felt her heart turn over hard.

He said something to both knights and started toward her.

And she realized that he was limping. Then she saw that his leine was splotched with blood, and his skirts were stiff and blackened. Margaret felt all the color in her face drain away, the sensation a sinking one.

He was removing his plaid as he approached, huge biceps bulging. "Lady Margaret."

"You've been wounded."

"I have a scratch or two."

She was angered by his indifferent tone. "Men die from war wounds every day."

He smiled a little. "So ye have a care, after all?"

She trembled. "I have already said that I do not wish you ill."

"So that is aye?"

Did she flush? "You have cared for me and in return, I will not let you die." She whirled, not about to analyze the depth of her concern. "Peg! Bring warm water, soap, my chest of potions, linens and more wine."

"Margaret," he said.

She turned back to him. Was he *amused?* "Would it please you if I did not care?"

"No. I am very pleased with my welcome here."

They were treading dangerously, she thought. "Then you are reading too much into a simple act of compassion, my lord."

"Mayhap." He shrugged. "Mayhap not."

Her cheeks burned. "Will you please sit? If you fall down, I am too small to catch you."

He laughed, the sound warm and pleasant. "I am not going to fall down, Lady Margaret."

"Oh, of course not. You're too mighty to fall, even if you've lost so much blood."

His smile faded as he studied her with that searching look she had become so familiar with. "The blood ye see is not mine."

She started, and then she looked him over with great care. She saw cuts upon his thighs that might have been caused by shrubs and branches, and an abrasion upon his arm. "You are not hurt?"

"I am not hurt."

She realized just how relieved she was. And he reached out to steady her, for she was trembling. She glanced up and their gazes collided yet again. "I am pleased," he said slowly, "that ye worry overly."

What could she say? She tried, "You must be tired. Please, sit down. Peg! Bring wine!"

He settled upon the bench, and seriously said, "A great many men have been wounded, Lady Margaret, and dozens have died. We fought for almost two entire days."

She sat beside him, carefully folding her hands in her lap. "I take it you were victorious?"

"Aye, but the cost was great."

Her thoughts now raced. He had won, she remained his captive.

"Ye have yet to ask about Sir Guy."

She smiled grimly. "I have prayed he is well," she lied, speaking rather tersely. "How is he?"

"Sir Guy suffered a mild wound to his shoulder—but he will live to fight another day." He finally sipped the cup of wine Peg had given to him.

Surely, Margaret was relieved. Surely, she had some small care for the man who would be her husband! "And I thank God he is not seriously harmed."

He was staring, his expression slightly bemused. "He is fortunate he did not lose his arm."

"You saw him receive the wound?"

"I delivered the blow, Lady Margaret."

Her tension instantly increased as she recalled how Alexander had stated that he might have to kill Sir Guy. She could imagine the two men wielding swords against one another, each intending to kill, and she shuddered.

Appearing very satisfied, Alexander drained his cup of wine.

Margaret refilled it for him and handed it back. She asked carefully, "Did you seek him out purposely? Did you wish to kill him?"

"Did he not vow to destroy me?"

Alexander had deliberately sought to attack Sir Guy, she was certain. And he had meant to kill him if he could.

"He will be back to fight another day—with more of the king's men."

She looked at him. "Are you certain?" she asked.

A long pause ensued. Alexander finally said, "He wants Castle Fyne."

Margaret flinched and looked away. Alexander was astute, and he had witnessed her entire exchange with Sir Guy. He knew, as she did, that Sir Guy had no care for her, except for the dowry she brought to their union. She thought about how angry he had been at the war parley. "Yes, I imagine he will be back—he must be enraged."

"Angry or not, Castle Fyne is a great prize. King Edward will want to control the route to Argyll—he will wish for Sir Guy to command Castle Fyne."

She stiffened as their gazes locked. "Just as Bruce now wishes for you to command Castle Fyne?"

"Aye."

Margaret looked at her hands. The implications of the war and how she was affected by it now hit her with great force. Castle Fyne was in the midst of the storm of war—just as she was. How those winds blew would decide her fate.

"Do ye pray fer Sir Guy's return?"

Slowly, she looked up. "It is my duty to be loyal to him."

He made a sound, as they both knew she had not answered his question. "Aye, and yer as dutiful as a woman could be."

She met his blue gaze instantly. If he knew how disloyal she was, and that she had been questioning her very future, he would not be speaking as he was. "I intend to be dutiful, yes."

He drained the cup of wine. "And what did ye think, Lady Margaret? Ye finally met the man yer uncle would have ye wed."

She stood up. "We met for but a moment, under very trying circumstances."

He held out his cup and Peg filled it. "Some women find him very noble—very gallant—with the blood of two royal houses in his veins."

Sir Guy was related to both the kings of France and England. "He appears honorable and brave."

"And if ye thought him injured, would ye cluck over him, as ye have me?"

She started. "Of course I would."

"Aye, ye would—because it would be yer duty." He stood up, and he towered over her. "Can ye tend my wounded knights? We must join Bruce soon."

Margaret had been absorbing how mocking he had been and now she froze. "You are joining Bruce?"

"Bruce needs his best men to seize lands, to defeat his enemies and all who think to stop him. I am one of his best men. I can hardly linger here."

She felt stunned, aghast. But why had she ever assumed that Alexander would placidly remain at Castle Fyne? A great war raged. Bruce was on the march. He was taking what castles and strongholds that he could, just as Alexander had taken Castle Fyne. He could not seize Scotland's throne if he did not have the great Scot barons and warlords behind him. He would need a great army to fight King Edward, he would need all of his best commanders—he would need the mighty Wolf.

"When will you leave?" she finally asked.

"When my army is whole. I will leave a hundred of my best archers and knights—enough to fight off anyone, including Sir Guy, or even Buchan."

"Have you news of either Buchan or Argyll?" Surely, by now, they had learned of the fall of Castle Fyne. Surely, they knew she and William were hostages.

"Buchan is enraged with Bruce, and he plots his vengeance now. As for Argyll, he is aiding one of his cousins against one of my brothers. Both men have probably learned of Castle Fyne's fall—neither will come to yer rescue anytime soon."

Margaret felt real despair. "So I am to remain a prisoner here, indefinitely."

"But ye will be safe."

Their gazes had met yet again. "I should put a salve on your abrasions."

He laughed at her. "There is no need, Lady Margaret. If ye please, tend to my knights."

She hesitated, but as she turned to go, he took her

arm, restraining her. "The news I have given ye now distresses ye."

She trembled, pulling away. "I have been expecting aid from either of my uncles."

"Come, Margaret, we both ken that is not the news that frightens ye."

He had the ability to disturb her to no end, she thought. "I hate war. It only brings death."

He stared at her, and she felt certain he realized that she was frightened—and not just for herself.

"Go," he said.

MARGARET KNEW THAT the best course of action was to avoid Alexander. She did not want to keep comparing him and Sir Guy, but every time she heard his voice or glimpsed him, that was exactly what she did. She did not want to have any concern for him, nor did she want to admire him, not in any way. Therefore she refused to even think about the war he was about to join.

But doing so wasn't easy, not when his injured men were recovering, and the rest of his knights and soldiers were being drilled for battle on a daily basis. She had only to look out of any tower window to know that this terrible war loomed. At Castle Fyne, she might be safely out of its path—for now—but Alexander was about to ride directly into the maelstrom.

One aspect of her captivity had changed. Each day she was allowed an hour's visit with William. Alexander had not told her why he had changed his mind, but she knew it was due to the affections evolving between them.

William had healed completely, and he was eager to plan an escape. He was impatient to join their uncle Buchan and go to war against Bruce. With an ever-present guard, they could not discuss such matters openly. William was an avid artist, and allowed to sketch, and he managed to slip her an occasional note, hidden within his drawings.

At least a week had passed since the battle of Cruach Nan Cuilean when she was sewing in her chamber by candlelight one evening. She had seen William earlier and she was concerned—he had used his eyes to communicate to her that he wished to speak with her. Margaret felt certain he had come up with a plan of some kind. She was going to have to use her sleeping potion on the guard so they could converse freely. She stabbed her forefinger with the needle, crying out.

"How did ye prick yerself?"

She tensed, her gaze slamming to her door, which was now open. Alexander stood there.

He smiled slightly. "Yer too skilled to make such a mistake. I wonder at yer deep thoughts."

She set the embroidery down, aware of a new tension. Alexander was such a big man that he dominated her small doorway.

"Ye have been avoiding me—dinna try to deny it." He stepped into her chamber and now she saw that he held a scroll, one tied tightly with twine.

"Is that a missive?"

"Buchan has written ye." Alexander's small half smile never wavered. He came forward. "He has written me as well, asking after ye—and demanding yer release."

She slid unsteadily from the bed, breathless with excitement now. "Have you replied?"

"No." His gaze moved over her—she was wearing a simple leine with a belt, instead of one of her usual gowns. "Ye look like a Highland lass."

She felt like hopping from one foot to the other, so

impatient was she. "I am a Highland lass. What will you say, Alexander?" A pleading note had crept into her tone.

He handed her the rolled-up parchment. "I will refuse, Margaret. The time isn't right for a ransom or yer release."

"Will it ever be right?"

"I dinna ken."

She sat down, untying the twine. "Did you read this?"

"No, but I will. He will expect me to read it," he added, rather unnecessarily.

Margaret barely heard him.

February 19, 1306
My dear niece Margaret,

I have received word of the siege of Castle Fyne and its fall. Your courage in defending the castle moves me to hold you in the highest regard. My brother would be so proud of you if he were with us today, as would the great lady Mary. Had I known of the siege, I would have come to your aid, but alas, the news has but reached me recently.

I need you to have courage now. The land is at war. Robert Bruce attempts to claim Scotland's throne. If you have not heard, he has murdered our cousin Red John in a church in Dumfries. We go to war, Margaret, for Bruce must never be allowed to take the throne, and he must be punished for our cousin's murder. As I write to you, asking for your patience, I am gathering our allies and soldiers. We will fight with England now, for Scotland's freedom from a bitter and conscienceless rival.

I have asked MacDonald for your and William's release. However, your value as a hostage is being widely discussed throughout the land, and whether he will release you or not is uncertain. It is also clear that he will hold Castle Fyne if he can. I have offered him other lands; he has refused. In such a time of war, between kings and traitors, it will be difficult to raise an army with which to rescue you.

However, I know you to be a strong, proud woman, capable of enduring captivity in his hands, so if all fails, you will have to wait for the Wolf's defeat in battle to attain your freedom. But have hope. That day will come. And know that you are not forgotten.

You are a boon to the great Comyn family, Margaret. Sir Guy sends his regards, as we all do.

God keep you safe.
Your uncle, John Comyn, the Earl of Buchan

Margaret was in disbelief at the significance of his letter. She was being abandoned.

"The news is not good?"

She thrust the parchment at Alexander. Then she stood, feeling as if her uncle had struck her. No, he had not struck her—he had tossed her away. "He is not coming. Not to free us—nor to take Castle Fyne back."

Alexander was reading the letter now.

"I am to have patience. I am to have hope."

He then looked up. "Do ye wish to keep this?"

Bitter tears filled her eyes. "Burn it."

He walked to the fireplace and dropped the parchment in the flames. Then he faced her. "I hardly wish to give ye hope. But if he meant to attack, he would never say so."

"He doesn't. I know him well. He expects me to wait

here, as a prisoner—as your prisoner—until you are defeated or this war ends! But it will never end, will it?" She wiped her eyes roughly with her fingertips.

"So ye feel sorry for yerself now?"

She blinked at him. It was a moment before she spoke. "Yes, I feel sorry for myself now." She heard how defiant her tone was. "I am just one woman, and you are the mighty Wolf. I cannot continue to fight you, Alexander, alone like this."

"But I do not wish to fight ye, Margaret. I never have."

"Don't. I am still intended for Sir Guy!" And now she realized that their union was more important than ever.

"When he has but one use for ye?" He was scathing.

She got to her feet. "I do not wish to discuss Sir Guy."

"Ye never do. But *I* wish to discuss him now."

She shook her head.

"When will ye admit that he was rude, unbearable— that he insulted ye, that ye deserve better?"

"It is late. You should leave."

"I dinna wish to leave." He folded his arms across his chest as if he meant to stand there in her room for a very long time. "Do ye think avoiding the subject of Sir Guy will change the truth? Do ye think that avoiding me will change anything?"

She decided to feign absolute ignorance of what he meant—when she knew his meaning completely! "The truth is that I am promised to an English knight, one reputed to be honorable and brave, and now, my family fights for King Edward, so the alliance is a good one."

"The truth is yer a great lady, too good for Sir Guy. And yer a Highland lass, like yer mother. Ye belong with a Scot or a Highlander."

"Do not ask me to be your mistress again!" she cried.

"I'm no fool. I ken ye'll be loyal fer as long as ye can—until there's no point."

It took her a moment. "Do not kill Sir Guy, Alexander. Not on my account."

He smiled, but it was chilling. "I almost killed him at the war parley. He insulted ye. I dinna like it. My blood boiled."

She was stunned. She hadn't known—he had been a master at hiding his anger.

"And if he's dead, there will be no point to yer loyalty," he said.

"You read the letter!" she cried. "We are at war! Now, we fight *with* the English, against you, against Bruce! Whether Sir Guy lives or not!"

"You prefer King Edward's rule to Bruce's?" He studied her. "One day ye will meet Bruce and ye'll change yer mind—and yer loyalties." He turned to the doorway, but then turned back. "Avoiding me will not change the kisses we shared, or that I want ye—or that ye want me back."

She trembled.

"I'm a patient man, Lady Margaret, and ye may take that as fair warning."

Margaret did not answer, watching him leave.

CHAPTER NINE

"LADY MARGARET! LADY MARGARET!"

Margaret leapt to her feet—she had been resting, even in the middle of the day, as she slept so poorly at night. Eilidh came running into her chamber, her eyes huge in her pale face.

"Ye must go to the ramparts!"

"What is it? What has happened?"

"It's Bruce! He is here—with his army!"

Margaret faltered—why would Robert Bruce come here with his army? She ran from her chamber and up the stairs to the ramparts. Most of the castle folk were already hanging over the crenellations to view the spectacle of Robert Bruce's arrival at Castle Fyne.

She ran to the closest wall, shoving past the men, women and children there. And she saw the dozens of men and horses rippling up the forest road. Huge yellow banners waved above them, etched with red. She could not see any foot soldiers.

An arm seized her from behind. Margaret knew it was Alexander before she whirled to face him. She was shocked by his hard expression.

"Bruce will be here for this night, and mayhap another one," he said fiercely.

"Why?" she asked, still shocked.

He did not bother to answer her. "Yer to go to the

kitchens and make certain ye serve a dinner fit for Scotland's next king."

Margaret now realized why Alexander had such a determined and intense expression on his face. He was Bruce's vassal. He expected Bruce to be his king. He was no longer the lord and master of Castle Fyne; Robert Bruce was.

"Of course," she said quickly. "He will be very pleased, Alexander, I will make certain of it."

His eyes flickered, perhaps with some relief. But otherwise, his hard expression did not change. "There is more. Yer to stay in the kitchens, or in yer chamber—yer not to come into the hall."

It took her a moment to comprehend him. She was being banned from Bruce's presence. Why? And then she realized that they would plot and plan their war against King Edward, they would conspire as to how to seize Scotland's throne. And she was their enemy.

"Ye'll obey me without question in this matter," he said harshly.

His tone was frightening—when she was no longer truly afraid of him. "I will stay in the kitchens or my chamber," she said softly. "So you will be at liberty to discuss what you must."

"Good." He then stared down at the approaching forces. "His army grows with every passing day." He sounded satisfied.

Fear rippled through her. She could still see only the dozens of knights at the army's forefront.

"He has hundreds of followers," Alexander said. "That is not enough to war upon England and all of her might, but as he marches through Scotland, he is raising men and arms from those he defeats, and those who gladly join him. We will be thousands strong in no time."

She glanced across the first line of knights. She could now make out the hundreds of men on foot behind them, the wagons and carts. She could even see the design of the great banners—Bruce also sported a great red dragon, his savagely rearing up, as if clawing apart the yellow flag it rode.

"Ye'll go in now," Alexander said.

Margaret hesitated, sensing that something else was at stake; she simply did not know what it could be.

She met Eilidh and Peg on the stairs, as Alexander vanished down them ahead of her. She quickly told them of their duties. Both maids were wide-eyed, at once filled with trepidation and excitement, for Bruce was a legend in the land.

But as she planned a great dinner for him, her mind raced. She turned to Peg. "Can you please begin the preparations?" she asked.

Peg glanced at her, as if she guessed that subterfuge was afoot, and she nodded, hurrying off. As she did so, Margaret pulled Eilidh into her chamber, shutting the door. "I have other duties for you."

There was a small voice in her head, warning her not to delve into the important affairs of powerful men. Margaret dismissed it. "Bruce is at war with King Edward, and we are allied with the king. Remember, Castle Fyne was stolen from me—Alexander is the enemy." She took the maid's hand. "I want you to listen very carefully to every word that is said tonight."

Eilidh gasped. "I'm to spy?"

"We must discover all the news that we can, Eilidh, and I am depending upon you."

Eilidh was incredulous. "What if I am discovered?"

Alexander was ruthless, and they all knew it as Malcolm had been hanged. "If they truly wished for a privy

conversation, they would bar everyone from the hall."
She hoped her smile was reassuring. "Alexander has
barred me from the hall, and that is why I need you."

Eilidh nodded, but she appeared frightened now.

Margaret gave her hand a reassuring squeeze. She was
not sure how any war news would affect her fate, but they
would be plotting and planning at her great table, in her
hall—she had to know what they discussed.

THE KITCHENS WERE so hot that Margaret had shed her
mantle and rolled up the sleeves of the blue surcote she
wore. She had also pinned her braid up into a coil, but
the heat was unbearable still. Perspiration gathered on
her brow, her temples and in her cleavage.

Fires burned in every oven and hearth as venison, hen
and lamb were roasted. Breads and pies baked. Oats were
rolled and boiled. The kitchen was the scene of constant,
frantic activity.

Bread, wine, cheese and smoked fishes had been
served. Eilidh now returned to the kitchen with an empty
trencher, her cheeks flushed.

Margaret rushed to her, taking the tray from her
hands. "Well?"

Her eyes were huge like saucers in her small face.
"He is so mighty, my lady, and so handsome, and so
much like a king!"

Margaret had never met Robert Bruce, but tales had
been told about him from the time he had ridden with
William Wallace as a young man, attempting to overthrow King Edward even then. He was renowned to be
not just a great soldier and a brilliant commander, but a
handsome nobleman and, in spite of a second marriage,
a ladies' man. "What have you heard?"

"They are talking of wars and battles, my lady, and it was so confusing."

Margaret was dismayed, but then, Peg returned with an empty tray, and Margaret smiled at Eilidh. "Get more fare and continue to eavesdrop," she said softly. It was too noisy in the kitchens for anyone to overhear them.

Peg put her tray down and came over. Her eyes were filled with respect. "He is a fine man, Margaret. I think he will be our king."

Margaret knew she must not trust Peg, but the maid loved to gossip. "Did you hear their conversation?"

"I did. Bruce cannot tame Galloway—he has just come from war there. He cursed the Gaels for their stubborn independence. And his men have lost Tibbers—and he will march on Dumbarton next."

"They have lost ground—they must be irate."

"No, they are boasting about the future—they think to win this war," Peg said.

Margaret remained amazed by the rebels' confidence. They truly thought to defeat King Edward.

"There is more, Margaret. They have gained new allies—the earls of Atholl and Lennox."

Margaret stared, stunned. The Earl of Atholl, John Strathbogie, was a good friend of her family—he would never turn his back on her uncle! She did not believe it.

A rising scent interrupted her thoughts. "God! Something is burning!" She rushed to an oven to help remove a shank of lamb before it was ruined, from the corner of her eye watching both maids leave, their trenchers full once again.

Having salvaged the shank, Margaret paused to sip some wine, wiping perspiration from her brow and her chin.

Eilidh returned a few moments later, very breathlessly. "Bruce leaves tomorrow, at dawn."

"Here." Margaret handed her a cup of wine and watched as she drank some of it. She could not decide if she would be pleased by such an abrupt departure. Bruce had upset the household, but if she did not learn anything of value that night, it was all for nothing.

Eilidh set her cup aside. "He is on the march to Scone, my lady, for the crown."

Margaret had been taking a sip of wine, and she choked. "Already?" she cried.

The maid nodded, but Margaret was disbelieving. It was March 5th. He could be at Scone in a week. And now she understood somewhat. He was advancing on Scone, and taking what castles he could along the way—including Dumbarton. He would need reinforcements if he were to claim the crown, as the act would launch the largest war with England this land had thus far seen. But the crowning of Scotland's king was a very traditional ceremony. A great many bishops and barons would have to be present. They would have to be summoned in advance of any coronation.

Did Bruce really plan to take the crown within months—or even weeks? "Have they decided upon a date for a coronation?"

Eilidh was so pale now. Nervously, she whispered, "I think they said March the twenty-fifth, but I am not sure, because they argued a bit."

Margaret went still, but her heart thundered. If a coronation had been set for March 25th, she must relay such information to her uncle, immediately. "When you go back, you must listen very closely—if a date has been set, we must learn of it."

Eilidh nodded, seeming tearful. "Will they really crown him, Lady Margaret?"

"I don't know. Eilidh—why did they argue?"

"The Wolf asked about the Stone of Scone. Bruce became angry. I do not know why."

"King Edward stole the Stone of Scone years ago—
and it is a part of the ceremony." Margaret wondered if
a coronation could even be valid, without the ceremo-
nial relic.

Peg came rushing into the room, directly to them. She
spoke in a rapid whisper, her eyes as wide as Eilidh's.
"Margaret, they're discussing a coronation! They have
summoned Scotland's great earls and bishops!"

So it was about to happen—Bruce would seize the
crown.

"Margaret! We will soon have a king!"

Margaret looked at Peg, realizing that she was filled
with excitement. She decided not to bother to remind her
that Bruce was the sworn enemy of her family.

But Peg stepped even closer, and lowered her voice
so it was almost inaudible. "They are speaking about
Isabella," she said.

Margaret became rigid. "Not Isabella—my cousin by
marriage?" Isabella was Buchan's young, pretty wife—
and a dear friend.

Peg nodded, her stare intense.

"Why would they discuss Isabella?" Margaret cried.

"There is a tradition for a king to be crowned. The
Earl of Fife must lead the new king of Scotland to his
throne, and there, he sets the crown upon his head. But
they have no Earl of Fife."

Isabella's young brother, Ed, was the Earl of Fife—
but he had been taken into King Edward's custody some
time ago. He was, in fact, a royal hostage. Isabella was
the Countess of Fife, as well as the Countess of Buchan,
now that she had married Margaret's uncle.

Margaret had not realized that this was a part of the

coronation ceremony. But then, she had never attended the coronation of a Scot king. "If Bruce wishes to follow tradition, what will he do? He will never be able to summon young Ed to the coronation."

"Bruce thinks they could summon Isabella to do the honor, in the Earl of Fife's stead."

Margaret gasped. "He must be a madman. Isabella is the Countess of Buchan now. She is against Bruce, not for him. Yet he would force her to commit treason?"

"I dinna ken, Margaret, and I am as surprised as ye."

Anger rippled through her. Isabella was her friend. They had met two years ago, when she was a bride. Isabella was only two years older than Margaret, which gave them some common ground, but more important, she had been somewhat forlorn at having left Fife. She had also been intimidated by her powerful, older husband— Margaret's new guardian. As Margaret had been rather intimidated by the earl as well, they had quickly become friends.

Surely, they would quickly realize that Isabella would never participate in the coronation. Or did they already know that, and not care? Would they abduct her and force her to help crown Bruce?

Margaret had to know what Bruce planned, and if his plan included her friend. She also had to warn Isabella, if she was in such danger.

"I am finished hiding here in the kitchens," she said, with sudden determination. She would not hide from Bruce any longer. She began plucking apart her braid. She shook her hair out and took off the apron she wore, then adjusted her gold girdle, and smoothed down her skirts. If they wished to plot and plan the theft of the crown, so be it—she intended to be present while they did so.

"My lady, the Wolf ordered ye to stay away from the hall," Eilidh protested.

"He did. But I cannot spy—Alexander would recognize me. Therefore, I am joining them. After all, I am the lady of this castle, and it is my right to welcome my guest."

Margaret left the kitchens, her pulse pounding. As she approached the great hall, she heard the conversation from within, which was loud and raucous and very male. She could now glimpse the many Highland men inside. She saw a great many English knights as well, and she was somewhat surprised—but Bruce was the Earl of Carrick, so he would have vassals from England, as well. Everyone seemed to be in good spirits, she saw, and her maids were mostly serving wine now, as the dinner was over. Glancing across the crowded hall, she saw Bruce and Alexander.

For one moment she hesitated on the hall's threshold, not to gain composure, but to assess the man who was bold enough to dare to seize Scotland's throne and fight off the might of England. He sat beside Alexander, his back to the wall, and his profile to her.

He was as tall as Alexander, meaning that he stood inches above most other men, as broad-shouldered, his arms those of a warrior accustomed to wielding swords and axes. Even from across the hall, she saw that his features were strong but pleasing. His hair was shoulder-length and reddish-brown. He was dressed in the manner more common to the borders and Englishmen, in a long-sleeved blue cote and a sleeveless brown tunic, his red mantle pinned at one shoulder. And then he turned aside from Alexander, as if aware of her presence, and instantly their gazes met.

Margaret trembled. He was exactly as she had thought

he would be—a mighty warrior, a powerful baron, the Earl of Carrick and, just possibly, Scotland's next king.

She started forward with as much dignity as she could muster. But there was trepidation. Alexander had seen her. She was careful not to look at him, but she felt his displeasure—and it was vast.

Margaret paused before their table as Bruce stood up, his blue eyes bright. He smiled at her. "Lady Margaret, I presume?"

Margaret curtsied deeply. "Welcome to my home."

His smile widened, as he now gave her a thorough appraisal, from head to toe. It was blatant—he made no attempt to hide it. "The rumors do not do you justice. You are even more beautiful than your mother."

Margaret was flustered by his open scrutiny of her figure, and also, by what she felt was a far deeper evaluation. She did not dare look at Alexander directly, but from the corner of her eye, she saw that he was angry. "You met my mother?" she asked Bruce.

"Upon a single occasion. But I am pleased you have decided to attend us. I was curious to meet the courageous lady of Castle Fyne." He indicated that she should sit with him.

Margaret approached, having little choice but to glance at Alexander. He gave her a chilling look, making it clear that she would pay dearly for her defiance.

"Are your duties truly over, Lady Margaret?" Alexander said coldly.

"I have done my best to see to it that our guests are well fed tonight." She smiled at him, and quickly turned her attention back to Bruce. "I hope you were not too displeased with the dinner I have served."

"I could not eat another thing, so I am well pleased." He glanced mildly at Alexander and then back at her.

"And I am always in a good humor when a beautiful woman is present."

Margaret did not blush as she sat down on the bench facing both men. "Then I am pleased, to serve you so well, my lord."

He sat and laughed. "Are you, Lady Comyn?"

He had stressed her last name. "I have no wish to displease you," she said, and she was being truthful, for the moment. "But I am curious. How could you have met my mother? The MacDougalls and the Bruces have been rivals for a great many years."

"We met during a truce—at a wedding. I was younger then—about your age," Bruce said. "I was instantly smitten, but your mother was not. I believe I asked her to ride with me in the forests. She struck me across the face."

Margaret believed his every word, and she was relieved that he was so amused, as she imagined her mother striking Bruce as a young man for his impertinence. "My mother was in love with my father, as odd as that may be."

"Your mother was a woman of great loyalty. As you take after her, I imagine you are, too."

She hesitated, unsure of how to respond, or if she was being tested. Her glance moved between the two men. "I am as loyal as my mother," she finally said. "I hope to emulate her in every way."

Bruce smiled and turned to Alexander, who sat very stiffly beside him, although he drummed his fingers against the table. "You must be charmed by your hostage, Alexander. And you have not said a word about her, other than to mention her courage during the siege."

Alexander smiled without mirth. "I find Lady Margaret to be a great many things—but around me, charming she is not."

"Well, you have taken her castle—her dowry. And she is a MacDougall as well as a Comyn—you are one of her greatest rivals."

"I do not consider Lady Margaret a rival—not usually," Alexander said. He gave her another cool look.

"Yet somehow, I am sure she considers you her rival—just as she considers me her rival. Am I correct?"

Margaret was uncomfortable. "I am a prisoner here. I have no time for rivalry, just survival."

Bruce laughed. "Well done!" he exclaimed. He turned to Alexander. "She is very charming, and it could not escape you. She is unusually beautiful, too—yet you have not extolled her beauty, not a single time."

"I felt certain her beauty would not escape *you,* Robert," Alexander said, taking up his wine. "There was thus no need."

Margaret now sensed a tension between the two men. She was alarmed.

"It would certainly escape me if she were hidden in the kitchens," Bruce said easily enough.

Her alarm increased. Had Alexander meant to keep her from Bruce, not so they might have privacy to discuss their war plans, but for other reasons? Bruce had not tried to hide his appreciation of her—and everyone knew he was a rogue when it came to the ladies.

"Lady Margaret does not know the meaning of *hide,* do ye, Lady Margaret?" Alexander murmured.

"I was hardly hiding in the kitchens." She wanted to alleviate the tension. "I had hoped to be able to come down to dine with you, my lord," she said to Bruce, "but preparing such a meal, in such haste, took a great deal of time."

"It has been a long ride from Galloway, so I am

pleased for every comfort, as are my men. Has Alexander allowed you to send word to Buchan?"

Her tension escalated. She glanced at Alexander. A warning look filled his eyes.

Where would Bruce lead? She swallowed. "No, but I received a missive from him the other day."

Bruce's brows lifted. "And were you pleased to hear from your dear uncle?"

She reminded herself that Buchan hated Bruce, as had their cousin Red John. Bruce seemed indifferent, but that could not be. "Of course I hoped to hear from him."

"But you are not smiling, my dear, thus you are unhappy. If he did not say so, I will tell you myself—he is too busy plotting revenge against me, Lady Margaret, to concern himself with you."

Margaret tried to smile. The upward curve of her lips felt ghastly. "He must see to the interests of the entire family."

"But you are a valuable hostage—a valuable bride—and a part of the family's great interests."

She became terribly uncomfortable now. She looked at Alexander, and he seemed grim. She had the oddest feeling, as if being on a hook, twirling in the wind, knowing that at any moment, she would be cut free—to crash to the ground.

"Buchan is in Liddesdale as we speak. He meets with his friends, Mowbray and de Umfraville, to plan a war against me." Bruce sipped his wine, entirely complacent, it seemed. "Unless Sir Guy bestirs himself to attack another time, I am afraid you will have to adjust to a lengthy period of captivity. And, of course, if Sir Guy returns to fight us, he must win."

She clasped her hands in her lap, but glanced at Alexander. He was very still, but his gaze held hers for a moment. And she was very aware that Bruce had used the plural, "us," instead of just referring to Alexander. "Alexander has made it clear he will not ransom me now. And my uncle also made it clear that I must have patience in these times of war. I have already imagined that I might be a hostage for far longer than I ever dreamed."

Bruce saluted her with his glass. "You are very brave, but you proved that during the siege. You know, the news of your alliance with Sir Guy surprised me."

She felt an impossible tension now.

"Your uncle—and your father—spent his life fighting the English, with your mother's kin at their side. Yes, a truce was made betwixt us all last year, but then, so suddenly, Buchan chose Sir Guy for you."

Alexander set his mug down, somewhat heavily. Margaret jumped. He said, "It is all politics."

"Aye, but to marry one's lifelong enemy? I cannot imagine." Bruce refilled his cup, Alexander's and a third one. He handed the latter to Margaret.

She clasped it but did not drink. "It turned out to be a fortunate alliance, did it not? As you are in rebellion, and we now find ourselves so firmly in King Edward's camp."

Bruce's eyes widened. "Hurrah! I must say, well done yet again!"

Margaret did not feel that she had done anything well. In fact, she did not feel well, and she regretted disobeying Alexander and coming to the hall. She glanced at Alexander. Why had Bruce wished to point out that she was nothing but a pawn in her uncle's political games? Why had he wished to suggest that her uncle did not care about her, except to use her for the family's ends? Did he want to drive the spike of misery into her? Did he think to make her waver in her loyalties?

"Do you not like wine, Lady Margaret?" Bruce asked.

Margaret took a sip. "I like it very much." She was ready to escape the table—thinking to outwit Bruce had been insane. "Will you be staying with us for very long, my lord?"

"I go to war tomorrow." He smiled. "Will that please you?"

"I merely asked so I might know what meals to plan."

"And you did not answer me, either." His smile did not waver—neither did his stare.

"You might be Scotland's next king. You have greatly affected our household."

"I will be Scotland's next king," he said easily. "Before you take your leave, lady, you must tell me one thing. How does the Countess of Buchan fare?"

Margaret had just begun to stand up; she froze. And all she could think was, why would Bruce ask about Isabella? "I last saw her at Balvenie, before we left for Castle Fyne. She was as usual, my lord, in good spirits."

He studied her for a moment. "You're about the same age—are you friends?"

What kind of question was this? "We are friends."

"Then you must know why she remains at Balvenie, whilst her husband plots against me with his allies in the south."

"I do not know why she did not go south."

Bruce sat back, glancing at Alexander. "Better the north than the south," he said.

Margaret became alarmed. What did that remark mean?

"We will break the fast before dawn, Lady Margaret, but the fare should be light, as we will travel hard and fast on the morrow," Bruce said.

It was a dismissal—and an abrupt one. Yet Margaret was relieved.

Alexander said, "Prepare my chamber for Bruce."

Bruce would sleep in the chamber adjacent her own? She told herself she need not worry, but the reassurance felt like a hollow one. She nodded, trying to meet Alexander's eye, but he refused to look up.

Both men were silent now. Clearly, they wanted her gone, so they could discuss the war—and the coronation.

Margaret curtsied and left. As she hurried away, a sinking feeling consumed her. Bruce had asked about Isabella, and she was afraid he meant to use her somehow, against Buchan, in his damned theft of the throne.

THE FIRES WERE out, the kitchen cleaned. The castle had fallen silent, most of its inhabitants asleep. It was several hours after dinner, and Margaret was exhausted.

Her mind would not stop racing with all the information she had gleaned. Yet she could not form any definite conclusions. She wondered if Alexander would allow her to write Isabella. She doubted it.

And tomorrow he would berate her for her disobedience, she was certain. He might even punish her.

But if there was any chance that her friend was in danger of becoming Bruce's pawn, she must warn her. Tomorrow she would visit William as she always did. If he had a plan to escape, it was time to learn of it.

Margaret went up the stairs toward her bedchamber. She was utterly fatigued, and she did not want to think anymore. She did not want to worry about Isabella, or Bruce, and she did not want to plot an escape. All of that could be done on the morrow.

But when she reached the upper landing, she tensed. She did not know when Bruce had gone up to his bed in Alexander's chamber, and she had no reason to think that he might disturb her now, but she was anxious. All of Scotland knew that he was unfaithful to his wife a great deal of the time.

His door was closed; hers was open. She could see into her room—Eilidh had stoked the fire there and it blazed. Her fur coverlet had been pulled invitingly down on the bed. Exhaustion claimed her.

But before she could enter her chamber, Bruce's door opened. Margaret froze as he stepped into the corridor.

He smiled.

She trembled.

"I can never sleep, not on the eve of war."

"I am sorry," she managed to say. He was clad only in his braies—the knee-length linen drawers favored by the English nobility. He was a very muscular man, with a hard, scarred body. She did not want to look at his rib cage or chest.

And from within her chamber, Eilidh turned and gaped at them.

"Why are you afraid of me? Is it because of Alexander? Or is it because I will be your king?" Bruce asked calmly.

Margaret was stricken. How should she respond? "All of Scotland speaks of you, my lord, and often. You are a legend, and rightly so."

He grinned, leaning against the wall. "Do go on, Lady Margaret."

"It is well-known that you adore the ladies, my lord, and that they adore you."

He laughed. "And what is wrong with that?"

She would not point out that he had a wife! "I am intended to another."

His smile faded. "Yes, you are—a poor deer, wide of eye, innocent and trusting, being led to the slaughter."

Margaret was disbelieving. "I am proud to do my duty."

"You should change your politics," he said, his tone suddenly hard.

She stiffened.

"I will be Scotland's next king. I will remember my friends. They will be rewarded—and well."

She did not have to ask how he would treat his enemies. Had his statement been a threat?

"You do realize, Lady Margaret, that I can arrange for your freedom?"

She started, for such a remark was hardly insignificant. He continued, "Alexander is my vassal. I am his liege lord—I will be his king. If I command him to free you, he will do so. If I command him to return Castle Fyne to you, he will obey."

Margaret heard her heart thundering in her ears. She wondered if Bruce heard it, too. But she already knew how much power he wielded—at least over those who followed him.

She wondered if Alexander would obey Bruce, should he order her release. She couldn't be certain.

"Why are you telling me this?" she whispered.

He softened and smiled at her. "I am telling you this because I like you, Lady Margaret, just as I liked your mother. I admire courage and pride, loyalty and even defiance, in both men and women—even in the enemy."

She swallowed. Was he suggesting a liaison between them? That if she joined him that night, he would surrender the keep to her—and give her back her freedom? "Are you offering me my freedom? What would I have to do to be freed? To have Castle Fyne returned to me?"

"No, I am not offering you your freedom—in return for a night in my bed." His smile grew. He was so amused. "Not that I do not desire you. But I am at war with England. I will soon attack Dumbarton. Alexander will be joining me very shortly. I need him at my side, for he is one of my best soldiers."

Margaret was overcome with relief. Bruce would not make advances—he was merely touting his power. But she then became torn with dismay. Alexander was going to war with him!

"When will Alexander leave here?"

"If he can ready the garrison here tomorrow, I expect him to ride out the following day," Bruce said flatly. "I cannot decide if Alexander's departure pleases or dismays you, Lady Margaret."

She inhaled, somehow smiling. "It pleases me, because I am his prisoner." She was shocked at how much her words felt like a lie.

Bruce laughed. Then he looked past her, toward the stairs. His smile changed.

Margaret turned and saw Peg standing there. She blushed and curtsied, murmuring, "My lord."

Bruce smiled at Peg, turned to Margaret, and inclined his head. Without bidding her good eve, he went into his bedchamber.

Margaret walked slowly into her room, only vaguely aware of Eilidh waiting for her. Bruce was powerful and frightening, and suddenly, she wondered if he could actually seize the throne, if he would one day be king.

She shivered. She did not want to be his enemy if that day came!

Peg came to her door. "Margaret? Will ye be angered if I go to him?"

Margaret turned to gaze at her. "No. If he is ever Scotland's king, it will serve you well."

Peg seemed relieved, and left the room. Margaret slid into her bed, as Eilidh lay down on the pallet she used on the floor. "Good night, my lady," she said.

"Good night." Margaret turned over, curling up. How she hated war. But Bruce loved it, Alexander loved it, fools that they were. And she did not want to worry now, not about Alexander or anyone, but she kept seeing him on the battlefield, sword raised, his hair in the wind, Bruce's banner flying…the images following her into sleep.

CHAPTER TEN

MARGARET GLANCED FURTIVELY into the great hall. Bruce and his men were finishing up breakfast, everyone eating determinedly, clearly intent upon an early departure. And Alexander was with them. Like the night before, he and Bruce sat together at the far table, their backs to the wall. Like the night before, they spoke quietly while eating. And they were so engrossed in the conversation that neither man ever looked up.

No moment could be better. She quickly rushed past the threshold of the room, expecting Alexander to shout at her to halt, but the command never came. Breathing hard, she raced down the corridor.

She had arisen well before dawn to help the women in the kitchens. Alexander had yet to summon her, but she knew such a summons would come. She expected it almost immediately after Bruce and his army left. In the light of this day, she anticipated far more than a rebuke for her defiance. And she could imagine how he would punish her—one choice would be to deny her the daily visit with her brother.

Therefore, she must speak with William now, in case such a punishment was inflicted.

She had so much to tell him; she so needed his opinion!

In the south tower, William's guard was eating a loaf

of bread with some cheese. He nodded at her, lumbering to his feet.

"Good morning." Margaret smiled. The guards changed frequently, but she knew them all. Still, it took her a moment to recall his name. "Duncan."

"Lady." He unlocked the door and opened it.

William was pacing, and he turned, clearly surprised to see her at dawn. He did not even greet her. "Bruce came last night—and they are leaving now?"

Aware of the guard in the doorway, who would listen to their every word, she smiled at him. "I was as surprised as you are. He rides on Dumbarton, William. There is a great deal of news."

He stared for a moment. And then, suddenly, he seized his right side and cried out, collapsing. Margaret started to rush forward, but so did the guard. She let him catch William, and as he did, she turned and emptied the contents of a small vial into his mug of wine.

The action took an instant, and then she was running over to them. "What is it?"

"God, I don't know!" William now sat down on the pallet, holding his side. "It was a terrible pain. But it is now gone."

"Ye had better hope so." Duncan returned to the door. He had dropped his bread, and now, he kicked it across the hall. Having lost the rest of his breakfast, he picked up the mug and drained the wine.

In five more minutes, he would be unconscious. Satisfied, Margaret turned to her brother. "Alexander is garrisoning Castle Fyne with a hundred good men."

"So he thinks to defend the keep if Sir Guy or Buchan attacks? Damn! Castle Fyne is easily defended with such a garrison. What other news, Meg?" William was hard and intent.

"Bruce has come from Galloway. He has not been able to gain support there."

William nodded, grim but briefly smiling. "The Gaels will never support him or anyone other than their own."

Margaret glanced at Duncan and saw him yawn. "I received a letter from our uncle, too."

William's eyes widened. He glanced at Duncan. "What did he write?"

"He is preparing for war against Bruce. He is hoping to ransom us, but Alexander has said he will not do so now. He says I am too valuable—even Bruce said as much. William, we will be captives for a lengthy time."

William gave her a smug look. She was certain he had a plan. "You will always have great value, for any man who weds with you will have a legitimate claim on Castle Fyne, as will his sons." Then, "Did you meet Bruce?"

She nodded. "He is a very strong man. I did not believe it possible for any man to go up against England and win, but maybe Bruce can do so."

"No. It will never happen. I won't allow it—Buchan won't allow it—King Edward won't allow it!"

A crash sounded and they turned; Duncan lay on the floor, unconscious. William laughed. "That was well done, Meg!" On his feet, he raced to the door and dragged Duncan inside, then closed the door solidly behind him. He bolted it.

"William! Bruce marches on Scone—to be crowned there!" Margaret cried.

William cursed. "He has always coveted the throne! Just as his father did!"

Margaret seized his sleeve. "He might plan to abduct Isabella. Peg heard him and Alexander discussing it. Apparently the Earl of Fife must play a role in the coronation ceremony, and they cannot get young Ed to attend, obviously. So they are wondering if they might use Isabella, instead. And Bruce asked me about her! I am very worried now. I have not been thinking about escape lately, but we must warn Isabella."

"I have a plan, and the timing is perfect!" William said.

"How could we possibly escape? I am no longer under guard, but someone is always close by—someone always has an eye upon me—except for now, when I made certain to use the chaos in the hall as an opportunity to see you. And you are under constant guard!"

William walked to the window and gestured. Margaret hurried over and looked out.

Perhaps a hundred knights were now riding out of the barbican and down the forest road, the sun just rising and shedding its bright light. The day was a clear one, with but a few fluffy white clouds in the sky, and Bruce was clearly visible at their forefront. Even from this distance, he made a proud, commanding figure, his huge yellow-and-red banner waving overhead in the midst of the cavalcade. The sight was at once powerful, sobering and frightening.

"The road is naught but a path, and it will take hours for his army to leave here," William said. "How many men does he have?"

"I don't know."

"The Wolf has five hundred men, does he not?"

She looked closely at him. He turned to face her, his back now to the window and the newly rising sun. "He has five hundred men, perhaps more, if his brother sent him an army, too."

"And he leaves in two more days? The day after tomorrow?"

"No. My understanding is that he leaves tomorrow, but

I have not yet spoken with him." She shivered. She was aware of her dismay as she spoke of Alexander leaving, to go to war with Bruce. "What do you plan?"

"We will leave the castle from the north door. From there, we must only cross a short patch of forest, and we will be on the road. We can slip into his army, where we will never be discovered."

Every castle had one or more small doors that could admit and expel a man on foot or even one astride, but no more than that. She stared, her mind racing. "You are guarded," she began.

"Leave the potion with me—I will administer it myself. I will wear my guard's clothes. You must disguise yourself, as well. As you just said, it was chaos this morning in the hall. It is chaos when the army leaves."

She trembled, beginning to understand. "Even if you and I can get to the north exit, it is also guarded."

"That is where Peg can be of value—do you doubt her ability to distract any man?" He smiled.

Could his plan actually work? She was incredulous. She knew she could slip away in disguise, so reaching the north door would not be difficult. And Peg could distract the guard at the small north exit. She would offer her some reward to do so. And once she left the castle, she could run into the forest....

Then she thought of Alexander and she sobered.

She knew he would be furious if she escaped—and he might even be disappointed.

She reminded herself that she had never given him her word that she would not eventually make such an attempt. It was her duty to escape, more so now than ever. Not only was she his prisoner, Bruce was seeking the crown. Isabella had to be warned, in case Bruce thought to use her against her will—and force her to commit treason.

William's plan might work. If they could merge into Alexander's army, they would never be remarked. And once at Dumbarton, they would be able to find friends to help them get to Buchan, if he was still in the south, or to return to Balvenie in the far north.

"What if I cannot bring you another potion? I have reason to believe that Alexander might not allow me to visit you again," she said slowly.

William shrugged. "I am friends with all my guards. I am no longer weak, but they do not know that. I will strike my guard from behind. I am leaving this place, Margaret, to return to Buchan lands, because we are at war and I must fight!"

In that moment, William reminded her of her father. He was very young—not even twenty—but he was fierce and proud, and so handsome. She felt herself nod. "Then we must decide upon the final details now—because we might not have another chance."

"He will leave after breakfast," William said. "Like Bruce, Alexander and his knights will depart first. You and I will meet two hours after he leaves, exactly, at the north door. Peg will distract the guard, and we will slip from the castle, run into the forest, and join the rest of the army as it is departing."

Margaret nodded, suddenly hugging herself. Was she dismayed? Wasn't she thrilled to finally be planning an escape—one that might be successful?

"And Margaret? If one of us fails to escape, the other must go."

She started. "I do not like the sound of that," she cried.

He held up his hand. "There is no choice now. We must warn Isabella, we must warn Buchan, and Bruce must be stopped before he ever reaches Scone. We escape tomorrow."

MARGARET RETURNED TO the hall, but slowly. She felt cold, and she hugged her mantle tightly to her. She did not know why she wasn't excited over William's plan. Tomorrow they might successfully escape; tomorrow they might be free! For it was a very good plan, and the odds might even be in their favor, now that Alexander trusted her enough to allow her some freedom of movement.

Was that the problem? That he trusted her somewhat? That she knew it? They were enemies, but in a way, an odd friendship had also formed. She had come to respect him; she had come to admire him. She was his prisoner, but she also knew he would keep her safe from all other enemies. He had even tried to protect her from Bruce.

What was wrong with her? As long as they were on opposite sides of this war, they could not be friends— and she must not forget that. He remained the enemy— and it was her duty to attempt an escape.

Tomorrow she might be on the road, hidden amidst his great army, as he rode to war. He would attack Dumbarton, and then continue to attack every enemy in Bruce's path as they marched to Scone, while she went home to Balvenie. There, she would embrace Isabella, warn her uncle, and plead with both her uncle and Sir Guy to retake Castle Fyne. She would probably stay in the north until her marriage in June. Alexander would remain at Bruce's side, as they fought to gain and keep Scotland's throne.

She faltered in the corridor, too dismayed to go on. Oh, how she hated this war! How she hated all war! She had lost three of her brothers in war, and recently, so many of her archers and soldiers, and Malcolm. She began to shiver. Briefly, she had started to believe Bruce could be victorious, but that had been when in his powerful presence. She wasn't overcome by him now. Bruce was one man, and a Scot at that, and he would never defeat King Edward!

Bruce would either die gloriously on the battlefield, or ingloriously, with his head upon the chopping block.

And Alexander's fate was tied to Bruce's. She did not believe he would be spared. If Alexander did not die in battle he would be executed alongside his leader. If he managed to escape King Edward, he would be in exile, an outlaw living in the forests....

She should not care. She did not want to care.

"Somehow, I dinna think yer looking for me."

She jerked out of her terrible reverie at the sound of Alexander's voice. He leaned against the doorway of the hall, his posture casual—his expression too bland. His eyes, however, were hard.

It was a moment before she could speak, and even so, her tone was strained. "Good morning, my lord. Bruce has left?"

"I feel certain ye ken that Bruce is gone."

"I saw him leave, yes."

"Ye disobeyed me directly, Lady Margaret. I am vastly displeased."

"I could not stand the rumors," she whispered.

"What rumors? And what excuse is that?" he demanded, anger now crossing his expression.

"The rumors of war. The rumors of a coronation. Does he march to Scone? Will he be crowned there?" she cried, trembling. She realized her fists were clenched. "And do you go to war tomorrow?"

"If he will be king, he will be crowned at Scone," Alexander said, more calmly. But his gaze was still searing. "I am leaving tomorrow."

"To attack Dumbarton? To attack every ally of King Edward as you march to Scone?" she cried.

"So yer maids were spying on us last night."

Tears seemed to arise. "Please leave Isabella alone."

"Ye discovered too much, Margaret."

"You already mean to punish me, do you not? Yes, my maids overheard you last night. But Bruce told me that you go to battle at Dumbarton. I can imagine the rest. God, Alexander—you go to war against King Edward's army!"

He studied her and began to smile. "Lady Margaret— are ye frightened for me? Even more now than before?"

She could not breathe properly. "I should not care. I know that. I really do not care! But I cannot wish you ill!"

His smile widened.

"You're amused? You think it amusing—to fight a legitimate king, to make an illegitimate one?" She felt like striking him, the way her mother had once struck Bruce! "This is not some silly blood feud over stolen cattle! This is a great war waged by a would-be king against a great king!"

"Scotland has been fought over before," he said, still smiling.

"Why? Why ride with Bruce? Six months ago you were King Edward's vassal."

"Yer worried about me."

She wanted to deny it. But she could not, not even to herself. "I did not wish you ill when you fought Sir Guy, and I do not wish you ill now. I may be your hostage, but you have been just."

He emitted a short laugh. "The lengths ye go to, to excuse yer affections for me!"

"I do not have affection for you!" she cried.

He studied her, his mouth soft. "I would be very dismayed," he finally said, "should you ever wish me ill."

Margaret had no response to make. She could not

fathom the depth of her distress now. She wished he had never taken up Bruce's cause. She wished he were not going to war tomorrow—and she even wished she were not planning to escape with William.

He moved away from the wall, saying, "We have digressed. There is no excuse ye can make fer disobeying my command."

She took a breath. "I am aware that you are angry."

"I meant to protect ye, Lady Margaret. I meant to keep ye out of jeopardy."

She had been right. He had wanted to keep her away from Bruce, but not so they could discuss their war secrets. "What will you do?"

Their gazes locked. "It gives me no pleasure, but ye'll be confined to yer chamber till I decide otherwise."

She tensed. How would she be able to escape, if she was confined to her chamber now? "If I tell you I am sorry—if I mean it—would you reconsider such a punishment?"

"No."

MARGARET LAY IN her bed, staring up at the ceiling. It was late and the castle was mostly asleep and incredibly silent. The only noise was from the wind outside, moving the trees, and a lone wolf, baying from a ridge somewhere.

She could not sleep. She had spent the day in confinement in her chamber, as promised, with Dughall standing outside her door as her guard. Eilidh had not been allowed to attend her. Dughall had brought her meals. Her window faced north so she could not see into the courtyard or barbican, but all day she had heard the footsteps and voices of Alexander's men as they provisioned the stronghold for his absence. Later, she had heard their voices from the great hall as they supped.

With nothing to do and no one to talk to, she had tried to take up her needlework, but that had been impossible. She was too worried.

She would never be able to escape now. William would have to escape alone. And tomorrow, Alexander would ride off to war.

WHY DID HE have to ride with Bruce? Why did he have to go to war against the might of England? What if he did not return from this battle, or the next one? She could tell herself a thousand times that he was a mighty warrior, that he would be fine, but three of her brothers had died in war. She knew better than anyone how feckless war was. How feckless fate was. Men like Alexander lived and died by the sword, and few lived to old age. She just hoped Fate would not take him at the battle of Dumbarton....

But they were marching to Scone. They meant to seize Scotland's throne. There would be too many battles to count, both before and after Bruce was crowned....

Suddenly she heard a footfall on the stone stairs. She sat bolt upright, aware that it was Alexander. She stared across her chamber, which was illuminated by the fire in the hearth. Would she even be able to wish him God-speed tomorrow?

Men were such fools, to take war so lightly!

And she was a fool, to have any care for him, when they were enemies!

She heard his door open and she flung herself back down on her bed, staring up at the dark ceiling. If only she could care this way for Sir Guy. And who knew? Maybe one day she would, but just then, she did not.

In a way, Alexander had become a significant part of her existence. In a way, he had become the center of her existence. Of course, he was her captor. One day, he would not be so significant.

But he almost felt like a mountain in the center of her world, one that was unmovable, and even insurmountable. Yet it was a mountain that was always there, a presence that was certain.

She tried to laugh at herself. He was like a mountain, but he wasn't an unmovable part of the land—he was a man. If he died, she would be saddened, but she would recover, just as she had recovered from the deaths of her three brothers and her parents.

"But I don't want him to die."

Margaret stiffened, realizing that she had spoken aloud.

She slid from the bed, barefoot and clad only in her chemise. He was leaving tomorrow at dawn, and earlier, she had refused to tell him that she cared.

She threw a fur around her shoulders and went to her door, helpless to resist her own impulses now. It hadn't been locked all day and it was not locked now. She opened it and Dughall instantly leapt to his feet. "Lady Margaret?"

He was incredulous, but then, she was barely dressed. "I wish to speak with Alexander," she said, very unsteadily. And she did not wait for his response. Margaret went to his door and opened it.

He leapt up from the bed, dagger in hand, held poised to attack.

She froze against the door, in surprise, dropping the fur.

His eyes were startled; instantly, they slammed over her and narrowed. He put the dagger down on the bed, then faced her, his eyes warm. "Margaret."

She was not surprised that he was alone—she was fairly certain he had been sleeping alone since the battle of Cruach Nan Cuilean.

She hadn't known what she would say to him a moment ago, but it was so easy now. "I don't want you to die."

His eyes widened slightly. His chamber was dimly lit from the fire in the hearth. He wore only his leine, and the fire made it possible to see somewhat through his tunic. Like all Highland men, he wore nothing beneath it.

His blue gaze now moved over her, slowly. "I am not dying anytime soon."

"That is what each of my three brothers thought."

"I am the Wolf of Lochaber," he said very softly.

"Alexander...I am worried about you." She had finally admitted it—and not just to him, but to herself.

"I am glad." He walked toward her and placed his hand over her shoulder on the wall. His gaze smoldered, meeting hers, but she saw questions there, too. He looked past her, into the hall. "Ye may leave us, Dughall."

Margaret did not turn, but she heard the boy flee. She realized she was staring at Alexander's broad, hard chest. Dark hair dusted its center. His nipples were erect.

He said softly, "How worried are ye?"

"I don't want to have this care. We are enemies!"

"I dinna wish to be enemies, Margaret, not now, not ever."

"I am afraid you won't return from this battle," she whispered.

"I will return, Margaret, ye may be certain, if yer waiting for me."

"Alexander—how can I?" she begged.

"Ye can because ye care. Alliances change all of the

time." He laid his mouth on hers, gently, a feathery brushing of their lips.

Desire exploded. Margaret seized his shoulders, her
body on fire, and the moment her hands closed upon
him, his kiss deepened.

She moved into his embrace, against his entire hard
body, and nothing had ever felt as right. His large body
encompassed hers. Her breasts were crushed by his chest,
and she could feel his manhood, rock-hard against her
belly. She moaned. He opened her mouth, thrust his
tongue deep. He cupped her buttocks and lifted her.

Margaret wrapped her legs around his waist as he
braced her back against the wall. She held on to him
tightly, kissing him back, blinded by the urgency in her
body and the sudden demands of her heart. A moment
later he was plunging deep inside her, and then they were
both crying out.

MARGARET AWOKE SUDDENLY, in confusion. For an instant,
she did not know where she was. She stared at the stone
ceiling, lying under a great many furs, in the bed that
had once been hers, in the chamber that was now his...
Alexander.

She inhaled, stunned. Too many images to count raced
through her mind, and in every one, she was in his hard,
heated embrace, burning with urgency, or in the throes
of ecstasy. She sat up, blushing. He had made love to her
with so much passion, so many times; she had returned
his passion, as wildly, as shamelessly.

Last night, she had been compelled to go to him, but
she hadn't consciously meant to join him in bed. Yet
somehow, the moment she had seen him, she had wound
up in his arms—and once there, she had not had a single
thought of retreat.

And now, as she glanced around the dark room, she saw that he was very much gone.

Dear God, surely he had not ridden off to war without saying a fare-thee-well? She sat up, glancing at the shutters, which were ajar. It was still dark outside—but she saw a glimmer of the rising sun. It was not yet dawn—he couldn't have left yet!

There was no time to dwell upon what had happened now. She leapt up from his bed, found her chemise upon the floor—it was torn and she blushed again—and she threw it on. Barefoot, without a mantle, she ran from his room.

Dughall wasn't in the hall, and for that she was grateful. But now, she recalled his presence there last night. She halted.

She was to marry Sir Guy in June. She was Lady Margaret Comyn—the enemy of both Robert Bruce and every MacDonald in Scotland. But she had slept with Alexander last night.

And Dughall knew.

Her chamber door was ajar. She glanced at the room—Eilidh stood there, smiling at her. "Ye'll catch yer death, standing there mostly naked like that," she said.

Her heart lurched with dismay and dread. Eilidh knew, as well. Margaret rushed inside, closing the door, as Eilidh handed her a clean chemise and cote. "I cannot explain," Margaret said briskly, taking off her torn undergarment and replacing it with the other ones. "But you are sworn to secrecy, Eilidh, you must vow now, on the lives of your mother, your sister and your nieces and nephews, that you will never tell anyone where I was or what I was doing last night." She did not add that her life might depend upon it.

For now she thought of her powerful guardian. Her

uncle would exile her if he ever learned of her infidelity. Of that, she had no doubt.

Eilidh blanched. "My lady, I would never betray ye! And I am pleased for ye. We all ken how his lordship has been lusting after ye, ever since the siege."

Margaret looked blankly at her. Everyone believed that Alexander had desired her from the moment he had first taken the castle?

"I hope he was a pleasing lover," she added, somewhat slyly. "Ye look satisfied, my lady. Ye have good color today."

Margaret thought that she blushed again. "Help me braid my hair!" She had no intention of sharing the details of her night with Alexander. As Eilidh handed her a pale blue surcote, she glimpsed a pile of clothes on the bed. Her heart slammed. "What is that?"

Eilidh picked up a hairbrush. "Ye asked for the clothes yesterday," she said, keeping her tone low.

Her disguise. Today, she was to attempt an escape.

Margaret fought to breathe, and with determination, she pulled the wool surcote over her head and shoulders, adjusting the long sleeves. She found her girdle and tied it as Eilidh began brushing her hair. Her heart now pounded with furious force.

William would be at the north door, if he could, in two hours. He would be expecting her to be there, too.

She could not think clearly. But her heart seemed to be shrieking in protest now.

Could one night change their lives?

"Hurry," Margaret snapped.

Eilidh stiffened, as Margaret never raised her voice, and quickly braided her hair into a long, single plait. Margaret turned and took her hand. "Eilidh, I am sorry. I am uncertain of what to do."

Eilidh smiled. "I ken, my lady."

Did she truly understand? But how could one night change anything? It hardly changed her name, her birthright, her loyalties or the facts of war. Impulsively, Margaret hugged her. Then she raced from the room and downstairs.

She forced herself to slow as she approached the threshold of the hall. She heard the voices of the many knights within, the clank of platters and mugs and swords.

She paused on the threshold of the great room.

Alexander stood with Padraig, already wearing his swords, and they were in a rapid conversation. She knew he was about to leave—she saw it in the set of his shoulders and in his hard, aggressive stance. Urgency rippled in his body, a very different kind of urgency from the kind that had afflicted him last night.

She flushed. Images flooded her, as did sensations… the heat in his eyes, the curve of his mouth…his arms were so strong, his body so hard. In his embrace, she had felt tiny and safe—she had felt cherished.

He jerked to stare at her, clearly ceasing conversation in midsentence.

As a result, Padraig turned to stare at her, too.

Her heart turned over, hard. She wondered how many of his men knew about them. Fear coiled. Buchan must never find out about the night they had shared. Sir Guy must never know.

Alexander left Padraig, crossing the hall with long, swift strides, and pausing on its threshold before her. His face softened. His did not speak, but his gaze held hers, and it was searching.

"I wanted to wish you farewell, Alexander, and God-speed," she said roughly.

His gaze remained probing. "Do ye have regrets?"

She hesitated, incapable of looking away. "I haven't had time to think."

"I have no regrets."

Her heart lurched another time. She wished he wasn't leaving…she wished they weren't enemies…she wished she were not intended to another man. And she realized she did not have regrets either—how could she? "I am glad," she whispered, "that we found a moment to share as we did."

He smiled at her. "It was more than a moment."

She trembled. "Alexander? Last night changes nothing. You go to war—as does my family—and we fight for different kings."

"Last night," he said as quietly, "changes everything."

Her heart turned over once more. But they hardly had time to argue. "Does it change my name? I am Margaret Comyn. Does it change who my uncle is—who my brother is? Does it change that I am to wed Sir Guy in June?"

"Sir Guy might refuse to marry ye, if he learned of this." His stare was sharp.

"He must never know! Buchan must never know! My uncle would lock me away in a tower for the rest of my life if he ever learned of this."

"Margaret, I ken ye fear Buchan—as ye should. But he cannot harm ye here. He cannot harm ye while yer under my protection."

Margaret tensed, realizing he was right—but she planned to escape. "Dughall must be sworn to secrecy," she said.

"Dughall has already been sworn to secrecy." He studied her. "But ye must have a care with yer maids."

"I know."

He glanced over his shoulder, into the hall. "I would like to stand here, speaking with ye, for some time, especially on this topic, but I canna. We are leaving. It is time."

Her heart lurched. "When will you return?"

"I dinna ken. Months, mayhap. Even after Bruce has the throne, the war will rage on. King Edward will have to suffer many defeats to ever accept the loss of Scotland—as will men like your uncle Buchan."

"I hate this war," she said, aware of how uneven her tone sounded. "Bruce said the war would be a long one."

"We fight for a throne. Such matters cannot be swiftly decided."

"I want to see you again, Alexander. Do not die."

His eyes blazed. "Then you will. God keep ye, Margaret."

Their stares held, and then he was turning and striding away, his swords bumping his thighs as he walked. Margaret hugged herself. "God keep you," she said harshly.

Then she realized that Padraig was staring, Sir Neil was staring, others were staring. She turned away, shaken, afraid her feelings had been written all over her face.

She heard them leaving, a thunder of booted steps across the stone floors and out the courtyard doors. Margaret told herself she must not feel such a sense of loss.

Peg stepped into the hall. "Margaret?"

Margaret understood and she looked at her. Peg wanted to know if they were putting their plan of escape into effect.

Alexander was gone. It would be months before he

returned. And one night did not change who he was or who she was.

She had betrayed her family and Sir Guy last night, but that did not mean she had changed her loyalties. Besides, she could not remain at Castle Fyne, Alexander's prisoner, knowing what she did.

"Be at the north door in two hours," Margaret said.

THE COURTYARD HAD been terribly crowded and filled with gawkers as Alexander and his knights had ridden out, but now it was quiet. Margaret paused on the steps leading into the yard, Eilidh behind her, both women in disguise.

Their hoods were full, their cowls long. Margaret wore Eilidh's clothes. Both women looked like Highland maids. But Margaret did not move down the steps.

William's plan would have been better, she thought, if they had left while Alexander and his knights were riding out, causing a great spectacle—most of the castle had turned out to watch and wave farewell. Now, the courtyard was too quiet. Some men and women were leading several cows into the yard, while a carpenter was making repairs to a door. Four children played in one corner and a pair of soldiers guarded the entry tower. On the ramparts, Alexander's archers stood, and the watch was in all the towers.

She knew his huge army was on the march, and slowly leaving the camp it had made outside the castle's walls, but from where she stood, she could not see it. Instead, she felt terribly exposed.

Her pulse raced. She told herself that no one would recognize her now, especially not from the ramparts above, and she started down the steps, Eilidh following. If they were to successfully escape, they must do so now.

She must not think about what she meant to do,

either—she must simply do it. Aware of Eilidh on her heels, Margaret hurried across the courtyard, away from the entry tower, toward its northernmost walls.

Ahead, she saw Peg there, laughing with the Highlander guarding the north exit. Peg had been eager to help—as long as she could escape and go home with them. Margaret glanced behind them and relief arose— William was hurrying toward them in his own disguise.

Even though he remained a careful distance away from her, so they would not become an obvious group, she saw that his eyes were bright with excitement. She tried to smile back at him, aware that she did not feel the excitement he was feeling.

Glancing ahead, she saw Peg move into the Highlander's arms. Beginning to kiss wildly, groping one another frantically, they moved against the wall—away from the door.

And a bell began to toll above them, loud and in warning.

Their disappearance had been noted, Margaret thought, stunned. Either someone realized she was missing, or, more likely, someone realized that William was not in his cell.

William cursed, looking back. So did Margaret—and she saw Padraig appear on the ramparts above the great hall.

And he looked down, right at William.

The two men seemed to make eye contact. Margaret could not see Padraig's expression from this distance, but she saw his posture change—stiffening with surprise.

"He has recognized me!" William cried. Then, "Run!"

But as Margaret turned to do just that, Peg and the Highland guard broke apart, the guard turning toward the ramparts. Margaret glanced back and saw Padraig pointing at William—he shouted something.

Margaret turned wildly back, faltering, as she could hardly run past the guard now. As she stood there with Eilidh, he came running toward her, and for one moment, she thought he meant to seize her. But he did not. He was running over to William.

William changed course, veering away from the guard, and from the north exit. And then she heard a horrible sound—a sound she hated and feared.

It was the hiss of an arrow.

William cried out.

Margaret choked in horror as William fell, an arrow protruding from the back of his shoulder. "Will!"

His face ravaged with pain, he looked up at her. "Go, damn it, go, run, go!"

Margaret did not want to leave him lying there in pain, wounded from the arrow. But Eilidh tugged on her hand. The guard was already upon Will, and now she saw that Peg had opened the north door—and it was not guarded—it was not even watched!

Trying not to run, they kept walking toward the small doorway, and as they slipped outside, she looked back into the courtyard. She could not see Will now—he was surrounded by soldiers. Peg slammed the door closed before she could see anything else.

Outside, they paused for an instant, staring at one another. Was William seriously hurt? "I must go back," Margaret began.

"No!" Peg seized her hand. "I dinna think they even ken we've escaped!"

Peg might be right, Margaret realized, as there were no rude shouts coming from within the courtyard. Surely, if they had been noticed, there would be cries of alarm and shouted orders.

And the thick, almost impenetrable forest was just steps away. She could not see through it, but she could actually hear the army on the road on its other side.

"Let's go," she said decisively.

They ran. And a moment later Margaret skidded into the first rows of branches, pine needles and wood scraping her hands and face, and catching her hair. She did not stop, and saw that Eilidh and Peg were right behind her. They plowed on through the trees, the ground frozen and hard now, until the only sounds in the woods were their harsh, heavy breaths.

Margaret held up her hand and they stopped, collapsing against a tree. Everyone panted heavily, catching their breath.

And when the sound of their breathing was softer, Margaret strained to hear, listening for sounds of pursuit. It would have been easy for Padraig and his men to follow their tracks into the forest, if they had been remarked escaping. But once they did so, it would not be as easy to follow them, not at all. The forest was too thick. The ground was at times muddy and thawing, and in other places, frozen solid. However, it would be easy to guess what they intended—that they meant to slip into Alexander's army.

But there was no sound of Padraig being anywhere close to them. Was it possible that their escape had yet to be noticed?

"I dinna think we're being followed," Peg whispered.

"I think you're right," Margaret whispered back. They exchanged looks. Margaret held up her hand, indicating that no one should speak. Very carefully now, they started south, at a slow pace, trying not to make a sound.

Perhaps a half an hour later they reached the other side of the forest. And there, upon the narrow road, was Alexander's army.

CHAPTER ELEVEN

BALVENIE SPRAWLED ABOVE them atop the hill, a massive red stone fortress.

Margaret halted her small mount. Peg and Eilidh had their own horses as well, and they also stopped, as did the three knights escorting them. She stared up at the welcome sight of Balvenie's curtain walls crossing the hillside, its towers jutting into the bright blue sky.

"Balvenie," she whispered, disbelieving. Three days ago she had awoken in Alexander's bed, and now, she was home.

The River Spey was below them, churning rapidly through the forested hillside. Its frigid waters still rushed over frozen rocks. But snow was melting everywhere. Patches of new grass and thistle with small, tight, un-opened blooms were emerging across the hillside and just beneath the thick castle walls.

"I will tell the watch that we have arrived," one of their knights said. He spurred his mount forward and up the hill at a canter.

"We are home," Peg cried, smiling. "I never thought to see the day!"

Margaret did not quite smile back at her. She was pleased to have reached Balvenie safely—she was re-lieved to have reached her uncle's largest, most defensi-ble home. But her happiness was somehow spoiled—and partly it was because Castle Fyne remained lost to the enemy, and William remained a prisoner there. But she knew that secretly, there was even more.

Secretly, she thought her homecoming spoiled by the night she had spent in Alexander's arms.

For, at random moments in the day, and then, in her dreams at night, she recalled not just the passion they had shared, but other moments, too, moments in which he seemed like a powerful champion. Yet she did not want to think of him at all! And she especially did not want to recall how she had betrayed her uncle and her betrothed.

"It's so grand," Eilidh whispered, wide-eyed with awe.

"It is very grand," Margaret agreed, and she started her mare up the hill, on the muddy road they traveled upon. Her two maids fell into line behind her, while the remaining two Highland soldiers rode abreast of her, having cast their furs aside.

They had stayed hidden in Alexander's army for two entire days, but when it had made camp not far from Dumbarton, they had stolen away. Peg had managed to get them inside the royal fortress there, where Margaret had been warmly received by its governor, John of Menteith. Already aware of the attack about to take place the next day, he had wasted no time in sending her on, with three of his men as an armed escort. They had arrived at Dumbarton in the fading light of the late afternoon, and they left just a few hours later, as twilight stole upon the land.

Margaret saw the gates of the barbican being opened, and now, she could hear surprised cries coming from the ramparts, as the news of her arrival spread. She looked up as men, women and children appeared on the walls above her, waving eagerly, clearly jubilant over her return. She smiled and waved back, but inwardly, she was grim.

She had said that one night could not change anything,

but apparently, it had changed a great deal. She could not shake an odd, lingering feeling of dismay. She was beginning to wonder if she regretted the night she had spent with Alexander, after all. Certainly, she no longer felt innocent. She had betrayed a great many loyalties, and she felt very grown up, a woman aged beyond her years.

They rode through the barbican and across the drawbridge. As Margaret entered the great cobbled courtyard, the huge door of the great hall opened. Isabella stepped outside, clutching a fur mantle, her red gown flowing about her. "Margaret!"

Margaret halted as Isabella ran down the steps and toward her. She was a tall, slim woman of nineteen, with surprisingly fair skin and thick brown hair, her eyes a stunning blue. "You are home!" she cried, beaming.

One of the soldiers helped her dismount, and before her feet even touched the ground, Isabella embraced her, hard. "Was there a ransom?" Isabella cried. "John said he did not think you would be ransomed!"

Margaret took her hand. "There was no ransom. We escaped. It is still cold out. Can we go inside?"

Isabella nodded, her eyes wide, and they hurried inside, followed by the other women and men.

The hall was filled with tables, tapestries and chairs. Rugs, not rushes, were on the floor. Fires blazed in two grand hearths.

"You must tell me everything," Isabella exclaimed. "But first, how could you escape the Wolf of Lochaber?" She seized her hand and clasped it again.

"The plan was Will's. We stole out the side door in disguise, and then joined Alexander's army as it left. But he was captured before he could even cross the courtyard, and he remains a prisoner, even now. We traveled with the army until Dumbarton. No one ever looked twice at us."

"Alexander?" Isabella's brows rose. She pulled Margaret toward a pair of chairs in front of one fireplace.

Margaret tensed. "Alexander MacDonald—the Wolf of Lochaber."

"It seems odd for you to call him by name. But then, you were his hostage for many weeks—for almost a month. Will you sit with me, Margaret? Will you share a glass of wine? You must be exhausted after traveling across half of Scotland! And I have missed you so!"

Margaret had missed Isabella, too. "Of course I will sit with you—we have so much to speak of."

Isabella grinned as they both sat. "Peg, please bring us wine. And prepare a feast! We must celebrate Margaret's safe return!"

Peg rushed off as Margaret handed her mantle to Eilidh, sighing, and stretched out her legs.

"Did you become friendly, then?" Isabella asked.

Margaret started. "I beg your pardon?"

"You call him Alexander now—you must have become somewhat friendly."

She hoped her cheeks were not pink—they felt warm. Yet she knew Isabella's question was innocently asked. She could hardly suspect that they had had an affair. "I do not know when I began to call him by name, but he remains the enemy. He is a MacDonald."

Isabella studied her. "You must hate him," she finally said. "He kept you prisoner, he holds Will even now and he has conquered Castle Fyne."

"Sir Guy already tried to take the keep back. He will undoubtedly try again. And now that I am home, I will send a letter to Argyll, seeking his aid."

"So you will not accept the loss of the castle?" Isabella cried.

"No, I will not. Would you?"

"I would not write letters to my kin, asking them to go to war for me! But then, I would have never thought to try to defend the castle in the first place. You are so brave!"

"It was a very foolish decision, Isabella. And I was terrified, and because I chose to fight, not surrender, many good men died."

"He must have been so angry with you," Isabella said after a pause. "If I had ever defied John in such a way, and attempted to battle against him, oh, he would hurt me terribly. Did he seek to punish you?"

Margaret rubbed her arms. Most men would have angrily punished such defiance, even though it came from a woman. "No, he did not seek to punish me. He was very angry but he was also reasonable. I did not suffer very much in his care."

Isabella blinked. "A warrior who is reasonable? Are we speaking of the same man? Is he then not like the legends?"

Margaret smiled a bit. "He is exactly like the legends, Isabella. He is strong, mighty and brave, a great warrior. I have wondered if he will ever be defeated in battle."

"You sound admiring!"

Margaret hesitated. "In some ways, I have come to admire him, and I certainly respect him."

Her gaze sharpened. "Is he as dark and handsome as is claimed?"

Margaret decided to dissemble. "He is dark, but if he is handsome, I never noticed."

Peg now returned, carrying a trencher with two mugs of wine. She gave each woman one, and Margaret thanked her. She sipped, aware of the extent of her lie.

She thought Alexander one of the most attractive men she had ever seen.

"If he is as mighty as you say, you may never win Castle Fyne back," Isabella said.

Margaret felt her momentary pleasure fade. "I am afraid of that. He has left a large garrison there."

Isabella made a harsh sound. "John is furious over Red John's murder, and he is spending all of his time planning war against Bruce. But my husband is very pleased with you. He has done little but boast about you since we first heard of the siege and your part in defending the keep. You may trust me when I tell you that you are high in his good graces."

"Buchan isn't here, is he?"

"No. He left weeks ago—to speak with our every friend, to raise men, to prepare for war—he fights with King Edward!" Her eyes darkened. "How he hates Robert Bruce."

Isabella was one of the least political women Margaret knew, but like the entire family, she despised the English.

"I have news of the war, Isabella. I must speak with my uncle. It is important."

"Can you write him?"

"No. I must speak with him in person," Margaret said. She was not going to describe Bruce's meeting with Alexander in a letter that could be intercepted by almost anyone.

"The information you have must be dear, indeed." Isabella did not seem curious as she sipped her wine.

"It is." This was as good a time as any to speak frankly with her sister in marriage. "Bruce spent a night at Castle Fyne."

Isabella sat up in surprise, spilling some of her wine.

Her entire demeanor had changed. Clearly, she was interested now. "You saw him?"

"I met him, yes."

"How is he?"

She started. The question seemed odd—as odd as her wide-eyed expression. "He is a powerful liege lord, Isabella. One arrogant enough to think he can be king."

She smiled. "I met him at Fife, before my marriage."

"I did not know."

"He was proud and arrogant then. I saw him after my marriage, too, at Lochmaben, and then at Dalswinton. He is a strutting cock of a man."

Margaret stared closely now. "He asked about you— now I begin to understand—I hadn't realized you had met one another once, much less several times."

"He asked about me?" She seemed clearly pleased. "So he remembers me?"

Margaret seized her hand. Did Isabella think that Bruce recalled her because she was a beautiful young woman? "I do not know if he recalls your having ever met, but he knows of you. And I am very worried." She leaned close and lowered her voice to a whisper. "He marches on Dumbarton—and then, to Scone. He will be crowned there soon."

Isabella's eyes were wider now. "He will be our king, Margaret—I am sure of it."

Margaret jerked. This was not the reaction she had expected. "He cannot hope to defeat King Edward, Isabella. It is mad to even dream of doing so!"

"Why not? He is next in line to be king—and we cannot remain yoked to England for much longer. God must finally be on our side!"

Was this her pretty friend speaking? Isabella never voiced an opinion, especially not when it came to affairs of state or matters of politics. Margaret was disbelieving. "You wish for Bruce to be king?"

She hesitated. "He is next in line—everyone knows it."

Margaret did not know what her hesitation signified. "Your husband will fight him to the end."

She flushed. "Yes, he will."

"Isabella! There is more. Bruce spoke of using you to aid him in his quest to be king."

She gasped.

Margaret hurriedly explained. "He cannot summon your brother to the ceremony, and apparently the earls of Fife have traditionally participated in the crowning of every Scot king. He and Alexander discussed the possibility of using you in the ceremony instead. After all, you are still the Countess of Fife."

Isabella's color was now high. She was speechless.

"I have come to warn you," Margaret said.

"Warn me? Oh, I am so glad you have told me this!"

Was Isabella *pleased?*

"But how would I get to Scone to help crown him?" she asked.

Margaret shot to her feet. "Are you mad? I thought to warn you *against* him."

Isabella stood. "I would love to help him be king!"

Margaret stared at her in horror.

Still red, her eyes bright, she cried, "I must get word to him! I must tell him I will help him in any way that I can! Or should I simply leave and go to Scone?"

Margaret seized her arm. "Buchan is against Bruce! He will disown you if you ever take Bruce's side!"

Isabella shook her head, almost wildly. "I don't care, Margaret. Let Buchan fret and fight, I don't care! Bruce should be our king!"

"You are suddenly political? Since when? If you help him, your marriage is doomed."

Isabella stared. "Then my marriage will be doomed."

THEY CAREFULLY AVOIDED the subject of Bruce for the rest of the evening, as well as the subject of Isabella's marriage, but the next morning, while Margaret was taking a much-needed hand bath, Isabella paused on the threshold of her chamber. Her smile was tentative. "Margaret? May we speak?"

Margaret was clad only in a chemise, warm and wet cloth in hand. She smiled, handing the cloth to Peg. They had not spoken very much last night after that first disturbing conversation. Margaret had retired early, immediately after supper. She had been exhausted. "Of course. Good morning."

Isabella glanced at Peg. "Could you bring us warm, spiced wine? I will help Margaret dress."

So she wished for a privy word, Margaret thought with some dread. Peg left, and Isabella waited a moment, until her footfalls could no longer be heard. "Are you angry with me?" she blurted.

Margaret toweled off her damp arms and legs. "Why would I be angry?"

"You are the most noble woman I know. I fear I have disappointed you."

Margaret set her towel down and pulled on a pale cote. "I love you, Isabella, no matter what you say or do. And you did not disappoint me yesterday—you surprised me."

"Please don't tell my husband about our conversation—and that I wish for Bruce to become our king!" she cried.

Margaret saw fear on Isabella's face—and she was glad. At least Isabella sensed the ramifications of her taking such an opposing viewpoint to that of her husband. "I would never betray you that way," Margaret said, meaning it. "But I am praying that you change your mind and support your husband in his causes—and in his war against Bruce. It is your duty, Isabella, as his wife."

"I have never been as honorable as you," Isabella said softly.

Margaret felt guilty—she was not as honorable as Isabella thought. "And surely you now realize that you could never help Bruce take the crown. Such an act is treachery against your husband."

Isabella smiled grimly, but it was almost a pursing of her lips.

And then, from outside, they heard cries from the watchtower.

Margaret tensed, her reaction an instinctive one, but no one would ever attack Balvenie! The fortress was too mighty a stronghold. Besides, the wars with England rarely brought battles this far north.

Still, someone was approaching. She ran with Isabella to the chamber's only window.

The shutter was open. It was a bright, sunny spring-like day. Most of the snow outside the castle walls had melted. And an armed group of riders was approaching.

The red, black and gold flag of Buchan waved proudly above them.

"John has come home," Isabella breathed, her tone terse. Margaret saw that she did not smile, and she was pale with tension.

Her gaze narrowed. Her father had died a year and a half ago—she had moved to Balvenie shortly after his death. Isabella had become Buchan's wife perhaps six months earlier. As Buchan was in residence often, she had seen Isabella and her husband together dozens of times. Their marriage had seemed quite usual.

But now, she paused.

She recalled watching Isabella at the opposite end of the great table, politely listening to her husband's every word. She recalled the way they would leave the company after supper, hardly exchanging a word, although Buchan always had his hand on his wife's waist. And she thought of how Isabella would greet him when he returned from attending affairs of state, or a hunting party. Buchan was usually boisterous, Isabella demure. Yet when he was away, the hall rang with her laughter.

She had never thought about the nature of their marriage before, and she did not know why she wondered about it now. Isabella had a lively nature, but she was usually quiet around her charismatic, handsome older husband.

"We should go down to greet them," Isabella said, a small flush upon her cheeks.

Margaret agreed.

THEY STOOD OUTSIDE the open front door, upon the top step of the stairs, awaiting the earl and his men. Although the day appeared benign, it was only early March, not even the fifteenth, and the breeze was brisk. Both women shivered, neither having bothered to don plaids or mantles.

The Earl of Buchan trotted into the courtyard with two dozen Highland knights. He was a tall man with dark hair—he was sometimes called Black John—and he rode at the group's forefront, his mount a black charger. He appeared a powerful figure of a man, and he was powerful—before his cousin's death, he had controlled half of northern Scotland. Now, he commanded the entire Comyn family, and no other family controlled as much of the north.

The horses were muddy, as were most of the riders.

The group paused, Buchan halting his charger before the steps where they stood. His expression brightened as he saw them, and then he was quickly dismounting, his smile wide.

"Margaret!" He rushed up the stairs, eyes wide with surprise, and he hugged her, hard.

Margaret felt tears arise. Of course he cared about her. How had she been in any doubt? She smiled as he released her. "Good morn, Uncle."

He clasped her chin and lifted it, his dark eyes searching. "We heard a rumor—that you had escaped—but we did not believe it!"

"I escaped, Uncle. It is a bit of a harrowing story."

"So the rumor was true!" His eyes widened with obvious admiration. "I should have known. You are exactly like your mother!" Then he turned and beamed at Isabella. "Wife! What a pretty sight you are!"

Margaret watched as Isabella smiled and as Buchan swept her hard into his embrace. He kissed her, and Margaret looked away. In that moment, there was no doubt that Buchan adored his beautiful young wife.

Turning back, Margaret gasped as she saw that Sir Ranald stood holding two horses, grinning at her.

She flew down the steps. "Sir Ranald! I heard you had escaped the Wolf during the battle in the ravine!"

"I did escape—and I rode directly to Badenoch—only to learn of the murder," Sir Ranald said, his smile disappearing. "My lady, how do you fare? We lost the battle of the ravine, and left you to defend Castle Fyne! I have heard the tale of how bravely you did so—and how many men were lost."

She hesitated, but she had no interest in dissembling now. "I hope to never be in a siege again, Sir Ranald.

My soldiers were terribly brave. So were the women, but there was never any hope, not against the Wolf."

"Thank God you escaped."

Margaret reached for his hand. She was about to answer, when she recognized the man who had just dismounted, and now stood behind Sir Ranald. She felt her expression freeze.

Sir Guy bowed, low. "Lady."

Her heart slammed. *Sir Guy had come to Balvenie. Of course he had.*

Sir Guy, whom she was to wed in June—whom she had so recently betrayed with another man.

Somehow, she swallowed, somehow, she breathed. And then she smiled, coming down the steps slowly, her gaze now locked with his. "Sir Guy! I am so pleased that you are here."

His gray stare swept her from head to toe. He still did not smile. "I will pray to God tonight, and give thanks, for His keeping you safe during your travails."

She bit her lip, nodding. "Thank you."

His gaze was searching, and she wished to avoid it. Suddenly she was terrified that he might guess her secrets—and suspect her infidelity. But he said tersely, "I owe you a vast apology, Lady Margaret, for my rude behavior when we first met."

She was taken aback. "You owe me no such apology, sir."

"I was dismayed to see you upon the battlefield—and in my worst enemy's hands. I fear I could not think clearly. Some think me gallant, but you could not, not after our meeting in such dire circumstances. I hope to redeem myself in the next few days." He bowed his head this time.

Did he regret his behavior, truly? If so, she should be

glad—she should be impressed! Margaret touched his sleeve briefly. He wore an armored breastplate over his brown surcote. Armored plates covered the hose over his knees. "You need not think about redemption." She smiled. "Thank you for offering an apology, but none is needed."

"You are as kind as you are beautiful."

He was a handsome man, his nose broad, his cheekbones high. Alexander had said that many women found him both charming and gallant, and of course, he had the blood of both the French and English kings running in his veins. She felt a new tension. Would she become charmed? And why did that idea disturb her? Why did Alexander's image now dare to haunt her?

"Margaret!" her uncle boomed. "We may all break the fast together, and you can tell us your tale of escape."

Margaret turned, almost relieved to have the intimate conversation interrupted. "Of course, Uncle," she said.

ISABELLA HAD LEFT to supervise the breakfast, and Margaret found herself seated at the table with her uncle, Sir Guy, Sir Ranald and a dozen other knights, some of whom she recognized, others who were English and clearly under Sir Guy's command. Wine, bread and cheese were served, the men instantly taking up the food and drink. Margaret wasn't hungry, and she toyed with her cup of wine, stealing glances at Sir Guy as he ate.

Her heart raced as she looked at him—not because she desired him, but because she would eventually be his wife. Thus far, he had been gallant. But she could not shake her first impression of him. She feared her initial opinions were correct.

Isabella returned to the table, taking a seat beside

Buchan. He smiled at her then turned to Margaret. "So? Will you tell us your story?"

Margaret tore her gaze away from Sir Guy. "There is not much to tell. We were disguised as common maids, and we stole from the castle while the Wolf's army was leaving, and then slipped into his ranks. It was easy to do, and we stayed hidden that way until they made camp outside Dumbarton. My maid Peg got us into the castle. John of Menteith received us warmly, then gave us an escort and sent us immediately on our way."

"How simple you make such bravery sound," Buchan said. "How is Will?"

"He was shot with an arrow while attempting to escape with us. Can you send a messenger to inquire after him?" Margaret asked.

"I will do so today," Buchan said, pushing his plate aside.

"Is there any war news? Did Dumbarton fall to Bruce?" Margaret asked him.

Sir Guy said, "John of Menteith refused to surrender and Bruce retreated."

She wondered where Alexander had gone. Margaret wanted to ask about him—and she wanted to ask about Castle Fyne. Did she dare? "MacDonald left a large garrison at Castle Fyne."

"I heard. Have no fear—Castle Fyne will be ours again, by the time we wed in June."

She stiffened. "So you have a plan to attack?"

"I am plotting with my brother. We will have Castle Fyne back, Lady Margaret, you may have no doubt on that."

She had so much doubt. "Will Aymer send his troops to fight with yours?"

"Aymer will give me men, yes." His stare remained riveted upon her. "You ask many questions."

"I want Castle Fyne back." She turned to her uncle hastily then. "Bruce was at Castle Fyne, Uncle, for a single night."

Buchan choked on his wine. "My God! Did you learn anything from him?"

It was on the tip of her tongue to tell him that there might be a coronation on March the 25th. But then she thought about the fact that if she said such a thing—and the date was right—Bruce and his allies would be attacked by King Edward. Alexander would be attacked. She shifted in her seat. She did not even know if Eilidh had heard the date correctly. "He marches to Scone to be crowned there."

"The world knows that!" Buchan exclaimed.

Sir Guy sent her a look. Was it as odd as she thought it was?

"They are seeking many earls, and I heard Lennox and Atholl will attend." Now, she was aware of Isabella staring at her. She did not look back.

"Atholl will never attend," Buchan said. "You must be mistaken, Margaret."

"I did not hear that myself—I had my maids spy on Bruce and MacDonald," Margaret said.

"You are clever," Sir Guy said thoughtfully.

She flinched, staring at him.

"I know Atholl well. He opposes Bruce, just as we do." Buchan was firm. "He is one of us."

Sir Guy smiled. "We have spies everywhere—even amongst Bruce's best friends. We will learn if Atholl is our friend—and we will learn when Bruce thinks to steal the crown."

Margaret wondered if Alexander knew that there were spies amongst Bruce's army.

"Bruce will be captured, and he will hang." Sir Guy drained his wine and set the mug down hard. "As will all of his damned friends."

Margaret hoped she did not appear appalled.

"We will be avenged, Lady Margaret, I vow it."

Somehow, she spoke. "I do not like this blood feud, Sir Guy."

His dark brows rose. "You opine against me?"

"I am afraid! Two great men—each seeking to kill the other!"

He stood, his stance wide, a warrior braced for attack. "He took Castle Fyne, he took you. And once, not long ago, we were friends! That bastard does not know the meaning of honor. So I will teach him the meaning of revenge."

Sir Guy was angry—his gaze blazed. She decided not to speak.

"Surely, Lady Margaret, you wish for revenge, too?"

She tensed. What should she say? "I despise war. I have suffered through too many wars to count! War only brings death. So no, I do not wish for revenge, as it only brings death, too."

"Then you will have to change your mind, lady. If I seek revenge, it must please you, too."

She looked down at her hands as they lay on the table. Most men thought as Sir Guy did, so she should not be dismayed. But she was both. "Of course," she murmured.

His gaze narrowed. "I will make certain," he said, after a pause, "that you are with me when we hang the mighty Wolf."

She trembled, looking up, wondering if fear was written all over her face.

EVENING HAD FINALLY fallen. Margaret thought that the day had been one of the longest of her life. She slowly went up the stairs, aware of the tension within her that she had not been able to shake all day. How she yearned for the privacy of her own chamber now.

She had caught Sir Guy watching her closely a dozen times that day. His enigmatic stare was so disconcerting! She could not imagine what he was thinking, but she had the terrible inkling that he suspected her of some grave failing.

But what was worse was that she did not care for him—not at all. In fact, she did not even like him. And she did not know how to change her thoughts. She did not know what to do.

Will had asked her if she were being sent to the gallows, would she meekly go? She had said no. Her impending marriage now felt like the gallows. Margaret paused by a ledge in the hall outside her door, a window above it. Outside, the night was a pale, soft purple, with many winking stars just beginning to emerge in the sky.

If she married Sir Guy, she would be told how to think. She would be told what to do. She would be criticized if she did not conform to his expectations of her. Margaret was certain.

Did she dare be honest with herself? She no longer wanted this marriage!

She thought of Alexander and felt a terrible pang—as if she missed him. But she must not miss him. What they had done was wrong. And even if she never married Sir Guy, Alexander remained a mortal enemy—in possession of both her brother and Castle Fyne.

Did she dare speak with her uncle about the marriage? He was so pleased with her now. Could she somehow convince him to change his mind about it?

Margaret instantly knew better than to try. Now that the Comyn family fought with King Edward against Bruce, her marriage had become more important than ever.

Despair immobilized her. She almost felt like crying. Instead, she lifted her face to the cool night air.

"I hope you are thinking about me."

She had been so immersed in her anguished thoughts, that she had not heard Sir Guy approaching. Slowly, with dread, she turned. "I did not hear you come up the stairs."

He smiled at her, pausing beside her. "I am a soldier, Lady Margaret. If I cannot steal silently upon you, how could I ever surprise the enemy?" His gray gaze slid over her slowly.

Margaret hugged her wool mantle more closely to her body.

"Are you cold?" He reached for her shoulders.

Margaret tensed. His hands covered her shoulders, slid down her arms, and adjusted the mantle for her.

Her body was now entirely in a coil. She did not like this man's touch.

He dropped his hands. "You fear me," he said softly.

She said slowly, "We are strangers."

"It is not the same." He slid the tip of his finger along her jaw. "You are so beautiful. I am pleased."

She stood very still, otherwise, she would flinch and pull away. "It is late," she said.

"Is it?" He trailed his finger lightly down the side of her neck. "You are only seventeen. In a way, you are so young. But most women are married well before such an age...by now, most women are well versed in their relations with men."

"But not I." She finally stepped backward, but into the wall.

"You have made me wonder," he said.

She almost choked. Did she dare lie monstrously now? "My lord?"

"Sometimes I look at you and I see a woman with experience far beyond her years. Other times, I think you are so innocent, and so ripe for the plucking."

She knew she must end this encounter. "I do not know why you see me in two such different ways. Sir Guy? It is late. I am tired, you must be tired, too. We should bid one another adieu."

He smiled. "But I am leaving in the morning, Lady Margaret. We might not see one another for some time— or even until our wedding in June. And I am enjoying being with you."

He would leave tomorrow. Her relief made her knees buckle.

He caught her by seizing both of her arms, pulling her close. "I have been waiting for a kiss all day."

She wanted to deny him, but she knew she could not.

Sir Guy pulled her against his lean body and claimed her mouth instantly.

Margaret felt tears arise. She did not move. She let him ply her lips with his, let him increase the pressure until his kiss became hard and hungry. Only then did she push at him. "Stop."

"Why?" He broke the kiss, breathing hard. "Let's go into your chamber, Lady Margaret. Lie with me. We will handfast tonight."

She cried out. "My uncle has arranged an English wedding—in a church!"

"But I do not wish to wait." He caught her face in his hands. "If you consent and take me to bed, the deed is done."

She opened her mouth to tell him no, but could not speak, for he kissed her again.

Fury began. Margaret hit his shoulders, once and then twice. He straightened, eyes wide. "You are fighting me?"

"We are not married yet!" She wrenched away, ducked under his arm and moved a great distance away.

He was incredulous. "What difference does it make, if we handfast tonight or marry in June?"

"If my uncle wanted us married today, he would have arranged it!"

"So you are loyal? Or are you afraid? Are you afraid of lovemaking?"

Margaret's mind raced. "I will not betray my uncle. I am his ward. I will do as he wishes."

Sir Guy began to smile. "If you will be as dutiful to me, I will be a very pleased husband."

Margaret trembled. "It is time to say good-night, Sir Guy."

He approached her in two strides, clasping her shoulders and pulling her close to kiss her soundly again. "I will forgive you your disloyalty now, as you should be loyal to Buchan. But now I expect the same fervor after we are wed." He caressed her cheek. "Good night, Margaret." Turning, his strides now hurried, he vanished down the stairs.

Margaret ran into her room, slammed the door and bolted it. She sank onto her bed, tears beginning. What was she going to do?

She knew the truth now. She feared Sir Guy—and she despised him.

CHAPTER TWELVE

MARGARET HAD BEEN summoned to her uncle in the great hall. She was worried as she traversed the castle. She could not imagine what he wished with her.

Suddenly Isabella appeared, falling into step with her. "Where do you go?" Isabella asked. "My husband has said he wishes to speak with me, immediately."

Margaret faltered. "He has also summoned me."

Isabella seemed alarmed. "He knows. There are spies everywhere. The first day we spoke, someone spied upon us!"

Margaret took her arm and tried to calm her. "Isabella, if he had heard about our conversation, he would have confronted you the day he returned. He would have confronted me." And Buchan had been in residence for five days—it was the eighteenth of March. Sir Guy had left for Berwick four days ago.

At Berwick he would rejoin his army, and then join his brother, Aymer, as they sought to engage Bruce and defeat him. By now, the world knew that Bruce raced across Scotland, seizing what castles he could, subduing what enemies he could, in defiance of King Edward, his ambition to become Scotland's king.

There were so many rumors now, so many tales, and in them all, Bruce was becoming a hero. The small keeps he threatened refused to rise up against him—instead, they opened their doors to him. Soldiers and knights were joining his army everywhere. He was, it was said, being happily greeted in every village he passed through. Farmers and fishermen were provisioning his growing army. Women with their children now followed him, as if he were a great piper.

King Edward was furious. His chamberlain had ordered Bruce to cease and desist. He had ordered Bruce to surrender. But Bruce had refused.

"I hope you are right," Isabella now said tersely. "But what would he want with us both?"

"We will soon find out," Margaret said. There were other rumors, too. Angus Og MacDonald was now actively aiding Bruce. But there was not one word whispered about Alexander.

Margaret knew she must, finally, ask about him. Was he with Bruce, still? Or did he go to war for Bruce on some tangential path? Had he even returned to Castle Fyne?

By now, he would know of her escape. It had been almost two weeks. She could not imagine his reaction to the news that she had left Castle Fyne—the morning after they had shared such passion.

Buchan was waiting for them in the great hall, standing before one hearth with two of his most trusted knights, whom he instantly dismissed. Margaret smiled hesitantly at him. "We are very curious, my lord, as to why you wish to speak to us."

"You must pack your trunks," he said, smiling. "We go to the shire of Aberdeen."

Margaret started. "May I ask what passes?"

"Of course you may. I am meeting with Sir John Mowbray, Sir Ingram de Umfraville, and the earls of Menteith and Atholl."

Margaret stared, her mind racing. Hadn't Bruce men-

tioned that her uncle had met with Mowbray and Umfraville already, in Liddesdale? Her uncle was going to
Aberdeenshire to continue to plot against Bruce; of that,
she had no doubt. And she would be going with him.

She was thrilled. She did not know why he wished
for her to join him, but did it matter? There, she would
hear so much more news of the war. There, she might
learn of Alexander.

"You wish for me to go, as well?" Isabella asked,
eyes wide.

"I always prefer you at my side, sweetheart," Buchan
said. "But in truth, my dear friends know that Margaret
was MacDonald's prisoner, and that she met Bruce when
he stayed overnight at Castle Fyne. They wish to speak
directly with her." He glanced at Margaret, still smiling.

Instantly Margaret felt some alarm. Mowbray was
warden of the Scot marches, Umfraville a great baron
renowned for the decades he had spent warring against
England. Menteith had just refused to surrender Dumbarton—and Bruce had decided to move on. The Earl of
Atholl had fought the English for most of his life. She
knew him well.

All of these men were powerful forces, not to be
lightly reckoned with.

She was to impart whatever knowledge she had of
Bruce and his plans to these men. Of that, she had no
doubt.

She had yet to reveal that the coronation might be in
seven more days. She knew her omission was treachery,
and she was afraid that if she made one false move, one
of these men would suspect her.

"I wish for you to accompany Margaret, actually,"
Buchan said to Isabella. "But we will not be gone long.
It is a day to the Peel of Strathbogie."

Peels were specially erected dirt fortifications, layered over the castle's walls, and Strathbogie was Atholl's seat. It had been fortified as a peel.

Isabella smiled, but so falsely that Margaret knew she did not wish to accompany them. "Whatever you wish, my lord," she said sweetly. She turned to Margaret. "Shall we pack?"

Margaret hesitated. "I'll join you shortly. I'd like to ask Uncle John about Castle Fyne."

Isabella nodded and left. Buchan said, "Nothing has changed, Margaret. I have yet to receive word about your brother. MacDonald has not returned, nor will he, I think. He remains with Bruce—they have just crossed the River Forth. Of course, you probably wish to know that Sir Guy has now left Berwick with a force of two thousand men. He means to meet Bruce head-on, with Aymer planning to outflank him. He will be trapped, sooner or later—you may be sure of it."

Alexander remained with Bruce, she thought. Surely they knew about the great English army attempting to engage them—hoping to destroy them.

"What is it? I can see you wish to ask me something."

"Have you heard how MacDonald reacted when he learned of my escape? I am worried he was enraged—that he will eventually take his wrath out on the people of Castle Fyne, or upon my brother."

"I heard he said not a word. I heard he was stone-faced. However, he had to have been surprised that a small woman like yourself could outwit him."

What did such an impassive reaction mean? Was it possible that he had not cared?

She was taken aback. She thought about Alexander a bit too much after spending the night with him, and she had assumed he was thinking about her, too. But now, she worried that he had forgotten the time they had shared together. Was it possible? She had so often gotten the impression that he cared about her, at least somewhat. But if he had not cared about her escape, did that mean that she had been entirely wrong?

"Is something amiss?" her uncle asked.

She quickly smiled. "No, of course not. But I do yearn to hear that Will is fine."

"As do I," her uncle said. "Is there anything else you wish to discuss?"

She should raise the subject of her marriage to Sir Guy. No opportunity could be better. Instead, she inhaled and smiled. "No, of course not."

ALTHOUGH THE ROADS were muddy from the spring thaw, the ride to Strathbogie was an easy one, accomplished in just eight hours. They were greeted by the Atholl himself, and ushered directly into his hall.

John Strathbogie, the Earl of Atholl, was a tall, handsome man of forty, with tawny hair that was forever tousled. Margaret had known him since she was a child—he had fought beside her father and her oldest brother at Dunbar ten years ago, where he had had the misfortune of being captured and then being imprisoned in the London Tower. Like a great many of his peers, he had only been set free when he agreed to serve King Edward in his army in Flanders.

Bruce and Alexander believed he would support them. Margaret did not know what to believe. She knew that Atholl hated the English, even though he had recently paid homage to King Edward. And his daughter had married one of Bruce's brothers.

But she could not imagine him betraying her uncle. Atholl and Buchan were friends. But clearly, both sides believed him their ally; therefore, he would have to betray someone.

He now embraced Buchan warmly. Then he kissed Isabella's hand. "You become more beautiful every day, lady," he said, obviously flirting.

She flushed and smiled, clearly pleased.

"Hello, Margaret," Atholl then said, turning to her. She began to greet him but was swept into his embrace instead. "So the little child has become the fierce woman, to fight the Wolf of Lochaber, survive capture and confinement, and then dare to escape." He laughed, releasing her. "If ever we are besieged here, I hope my wife will be as brave. You have set the example!"

"I wasn't brave, I was afraid," Margaret said.

"And you are so modest," he teased.

Atholl led them to the table inside his hall, where the others waited. Greetings were exchanged as everyone sat down, the women together at the far end of the table.

"These proceedings will be kept secret," Buchan declared. "Bruce must never learn of our plans."

Murmurs of agreement sounded, all from the men. The women pretended not to listen.

"How was your journey?" Marjorie asked. Atholl's wife was a pretty blonde and the daughter of the Earl of Mar.

Margaret told her it had been swift, but she was listening to the men, stealing glances at them, as Marjorie turned her attention to Isabella. She did not know Mowbray, the young warden of the marches, and she had only briefly met Menteith, at Dumbarton, after her escape from Castle Fyne. But Ingram de Umfraville's mother had been a Comyn, and he was a legend in his own right. Middle-aged, he had devoted his life to the war against England. It was shocking to know that he hated Bruce even more than he hated King Edward, and that he now fought on the side of England.

Umfraville pounded his fist on the table. "Bruce murdered our blood. I have vowed to God to make him pay for his treachery and his sacrilege. No matter how I despise King Edward, Bruce must pay for what he did."

"Hear, hear," Atholl said fiercely.

"If Bruce becomes king, he will destroy us all—he has vowed it," Menteith said. "At Dumbarton, his terms were clear—surrender and become his friend, or fight and suffer all consequences."

"His threats are not empty," Umfraville said. "I have known him since he was a boy. And any man who can commit murder in a church knows not God or honor."

A discussion ensued about Bruce's character, and it was agreed that he would be merciless if he ever became king.

"And we are his greatest enemy. We have always been his worst enemy," Buchan said. "If Bruce gains the throne, he will seek to destroy every Comyn in the land."

Buchan believed his every word, Margaret realized. But was it true?

She thought of how ruthless Alexander had been upon taking Castle Fyne. He had been prepared to hang all of her men. And it had taken him but a moment to hang Malcolm.

In war, men like Bruce and Alexander knew no mercy. She had not a doubt.

But she was a Comyn, too.

"Bruce must be stopped before his army grows too large to be defeated easily," Mowbray was saying. "The people love him. They are cheering him now as he marches through their villages. There is talk growing of how he should be Scotland's king! That it is his right!

If he is not stopped by summer, I fear this war will be endless."

A brief silence fell. Margaret now realized that all of the women were listening intently to them, each female face pale.

"He will be stopped well before summer," Buchan finally said. "Bruce cannot defeat the might of England."

"I wish to speak with Lady Margaret," Umfraville said, looking boldly at her. "I have thanked God, Lady Margaret, that He kept you safe during the Wolf's siege, and that He aided you in your escape."

Margaret flushed. "Thank you."

"How many men did MacDonald have when he left Castle Fyne, lady?" Umfraville demanded. "I wish to know his numbers in fact!"

Margaret could not breathe properly now. Of course she had to tell the truth! "He went to war against Sir Guy at Loch Riddon with six hundred men, I think. But he had asked his brother for five hundred more. I do not know if they were raised."

The men now nodded, absorbing this.

"If MacDonald only has a thousand men, his army is the lesser one—we should isolate and destroy his men first," Atholl said.

Margaret stared at him, hoping no one would notice her anxiety. She wished to warn Alexander.

"Tell us about Bruce's stay at Castle Fyne," Umfraville said.

Her heart leapt. "I have told my uncle everything I know," she said, aware that she was most certainly lying. She had not divulged the possible date for the coronation—and she had not divulged their plan to use Isabella in the ceremony.

"Tell us what you remember, Margaret," Atholl said, smiling pleasantly at her.

Her heart pounded now, not knowing Atholl's allegiances. "I had my maids spy upon them as they supped. They worried about the coronation—about the missing Stone—and about the fact that the Earl of Fife is the king's ward."

"They will have to crown him without the boy," Buchan said.

"And they did not discuss a date for the coronation?" Umfraville asked harshly.

She met his dark, heated gaze, knowing she must lie to save Alexander from capture and maybe death. "No."

"Who will they ask to attend?"

She did not look at Atholl now. "I do not recall."

"You said Lennox," Buchan said. "You said Atholl."

Atholl's eyes widened as every face turned to him. Then he laughed.

"Did I?" She squirmed. "I cannot recall—it was so long ago! But I do recall my impression of Bruce."

All eyes were upon her now.

"He was so powerful, so royal! Everyone knows no single man can fight England and win. Yet when with him, I wondered if he might become Scotland's king." She deliberately hoped to divert the men by inflaming them.

There was a brief silence, and then someone—her uncle—slammed his fist furiously down. The table jumped. Wine spilled. "He will never be our king!"

A fierce argument began—every man speaking at once. Margaret felt her cheeks flaming, and finally, she glanced at Atholl.

He was studying her. Instantly, he looked away.

Did he suspect her of duplicity? Of treachery? What had that odd look meant?

And did he ride with Buchan—or Bruce?

Beneath the table, Isabella took her hand. Somehow, Margaret smiled at her, in spite of how frantically her thoughts were racing. Then she beseeched her uncle. "This talk of war has given me a terrible headache. Could I be excused?"

"I think we are done—for now. But Margaret? They may wish to ask you more questions before we leave on the morrow."

Margaret nodded and got up. Isabella leapt up to join her. "Husband? May I go up, as well?"

He smiled fondly at her. "Of course you may."

"Shall I show you to your rooms?" Marjorie asked, also rising. She seemed relieved to be able to leave the table.

As she followed Marjorie and Isabella up the stairs, Margaret thought about what she had just learned: they might try to divide Bruce's army from Alexander's. They would then destroy Alexander first.

"Marjorie? I must use the privy chamber," she said.

Marjorie smiled at her over her shoulder, and she and Isabella turned the corner upstairs.

Alone on the stairwell, Margaret turned and raced down the winding steps. She hurried to the threshold of the great hall, but did not step across it. Instead, her heart pounding, she pressed against the wall, trying to hear.

The men were speaking loudly enough that she caught bits and pieces of their conversation. She heard Bruce's name being mentioned several times, as well as Alexander's. She heard them mention Scone.

"What are you doing?" Sir Ranald seized her arm.

She gasped, facing him. His expression was hard.

He did not wait for her to answer. "You must go up-stairs, Lady Margaret, before Buchan catches you."

She tried to devise a plausible explanation for her eavesdropping.

"Go," he insisted.

Margaret fled.

MARGARET WAS ABOUT to climb into her bed in the chamber she had been given when Isabella stepped into the room.

She started. It was very late now, but if Isabella had come to speak with her, it meant that the men were still downstairs.

"You gave me such a fright," she said, closing the door. She wore but a long, loose robe, her hair in plaits.

Margaret knew she was speaking of the interview that had taken place an hour earlier in the hall below. "I was not going to reveal Bruce's plans for you," she said. "But surely, after seeing how angry all the men downstairs are, you realize you must never acquiesce in his attempt to steal the throne."

"If he comes for me, I will go with him," Isabella said.

"What would make you think that he will come for you? Surely, you have not received a message from him?"

Isabella flushed. "How could I receive word from him? But if he wants me at Scone, I would need men and horses in order to get there. He would have to come for me."

Margaret was filled with doubt. Had Isabella received word from Bruce or a crony? Was it possible?

"What about you, Margaret?" Isabella approached her and sat down on the bed as Margaret stood beside it. "Do you support Bruce now?"

"Why would you think that?" But hadn't she betrayed

her uncle and his allies a moment ago? By failing to reveal all that she knew?

She had done so not to support Bruce, but to protect
Alexander.

Isabella's stare was steady. "Because you did not tell
them everything that you know. You did not tell them
that there is a date for the coronation, or that they wish
for me to stand beside Bruce when he puts on the crown."

"I am against Bruce!" she cried. But she felt a nagging
doubt—her actions thus far said otherwise.

She could not be entirely against Bruce as long as Alexander rode with him, she realized. She simply could
not.

"But if you had spoken up," Isabella said, "Buchan
would keep me under guard, and there would be no possibility of my ever being at Scone. If you had spoken up,
they would ride for Scone shortly, and lay a trap there
for Bruce."

Margaret's heart thudded. She did not know what to
say.

Isabella stood up, their gazes locked. "Is it Bruce?"
she asked, low. "You met him. Did he persuade you that
his cause is the just one?"

She wet her lips. "No."

Isabella began to shake her head. "He has an eye for
the ladies. You are so beautiful. He must have flirted
with you—perhaps tried to take you to bed? And he is
a handsome man. He has convinced you, Margaret, to
betray the family, hasn't he?"

"He has not!" she cried, in real horror. "He flirted a
bit, but most men do. And he did try to impress upon me
that it would be advantageous if I changed my loyalties—
but I refused. I am loyal to Buchan. I am a Comyn!"

Isabella studied her intently. "I believe you. But from

your actions, you are not as loyal to my husband as you think." She walked to the door, then swiftly returned and kissed Margaret's cheek. "Good night, Margaret. And thank you for keeping my secret."

THE WIND WHIPPED the trees that lined the road they traveled upon, the skies above gray and threatening rain. Margaret rode beside Isabella, huddled in a fur, their horses restlessly tossing their heads. Buchan and Sir Ranald rode ahead of them, the rest of the escort behind. It was midafternoon and they were but a few miles from home.

"I am frozen to the bone," Isabella said, her teeth chattering.

Margaret was as cold, but before she could speak, Sir Ranald called out, holding up his hand, and every horse in the cavalcade halted. Ahead, a rider was streaking down the road toward them, at a full gallop.

Buchan nodded and Sir Ranald galloped toward the oncoming rider, the two meeting some ways down the road, neither man very visible from this distance. A moment passed as they spoke to one another, and then Margaret watched as Sir Ranald and the rider turned as one, riding back to their group.

When they were close enough to be identified, Margaret recognized the rider as one of Buchan's soldiers. Sir Ranald said, "The Wolf of Lochaber is camped upon the River Spey, not far from Balvenie."

Margaret almost cried out. Instead, she clamped down on the cry, and stared, disbelieving. Why would Alexander be at Balvenie?

Sir Ranald rode up to Buchan and held out a rolled-up parchment. "He has sent this to you, my lord."

Feeling dazed, Margaret watched her uncle leap from

his stallion and take the parchment. Sir Ranald also dismounted, and Buchan handed his horse's reins to him. He immediately untied the parchment, unrolled it and began reading.

Margaret realized she was holding her breath. What did the Wolf want? If he sent but a letter, she would assume it was news of Will—or a request for a ransom. But he was camped just down the road on the banks of the river.

It was incredible.

And then she saw an expression of disbelief cross Buchan's face. He whirled and looked up at her.

A terrible tension struck her. "What is it? What passes?" she managed to ask.

"He wishes to trade Will for you—for you as his bride."

For one moment, Margaret did not understand him.

Buchan tore up the parchment then, furiously.

"He has asked for my hand?" she gasped, as comprehension began.

Buchan faced her, red-faced. "The bastard! He wishes to strengthen his control of Castle Fyne! If he marries you, no one will question his command!"

Margaret was reeling. She felt Isabella reach out and touch her arm. She could not look at her—she stared at her uncle, instead.

Alexander had proposed a marriage between them.

She could marry Alexander instead of Sir Guy.

And for one instant, her heart leapt. For one instant, she was relieved.

"He has said he will await your answer, my lord," the outrider said.

Buchan turned. "Damn him to hell! My answer is no!

Tell him I demand a ransom for my nephew, and he will suffer my wrath if he does not ask for one!"

Margaret gripped the horn of her saddle tightly, and her mare was prancing about, as she sensed her rider's tension. What had she been thinking?

Her family hated Alexander's family; the clans were rivals and blood enemies.

A war now raged, pitting the Comyns against him and Bruce.

Of course they could not marry. He was her enemy!

And he had only asked for her hand in marriage because of Castle Fyne.

The rider was galloping off toward the north, where Alexander was camped, and would soon tell him that her uncle had refused his offer.

She began to shake. Did she feel dismayed? She must be mad, if so.

Buchan faced her. "You are to marry Sir Guy and he knows it." He then seized his horse's reins and leapt astride. "To Balvenie," he roared, still enraged.

Margaret watched him gallop away, and then realized she must follow, when she was so stunned, she was merely sitting there in a daze.

"Come, Lady Margaret, as it will rain soon," Sir Ranald said, having ridden up to her.

She flinched, as he had taken her by surprise, she was so enraptured in her thoughts. She had avoided looking at him the entire day, after he had caught her eavesdropping the night before. Now she was surprised, because his expression was kind.

She took a deep breath. "Yes, we must hurry to Balvenie—before it rains."

MARGARET DARED TO cross the great hall, where Buchan paced, still in a temper, and now surrounded by his men. He did not even see her, and for that, she was relieved. She ran upstairs to her chamber. Once inside, she halted, breathing hard.

Now what should she do?

Alexander was but a few minutes away, and Buchan had refused a union between them, and rightly so.

She hugged herself. If only she could think clearly. But now, she had one thought. She kept thinking about how different it would be if she married Alexander instead of Sir Guy.

Peg rushed into the room, her eyes wide. "MacDonald offered marriage? And he is at the River Spey?"

Margaret nodded. And as she stared at Peg, she thought about Will, who would have been freed if Buchan had agreed to such a union. Poor Will.

Peg said, "He is a MacDonald. The enemy of yer mother's kin. But Sir Guy is English—and every bit as much an enemy."

"We ride with the English now."

"Fer how long?" Peg challenged.

Margaret shrugged helplessly and said, "Peg, we are at war."

"Fer how long?" she repeated relentlessly.

Before Margaret could respond, Isabella came to the threshold of the room and stared at her. "Ye are white," she finally said. "What has happened?"

Margaret bit her lip. "I never imagined he would ask to marry me."

Isabella stepped into the room and closed the door. "What did you imagine?"

Margaret tensed. Isabella suspected something. But she could never know the truth. It was too dangerous. "I imagined that eventually we would war against him and take Castle Fyne back," she finally said.

"But he has decided marriage is better than war. How interesting—but then, you are so beautiful. Is he smitten?"

"I doubt Alexander would be smitten by any woman, Isabella."

"He was smitten by his mistress, the woman he fought to make his wife—the woman who died giving birth to his child."

Margaret tensed. "That is legend."

"Everyone knows it is true."

She folded her arms. "He is not smitten with me. He wishes to keep Castle Fyne securely in his control."

"You seem distraught, Margaret."

Isabella was right. She was upset as never before. She could not marry Alexander, and it had more to do with the war for the throne of Scotland than it did the ancient enmity between their clans.

I would be proud if ye ever fought to defend what was mine.

She froze, having just heard Alexander as clearly as if he stood beside her. He admired her. He respected her. And he had spoken those words to her after Sir Guy had berated her for defending Castle Fyne from his attack.

Alexander had appreciated what she had done. Sir Guy had not.

And when Alexander touched her, desire swelled; when Sir Guy touched her, she was repulsed.

"Do you have some interest in the Wolf of Lochaber, Margaret?" Isabella asked, taking her hand.

Margaret jumped as if burned. "Of course not." She felt her cheeks heat.

And then Margaret heard her uncle roar from the hall below. If she hadn't misheard, he had shouted her name.

Isabella blanched, dropping her hand.

Margaret ran to the door and opened it, and as she did, Eilidh appeared, running as hard as she could toward her. "The earl wishes ye downstairs," she cried, appearing pale and frightened.

"Margaret!" Buchan shouted again.

Something had happened—another message from Alexander, perhaps? As frightened as the rest of the women, Margaret lifted her skirts and ran down the hall and downstairs, Isabella and her maids on her heels.

Buchan was pacing, flushed with anger once again. As she skidded into the hall, he halted, facing her, arms akimbo. "You know him, do you not?" he asked. "You must know him well!"

Had someone betrayed them? Peg? Dughall? Did Buchan speak of her infidelity now?

"Well?" he demanded, striding to her. "What does he want? He has just demanded a meeting!"

She almost fainted; she was so relieved. Isabella steadied her and said, sharply, "John! She is distraught! You must not shout at her."

He glanced at her and said, "I am distraught!" But he did not shout now.

Margaret caught her breath and faced him. She sought composure. "I cannot imagine what he wants. But he has Will." Her mind began to race, frantically. He had Will; he wanted a meeting. "You must go!" She caught herself and softened her tone. "Uncle, can you please speak to him? Perhaps you can arrange Will's release!"

"Of course I am going to speak to the bastard—he has your brother and Castle Fyne!" He whirled to Sir Ranald. "Tell him we will meet at the red rocks in two hours. He may bring ten men, no more. I will do the same. Then have a hundred of our best soldiers ready, and fifty knights. We go to the red rocks in an hour."

Margaret tried not to tremble. As Sir Ranald left, she said, "You will deceive him—and ambush him?"

Buchan stared sharply. "I will meet him with ten knights, as I said I would, because I wish to know what he will do this time. But my small army will be close enough to protect us if he thinks to deceive *us* in any way. He is camped here with two hundred men, Margaret. I cannot simply meet him without a small army of my own."

"I want to come with you," she said.

"Why would you wish to come?" he demanded.

He hadn't refused. She said tersely, "He has Will. And he has my castle. I also want to hear what he will say." She boldly approached and touched his arm. Suddenly nothing had ever been as important; suddenly, she had to see Alexander. "Uncle. I fought almost to the death to defend my dowry. I fought him for an entire day, at times, throwing burning oil on his soldiers. I stabbed a MacDonald man. I have earned the right to join you. If you negotiate with him, perhaps, I can help."

His eyes widened. A brief but terrible silence fell. No one in the hall moved. Perhaps she had been too bold, gone too far—she was but a woman!

But Buchan finally said, "You have earned a great many rights, Margaret."

She nodded, barely able to draw a breath.

"In fact, I want you to come to the red rocks with us."

THE POUNDING RAIN had stopped, but the skies were so dark they were almost black, indicating that more rain would come. Margaret rode just behind her uncle, Sir

Ranald at her side, as their horses walked slowly down a narrow, muddy path toward the river.

Ahead, she saw a shadowy cluster, just barely formed against the dark sky, but then the images began to take on the shape and appearance of horses and men. She could now see the red boulders that designated their meeting spot; she could make out the white water of the swollen river, as it rushed torrentially through the glen.

And she finally saw Alexander.

He sat his gray steed at the forefront of his men, neither horse nor man moving.

Margaret felt her heart lurch and then thunder. She had not seen him in almost three weeks. She could not look aside now. Her cheeks began to burn.

He was staring at her, too. She felt certain—though he was still too far away, and she could not see his eyes....

He had asked for her in marriage, but she could not imagine how he truly felt about her having escaped.

They continued to slowly approach, the ground dangerously slick beneath their horses' hooves. Her uncle finally paused his horse, a small distance separating him from Alexander. Margaret halted her mare beside him.

Their gazes met. Alexander's expression was hard, but it was also impassive—it was impossible to discern any of his emotions. He nodded slightly at her.

Oddly, the small gesture seemed too intimate and Margaret tensed, glancing at her uncle, who was observing them. She did not nod in return, or in any way acknowledge the salutation. She was suddenly so afraid that her uncle would guess at the intimacy they had shared.

Buchan's heated regard was on Alexander. "You hold my nephew, you hold my castle—and you've taken me out of my fine hall in the middle of a storm. What do you want, MacDonald?"

Alexander's gaze was cool. "I suggest ye reconsider my proposal, Buchan."

"There is nothing to reconsider! I gain nothing from such a trade!"

Margaret tensed, horrified—surely, her uncle did not consider Will nothing.

"I dinna think ye had any care fer yer nephew. He is fine, by the way. Angry, but fine."

Briefly, Margaret felt a great relief.

"I have a great care for Will," Buchan flared. "Is this why you have called me outside in such weather? To berate me for my refusal to give you my niece? To accuse me of not caring about my nephew?"

"I have called ye here," he said, staring at Margaret now, "to make a second offer."

She froze. Their gazes locked. He would offer for her another time?

Alexander tore his gaze from her and said to her uncle, "I'll add Glen Carron Castle to the trade."

Buchan started.

Margaret began to tremble. When he did not speak, she wondered if her uncle was considering trading her to Alexander—for her brother and a castle.

"I rebuilt the keep after I razed it to the ground—it is a fine, defensible fortification," Alexander said flatly. "An' ye ken, it abuts Badenoch land. Ye'll grow yer borders there."

Stunned, she stared at her uncle, who was gazing at Alexander, his expression now one of calculation. She could see that his mind was racing.

He was considering such a trade! He might accept, she thought, feeling almost frantic. A part of her was dismayed—that he could be so easily persuaded to give her over to the enemy—but another part of her was desperate.

She knew Alexander would be a reasonable husband, knew she would enjoy being in his arms and bearing him children…. But dear God, then what? He would go to war against her brother, her uncles, her aunts and cousins….

"She is to wed Sir Guy in June," Buchan suddenly said harshly. "Surrender Castle Fyne and Glen Carron, and I will give her over as your bride."

Margaret felt her heart lurch. She looked from her uncle to Alexander, stunned.

He *would* trade her—but only for two castles, one of them being Castle Fyne.

Alexander was staring at her—she thought she could see a flicker of compassion in his eyes. But when he spoke, his face was hard, cold and set. "I will not give up Castle Fyne."

Buchan's expression became savage and mocking at once. "You think yourself a great lord? My niece is worthy of princes, and she's to marry a man with royal blood—not a Highlander from the far isles who cannot speak French properly."

"So ye insult me now?" But Alexander smiled coolly, amused.

Margaret felt a chill sweep her, and she begged silently, *Don't!*

He glanced at her—as if he had heard her innermost thoughts. Then he turned a frightening look upon her uncle. "Ye should think one more time about refusing me. Ye dinna wish to suffer my wrath."

"And now you threaten me?"

"I have Will, I have Castle Fyne—and I am here, at Balvenie."

Buchan started. "What do you intend, Wolf?"

"I promise ye great loss," he said, picking up his reins. His stallion pranced, snorting. He turned to Margaret. "Are ye well?"

She froze. He was speaking directly to her?

"Lady Margaret," he snapped. "Are ye well?"

She knew she must not answer—she knew she must look away—but she could not do as she must. She whispered, "Yes, I am well."

He spurred the gray stallion toward Buchan. "I became fond of my captive, Buchan. Ye keep her well."

Buchan was turning red. "When we capture you, Wolf, I will be the one to take off your head and place it on a pike!"

Alexander laughed at him.

"Stop," Margaret tried to say, but her whisper was low and hoarse. How could they do this, now?

Sir Ranald seized her wrist in warning.

"And when yer favorite castle lies in ruins, and Sir Guy is dead, I will take her as my bride," Alexander said.

Margaret was horrified.

Alexander whirled his horse, sent her a searing look, and then spurred the beast hard. It screamed in protest and galloped away, blood on its sides. His knights all followed.

And then there was no one at the red rocks and the river's banks but Buchan, Margaret and his men.

"I will kill him," Buchan said. And then he turned his furious gaze upon her.

She wanted to cringe. *He knows,* she thought. But she did not move.

"If he wants you, you have become more trouble than you are worth!" With that, he spurred his horse and began to gallop up the muddy hill.

Margaret was ready to collapse. Sir Ranald reached

out and caught her as she swooned, dragging her from her small mount to his larger one. "Lady! I will have you safely home."

Hot, blistering tears arose. Margaret nodded, now in Sir Ranald's arms.

CHAPTER THIRTEEN

EILIDH WAS STOKING the fire in the hearth in Margaret's chamber when Sir Ranald led her in. She was trembling. On the way back to the castle, it had rained torrentially, and she was soaking wet. But she was not shaking from the cold. She was not on the verge of collapse because of the rain.

Eilidh blanched. "Lady?"

"She has had a trying afternoon," Sir Ranald said. "You must help her into dry clothes, sit her before the fire and bring her warm wine."

Margaret felt shocked. And she was terrified.

Did Buchan suspect that she and Alexander had been lovers?

But there was even more. Did Alexander mean to marry her, no matter the consequences—and would he attack her uncle to do so?

"Please sit down, Lady Margaret, before you fall over," Sir Ranald said kindly.

Margaret had been guided to the chamber's sole chair, which had been placed before the blazing fire. Somehow, she did as asked; somehow, she looked up at him and smiled. "Thank you, Sir Ranald. I am fine."

"You are not fine." His green gaze was searching. Then he dropped abruptly to one knee and took both of her hands in his. "I wish to protect you, Lady Margaret!

I wish to aid you! But if you play a dangerous game, then you must tell me."

What did Sir Ranald think? She had not considered what everyone else who had been present at the red rocks might think of the encounter. But Sir Ranald had caught her eavesdropping at Strathbogie; he had seen her exchange with Alexander.

As she stared at him, terribly uncertain now, Peg and Isabella ran into the room.

"What happened?" Isabella cried. "John is vowing to murder the Wolf the next time they meet! He is furious, and already in his cups!"

Margaret looked back at Sir Ranald. "We will talk another time, when I have had a chance to think," she said. If Sir Ranald meant to be her ally, she would accept him as one. She so needed allies now. But she would not make him her confidant.

He nodded and left the room.

Peg closed the door behind him. "Margaret?" she asked, eyes wide.

She could no longer contain her distress. She covered her face with her hands, trying not to cry, thinking of Alexander, who had decided he must marry her, no matter the cost, the pain. She could not imagine his motivation, other than his desire to control Castle Fyne for all of his lifetime, and to pass it down to his sons.

But what of her and her desires?

The chamber seemed to rock wildly, as if a boat in storm-tossed seas.

She thought of Buchan, who had hated Alexander before, and would hate him impossibly now. The two had been enemies for a great many reasons before this war had come between them, but now, their enmity had become personal. Alexander had threatened Buchan;

Buchan had threatened him in return. It felt certain that in the end, one man must die.

It was Isabella who came to her and put her arms around her. "What did he do?"

She tried to wipe the moisture from her face, desperate to find composure. She met Isabella's worried gaze. "He made a second offer of marriage—and when Buchan refused, he threatened to destroy him and his castles."

Isabella said, "No, I meant what did my husband do?" Then, "He is angry with you—he told me so! I assumed you are near tears because of him."

Margaret inhaled. "He considered trading me to Alexander, not just for Will, but for Castle Fyne and another keep."

Isabella was dismayed. "I am sorry. But he does love you, Margaret."

"He would give me over to the enemy if the trade was advantageous enough." The pain stabbing through her breast felt like a knife. "He would give me over with hardly a second thought." Hadn't he abandoned her while she was being held hostage at Castle Fyne?

And hadn't Will complained all along that her marriage to Sir Guy was an act beyond expedience—that she was being tossed aside, as if a *thing* of little worth, a *thing* without feelings?

She had refused to believe it, but it was true. Her father would never have treated her in such a way. He had loved her for who she was, from the time she had been born. He would have wanted a marriage for her that was expedient, but he would have also wanted her to care for her husband. Margaret had no doubt.

He would never have bartered her away, not even in a time like this, when a kingdom was at stake.

"Of course he would seek a trade if doing so would

make a good alliance—you are only a woman." Isabella clasped her hand tightly. "We are all disposable, Margaret. You must know that."

Margaret had not realized that Isabella was so worldly. "What if Alexander makes a third offer? What if he offers so much that Uncle John cannot refuse?"

"Will he make another offer?" Isabella asked, surprised.

"I never expected any offer!" Margaret cried.

Isabella paused. "The truth is, if Sir Guy fails to take Castle Fyne back, you will have lost your value to him—but you are a great prize for Alexander."

"The Wolf is smitten," Peg said, stepping forward. "He was smitten with Margaret from the moment he first conquered Castle Fyne."

Isabella turned an incredulous look upon Margaret. "Is it true?"

"He is hardly smitten," Margaret said, standing. But she wasn't angry with Peg for speaking up. She wondered if she could be right. "Can you help me out of my clothes?"

Eilidh rushed to her chest to pull out dry garments as Peg came over, and they began to pull off her wet cotes. Isabella watched them and said, "Margaret, the Wolf has already proven he will go to great lengths to take a woman to wife."

Margaret had just shrugged on a dry chemise and surcote. Peg began to unbraid her wet hair as she faced Isabella. "You are right. He is relentless."

Isabella studied her. "Is he repulsive?"

Margaret laughed, somewhat hysterically. Should she confess all to her friend? Did she dare?

"He is very handsome," Eilidh whispered. Peg nodded in agreement.

Isabella started and Margaret winced. "He is handsome—and there is more. He said he would kill Sir Guy if he had to."

"He will not let a marriage stand in his way?"

"No." Her gaze locked with Isabella's. She knew that even if she married Sir Guy, Alexander would come for her.

Isabella knew it, too. Her color high, she slowly said, "He may be your savior, Margaret, in the end."

Margaret shook her head. "Please don't say that."

"He has stolen Castle Fyne from you, and now, you have nothing but the hope that Sir Guy will take it back. But if he marries you, you will be lady of Castle Fyne again."

MARGARET COULD NOT sleep. She stared up at the ceiling of her chamber, watching moonlight play across it. Her uncle had left with his great army that morning.

Buchan would take his army south to join King Edward's as it marched north, in an attempt to stop Bruce in his westward march across Scotland.

She wondered if Bruce would attempt to be crowned in four more days; she wondered if Aymer de Valence, who now commanded most of England's army, would learn he was marching for Scone and somehow stop him. She turned over onto her side, hugging her pillow. To stop Bruce, if he was intent on a coronation, would mean a battle to the death. Of that, she was certain.

She trembled. She had done her best to avoid Buchan ever since that meeting with Alexander at the red rocks. Buchan had been preoccupied with his war preparations, so it had been easy to do. Still, she knew he was not pleased with her now.

Could Alexander be smitten? If he was, wouldn't she know? And didn't he realize how devastating his ambitions were for her—for her entire family?

More dismay arose, as did a lump of fear. Margaret wished she knew if Atholl and the others had a plan to separate their armies. If she had, she would send word. No matter what happened—even if she married Sir Guy—she did not want Alexander to die.

Tears arose. Hugging the pillow, she rocked herself finally to sleep.

And then she was wide-awake and terrified—for a hand was clasped over her mouth, preventing her from screaming, and a viselike arm was around her waist. She was pressed hard against a muscular male chest. A man was in her chamber—in her bed!

"Dinna scream. I willna hurt ye, Margaret."

As her eyes flew open, as her scream was choked off, she knew it was Alexander.

She looked upward, into his intense eyes, while he loosened his grasp of her mouth and his grip on her body. Her heart turned over wildly.

He slowly removed his hand, saying, "And if ye do scream, no one will hear—the watch has been rendered useless for the next few hours."

Now she began to realize what he had done—he had stolen into an enemy fortress, one filled with Buchan's finest soldiers! "Alexander! Are you mad? If they catch you they will hang you!"

He slowly smiled at her. "Ah, so nothing has changed, ye canna wish me ill."

She went still, acutely aware of being in his embrace— overcome by the sensation of his hard muscles against her softer flesh, by the scent of man and pine, by the knowledge that he was there for her. "I cannot wish you ill." She breathed hard, almost lifting her hand to touch his face, but she must not act as if they were lovers. They were not lovers—that one night had been long ago! "You cannot be here."

"I can and I am." He did not smile now. "Ye ken the man I am. I never say what I dinna mean. I'm taking ye away, Margaret, and ye'll be my wife."

Her mind spun, incredulously. "You will force me to marry you?"

"I dinna think there will be force involved," he said softly. His gaze moved to her mouth.

Desire pummeled through her. Margaret did not move.

He slowly looked up and into her eyes, a slight curve to his mouth. "Dinna tell me ye remain loyal to Sir Guy and yer uncle."

"I despise Sir Guy."

He smiled. "As ye should."

"But I cannot betray my uncle by marrying you."

"Come, we must go. This discussion can wait." He stood, taking her with him. "Get dressed."

Margaret started for her clothes chest. "Where are we going?"

"Scone."

Margaret froze.

"Surely ye wish to come. Surely ye wish to be there fer Isabella—she will need a friend."

Margaret began to shake. *He had come to Balvenie for Isabella!* Her thoughts tumbled. "Alexander! If you must pursue me, so be it! But leave poor Isabella alone! Do not make her betray her husband! Please!"

He hardened. "Get dressed, Margaret. Now."

She began to shake wildly, but did as he demanded.

She rushed to her chest and took out her clothing, thinking about the fact that he hadn't just come for her—although she had no doubt he meant to marry her, if she would ever relent. He had come to abduct Isabella and force her to commit treachery against her husband—and treason against King Edward.

She turned to him. "Treason is a hanging offense."

"Isabella will be kept safe."

"Buchan will hang her himself!" she cried. "And if he does not, King Edward will hang her!"

He strode to her and took her arm and shook her, once. "Get dressed, now." His eyes were hard. "We killed a few of the guards, but the others will soon awaken."

Immediately she thought of Sir Ranald, who had been left behind to take care of her. "Sir Ranald? Please, tell me you did not kill him!"

"Get dressed."

Again he was the man she so often feared and hated, a man who would not compromise, not when driven to achieve his own ends. Margaret turned away and now saw that her door was wide open. Torches lit up the hall beyond it. She suddenly glimpsed one of her uncle's soldiers, lying crumpled upon the floor. She did not know if he was dead or unconscious.

She gave him her back and stripped off the ankle-length robe she slept in. She quickly donned her cote and surcote. She was frantic as she tried to do the cords of her girdle.

How could she help Isabella? Her friend was not strong. She was gentle, playful and young for her age. Margaret could manage these intrigues. But Isabella did not deserve to be a political pawn.

Buchan would hunt her down, she was certain. If Isabella consensually helped crown Bruce, he would hurt her terribly for such disloyalty.

Alexander seized the girdle and took it from her. "Yer shaking as if yer afraid of me."

"I do fear you," she said, looking up. "But right now, I am afraid for Isabella, not myself."

He handed her the soft boots she wore when riding. "When will ye ever trust me? If I tell ye we'll keep her safe, that is what we will do. Bruce is not like Buchan. He rewards those who are faithful to him." Grasping her arm, he guided her into the hallway.

Margaret was relieved that the men who lay in the hall were clearly unconscious, and not dead. But Sir Ranald was not amongst them.

Isabella's chamber—which she shared with her husband—was at the far end of the corridor. Her door was wide open, and she was rushing out as Margaret approached, her dark hair in one long braid, her eyes bright with excitement, her cheeks flushed. "Margaret! You are coming with us?" She sounded surprised and pleased. And she was smiling.

"Isabella, do not voluntarily go with these men!" Margaret cried. "If ever there is a time to come to your senses, it is now!"

"I haven't lost my common sense," Isabella returned, her smile fading. "Oh, Margaret, be happy! Bruce will be crowned at Scone!"

How could she dissuade her now? "You must stop now and think about the consequences of what you intend to do! What of your marriage? You have a good marriage, Isabella, and Buchan loves you. He will be furious and he will never forgive you."

A very stubborn look crossed Isabella's face. "I don't care."

"You don't mean that," Margaret cried. "You can't mean that!"

"I do mean it. I do not care about John! Will you come with me? Please? I need you, Margaret!"

"I doubt I have a choice, but I would not betray my uncle, or this family, Isabella. If I go with you, I am being forced to do so." But as she spoke, she glanced at Alexander, feeling as if her words were hollow.

"Of course you wouldn't! For some reason I could never fathom, you are so loyal to my husband."

"He is my uncle. He and Will are all I have left!" Margaret made one last attempt to dissuade her from her suicidal course. "Have you considered that you will be committing treason if you place that crown on Bruce's head?" They had yet to broach that subject.

Isabella lifted her chin. "Then so be it. I am the Countess of Fife!"

"You are the Countess of Buchan and the Earl of Buchan's wife!"

A movement sounded behind them. Margaret turned, and saw one of Alexander's men at the top of the stairs, signaling him. Alexander took her arm. "She made up her mind long ago, Margaret, and even if ye could change it, I'd take her with us—just as I am taking ye."

Margaret met his hard gaze for a moment, knowing that his mind was made up. They started down the hallway, two of Alexander's men in the lead, Alexander behind Margaret and Isabella. When they reached the great hall, Margaret saw that six knights lay unmoving upon the floor, and one was Sir Ranald.

She cried out, for most of those strewn on the stone were clearly dead. Blood had pooled beneath one soldier's head. She rushed to Sir Ranald, who was terribly pale, and laid her fingers upon his throat.

It took her an instant to realize that his pulse beat there, sure and strong. Relief filled her. A shadow fell over her and she looked up. "This is Sir Ranald—and he is important to me."

"I will remember it." Alexander reached down and dragged her up. "Be silent now," he said to her and Isabella.

They hurried from the hall, outside and into the night. The courtyard was eerily quiet, as if deserted. But a dozen of his men appeared, stepping out of the night shadows, as silent as wolves on the hunt. And there were no cries from above.

She glanced up. The watchtowers were deserted. She feared the watch lay dead.

And a moment later they were stealing out of a small south door, where dozens of horses and riders awaited them in the dark.

IT WAS HIGH noon when Alexander held up his hand, halting their cavalcade.

They had been riding at a rapid pace, away from Balvenie, ever since leaving the castle in the middle of the night. Margaret rode beside Isabella, between two of Alexander's men. There were about fifty Highland knights in their group. Nine or even ten hours had to have passed. They were deep within a forest now, but they had been using deer paths that had clearly become roads for warhorses for most of the journey. Initially their pace had been as rapid as possible in the dark of the night, but at dawn, when it seemed that any pursuit would be far behind, Alexander had slowed the pace to a walk. Now, he turned his mount to face them. "We will rest here until dark," he said.

Margaret was relieved. She was stiff, sore and exhausted—in fact, she was even more fatigued mentally than she was physically. Conversation had not been allowed. She had had hours in which to think.

She could not bring herself to feel genuinely dismayed over her abduction. But she remained terrified for Isabella. If she could, she still hoped to convince her not to participate in Bruce's coronation.

She glanced at Isabella, who also appeared pale and exhausted, and they smiled grimly at one another. Margaret could not wait to dismount. She imagined Isabella felt the very same way.

Alexander had already leapt from his horse. Dughall was leading it away. He smiled at Isabella, striding to her. "How do ye fare, Countess?"

"I do not know if I can stand up," she admitted. "My entire body hurts."

He caught her around the waist and helped her down. When Isabella's feet touched the ground she fell against him. Alexander righted her, but for a moment, Isabella was in his arms.

Margaret watched, feeling oddly annoyed, and her annoyance increased when Isabella smiled at him and murmured her thanks.

Margaret pretended to ignore them as Alexander led her toward a pallet recently put down; a tent was being erected for her. She slid from her horse with some difficulty, wincing. But Alexander caught her arm from behind. "If ye would wait, I would help ye down in turn."

Margaret faced him, and then she pulled away. But his touch seemed to linger. His touch affected her as no other man's could. She was so acutely aware of him now.

But hadn't she been as aware of him all night? She had found herself staring at him as he led the way, time after time. And as frightening as the night was, there had been something reassuring about the broad set of his shoulders, the proud tilt of his head.

But she should not be reassured. Their disappearance had been remarked by now. Sir Ranald must be in hot pursuit. Word would have been sent to Buchan.

"You seemed occupied tending to Isabella," she said, unsmiling.

"Are ye jealous? Because ye need not be, Margaret."

"I do not wish to be jealous, Alexander, just as I do not want to have any care for you." She then shrugged. Some feelings were simply impossible to control.

"But ye do care." When she didn't respond, he said, "Ye should eat and sleep. We'll ride again at dark—through the entire night."

His stare was unwavering, but she could not look away, for she had not seen him for so long. But she must rein in her affections. "There will be pursuit."

"Do ye warn me?"

Was she warning him? "Sir Ranald is devoted to me."

"Of course he is. I am prepared, Margaret. Six of my men ride far behind—if they discover pursuit, they will relay the news to me."

"Is there any way that they can catch us?"

"'Tis unlikely. We turned all their horses out of the stables. They will have to catch them before they can chase us. And we rode very hard fer the first few hours, and I have taken an unusual route. We do not travel in the most direct manner." He gestured, indicating that she should join Isabella, whose pallet was now beneath the open tent.

Margaret did not move. "How long will it be before we reach Scone, Alexander?"

"It depends on whether we are being pursued, and if I have to take an even more unusual route. It also depends upon ye and Isabella. I dinna think either of ye will be able to ride as long tonight."

"Is he to be crowned on the twenty-fifth?"

Alexander started. "Why should I be surprised by anything ye say or do, Margaret? I already knew ye spied on us when Bruce came to Castle Fyne."

"I was your prisoner—it was my duty to spy—to learn of what was happening in the country."

"And will it be your duty now—again?" His eyes remained dark and hard.

"I wish not!"

"So yer answer is aye." He turned away from her, anger and disgust in his strides.

She stared after him. She did not want to argue or fight! But what did he expect from her now? Her family was at war with Bruce. Of course she must spy!

But that did not mean she would relay everything she learned.

Margaret turned and slowly approached Isabella, whose eyes were wide. She sank down beside her, knees buckling.

"Are you lovers?"

Margaret flinched.

"You have kept my secret—I will keep yours."

"That isn't fair," Margaret breathed.

"Why not? We are friends. You have helped me—perhaps I wish to help you, too."

Margaret had no intention of telling Isabella the truth. She was afraid Isabella might inadvertently let the truth slip. "I need a privy moment."

"I think I know your answer, Margaret," Isabella said.

Margaret's head ached now, along with her body. Alexander's men all glanced at her as she veered away from the small camp, and she quickly realized that she was to be watched—and she would not be allowed to simply walk away into the forest, to attend to her own needs… or to escape.

Was she Alexander's prisoner now? Somehow, she did not think that he would actually keep her against her will.

Dughall had detached himself from a group of men who were seated around a fire. He was following her, but at a discreet distance.

"I am not going far," she said over her shoulder.

"Good." He smiled at her. "But I must go with ye—I will turn away, Lady Margaret, so ye can do what ye must."

She was somewhat angry, but she knew she must not blame Dughall—if she was to blame anyone, it would be Alexander.

And escape was not on her mind. Isabella needed her. And she and Alexander had to speak. It felt as if they had so much to say to one another. She just wasn't sure how to begin, or what to say, or how to get through an entire conversation without anger and accusations.

She hurried into the trees. Dughall stayed back, and she found a private place to take care of her needs.

Then she paused in another small glade, Dughall not far from the camp, where he kept one eye upon her, leaning against a tree. She rubbed her temples tiredly, walked over to a flat rock and sat down on it. Then she hugged her knees to her chest and laid her cheek there.

What should she do now?

She remained terribly attracted to Alexander. She continued to care for him. When they had spent that one night together, nothing had really changed. Now, everything had changed.

She did not want to marry Sir Guy. Alexander had taken her forcefully away, so now she could not marry Sir

Guy, and for that, she was grateful. But he had decided he wished to marry her himself, undoing her every conviction. If ever such a marriage came to pass, she would be giving up her every significant loyalty—all would be transferred to Alexander.

"Ye will not rest?" she heard Alexander ask.

She shifted to face him, suddenly a bit breathless, dropping her legs over the side of the rock. "I will gladly rest, after we have had a chance to speak."

"I wish to speak with ye, too, Margaret," he said, very seriously. "We shared a bed, and the morning afterward ye left me."

She could not look away from his searching gaze. He was so solemn, and she felt guilty. "Will had devised a good plan. It seemed likely to succeed. In a way, I did not want to leave, Alexander. But Peg had heard of your plans for Isabella. I had to warn her."

"I trusted ye."

She flinched. "I had to escape. It was my duty, Alexander."

"Did ye sleep with me to soften me fer the escape?" he asked, his gaze direct.

She gasped. "How could you think such a thing?"

"I would be foolish not to consider such a possibility."

"I came to you because I was afraid you might go to war—never to return. I did not know we would make love. I came only to tell you that I had become fond of you, against my better judgment, in defiance of my loyalties."

"When I heard ye'd escaped—that very morning— the news was like an ax striking my chest."

"I am sorry!" she cried.

He tilted up her chin. "I believe yer sorry—I also believe ye'd escape again, if ye could."

"From here? No. I can't leave Isabella yet."

He studied her. "Isabella was expecting us—ye warned her. But ye dinna warn Buchan. If ye had, I would never have been able to get inside Balvenie. Why?"

She flushed. "I could not betray Isabella, not once I realized how eager she was to aid Bruce."

"So ye put her before yer uncle."

She hesitated. "She isn't my blood, but she is my friend."

"Blood always comes before friendship."

He was right. She had put Isabella first. "I was protecting her."

"The way ye think to protect me?"

She started. Before she could ask him what he meant—afraid of what he meant—he said, "Ye ken Bruce will be crowned the twenty-fifth," Alexander said, staring. "When did ye learn that?"

She flushed. "Eilidh thought she heard such a date, Alexander."

"Did ye warn Buchan about that?" His gaze was searing.

"No. I could not bring myself to tell him of the date—which Eilidh was uncertain of, anyway."

"Why not? The great Comyn family hates Bruce. Yer a Comyn. Why not, Margaret?" he demanded. "Or have yer loyalties finally changed?"

She slipped to her feet. "My loyalties haven't changed! I wasn't sure the date was correct!"

"Tell me the truth. Tell me the real reason ye did not tell Buchan when we will crown Bruce."

She inhaled. "If I told him, he would ambush Scone on that date—and you would be there with Bruce. I am afraid for you!"

He reached out and clasped her shoulder, pulling her closer. "So yer loyalties *have* changed."

"Don't do this, Alexander. I do not want to be enemies, but that is what we must remain." Yet how could they truly be enemies when she wanted to be in his arms?

"We ceased being enemies when we shared the same bed."

He was so resolute. And she knew that when resolute, Alexander was impossible to move. "I'm your prisoner—again! And that makes us enemies."

"Yer a prisoner here only if ye want to be one." He clasped her other shoulder and pulled her entirely into his embrace. "I think yer loyalties have already changed, but as stubborn as ye can be, ye refuse to recognize it."

If he was right, she had to warn him of all she'd learned. "Alexander, there is more. Buchan and his allies hope to divide your army from Bruce's. They hope to isolate you and then destroy you."

His eyes gleamed. She knew he was thinking that he was right after all—that her loyalties had changed. "Are ye certain?"

She nodded. "But I have no other details."

He tilted up her chin. "See, Margaret? Ye think to warn me now."

"Yes, I am warning you. Can't I be loyal to my family, and try to keep you safe, too?"

He shook his head, an odd, tender light filling his eyes. "Mayhap for a day, or two, or ten. But in the end, ye will have to choose. In the end, it will be me—or them."

She would never be able to abandon her family, she thought, feeling frantic. But she would never purposefully place Alexander in jeopardy. "Why can't you understand? Buchan and Will are all I have left of my mother, my father, my other brothers!" But his hand was now caressing her back, causing desire to fist within her.

And he clasped her face in his large hands. "Buchan would sell ye to me fer the right price. And Will would understand—if ye told him that ye love me."

She went still. What had he said?

When she didn't respond, he seemed disappointed. "Will ye ever give an inch?" he murmured. "Tell me ye still care. Tell me yer glad I came to Balvenie. Tell me ye wish to be my wife."

Her heart thundered. "I can never marry you."

"Ye can," he said softly. "Ye will."

"I am always afraid for you. I'm afraid you will die by the sword."

"I will die like my father, sword in hand, upon the battlefield, in God's grace," he said fiercely. "But if yer waiting fer me, I will not die soon."

She clasped his face. "Is that a vow?"

"Aye, 'tis a vow, Margaret."

Her heart turned over, hard. What if? her mind began. But then he kissed her, hard, with a hunger pent up from the past weeks, and her thoughts simply ceased. There was only sensation—his hard, inflamed body, her taut, heated skin, the urgency racing between them. And there was emotion—desperation, relief and elation.

She had forgotten how much she needed to be in his arms. She had forgotten the rush of dizzying pleasure, the budding desire, the building pressure. Margaret ran her hands over his hard back, their mouths fused.

He broke the heated kiss abruptly. "I missed ye," he said, eyes hot.

"I missed you," she admitted breathlessly.

His smile was satisfied, yet savage. Alexander lifted her abruptly into his arms, shoved his way into the forest, and laid her down on a bed of pine needles. He paused on all fours, a question in his eyes. And Margaret reached up and pulled him down on top of her.

Their mouths fused frantically as he reached for the hem of her clothes. A moment later Margaret gasped as he impaled her amidst an explosion of stars....

CHAPTER FOURTEEN

MARGARET LAY IN Alexander's arms, their naked bodies entwined. She did not move, afraid that if she did so, reality would intrude. Just then, she wanted to be held, and to hold him. She did not want to think about anything other than how wonderful their lovemaking had been.

She closed her eyes and kissed his chest. "You are an excellent lover, Alexander."

"And ye would ken, how?"

She looked up at him, cradled in his arms. Then she reached up to touch his rough jaw. "I would know because I am so pleased." But now, with her pulse having returned to normal, she felt the cool breeze on her back and shivered.

He reached over her and pulled her mantle over them both. "Will ye admit yer glad that I came to Balvenie for ye now?"

She snuggled against him, her cheek pressed to his chest. "You are shameless to ask such a question now."

"I ken when triumph is at hand, Margaret."

He was a warrior. He knew when to strike—he knew that she was so pleased that she must answer yes. "Yes, Alexander, I am glad you came to Balvenie."

He lowered his face and kissed her slowly. "I came fer Isabella, as Bruce commanded," he said. "But I also came fer ye, Margaret." His eyes darkened. "Buchan only cares fer himself. Sir Guy is as filled with ambition."

She trembled. She had been trying not to think about anything other than the past hour they had shared. She did not want to face reality now, not if she could avoid it, just for a bit more. "You are filled with ambition as well, Alexander."

He was gruff. "Aye. But I care fer ye. The others only think to use ye as their pawn."

"I don't want to think about this now," she whispered. But it was too late, reality had intruded upon their brief moment of happiness.

His grasp tightened. "I'm sorry. I dinna mean to distress ye."

She quickly smiled. "I am not entirely distressed." And then she pressed herself even more closely to him.

"Good," he said, and he fell silent. He continued to hold her, but she knew he was brooding, as she was.

It felt right, being in his arms, when it was so terribly wrong. What was happening? He had admitted caring for her, even to her uncle. She had admitted caring for him. There was a strong bond of affection between them, and there was so much passion. But she also respected and admired him—he was a man of courage and honor, and he was just. And he had proven that he respected her.

So many emotions were swirling within her—confusion, fear, but there was also joy, and a swollen emotion that felt suspiciously like love.

Oh, God. She must not fall in love with Alexander!

"Margaret. What is it?"

She realized that panic had jolted her.

"Sir Guy will kill us both if he ever finds out, and my uncle will banish me from his lands."

He sat up, helping her to do so, too. Then he adjusted the mantle about her shoulders and chest, aware of her modesty.

"If ye wed me, I'll keep ye safe."

"I cannot argue with you now."

He studied her. "Ye'll bend, Margaret, sooner or later."

"Have you ever been thwarted, Alexander, when seeking ambition?"

"No." His gaze was direct.

And she was his ambition now. She stared at him, suddenly thinking about his deceased wife. "Did you really besiege Glen Carron Castle for the sake of a woman you wished to wed?"

He eyed her carefully now. "I was young and ill-tempered."

"So it's true?"

He said with equal care, "'Tis a bit of the truth."

She suddenly straightened. "You don't want to speak of your wife, Alexander? Did you love her that much?"

He sat up straighter, too. "I probably loved her. It's hard to recall. 'Twas long ago, Margaret. I was angry—I wanted to go to war and avenge my clan."

"What do you mean?" Margaret asked, wondering how he could forget whether he had loved her or not.

"The massacre of Clan Donald had been just months before. Her father rode in that battle. I wanted revenge—any kind of revenge—and so I took her to bed. She became my mistress, she was carrying my child. I decided to marry her." He shrugged. "Glen Carron is a fine castle and I wanted the keep. MacDuff refused. So aye, I besieged the castle and took him prisoner, until he agreed to the union."

Margaret felt how wide her eyes were. It did not sound to her as if he had loved his wife. The match had been the result of his need to avenge his kin.

"Why do ye ask about something so ancient?" he asked.

She tried to be nonchalant. "Legend has it that you had an undying love for her."

He laughed, but roughly. "Perhaps I did, at the time." His smile faded. His stare became direct. "The only woman I have affection for is now is the woman before me."

She flushed. "We should go back, before someone suspects."

"They suspect, Margaret, we've been gone fer an hour." But he stood up.

She leapt to her feet. "I cannot have gossip about us reaching Buchan and Sir Guy."

He steadied her instantly, reached down and handed her clothing to her. He did not reply, and she wondered if that meant the gossip *would* soon reach Buchan and Sir Guy.

Margaret watched him for a moment as he began to don his belts and swords. Her heart was thundering, partly from desire, and partly from fear. She was afraid of the extent of the affection she felt for him.

She did not want to fall in love with Alexander Mac-Donald. That would be a terrible twist of fate. If she ever realized that she loved him, surely, she would have to decide where her loyalties lay—for the very last time.

"You said Will would understand if I told him how I felt." She shook her head. "I think you are wrong. I think he would be furious."

Alexander came over to her. "There is one way to find out."

She gasped. "You will take me to him?"

"If he gives ye his blessing, will ye then accept me as yer husband?"

She began shaking her head. "Even if he did, we are at war!"

"If we were not at war, would ye marry me?"

Margaret went still. She owed him the truth. She owed it to herself.

In that moment, she knew that if this war ended, she would beg her uncle to accept him as her husband, never mind the feud between their clans.

"I would try to make amends with everyone first, but yes, Alexander, if we were not at war, I would wish to marry you," she said.

He smiled at her with hard satisfaction.

"But we *are* at war! And we remain at an impasse, Alexander."

"Do we? I think not."

March 26, 1306—Scone Abbey

SCONE ABBEY ROSE so abruptly out of the mists that their horses shied.

Margaret had been riding beside Alexander, with Isabella at her other side. They were behind three Highlanders who had led the way since dawn that morning. The horses in front of them were taken by surprise at the sudden sight of the pale stone ahead, and they leapt wildly aside. Margaret's mare reared, as the bells in the abbey watchtowers began to ring.

Alexander reached down to seize Margaret's reins. As he halted her prancing mare, the bells kept tolling above them.

Margaret glanced at Isabella, to make certain she was well. Her mount was also at a standstill, for Dughall was with her. The three foremost men had all halted their unruly chargers, too.

"Scone," Alexander quietly said.

Margaret had never been to Scone before, much less

the centuries-old abbey. Massive walls seemed to stretch endlessly before them, behind which a huge central tower soared, a spire atop it. And alongside the spire a great yellow flag waved, a red dragon in its midst.

"It is done," Alexander said, sounding savagely pleased. "Bruce is king."

For one moment, Margaret stared at the yellow flag, transfixed. They were late. A terrible storm had made travel impossible for almost an entire day. Bruce had been crowned yesterday anyway.

She glanced at her friend, who had been staring up at the flag, too, her eyes wide with disbelief. Margaret suddenly realized the implications of Bruce being crowned as planned on March 25th. Isabella had not been part of the ceremony; she had not betrayed her husband, or her king!

Before elation could take hold, Alexander stood in his stirrups and signaled the fifty or so men behind him. Then he turned to face forward, but he glanced at her, briefly smiling before spurring his horse over to Isabella. "Countess. If ye will join me?"

Margaret tensed, watching as Isabella and Alexander rode together, side by side, up the road. The front doors of the entry tower were slowly opening. She suddenly worried about Bruce, remembering his intimidating presence. Would he be angry with Alexander for their late arrival?

Margaret rode through the entry tower with Dughall, keeping their mounts to a sedate walk. Their horses' hooves echoed on the cobbled stone in the archway.

It felt eerie. She glanced up at the vaulted ceilings above them, feeling trapped.

Dughall grinned at her. "'Tis good we're not the enemy."

But she was the enemy, Margaret thought with a shiver.

They emerged into the early daylight of the court-yard. It was full. Tents had been erected everywhere, and horses were tethered by the far walls. Yet as full as it was, it could not contain Bruce's entire army—just his most important men.

Alexander and Isabella were riding directly to the steps before the central hall. A group of men stood there to greet them.

Margaret tensed, espying Robert Bruce immediately. He stood a hand above everyone else, in a dark red sur-cote with long sleeves and an ermine-lined gold man-tle. A brooch winked from its claspmantle and jewels glinted from the hilt of his sword. He was surrounded by equally well-dressed noblemen—one of whom was the Earl of Atholl.

Her heart turned over, hard. Her instinct had been cor-rect. Atholl had betrayed Buchan that night at his home. Atholl rode with Bruce.

Alexander had dismounted, and he was helping Isa-bella to do so, as well. But Margaret's gaze was riveted to Atholl's, and the moment he met her eyes, he smiled and bowed his golden head.

Margaret did not smile back. Atholl had betrayed her uncle, after so many years of friendship. She wondered if Buchan knew. And she wondered what Atholl thought of her—and Alexander.

Bruce was hurrying down the steps. "Alexander! You have brought me the Countess of Fife!" he exclaimed.

Alexander dropped to one knee. "Yer Majesty," he said. "I have gladly done as ye have demanded."

"Rise up, you may pay me homage tomorrow. And I had no doubt you would bring her here."

"The storm delayed us," Alexander said, standing. "And I am sorry."

"Do not apologize for God's will."

Margaret was relieved that he seemed only happy at their arrival, despite its delay. He was positively expansive as he turned to Isabella. But suddenly a beautifully gowned and heavily bejeweled woman stepped outside the central hall, also clad in red and gold, her hair tightly braided beneath a gold circlet. The woman was younger than Bruce, but older than either Margaret or Isabella, probably in her late twenties. She stared, unsmiling, at Bruce and Isabella, and Margaret felt certain that this was his second wife, Elisabeth de Burgh.

"Countess!" Bruce boomed. Margaret's attention was jerked back to Bruce and Isabella. He clasped her hands tightly and said, "Welcome to my royal court."

Isabella beamed. "Your Majesty!" She started to curtsy, her color high.

He hauled her upright, and then held her by both arms. "Do not bow to me yet. Isabella—how beautiful you remain!"

Her eyes shined. "Thank you, Rob—Your Majesty."

Margaret was horrified. Isabella was smitten with Robert Bruce. Her feelings were so obvious; they were expressed all over her face.

"I am so pleased you have come, Isabella. I have a great need of you."

"I could not wait to come and help you to become king!" she cried earnestly. "I have dreamed of this day!"

Margaret felt despair stab through her. Isabella was not worldly, never mind that she had thought so for a moment at Balvenie. She was young and flirtatious, she was impressionable and impulsive. But most of all, she was in love with Robert Bruce.

"Do ye wish to stay astride forever?"

She jerked as Alexander spoke, rather teasingly, but so softly no one could hear.

But her attention returned to Bruce and Isabella. "And you will be a great help to me! We despaired, Isabella, when Alexander did not arrive yesterday, and I was crowned anyway. But we will hold another coronation tomorrow!" He turned, scanning everyone present. "Tomorrow, at Caislean Credi, the Countess of Fife will lead me to my crown!" he roared.

Everyone present roared back in approval.

And Isabella gazed upon Bruce with open adoration.

Margaret looked past Bruce. His wife stood unsmiling on the top step before the central hall, surrounded by several noblewomen. She was as still as a statue, and clearly displeased.

Alexander laid his hand on top of her knee.

She inhaled. As distraught as she was, as frightened—for Isabella, who would apparently still be used by Bruce as his pawn—Alexander's touch aroused her in many ways. He had her attention, and he also made her instantly wonder what they would do now. Were they to continue their secret love affair? An insane part of her hoped so!

But if she was ever found out, she was doomed.

He smiled at her and took her hands, tugging her down from her horse. Margaret landed in his arms.

"All will be well," he said softly, and then he released her.

"Lady Comyn."

Margaret froze at the sound of Bruce's voice. Slowly, she turned, wishing he had not noticed her.

He smiled at her, though it did not reach his eyes. Instantly, she dropped into the lowest curtsy she had ever performed. Keeping her head bowed, she said, "Your Majesty."

"You may rise," Bruce said, his gaze sharp.

She was a Comyn and Bruce's rival—but she was now in his court. She shifted, stepping closer to Alexander, aware now of a rising sense of fear.

"Is it Lady Comyn? Or have you wed Alexander?"

Margaret did not know what to say. "My uncle refused Alexander's offer, Your Majesty."

"And you, Lady Margaret? Have you refused his offer, as well?"

She inhaled. If she confessed that she had refused Alexander, what would Bruce do? If she admitted to maintaining loyalty to her family, would he imprison her?

"Lady Margaret has decided to speak with her brother." Alexander stepped between them. But he spoke casually, as if they were discussing the recent storm and nothing more. "If he gives her his blessing, she will defy her uncle and marry me."

She hadn't said any such thing, but wisely, Margaret did not speak.

"Good." Bruce confronted Margaret, his stance wide. "At Castle Fyne, I tolerated your politics. But I have no patience for such loyalties now. I have given Alexander my approval for your marriage. The sooner you wed him, the better it will be—for you, for him…for me."

He was threatening her. She nodded and cast her head down, but inwardly, she was shaken and afraid.

"Lady Margaret," he snapped.

She flinched at his tone and looked up.

"Beware. I have no use for spies." His blue eyes blazed.

She wished to cringe. Did he think she meant to spy on him? Did she?

"She will not spy," Alexander said.

"If she spies, she will pay the price for such actions, no matter how you care for her. I suggest you guard her well." And then he smiled at them. "Come, we will continue to celebrate my crowning." Bruce turned, indicated for Isabella to join him, and hurried back up the stairs.

Margaret stared after him and Isabella, watching him as he put his arm around his wife—the queen. Isabella seemed taken aback by the gesture, and having no choice, she fell into step behind him and his wife. They vanished inside, followed by their coterie of soldiers, hangers-on, ladies-in-waiting and gentlemen in attendance.

Margaret began to shake. "I am Bruce's enemy, Alexander."

Alexander put his arm around her. "No. Yer with me." His face was hard. "Dinna do anything foolish. I can protect ye, but not if ye betray the king."

Margaret nodded. She had no wish to become Robert Bruce's prisoner, not now, not ever.

MARGARET FOLLOWED ALEXANDER into the central hall of the abbey, entirely aware of the position she was in. A terrible tension beset her. She was Margaret Comyn, the Earl of Buchan's niece—a rival to the king. Indeed, she was the only rival to the king present. She would be considered a traitor by everyone at the abbey.

And now that Robert was King of Scotland, she was very much at his first court. She glanced swiftly around. The hall was filled to overflowing with ladies and noblemen. The queen and her women had taken up one end of the hall, where they were seated at a long table, Isabella with them, along with Marjorie—Atholl's wife.

The women were conversing quietly, but Isabella was distracted—her gaze was on Bruce.

Margaret watched her for a moment, grimly. In a short amount of time, everyone at Scone would realize how Isabella felt about her king. She then realized that Elisabeth was watching her, as well. The queen was not quite scowling, but her expression was dismissive and filled with disdain. She disliked Isabella already.

Margaret turned her gaze. Bruce was surrounded by a great many of his noblemen, including Atholl. They had gathered by the hall's single hearth. Servants were giving everyone cups of wine. Other followers stood about in groups, everyone animated and pleased.

Alexander leaned close. "I must attend Bruce, Margaret. I will find out where ye will reside while we are here."

She almost asked him not to leave her, but managed to refrain. "How long will we stay here?"

"Bruce will not linger. Unless he has changed his plans, he will march on Monday."

"Where will you go on Monday?"

His gaze held hers. "I will march with Bruce, and we will discuss that later." He gave her a significant look, then strode away, approaching Bruce.

He would go to war in two more days! And what would her fate be on Monday? Where would she go?

She thought about what he had told Bruce—that she would go to Castle Fyne to speak to Will. Surely that had been a ploy to please Bruce—hadn't it?

Margaret hugged her mantle close, watched him speaking to Bruce. A moment later a woman paused directly before her. Golden-haired and blue-eyed, she did not smile. "I am Lady Seton—Christopher Seton's wife. Robert has asked me to introduce myself and show you to your chamber, Lady Comyn."

Surprised, Margaret met her cool gaze and thought,

She does not like me. She had called Bruce "Robert," indicating that they were familiar, and hadn't Christopher Seton been with Bruce at Dumfries during Red John's murder? Rumor had it he had even deflected blows sent toward Bruce. "You may call me Lady Margaret," she said carefully.

"Very well. And you may call me Lady Christina. How odd this is, that you are here." She started to walk from the hall.

Margaret followed. Several responses came to mind, but she held them all back. This woman was married to one of Bruce's closest knights. They were, most definitely, enemies.

They left the hall and walked up a narrow stairwell in silence, Margaret deliberately remaining behind her. Christina went past several chambers, finally pausing before a small room filled with pallets and chests. Margaret suddenly felt a pang, wishing Eilidh and Peg were with her here, and not back at Balvenie where they remained when Margaret and Isabella were taken.

Christina stood aside, gesturing into the room. "You will sleep here, Lady Margaret. The abbey is a large one, but Robert already has a great many followers and a large court, so we are terribly crowded."

Margaret now realized that Christina had the same hard blue eyes as Bruce. "Are you his sister?"

"You did not know?" She was cool, but surprised.

Margaret managed a smile. "You have a passing resemblance."

She folded her arms across her chest. "That is what everyone says. In any case, I am going back downstairs. You may rest here or you may join us." She shrugged, clearly indifferent.

Margaret suddenly touched her sleeve, forestalling her. "I am not a threat to you."

Her stare was as cold as ice. "Really? You are the Earl of Buchan's niece and ward. I am Sir Christopher's wife—and King Robert's sister. You are very much a threat. You should not be here, Lady Margaret."

"I did not think Isabella should come here, to commit sheer folly, without a friend."

"Do not think to turn her against us."

Margaret froze. Christina Seton was as ambitious as her brother, she realized. She would see him crowned king, no matter the consequences.

"Unless you mean to marry the Wolf and pay homage to my brother, you should go home, Lady Comyn, back to Buchan, back where you otherwise belong." Christina turned abruptly and left.

Margaret sought the closest pallet—her legs would not hold her—and sat down.

Christina Seton *hated* her. That much was clear. But then, wasn't Margaret one of Bruce's greatest rivals? Not by will, but by legacy?

She was afraid to go back downstairs; she knew that every one of Bruce's supporters would regard her with suspicion and hostility—everyone except for Isabella and Alexander.

Maybe Christina Seton was right—she should choose. Either marry Alexander or go home to Balvenie.

The mass was almost over. Margaret sat with Isabella behind the queen and her ladies, Bruce seated on the other side of the aisle with all the men, in the abbey's grandiose church. No seat was to be had, and behind the last row of benches, his soldiers stood, crowding into all the available space of the old church.

Margaret did not move as the worshippers were dismissed and everyone began to rise. Conversation and some laughter filled the ancient church. The women in front of her began to chat eagerly and happily; only the queen did not speak. On the other side of the aisle, the men were behaving boisterously. Bruce was in especially high spirits. He turned toward the women, smiling at his wife. Then he gestured to Isabella.

Isabella smiled widely and hurried over to him.

Margaret watched them stoically. Yesterday she had been kept away from Isabella. Christina Seton must have decided it would be dangerous otherwise. As worried as she was about Isabella's fate, she must worry about her own future. For she and Alexander had not had another moment in which to seriously speak. Tomorrow he would go to war, and she did not know if he meant to send her home. Yet she could hardly remain at Bruce's court.

As she stood up now, her gaze moved across the aisle to where Alexander stood, his smile pleased, his posture indolent and relaxed. He was so rarely in such a frame of mind that she paused to stare openly at him, and in spite of the dire situation, her heart raced. If he was leaving tomorrow, they must find time to spend together tonight.

He was speaking with Atholl and Marjorie, but he glanced immediately back at her, his smile vanishing. She knew he felt as she did; that they must seek some privy time together.

The congregation was filing outside. They would all walk from the abbey to Caislean Credi, the Hill of Credulity. There, Bruce would be crowned another time.

Margaret was one of the last to leave the church, and when she stepped into the courtyard, Alexander fell into step beside her. He took her arm. "How did ye sleep last night?"

"Surprisingly well, considering that I have resigned myself to watching Isabella destroy her marriage." She would not share how difficult it was to be at court, surrounded by so much animosity and suspicion.

"But she crowns Scotland's king." His eyes blazed. "Today, the Countess of Fife earns her place in the legends of this proud land."

Margaret decided not to comment, as she did not think becoming a part of a legend the kind of fortune her friend needed. They walked in silence from the courtyard, following the huge crowd up the hill, Bruce and Queen Elisabeth clad in crimson and gold, and mounted on fine white horses.

A great crowd had gathered atop the hill; men, women and children having come from all over Scotland, both on Friday and now, to witness this second coronation of Scotland's king. Margaret and Alexander walked past the crowd until they had reached the very front row, where Atholl, his wife and the other earls and countesses stood. She saw Christina Seton with a handsome, golden-haired man. They were holding hands, speaking quietly to one another, smiling. And Christina seemed entirely changed—somehow, she was soft and pretty now—and it was almost impossible to recall how cold and cruel she had been yesterday.

Bruce stood alone in the center of the cleared hilltop, not far from a handsome throne. He looked very much like a king, in his red-and-gold surcote and hose, his head erect with pride, his blue gaze brilliant and burning.

Elisabeth, the queen, stood apart from him with the bishop of Glasgow, who was unfolding various vestments and a robe, long guarded and kept in secret for just such a day. Today, Elisabeth was as impassive as usual, but she was almost pretty, in her red ermine-trimmed gown.

She stared at her husband unblinkingly. It was impossible to know what she felt.

Isabella waited with the other bishops, a short distance from Bruce. She was stunningly beautiful in a pale white robe, her long dark hair loose, her cheeks flushed, a gold circlet in her hands.

The crowd had become terribly silent. Bishop Wishart now approached, a sword in hand. Margaret realized she was watching with bated breath. She glanced at Alexander, and saw he was as rapt as she was—as everyone was. She looked back at the ceremony.

Bishop Wishart had handed the sword to Robert, and now, he placed the ancient robes about his shoulders. Then he began to administer the oath Bruce must take to become King of Scotland. Bruce's head was bowed.

"And from this day, you will be King Robert I, the king of every man born in Scotland." Wishart now turned, gesturing to Isabella.

Margaret inhaled, as Bruce looked up and as Isabella started forward.

A great many gasps and murmurs sounded as Isabella hurried toward Bruce, her eyes filled with excitement, the circlet in one of her hands. She had never been as beautiful. She appeared to have come from a dream—as if an angel. Bruce's blue eyes burned with fervor, with heat, and they were riveted upon her.

Isabella paused before him, their gazes locked. Then she took his hand, almost shyly, and he smiled at her. Blushing, she led him a few short steps to the throne.

Margaret felt chills. She glanced at the queen.

There was no expression on her face, none.

Bruce sat down, adjusting his robes. Isabella placed the circlet on his head.

Margaret felt more chills racing up and down her arms

as the crowd roared in approval. Alexander, Atholl and the noblemen standing with them all roared, as well.

She hugged herself, feeling very much as if swept up in an avalanche. Yet it wasn't exactly frightening....

A poet stepped forward, a parchment in hand. Smiling, he began to read the long genealogy of this king, going back centuries, naming ancient kings Margaret had never heard of.

Alexander slipped his arm around her.

Startled, Margaret looked up at him and saw how widely he was smiling. She realized the bard had ceased his litany, and Wishart cried, "King Robert of the Scots!"

Margaret stepped closer to Alexander, so their bodies were melded, as the crowd shouted back, "King Robert of Scotland!"

Tears arose. Wasn't it better to have a Scot king, than to answer to King Edward?

"King Robert! King Robert the Bruce!" the crowd chanted.

Alexander suddenly grasped her waist and lifted her high.

"What are you doing?" she cried. He was twirling her about, as if in a dance, but then, a great many men and women were dancing wildly now.

He suddenly set her down, his hands on her shoulders. "Will ye celebrate with me?" His eyes gleamed.

Her heart lurched. She knew exactly what he wished. "Yes."

He grinned at her. And then he swept her up against his chest and kissed her, deeply.

Margaret gasped for air when he was done and he had set her back on her feet. Then she realized that the Earl of Atholl was staring at her. He smiled slightly at her before turning to Scotland's king and queen.

She tensed. He knew she and Alexander were lovers. If Atholl was still pretending allegiance to Buchan, would he tell him of Margaret's betrayal? But he was with Bruce—he had betrayed Buchan himself—and she knew that. Perhaps he wouldn't be so quick to share what he knew, then.

ALEXANDER PUT HIS arm around her and they approached Bruce, who stood with Elisabeth now. Isabella stood behind him, and he and the queen were surrounded with the noblemen and women of his court. Margaret saw Bruce take Elisabeth's hand and kiss it.

And Robert Bruce said, very loudly, for a great many to hear, "From this day forward, you are queen and I am king of Scotland."

His wife widened her eyes. "Really? For I think we are only playing at being king and queen, very much like small children."

Margaret bit back a gasp.

Bruce darkened. "You are queen, Elisabeth," he warned, "and I am king of the Scots."

Elisabeth smiled and did not speak.

ALEXANDER GAVE HER such a promising look that she failed to breathe, and then he pulled her down behind a line of trees. Margaret seized his broad shoulders as he came down on top of her, and their mouths fused wildly.

As they kissed on a bed of grass and pine needles, she could hear the crowd atop the hill; there was so much happy laughter. Alexander's tongue moved deep. Margaret kissed him back as thoroughly, briefly blinded by her need. How she had missed him during her time at Balvenie. In a way, she missed him still, for she was acutely aware that little time remained for them to be together now.

But the crowd that had just witnessed Bruce being crowned for a second time was beginning to disperse. The sound of their conversation and laughter was growing louder, as the noblemen and women, the farmers and their wives, the soldiers, began descending the hill. In a moment, the crowd would be walking just past them, unaware of where they lay hidden among the trees.

Alexander tugged her skirts up to her waist. "Ignore them," he whispered.

His touch was deft and Margaret gasped. But then she heard the gentlemen who were walking so closely by them.

"The queen is furious with Bruce," a male passerby said.

Alexander went still, listening now as she did.

"He has made her Queen of Scotland, she should be pleased," a familiar voice answered. It was Atholl.

Margaret had frozen as Alexander held her closely. She could just glimpse the line of people walking past the trees that hid them, and she could see the three closest men—Atholl walked with Lennox and another nobleman whom she recognized but did not know. A part of her wanted to listen, a part of her feared discovery and part of her did not want Alexander to stop making love to her.

"Bruce will do as he pleases," Lennox said. "And Isabella is very pleasing." He laughed.

"I know Isabella well. I also know Buchan. I fear for her," Atholl replied.

"The queen will not tolerate her for long," the third man said. "But she will never harm Isabella while she is in Bruce's favor."

"And for how long will that be?" Lennox asked.

"She has risked her life to crown him—Bruce will never forget that," Atholl said with vehemence.

And the three men were gone.

Alexander suddenly moved over her. Margaret's gaze flew back to his strained face.

"How can ye be distracted now?" he asked softly.

"You were listening, too," she managed to say.

He slowly smiled at her. Margaret lost her ability to breathe as he pushed slowly into her, watching her every reaction. She gave up all coherent thought, surrendering to the shocking pleasure. And she collapsed beneath him, trying not to cry out.

"Now that is better," he said roughly, but low.

Sometime later, when Alexander had grunted in satisfaction, he held her, hard. Margaret held him in return, as he rolled to his side, taking her with him. She did not move, waiting for her pulse to subside. Alexander kissed her temple.

She took a long breath. Sanity returned. So did coherent thought. And the only sounds in the forest were the birds singing in the trees above them and their own labored breathing. Margaret could see through the trees to the path leading down the hill to the abbey. It was empty.

"Do ye have to worry about Isabella now?" he asked, his mouth moving against her temple.

"Yes. You heard them. She is causing gossip. Gossip that will surely reach Buchan. If Robert ever sends her away, I fear for her."

"He is a man of great loyalty. He always rewards his allies. She may be his lover now, but Lennox is right, he will never forget what she has done for him." He shifted to his side so he could look more directly at her.

How she wished she was as certain as Alexander and Lennox, but she had doubts. Now Bruce meant to reward

Isabella. But what about a year from now—or even ten? "I wonder if Bruce's ambition dwarfs even his loyalties."

Alexander sat up. "That is a dangerous remark, Margaret. For it would mean that he would give up those who have stood by him, if ever his ambition demanded it."

She had made her terrible point. Dismay claimed her. No good was going to come of Isabella's actions, she was certain. Her marriage was in ruins, and her fate was uncertain. Then she recalled that terrible instant when she and Atholl had made eye contact at the coronation. "I think Atholl knows about us."

"And if he does?"

"He has been friends with my uncle for years—since I was a child, at least. What if he tells him?"

"If he returns to the peel at Strathbogie he will hardly be inviting Buchan to dinner. And ye ken his secrets."

"I HOPE YOU are right," she said. "What if he has told his wife? Isabella suspects us, as well. She is so naive—she might say something by mistake."

His gaze turned searching. "I said I'd protect ye, Margaret. I mean to do just that. If ye stay with me, it will not matter what Buchan knows."

Margaret stared into his unwavering gaze. He would not be able to protect her from Buchan's wrath if she returned to Balvenie, and he was at war. "And for how long will I be with you? You are going to war with Bruce tomorrow."

Alexander's expression changed as he stood lithely up. He held out his hand and Margaret gave it to him, so he could pull her to her feet. "We march north, on Dundee," he said in agreement.

She shivered, her mind suddenly filled with ghastly and bloody images of battle—all far too real—all with

Alexander in the midst of the fighting. "God, I do not like it when you go to war."

"I am a warrior."

She wet her lips as they exchanged long stares. Her mind returned to the dilemma she faced. Where was she to go? Was she free to leave if she wished? She did not believe that Alexander would detain her against her will. Not now. "And what of me? Where will I go tomorrow?"

"Bruce sends his women to Aberdeen. In the north, they will be safe."

"Does he fear that his enemies will capture his queen and her ladies?"

"'Tis possible. He must make certain to keep them safe. Ye could stay with Queen Elisabeth, Margaret."

He had spoken as if he was making a suggestion. "Are you giving me a choice?"

He glanced aside. "Ye would not have to face Buchan if ye stay with the queen. Ye'd not have to face Sir Guy."

He hadn't answered her. But she did not believe that Alexander would keep her forcibly now. And that meant she did have a choice—to stay with the queen and her women, or return to Balvenie. "Even if the queen would allow me to join her court, how could I do so? Bruce doesn't trust me. The women do not trust me. I am a Comyn—I am one of his enemies. Surely, I would have to pay homage to King Robert." She recalled Christina Seton's words—either that, or she could marry Alexander.

"If I speak fer ye, ye will be allowed to join Queen Elisabeth's court," he said flatly. "If ye stay with the women, ye could wait fer me."

Margaret felt torn. She wanted to wait for Alexander to return to her. But then what? Was she to simply disavow her loyalty to her uncle, her brother and the entire Comyn family?

Was she to stay with Queen Elisabeth during this terrible war, while her family fought Bruce from its other side?

"Isabella will stay with the queen," Alexander suddenly said. "She wishes to stay—as she cannot go home. Will ye stay at court to protect Isabella?"

Margaret was aware that Alexander thought to manipulate her. She hesitated. She was truly reluctant to go home to Balvenie. But the idea of staying with Queen Elisabeth was frightening—even if she wished to protect Isabella. God, what would her dear mother do in such a circumstance, in such times? "You are trying to convince me to choose to stay. Unfairly, you are using Isabella to do so."

"Aye, I am trying to convince you to stay with the queen and her women," he said. "I want ye here—waiting fer me."

She was so tempted to stay. But he was asking for so much. "You are asking me to change my loyalties—again," she said slowly. "But if I stayed here, I would not remain as your lover. You are actually asking me to stay—and marry you."

"I haven't hidden my true desire," he said harshly. "So what will ye choose, Margaret?"

She felt as if she approached the precipice of a dangerous cliff. One more step, and she would surely leap off—but to what fate? "It is probably best that I return to Balvenie, for now."

"Fer now?" He was angry and incredulous at once. "Ye will stay loyal to yer damned uncle?" he exclaimed. "Ye will marry Sir Guy?"

"It's not just Buchan," she cried. "And I cannot marry Sir Guy now—you must know that!" And as she spoke, she faced her innermost thoughts and feelings. It was true. She could not marry the Englishman. "Maybe, just maybe, this damned war will end, sooner, not later!" She reached for him.

He dodged her efforts. "Buchan will never release ye from the union." He was hard now. "Very well. If ye wish to return, ye shall."

And before Margaret could thank him, he spun on his heel and strode away.

IT WAS LATE, and there was little revelry in the abbey's great room now. The fires in the hall's two hearths were dying. A great many soldiers were taking to their pallets upon the floor there. A few men and women remained at the tables with their wine, but most of the court had already retired, as had the king and queen.

Margaret was exhausted, and she had wanted to leave the celebration hours ago, but she had decided to remain because of Alexander.

Tomorrow Bruce would take his army north, while his women went to Aberdeen under his brother's care. She would ride with them, and be given an escort to continue home once they had reached the city.

Tonight was her last night at Bruce's court, and for that, she was relieved. On the other hand, it was also her last night with Alexander.

He had been in conversation with Atholl for some time, and she could not imagine what they were discussing. But he had not looked her way even once, and she knew he was very angry with her.

She wondered if he would signal her to join him later, so they could spend one last night together.

Her heart hurt terribly now. Leaving him this time was so much harder than before. She cared far too much.

And she was so worried now about her return to

Balvenie—and the confrontation she must have with her uncle.

Isabella also remained in the hall, having drunk a bit too much wine. She now came over to Margaret, having unsuccessfully tried to converse with the queen's women for some time. She sighed. "You have been staring at Alexander all night!"

Margaret felt herself flush. "I am returning to Balvenie, Isabella. I intend to try to convince Buchan that you were coerced into participating in the coronation."

Isabella shrugged. "I would not waste my breath, Margaret, but you are a dear friend." Her gaze now settled on Alexander. "Why don't you admit that you are smitten? Why don't you surrender to him? Why not marry a great warrior who can keep you and your lands safe?"

Margaret tensed. What would Isabella say if she knew just how tempting such a decision was? "I do care deeply for Alexander, but my mother raised me to be loyal. How can I forget her now?"

Isabella shook her head, confused. "Your mother is dead, Margaret, but you are very much alive!"

Margaret did not bother to tell her that her mother's legacy remained very much alive—and that it always would. She glanced at Alexander again, now conversing with Sir Christopher Seton. He had drunk a great deal of wine, and he was finally smiling. But she was not deluded. He remained upset with her.

Suddenly a squire tapped upon Isabella's shoulder. Isabella whirled, relief written all over her face. "Will you come with me, Countess?" the boy asked politely.

Bruce was sending for her, Margaret thought, amazed. Never mind that he was upstairs—as was his queen.

"I must go," Isabella cried, hugging her. Her eyes

were bright—shining. Then she dashed off, the squire behind her.

Dread began. There would be no discretion then, between the king and his lover?

Christina Seton paused before her, unsmiling. "You are a very fortunate woman."

"It is late, Lady Seton. Can we spar another time?"

"My brother is a fool, to allow you to return to Buchan after you have been with us! But Alexander has somehow convinced him you will not harm us. I do not believe it, not for a moment!"

Margaret realized Christina wasn't hateful, she was afraid. "I have no secrets to tell," she said.

"I worry for my husband and my brother every day." She whirled and hurried away.

Margaret bit her lip, suddenly filled with compassion and understanding—how could she not be? She worried every bit as much about Alexander. And as she had that thought, he caught her arm from behind.

She turned, her heart slamming. "My leaving doesn't mean I don't care."

"One day, ye will realize ye changed yer loyalties long ago, and ye now live a charade." He was unsmiling and grim. "Let us hope that day isn't a day too late."

She took his unyielding hand. "Is it true? Did you have to convince Bruce to let me return home?"

"He wants us wed." He glanced down at their locked hands. "He thinks I'm a fool."

"Then how did you ever manage to persuade him?"

"He needs my sword and he needs my men. He needs my brothers and their armies." His grasp suddenly tightened. "I am trying not to be angry, because I ken ye so well. It is late. Let's go to bed. We leave early on the morrow."

Her heart raced. Even such a strong disagreement could not diminish the attraction and affection they shared. And they had so little time, she thought, gripping his hand more tightly. She didn't want to even ask when she would next see him again.

She heard rushed footsteps, and then someone was calling Alexander's name as the front doors to the abbey slammed. Padraig's son and the messenger, Seoc, rushed into the hall, his brat dusted with snowflakes.

She felt frozen. Hadn't Seoc come from Castle Fyne?

Alexander hurried to him. "What has happened?" he demanded.

Seoc was muddy, damp and breathing hard. "My lord! Castle Fyne is under attack."

Margaret felt the floor tilt. *Sir Guy had finally attacked.*

"Is it Sir Guy?" Alexander demanded.

"Aye, and he has two or three thousand men and perhaps a hundred knights!"

Margaret could not breathe. Sir Guy was no fool, oh, no! He probably knew she was with Alexander, and perhaps even at Scone with Scotland's new king!

Alexander was already striding past her, toward the stairs. Margaret rushed after him, tripping in her haste. He did not stop for her, hurrying up them with long strides. Lifting her skirts, she followed.

And at the top of the steps, two huge Highlanders barred his way. Both were heavily armed.

"I must speak with the king," Alexander said. "I have urgent news."

Panting, Margaret paused behind Alexander as one guard went to the first closed door and knocked upon it. "A messenger has come, Your Majesty, and Alexander MacDonald says he must speak with you!"

A brief moment passed. But then the door opened, revealing Bruce, barefoot and in a simple leine. His hair was disheveled, his color high. Margaret could see past him into a large chamber, illuminated by the fire within. Isabella lay there in its bed, amidst the blankets, which were loosely draped about her obviously naked body, her long hair loose and flowing about her bare shoulders.

Margaret knew she could not worry about their open affair now, but she was terribly dismayed.

"What passes?" Bruce demanded, his eyes flashing.

"Sir Guy has attacked Castle Fyne with two or three thousand men. May I have yer permission to relieve the siege and defend the keep?" Alexander asked, speaking swiftly and sharply.

"You have my permission. And Alexander—make damn certain we do not lose Castle Fyne to the English!" Bruce said harshly.

Alexander did not reply, but Margaret knew he meant to do more than keep the castle; he meant to finally kill Sir Guy. She stepped forward, trembling, aware of her own audacity now. "Take me with you."

Both men saw her at once. In unison, they turned to regard her. Alexander seemed incredulous, but Bruce stared, his speculation obvious.

Their scrutiny was unnerving. She inhaled. "Castle Fyne is mine—it is my legacy from my mother. I must go with Alexander!" She was pleading with the king, her gaze locked with his.

She instantly saw that Alexander meant to object. But before he could speak, Bruce held up his hand.

He stepped forward, past Alexander. His relentless gaze upon her and her alone, he spoke to Alexander.

"Defeat Sir Guy—kill him, if you can—and take Lady Margaret with you." He slowly smiled at her. "After all, it is her home—and that is where she should be."

CHAPTER FIFTEEN

THEY MADE CAMP along the pebbled shores of Loch Riddon, the high, rocky peaks of Cruach Nan Cuilean looming over them. They had ridden without pause for two days and two nights. The firs and pine crept almost to the shores of the loch itself, leaving a long but narrow clearing for Alexander's men. Margaret hugged herself, so exhausted she could barely stand, as Dughall and another lad erected Alexander's tent at the forest's edge. Around her, his men were swiftly preparing for the night ahead. She ignored the sight of so many tents and cook fires being prepared, so many horses being watered and fed, so many arrowheads and knives being sharpened. Instead, she stared at the mountain.

Sir Guy had attacked Castle Fyne.

Even now, her home was under siege.

She rubbed her forearms, the afternoon chilling. Inwardly, she felt sick, as she had for the past two days. The prospect of her home falling under Sir Guy's control was terrifying. She had finally realized she could not marry him, no matter how Buchan wished for the alliance, no matter how greatly it served the Comyn family. But if it did fall, what would happen to her?

She knew she must worry over far greater matters than her own tiny future. But if Castle Fyne fell, Buchan would never release her from the impending union with Sir Guy.

She glanced across the encampment, where Alexander spoke with some of his best Highland soldiers. His expression had not changed since they had left Scone Abbey—it was set with determination. He would not lose Castle Fyne.

She did not want to think about what he had told her about his deceased wife now, but she did. He had become involved with her for revenge—he had said so. And he had gone to battle, not for his mistress, who would later become his wife, but for Glen Carron, the stronghold he wished to possess.

She was certain that Alexander cared for her. But if Castle Fyne fell, would he be as eager to take her to wife? Would he wish to take her to wife at all? After all, she was already his mistress, and she would bring nothing to their union!

But she might not even have that choice. She wished her last thoughts were not screaming at her, but they were. If Sir Guy conquered the castle, there would be so much pressure brought upon her to go forward with the marriage....

The shadows of the late afternoon were lengthening. Alexander had dismissed his men, and he was starting toward her. Margaret glanced up at Cruach Nan Cuilean, remembering the last time she had been within its reach. She would never forget how Alexander had fought over her—and Castle Fyne—with Sir Guy then. She would never forget how it had ended—in hatred, with threats. Sir Guy had sworn to kill Alexander. Since then, his desire for vengeance had escalated. Since then, his hatred had grown. And since that battle, Alexander had vowed to kill Sir Guy.

It had become a blood feud.

She was afraid of what might happen when they next met—perhaps tomorrow—on the battlefield.

Alexander's tent now stood entirely aloft, his banner flying above it. As he approached, she felt her knees buckle.

He caught her, some alarm in his eyes. "I would never wish ye here!" he exclaimed. "Only Robert would think to send ye with me."

"I am tired. Some rest and I will be fine," she said, but it felt like a lie. She was so frightened about the morrow. She was so frightened about the entire future!

"I canna worry about ye now, Margaret, yet that is what I must do." He released her grimly, his gaze veering past her, as if he wished to espy the enemy upon the horizon.

She studied him. His focus was on Sir Guy and Castle Fyne, not her. She said softly, "He plots to marry us, even with Castle Fyne under attack."

He started, his gaze veering back to her. "'Tis in everyone's better interest, Margaret, even yers."

She would not argue that last point now. She did not know if he was right or wrong. But it was even more tempting now than before to accept his offer of marriage. If she did, no matter what happened next, she would be out of Sir Guy's reach. Buchan could not force her into wedlock.

She thought about her mother, wishing she were alive to advise her.

"Ye should rest. Go lie down, Margaret, as I have a great deal to do."

"How can I rest—when I am so worried?"

"I will turn the English back," he said fiercely. "Sir Guy is a coward, and tomorrow, ye will see as much."

Once again, she thought of how much the two men

hated one another, and of the vows they had made. "If only there were a way to negotiate!" she cried. "If only there were a way to avoid all the bloodshed and death!" And if only there was a way to ensure that Alexander and Sir Guy did not come face-to-face. Yet that was unlikely, and she knew it.

"This is war. I must take Castle Fyne back." His blue eyes had never been as hard, as dark.

She stared unhappily at him.

"Come, Margaret. We both ken ye dinna wish to marry him now. We both ken ye'd rather I win the keep."

In that moment, she knew what her heart wished—it finally, truly wished for Alexander to defeat Sir Guy, for him to retake her castle! "Yes," she whispered.

"Of all of us, ye ken how much Sir Guy lusts fer Castle Fyne. No matter the size of my army, he willna surrender now. There is nothing to negotiate," Alexander added, his expression hard and set, his tone final. Then, "Yer dismayed. Why?"

"You always speak the truth." She could not smile. "What if the battle does not go well?"

"It will go well." He was even more adamant now. "I won Castle Fyne and it is mine. And I want ye, Margaret, as my wife. I will have both."

She met his intent gaze. Just then, it was impossible to think he would not succeed in attaining his ambitions.

Alexander suddenly stiffened. Margaret realized that he was listening to the sounds of the impending night, and then she heard approaching hoofbeats. A rider was coming into their camp at a reckless gallop—but why?

Alexander's expression changed and he turned toward the sound, as did Margaret. A horseman approached from the west. The direction of Castle Fyne.

"I sent my spies ahead this morning," Alexander said

tersely. He started toward the horseman, who was now trotting through the makeshift tents and standing men.

Margaret quickly followed Alexander, although she could not keep up with him. Padraig appeared from some other corner of the camp, as did several more of his most trusted Highlanders. She tried to increase her pace, now outdistanced, as Alexander reached up and seized the spy's bridle.

She lifted her skirts and ran, staggering somewhat. By the time she reached the group of men, Alexander's face was dark with anger. "What is it? What has happened?"

He slowly turned, his blue eyes aflame. "We're too late."

"What do you mean?" she cried.

"He breached the gates hours ago—Castle Fyne has fallen."

Margaret felt as if she had been struck in the chest. Her mind began to race.

Sir Guy had Castle Fyne—finally. She trembled, suddenly ill. Oh, God, now what should she do? She could not marry him, not for her family, and not even to get her legacy back! But he had just positioned himself in such a manner that she might have no choice. She flinched, tears arising, and met Alexander's burning gaze.

"I will not let ye go to him." His tone was hard, but controlled. It was a warning. "Ye will not return to Balvenie."

She breathed hard. She didn't want to go to Sir Guy! But did he deny her freedom now?

She rubbed her temples, trying to sort through this new, terrible crisis. "Will we now attempt a siege? You besieged the keep once—and you triumphed."

It was a moment before he spoke. "We besieged the

keep when there were but forty or fifty men within. Sir
Guy has a huge army."

His meaning dawned. "You will not attempt a siege?"
She was disbelieving.

"There is no time," he said, fists clenched.

"What do you mean?" she cried.

Alexander strode to her. "I was to defend the castle—
and return to join Bruce. He needs me and my army in
the north."

"So you will turn your back on Castle Fyne? You will
allow Sir Guy this triumph?"

"I allow nothing," he said harshly. Then, "I had
planned to attack his flank, Margaret, while he besieged
the keep. But the garrison there fell too quickly. A siege
now could take weeks—but more likely, it would take
months—and Bruce does not have weeks or months. As
soon as word of his coronation spreads, King Edward
will send forth every single man he can muster. The war
for Scotland's crown begins."

She hugged herself, still in disbelief. God, Buchan
would put her under terrible pressure to marry Sir Guy.
And all while Alexander fought with Bruce to keep Scotland's crown! And where would she now go? To Queen
Elisabeth's court?

"There is more."

Alexander had spoken so tersely that she cringed.
Margaret dared to look up at him, knowing whatever he
meant to reveal it would not be in their better interest.

"Yer brother was wounded in the siege."

She gasped. "William was hurt?"

"Aye."

Margaret began to shake. William had been wounded.
Her only living brother, whom she had not seen in over

a month.... Fear clawed at her. "Oh, God—how badly is he hurt?"

"Badly."

She could not move, and for a moment, she could not speak. Then, "Is he dying?"

Alexander grimaced.

She hit him, hard, across his huge forearm, and pain shot through her hand. "Tell me!" she screamed. "Is he dying?"

"I dinna ken," he shouted back, a roar. "But he is badly wounded, so aye, he could die, there is that chance!"

She hit him again, but weakly, and this time, she was crying.

But she knew what she must do—what her duty was now. Then the words came forth, unbidden. "I am going to him."

He grasped her by her arms. "If ye go to him, Sir Guy willna let ye go, ye will be his prisoner—and then ye will become his wife."

She fought for air. She knew he was right. Sir Guy would hold her against her will. He would control her fate. She would become his wife.

But if William died, and she did not see him first, she would never be able to live with herself. "Let me go," she managed to say. "Get me a horse. Take me to my brother."

Roughly, he released her. He gave her one last look— his expression hard. To his men, he said, "Take her to Castle Fyne."

And she began to realize what was truly happening. Tears fell. "Alexander," she whispered.

But his back was turned; he walked away.

CASTLE FYNE WAS ahead. Everyone halted their horses at the edge of the woods, the castle above them, atop the hill. And then the bells in the watchtower began tolling.

Margaret felt sick. They had ridden out of the camp immediately, as she could not wait until dawn to see William. By dawn, he could be dead.

There had been no time to send a messenger, no time to do anything other than to mount up and ride out. The shadows of the late afternoon had given way to the fading light of dusk. A crescent moon was emerging in the purple sky above the keep.

A dozen Highland soldiers had accompanied her. Margaret's mare was in their midst, Alexander astride his gray stallion at their forefront. He had not spoken to her since she had decided that she would go to William—and put herself in Sir Guy's command.

If she were not so frightened for her brother, she would be deathly afraid of what her actions meant, not just for her, but for her relationship with Alexander. But she only knew she must see William, and that he must not die. He was the only family that she had left!

Alexander turned his stallion so he partially faced her—but he did not look at her. "Ye will ride alone from here. Identify yerself to the watch."

She flinched, for his tone was so impassive. It was as if he had also made a decision not to care. She stared, but he would not make eye contact with her.

She lifted her reins. "Alexander."

He signaled his men, who turned their mounts around, in preparation of returning to Loch Riddon. "Ye should hurry, while there's still some light," he said. He waved his men forward.

"Alexander!" she cried. But she did not know what to say, because the only words that came to mind were wildly inappropriate: *I love you.*

"Godspeed." He spurred his stallion into a trot and then a canter.

She watched, incredulous, as she was left there alone, a short distance from the barbican. He had not looked at her, not even once. And that hurt so much.

But what had she expected? She was riding into a castle under Sir Guy's command. Of course he disapproved.

But if he cared for her, wouldn't he say something in farewell?

Alexander had caught up to his men, but he suddenly halted. He turned and, from across the glade, he looked at her.

Tears blurred her vision. And she almost considered giving up her desperate need to see William—she almost spurred her own mare and galloped back to him.

But what if Will died? She could not live with herself if she turned her back on him, and she knew her mother would feel the same if she were alive.

Margaret lifted her hand.

That brief instant stretched into an eternity. Then Alexander whirled his stallion and galloped into the forest, disappearing from her view.

She choked on her grief, staring at the woods where she had last seen him. And then she summoned up every ounce of determination she had. It was over; it was time.

Margaret turned her mare and urged her into a trot, up the hill and toward Castle Fyne. As she did, archers appeared on the ramparts above her. The bells continued to toll.

She realized she was crying—that tears were sliding helplessly down her face. She already missed Alexander. She would always miss him.

But so be it. Margaret used her sleeve to dry her cheeks, and then she drew her hood down to reveal her unusually colored hair. Cries began to sound from the castle's walls. She had been recognized.

And by the time she reached the barbican the front gates had been opened. But before she could pass through them, a group of armed knights thundered through the entry tower, over the drawbridge and across the barbican toward her.

They were heavily armed, clad in mail, their visors down. Abruptly, she halted her mare. Her heart skidded in fear and alarm.

The dozen knights surrounded her. One lifted his visor as he trotted directly to her. It was Sir Guy, and he stared, surprised. "Lady Margaret!"

She somehow wet her lips. "Sir Guy. Good evening. I have come to see William. Is he still alive?"

His eyes wide, he studied her. "Yes. Is this a trap?" He scanned the land beyond her.

"No, this is not a trap—I am entirely alone," she said tersely.

His gaze slammed back to hers. "He let you go."

"Please—we can discuss this later. I am desperate to see my brother."

His stare remained searching—and now, she did not think his expression particularly welcoming. She tensed. She hadn't had the time to wonder if he might be suspicious of her relationship with Alexander—now that so many knew that they were, indeed, lovers.

He moved his steed against her mare and caught her arm. "This is a surprising but pleasing turn, Lady Margaret." And before she could object, he lifted her from his horse and placed her in the saddle in front of him.

Heat exploded in her cheeks. His arm tightened around her waist, and he was galloping back over the drawbridge and through the entry tower. "I look for-

ward to your tale, Margaret, for I cannot imagine how
you persuaded Alexander to release you."

His breath brushed her ear as she spoke. She shuddered with distaste. "I have no intention of escaping, Sir
Guy, if that is why you removed me from my mare. I am
here of my own free will, sir."

"I take no chances now," he said, sounding pleased.
"My God, I have Castle Fyne—and I have you."

She trembled again, deciding not to speak—as any
response that came to mind would most likely annoy or
provoke him. But one thing was clear. Twice he had referred to her having been released; he believed she had
been kept against her will.

He did not know of her affair. Not yet, anyway.

"Can you take me immediately to my brother, sir?
Please?" Margaret asked, as calmly as she could.

"Of course. And afterward, we will…discuss…mat-
ters."

She closed her eyes in sheer dread. She now recalled
how he had wished for a Highland handfasting at Balvenie, and she had little doubt he would wish to marry
her and consummate their marriage as swiftly as possible now.

But she would worry about Sir Guy later. First, she
must see Will.

And as they trotted across the courtyard, a great many
men and women waved at her, calling out to her. Margaret recognized most of them.

"Wave back," Sir Guy said softly. "They adore you. I
see that now. They adore the lady of Castle Fyne."

Margaret waved dutifully back.

"Alexander was a fool to release you to me," he said
in her ear.

They had reached the stairs leading to the great

hall. Sir Guy had only halted his horse and loosened his grip upon her, but Margaret was already leaping to the ground. She did not want to consider his meaning. "Where is Will?"

"He has the chamber next to mine."

Margaret lifted her skirts and raced up the wooden steps, running through the hall. Several maids rushed after her. "Can we help ye, Lady Margaret?"

Margaret recognized Eilidh's sister, Marsaili. "Is my chest still here? I will need my potions, surely, to attend my brother."

"Yes, and I will retrieve it fer ye," the second woman said.

Margaret recognized the woman who had been beside her on the ramparts, fighting off the invaders, during Alexander's siege.

She reached Will's door. It was open, and she halted there. There was so much blood. Will was so pale. And he was unconscious.

Margaret steeled herself, then she strode into the chamber.

Before she woke him up, she looked at his bandaged thigh—the linen soaked through with blood. A sword had clearly sliced through an artery. If he was still bleeding, he would certainly die!

"I need more linens," Margaret said, praying she sounded calm. "And I need a strong pair of hands— preferably male hands—in case we must stanch this again."

Will's lashes lifted. "Meg?" He was weak and disbelieving.

She knelt beside him, clasping his face and kissing his cheek. "Yes, I am here. I am going to take care of you, Will."

"I can't believe it…how did you come? And did I dream it or is Sir Guy here, as well?"

Will did not know of her divided loyalties. "Sir Guy has taken Castle Fyne from the Wolf, Will. And you must not speak, you must save your strength! I will look at your leg."

"Thank God," he murmured, eyes closing.

She touched his forehead, which was damp with sweat and hot with a fever. He was already fighting an infection.

Margaret waited until the maid had returned with a young Highland lad before she began to peel away the bloody bandages. To her relief, the wound had been cauterized and the bleeding had stopped. But the terrible gash was inflamed with an infection.

Marsaili returned with her chest. Margaret smiled at her grimly. "Now we will save my brother's life," she said.

SIR GUY WAS seated at the table in the great hall, still, when she paused on its threshold several hours later. She tried to control her dismay. She had hoped he would have gone to bed, though she had not thought that likely.

Instead, she had suspected that he would wait up for her—and she had been right.

Sir Guy looked at her, a mug of wine in his hands. He did not stand. But his gaze skimmed her bloodstained gown.

"I apologize for my appearance, Sir Guy," Margaret said, refusing to enter the hall. Everyone else within it was sleeping upon their pallets, except for two serving maids. They hovered not far from Sir Guy.

"Is your brother alive?"

Margaret tensed. She did not think Sir Guy cared

whether William lived or died. "Yes. But he has lost a great deal of blood and an infection has set in."

"Do you think he will live?"

"He will live," Margaret flared, and then she reminded herself to hold her emotions in check.

Sir Guy slowly stood. "If you are angry, be angry with MacDonald, not me. His men delivered the blow to your brother's leg, not mine."

She trembled. Of course William had been fighting with Sir Guy, against Alexander, to liberate the keep. Yet she hadn't had time to dwell on that fact.

"And William was only here because MacDonald refused to ransom him," Sir Guy added with a slight smile.

Was he trying to drive a wedge between her and Alexander? Yet why would he even think to do so? He did not know they were anything other than a captor and a captive. But he did speak the truth. If Alexander had ransomed William—or simply freed him—he would not have remained at Castle Fyne, and he would not be fighting for his life now. "William has been a prisoner here since February. As soon as he is well, I would like to send him home to Balvenie."

"Are you asking my permission?" Sir Guy seemed surprised. "I am lord here, but I am not lord over your brother. I already sent word to Buchan, by the way, telling him of my conquest, and of Will being wounded."

She wished he hadn't done so. "Then we will hear from him in return." She forced a smile. "Sir Guy, I must beg you to dismiss me. We rode for two days straight, and then I tended my brother. I am exhausted, I must change my clothes—and then I wish to stay with William. He needs my care."

Sir Guy smiled oddly. "We have a great deal to discuss, Lady Margaret. If you wish to change your soiled gown, you may do so later." He gestured. "Sit down."

It was not a request, nor was it uttered as one. Margaret felt her heart lurch with dismay, and she slowly crossed the room. Sir Guy did not move, his stare unwavering upon her. When she sat, he poured wine from a vessel into a mug and handed it to her. Then he glanced at one of the maids, standing nervously in the corner, and ordered food for her.

Margaret stared grimly at her wine, as Sir Guy sat down on the bench beside her. "There is great talk in the land," he said.

She tensed, but not because his big thigh was against hers. She looked up at him, praying gossip of her affair had not reached him.

His gray gaze was steady upon hers. "Bruce was crowned king at Scone," he said flatly. It was not a question.

Was she to admit having been there? She had come with Alexander, so of course she would have been there.

"Not once, but twice," he continued, almost softly. "Will you deny it? Will you deny being a witness to the coronation?"

She held her mug now tightly with two hands. "No."

"And the Countess of Buchan led him to the throne?"

She inhaled. So the news was out. "Yes."

Sir Guy smiled. "They say MacDonald came for her in the middle of the night, that he took her directly from her own bed."

She was shaking now. "Yes, that is what happened."

"They say she was not forced—they say she was more than willing."

She wet her lips and shook her head. "No."

"No?" His brows lifted.

She must lie for Isabella, she thought, feeling desperate. "Bruce meant to use her no matter what, Sir Guy. She decided to cooperate. She did not have a choice!"

He studied her. "The gossip is vicious, Lady Margaret, truly vicious. They say she was thrilled to crown him… and that she shares his bed."

Margaret looked helplessly at him.

"I have spies," Sir Guy said, "in a few places, mostly in the south. But Aymer, my brother, has spies amongst Bruce's most trusted men."

Margaret went still, immediately thinking of Atholl.

"You are pale," he said softly. "Surely, you do not have something to hide?"

"No," she managed to answer. And she said, not just because she wished to change the topic, "Isabella had no choice!"

"She had no choice but to crown Bruce—or to bed him? Please, do not tell me the mighty Bruce forced her to bed! The man has slept with half of the women in England. Soon, he will sleep with half the women in Scotland."

She was silent, thinking frantically, wishing she hadn't seen Isabella in Bruce's bed—for then it would be so easy to dissemble. And if Sir Guy knew all of this, didn't her uncle?

There would be no saving her marriage, she realized. But Isabella did not wish for it to be saved, anyway.

"And you, Lady Margaret?" he asked softly.

She flinched. "I beg your pardon?"

"What choices have you had?"

His gray stare was mesmerizing. "I do not comprehend you," she tried, but she did. She knew exactly where he meant to go.

"You were at the coronation."

"Yes."

"And you had no choice but to attend?"

She felt her cheeks begin to warm. "I was curious. And I was there—at Scone Abbey…." She trailed off. Oh, God, what would he say and do, next?

"Yes, you were there…. When he came for Isabella at Balvenie, did MacDonald take you from your bed, as well?"

She wanted to glance away, but his stare was so relentless that she could not look aside. "I was asleep when they intruded."

"I can only imagine," he said, unsmiling. "You were asleep, and you awoke to what? A fight in the hall below?"

She stared into his expressionless gray eyes. "The fighting did not awaken me. I awoke…when he seized me."

He made a harsh, amused sound. "Of course he seized you in your bed. How frightened you must have been."

Her cheeks were on fire now. "I was not frightened, Sir Guy. I had already been his captive for almost a month. Had he wished to hurt me, he would have done so while I was a prisoner here."

"You are such a clever woman," he murmured. "And now you will tell me that he abducted you, as well?"

"No." She shook her head, her heart thundering. "I was afraid for Isabella. I knew what they intended. I had overheard them discussing her here, at Castle Fyne, that single night Bruce was with us. She is so young, so reckless! I decided to go with them to attempt to keep her safe—to try to thwart their schemes to use her! But as you know, I failed. Isabella is headstrong."

He studied her. Then he turned his relentless gaze

away, finally. As he reached for his wine, Margaret almost collapsed.

But she knew this respite would be brief, she knew another attack was forthcoming.

He drank for a moment, then he glanced at her. "You went willingly with him."

"Because of Isabella."

"Yes, because of Isabella, because you are such a loyal friend—when you do not share a drop of blood."

"She is married to my uncle. I advised her, again and again, of the fate of her marriage, should she help his worst enemy."

"And did you advise her to stay out of Bruce's bed?"

"Yes, I did!"

"And you, Lady Margaret? All this advice you dispense, out of loyalty, with such sincerity, do you follow any of it, yourself?" He stood, legs braced.

She was too tired to stand, yet she did not like him towering over her—and she was afraid of his insinuations. "I am doing my best, Sir Guy, in these treacherous times."

"MacDonald has become fond of you. *Fond.* I comprehend his offer of marriage—he seeks what I seek—legitimacy of ownership here. But now he is *fond* of you. Just how fond has he become?"

She managed to stand up. Did he know of her affair, or not? Was he fishing—or was he playing cat and mouse? "I refused his offer of marriage, Sir Guy!" she cried. "Not once, but several times."

"So he has asked you directly?" His eyes were wide. "That begs the question then—has he seduced you?"

She was overcome with panic. How could she answer when she was a terrible liar? When lying was the only possible answer?

"Why do I even ask?" He shook his head then. "You are so loyal—even to Isabella—you are too loyal to Buchan to betray him by sleeping with the enemy! But he has tried, hasn't he? He has tried to seduce you."

Tears had arisen. It was a sign of her desperation. Why hadn't she married Alexander? This man would learn the truth, eventually, and then he would hurt her! Somehow, she nodded.

"Why did he release you?" Sir Guy demanded. "Did you use your wiles upon him?"

"No! He never kept me prisoner—because he is fond of me! I went to Scone with Isabella of my own volition! And Alexander had agreed to allow me to return to Balvenie when we received the news of your attack here." She was shaking now. She felt as if she would soon fall over.

Sir Guy was now truly surprised. "MacDonald let you return here—and he was about to allow you to return to Balvenie! And you are a valuable prize!" Sir Guy was thoughtful now. "MacDonald has become a fool. But why would Bruce release you?"

"I begged Bruce to let me go with Alexander when we heard of your attack. I do not know why he agreed, I swear to that! But he also wishes for a union between myself and Alexander—I think he thought Alexander would take Castle Fyne from you, and I would then marry him."

"A grave miscalculation on Bruce's part—and it will not be his final error," Sir Guy said. Mug in hand, he slowly paced back and forth in front of it.

Margaret had to sit back down. She could not stop trembling. "Sir Guy? I do not feel well," she said, and she meant it. She was dizzy and light-headed now. The room was beginning to sway.

He planted his hands on his hips. "I cannot believe

they let you go! But they did—MacDonald, the mighty Wolf, and Bruce, the mighty king. And now, all is to my advantage." He smiled, hard, with satisfaction.

She was going to swoon, she thought, from sheer fatigue, yet she must not do so, because Sir Guy was the enemy, and William needed her!

"Lady Margaret, we will be married this night," he said.

Margaret heard him, in horror, as the hall turned black.

CHAPTER SIXTEEN

MARGARET AWOKE AND instantly recognized the chamber she was in. It had once been her parents', and then so recently, it had become hers, but only briefly—only until Alexander had besieged Castle Fyne. Her gaze veered to the suit of mail hanging on a peg on the wall.

The bedchamber was now Sir Guy's.

She trembled. She was at Castle Fyne, and William was seriously ill, but she was Sir Guy's captive, whether he said so or not.

"My lady!" Marsaili cried, rushing to her side. "Here, take a sip of wine."

Her heart had sunk with dismay and even fear. She recalled the terrible conversation she had just had with Sir Guy. Was he suspicious of her loyalties? It seemed so. And he had said that they would consummate their marriage that very night.

Margaret quickly looked past the maid, but no one else stood in her bedchamber, much to her relief. She sat up breathlessly, her heart thudding, but she no longer felt faint. Could she fend off Sir Guy? She must—but how? And even if she succeeded in denying him the consummation he wished for, what would happen when he heard the rumors of her affair with Alexander? Would she believe her denials? Her lies?

For those rumors would reach him, sooner or later.

Margaret took a sip of the wine. She had fainted in the

great hall below once before, only to be carried upstairs by Alexander. It felt like a lifetime had passed since then.

And now, she compared the two times, the two men. When Alexander had rescued her from a swoon, she had been oddly grateful. There was no gratitude now. Even when she had been Alexander's prisoner of war, she had felt safe and protected. She was not confirmed as Sir Guy's prisoner, but she had no doubt she would not be allowed much freedom of movement, making her a veritable captive. And this time, she did not feel safe, not at all. She felt as if she were in dire jeopardy.

And she was in danger, was she not? Her entire future was at stake. What was she to do?

Would Sir Guy come for her shortly?

If he forced her to bed, they would not be considered man and wife, under Highland tradition. Tradition held she must consent to the marriage. But he could claim otherwise, and who would know the truth?

Margaret slid her legs over the bed, standing. "Did I sleep for very long?" she asked. How she hoped it was close to sunrise!

"Only a moment, my lady." She smiled, but with concern.

Margaret did not know if the maid was worried because she had fainted, or because she now lay in Sir Guy's bed. "I wish to tend my brother." William needed her, and she could use William as an excuse to hold off Sir Guy. "But first, I would like to get out of this gown."

"I can wash the gown fer ye tomorrow, lady, but in the meantime, I only have a leine fer ye."

Margaret now saw the pale, saffron-colored tunic lying upon the foot of the bed. Clearly it had been left there for her. "That will do. I am hardly a stranger to Highland garb."

"Aye, I recall ye wearing just such a leine the last time ye were with us," Marsaili said, smiling. "How is my sister?" She began helping Margaret remove her surcote.

"Eilidh is a wonderful help to me, and I wish she were here," Margaret said, meaning it. By now, both Peg and Eilidh knew she had gone with Alexander to Scone and that Bruce had been crowned there. They would not be very worried about her.

"She is a good woman," Marsaili said, with pride.

Margaret trembled from the cold as she removed her cote, left only in her chemise, which came to midthigh.

"I'll add more wood to the fire, lady, before ye come back to bed."

Margaret was going to tell her not to bother, as she would spend the night in William's chamber, when she heard a movement outside her closed door. Dread arose. And then the door opened.

Sir Guy smiled at her.

Margaret seized the leine and held it against her breasts as Sir Guy leaned against the door, smiling. Staring at Margaret, he said to Marsaili, "Leave us."

Margaret was afraid. Worse, she was almost naked. She did not like Sir Guy's stare or his smile, and she did not want the maid to leave, but she could hardly ask her to stay. Marsaili glanced at her for approval, but Margaret could not look away from Sir Guy.

"Leave us," Sir Guy snapped, annoyed at her failure to obey.

Marsaili fled past him.

SIR GUY'S HARSH expression eased as his gaze moved to the tunic she held, and then to the hem of her chemise, as if he could look through it, and then down her bare legs. "I have always thought you beautiful," he said flatly.

Oh, my God, Margaret thought, her grasp on the tunic tightening. She knew what he wanted. "Sir Guy, please allow me to dress."

He pushed himself off of the door and strode toward her. "So you are modest?" He took the tunic from her hands and tossed it to the floor. "I am enjoying the sight of you. You please me, Margaret—and we will soon be wed."

Margaret backed up, certain he could see through her thin chemise. She debated telling him they would never wed—but was afraid that would inflame him. "Our wedding is in June." She tried to sound calm.

He caught her by her arm and pulled her forward. "Do not be afraid of me, my dear," he murmured.

"If you wish to speak with me, please, allow me to clothe myself!"

His gaze moved over her thinly veiled bosom before rising. "I have conquered Castle Fyne, Margaret, as I said I would—I have defeated the damned Wolf and I am the victor here."

"I know," she breathed, when she wished to point out that he had not, precisely, defeated Alexander. He had not been present to defend the keep from Sir Guy.

"Do you know how it feels, to triumph in war?" he asked, softly, his hand warm on her arm.

"No," she answered breathlessly.

"It is a glorious feeling—there is no other feeling quite like it."

She bit her lip, not responding—she had nothing to say. But she recognized the heat in his eyes.

"I want you, Margaret, very much."

"You want Castle Fyne." The moment she spoke, she was horrified. But she could not stop. "And you have Castle Fyne."

"I want Castle Fyne, and my bride."

His thighs were rock-hard against hers. And she recognized the state he was in. Alexander had taught her that. "You are holding me too tightly," she gasped.

"But if I let you go, you will flee—I am certain. You cannot elude the man you are to wed, Margaret."

"You are hurting me," she cried, when that was not quite true.

He eased his grip, his regard puzzled. "Why do I frighten you so? Why do I believe you intend to resist me?" he asked, stroking his thumb across the line of her jaw. Margaret knew he was about to kiss her and she stiffened.

His mouth covered hers, and as it did, he closed his other hand over her breast.

Margaret cried out in protest, jerking back frantically. He locked her in his arms, kissing her deeply, thoroughly. Margaret wanted to scream at him, but she could not push away and break the kiss in order to do so.

He finally straightened, breathing hard, his gray eyes heated with lust. But he did not release her. "Why must you play the virgin now? A union is in both of our best interests."

"My brother could be dying. He needs me."

"I need you," he said harshly. "I need to consummate this union, immediately, so no man can dispute my rights here." The lust was gone from his eyes. Determination burned there.

"There is no one disputing your claim tonight!" She thought frantically. "William is deathly ill, and Buchan wishes for us to have a public wedding, in an English church!"

"God, you are disputing me!" His stare became searching. "Buchan would agree—all has changed, Margaret. I would expect you to be as eager as I am to have our union consummated—and to have my claim here strengthened, by right as well as might, so no man, not even the Wolf, will ever think to take Castle Fyne from us."

"I cannot think straight, with William so badly wounded! But I know I must obey my uncle, Sir Guy." She trembled, trying to put a small distance between them—he would not allow it. "Perhaps you should send him a letter?" She hoped to merely delay what seemed inevitable now.

"I am not sending him a letter, Margaret." He pulled her abruptly into his embrace. "You are here and we will be man and wife in a matter of minutes." He locked his arms around her and began to kiss her, hard.

Margaret struggled. "I do not consent to this marriage!" she screamed, tearing her mouth from his.

His eyes widened in shock. His grip became bruising and brutal, as if he might break her waist. "You do not consent?"

She shook her head. "I cannot marry you. I do not know you, you are English—I will not!"

"So your professions of loyalty to Buchan were a ploy?" Fury covered his face. He shook her hard. "You will not thwart me!"

She was crying as he used his body to push her backward toward the bed. Margaret tried to hit him with her fists. He ignored her blows, driving her down onto the bed and coming down on top of her. He caught her by her hair so hard she froze. His stare was ruthless now.

"Is it MacDonald?" he asked softly.

He meant to hurt her anyway, but she was afraid of what he would do if she ever admitted her love for Alexander. "Do not force me," she whispered.

His grasp on her hair tightened, he kneed her thighs

apart, and she cringed. But she knew better than to provoke him. She closed her eyes tightly, so as not to look
at his savage, ugly face.

Suddenly, Margaret heard racing footsteps coming up
the stairs, beyond the closed door and the corridor. Sir
Guy heard them as well, for his entire body went still.

The booted steps were louder now, rushing toward the
door, urgency filling the sound. The door flew open, and
one of his men stood at the threshold.

"Sir Guy! A messenger has come—from your brother!"

Sir Guy's eyes widened.

Margaret was still—she was afraid to move.

And then he looked at her, once. The look was hard
and ugly—he would return. He leapt from the bed and
strode across the chamber. And then he was gone.

For one more moment, Margaret still could not move.

And then her thoughts began. She had been given a
respite—and it was the miracle she had prayed for.

Margaret leapt forward, seizing and shrugging on the
leine as rapidly as possible. And then, about to run for the
door, she collapsed by the wall, tears blinding her. She
began to shake, wildly, uncontrollably. And she began
to retch.

He had meant to rape her.

She gasped and gagged, hugging herself, in a ball,
on the floor.

WHEN WILLIAM'S FEVER broke, it was dawn.

Margaret was disbelieving as she clasped his damp,
cool brow. For until that moment, he had been burning
up with a raging fever. But he was suddenly cool now—
the fever was gone.

Was it another miracle?

Silently, she closed her eyes and thanked God.

When she opened them, she saw her brother, resting peacefully. Pale morning light was streaming into the chamber. She had been sitting with him ever since she had left Sir Guy's chamber—when Aymer's messenger had arrived. She had spent the past few hours keeping compresses with icy lake water on his body, forcing him to drink, and alternately begging him to get better. Doing so had made it easier for her not to think about what Sir Guy had tried to do—or what he might try to do another time.

Now, she grasped her brother's damp, cool hand, hard. "Will! You have beaten the fever!" She raised it to her mouth and kissed it.

His lashes lifted and fell.

She leaned close and kissed his temple. "It is I, Margaret. You have been ill with fever—fighting an infection. We are at Castle Fyne."

Will's lashes rose again, and this time, blearily and without focus, he looked at her. "Meg?"

Before she could respond, she heard the door open. She stiffened, not turning as her stomach roiled, as dread consumed her, as fear laid its icy claws upon her.

Sir Guy said, "He will live?"

She inhaled, summoning up all of the strength and courage she had. Determined to pretend their previous encounter had not happened, she turned to him. "Yes, I believe so."

His gaze moved over her before he glanced at William briefly. He was unshaven and bleary of eye; clearly, he had been up all night, also. "King Edward has appointed my brother Lord Lieutenant of Scotland."

Margaret stared, keeping her expression blank. There had been talk of Aymer de Valence being given command of Scotland for months. She did not know how it affected her, Alexander or the war against Bruce, but it certainly gave Sir Guy great power. Had he been called away? How she hoped so. How she prayed it was so!

"Why are you not pleased? My brother now the might of England here! I will become one of the most powerful lords in Scotland, Margaret. You will become one of its reigning ladies."

They would never be man and wife, not if she could help it. "Then this is a fortunate turn."

"It is very fortunate—but not unexpected. Aymer is one of King Edward's favorites—as he should be. Bruce cannot go up against my brother and win."

Margaret stared expressionlessly—she wanted nothing more than to have Robert Bruce defeat Aymer—and Sir Guy.

Her loyalties had changed. There was no further doubt now.

The English were the enemy; Sir Guy was the enemy.

Her tension escalated impossibly at the realization.

Sir Guy glanced briefly at William again, who was watching them both as he listened to their conversation. "I must take my army back to Berwick to join my brother and his forces there. But when you are well enough, I imagine you will wish to return to Balvenie, or join us in this war."

She trembled, praying for another miracle—his immediate departure.

Will nodded. "I long to fight Bruce, with the rest of my family."

Margaret managed to remain impassive, but inwardly, she cringed. So swiftly, they were on opposite sides of the war, as he had feared—as she had feared.

Sir Guy now stared at her. "Bruce sent his wife and

her women to Aberdeen. King Edward wants them captured. Aymer has offered me the task."

Alarm flooded her, and she feared it was evident. "Is it possible to capture them? They must be well guarded."

"I have heard they are not well guarded—that they are in the care of Bruce's brother, Sir Nigel, and a handful of his best men. Are you now fond of Elisabeth de Burgh?"

She wondered if she could send word to Queen Elisabeth, and warn her that Aymer de Valence wished to capture her and her ladies-in-waiting. "I have barely said a word to her—and she has barely said a word to me."

"Ah, yes," he mocked. "You fear for Isabella."

She hadn't given Isabella a thought until then, but she imagined her fate would be dire if the queen and her women were captured. She decided not to speak.

"We have matters to discuss before I leave," Sir Guy said. "I will speak with you downstairs." He nodded curtly, spun on booted heel and left.

Margaret's shaking increased. He wished to speak with her *downstairs?*

He hadn't summoned her to the adjacent chamber. Dear God, was she being given another respite? Relief began to flood her. Moisture gathered in her eyes. Images flashed of that brutal encounter. But now was not the time to think about it.

"You are afraid of him!" Will cried weakly.

She looked at Will and nodded. And she did not think she should confide in William about what had happened—not because he was weak, but because he would be enraged.

"I knew you should not marry an Englishman! But what has happened—does he dislike you, too?"

She leaned over him. "Do not bother yourself now! You are too weak to become impassioned."

Will panted and said, "At least he got Castle Fyne back for us."

Did she dare tell him about her relationship with Alexander? Did she dare share her feelings? Was Alexander right? Would he approve of their union?

"Are you going to marry him, Meg? Is the marriage still planned?" Will asked feebly.

She stroked his hair. "I am supposed to marry him, but I cannot. Even if it means losing Castle Fyne, I cannot marry him—I despise him." She felt ill again—enough so to use the chamber pot.

Will stared widely in surprise. "Is he that horrid?"

"I do not like him, and I never have." She paused, tears filling her eyes. How she needed Will's support, his blessing. "I love someone else." And it was true. But hadn't she known on some level, for some time, that she loved Alexander?

She did not know when she had come to love him. Perhaps it had been at Balvenie, when he had come for her and Isabella in the middle of the night. Or maybe it had been the morning after the first night they had made love, when they had met in his hall, and each had admitted to not having a single regret.

But he had been so disappointed and so angry when she had left him to attend William. Was he angry, still? Surely he would forgive her eventually, and understand why she had gone to Castle Fyne.

But now what? She looked at William, who was stunned. "You have fallen in love? In such a short time?"

"Yes. I wish to marry someone else."

And dear God, it was true. Her heart leapt with excitement now. She wished to marry Alexander. Even though it meant changing sides in this war—she had already changed sides!—and it meant giving up every loyalty she had lived with for her entire life. The time had come to choose. Sir Guy had made that very clear.

"Who has claimed your heart?" Will asked harshly.

It was a moment before she spoke, fearful of his response, yet praying he would approve. "Alexander Mac-Donald."

Will choked in disbelief. "Meg? Is this a jest?" When she did not speak, when she sat stiffly, staring, he flushed with anger. "Are you mad? He is not just our blood enemy—he does not just have MacDougall blood on his hands—he rides with Bruce, in a war against us. Against me—against you!"

She trembled. "Bruce is king, Will. He was crowned a few days ago at Scone."

Will sat up, as white as snow. "And he will be hanged as the traitor he is! You have lost your wits! We are fighting Bruce, Meg—we are, you and I!"

"Did you not once say that any Scot, even Bruce, would be a better king for Scotland than King Edward?"

"You dare to argue?" He now collapsed against the pillows, panting.

"You are tiring yourself!" she cried. She quickly placed a linen compress in the icy lake water, and laid it on his forehead. "You will become ill again. Please, we should not discuss this, now."

"Does Buchan know? Of course he does not!" Now, his eyes closed.

She decided not to answer, but it was very clear—Will was not about to approve of her feelings for Alexander, and he was not going to bless a marriage between them.

"I am sorry," Margaret whispered, choking.

But Will was now asleep.

WHEN MARGARET ENTERED the hall, she saw that Sir Guy was immersed in a deep conversation with three of his men, and she overheard them discussing the transportation of three siege engines. She folded her arms, standing by the threshold, trembling. She could not have a natural reaction to him; she remained utterly afraid of Sir Guy.

"Where is Bruce now?" one of his knights asked him.

"He is on his way to Dundee, and that will be a lengthy battle." Sir Guy turned, having become aware of her.

Margaret stared back at him, aware of how ill she felt. But she dismissed the terrible, haunting sensation. In the heat of their struggle, she had lost all discipline, shouting her true feelings about their marriage to him. Now, they were serious rivals.

Her mind raced. If he believed her in opposition to their marriage, she would be held a prisoner, certainly. She might be held prisoner anyway. No matter what, no good would come of her having disclosed the truth of how she felt and what she wanted. She must somehow convince Sir Guy that she would meekly obey him, even if she did not mean it.

Sir Guy was staring at her. Not looking at his men, he said, "These matters can wait. Leave us."

The three knights turned and hurried out, leaving them very much alone in the great hall. Somehow she asked, "When are you leaving?"

"As soon as we can, within hours, or less," he said, starting toward her. He paused before her. "How that must please you."

She did not reply and she did not allow her facial muscles to move.

He smiled unpleasantly at her. "I am leaving a very strong garrison here. But MacDonald will not attack—

if that is your hope. He is with Bruce now. Castle Fyne remains ours."

She fought to keep her expression unchanged as she prayed to God to keep Alexander safe. And it did not escape her attention that Sir Guy had referred to the stronghold as theirs. "I hardly wish for Castle Fyne to be attacked another time."

"Then, finally, I am pleased with you," he said.

She had her opening. "I am also sorry to have displeased you."

"Really?" His single word was a challenge. "I am a knight, and when called to battle, I go," he said harshly. "But I will return here as soon as I can, to finish this consummation. And Margaret? I will write Buchan immediately."

Of course he would. Perhaps she could get her own missive to him, defending herself, and begging him to support her decision to abandon his plans for her marriage to Sir Guy. If Buchan could be dissuaded from their union, it would change everything! But she knew that was not likely.

"You are a mere woman. You do not get to choose whom you will wed, or whom not to wed." His gaze narrowed. "While I am gone, you should think about our upcoming nuptials, and what serves you best when I return. Fighting me is not in your better interest."

"I know I do not get to choose my husband, nor do I get to refuse a husband. And I regret losing my temper, Sir Guy, but you frightened me terribly."

"So the fault is mine?"

"Of course not." Carefully, she said, "Sir Guy, I became frightened last night. I have been expecting a June wedding. And I am also afraid that we do not suit—that I continually displease you. I lost all reason. I wish to apologize."

He made a harsh, disparaging sound. "I have always thought you clever—too clever. Do you think to convince me that you are not opposed to our marriage? You will have to do better. You will have to change your nature, and your ways. And Margaret? If you are being insincere, know this—what you wish doesn't matter. We will marry, either here, in a handfast, or in June."

She somehow nodded.

"At least you are obedient today." His stare hardened. "I hope you are sincere. It is claimed that you are an honorable woman. If so, you will do your duty, cease your disputes, and gladly."

"I am a woman of honor."

He seemed skeptical, still. "Time will tell. In the meantime, you will remain here, behind these stout walls, where you will be safe. You remain a valuable prize to MacDonald, to Bruce—and to me." With that, he turned and strode across the hall and left.

Margaret heard him calling to several men. Slowly, she walked over to the table, and there she sank down.

In a few more hours he would be gone. She could not wait.

THE ENTIRE CASTLE was asleep. Alone, Margaret sat at the table in the great hall, one taper burning. She dipped her quill in the ink and wrote upon the vellum spread out before her.

April 15, 1306
My dearest friend Isabella,

I am safely arrived at Castle Fyne, attending to my brother. William was wounded when Sir Guy attacked the stronghold, but he is out of danger now.

Sir Guy has ordered me to remain here, while he marches to Berwick to join his brother, Aymer. He has left a strong garrison behind, leaving us secure and defensible. Soon William will be well enough to return to Balvenie. I am to await Sir Guy's return.

Margaret thought she heard a footfall and she froze, listening. Sir Guy would never allow her to write to Isabella. But Marsaili would smuggle the letter from the keep to the village below the castle, on Loch Fyne's shores. There, one of the villagers would be well paid to forward the letter to another courier, in another village, and eventually, the letter would arrive in Aberdeen.

Without a single messenger, it was a painstaking way to get her message to Isabella, and there was always the possibility that Isabella and the queen and her court would be gone by the time the missive arrived. Still, there was no simple way to send the letter, not when she was writing to her friend who was behind enemy lines.

And there was always the chance that her missive would be intercepted. Margaret knew she must be careful about what she said and how she said it. She wished to warn the queen that Aymer had been instructed to send his men to capture them, and she also wished to inquire after Alexander. She continued.

I am praying you are well and safe, in a time of war and intrigue, when spies are everywhere, when even women can be pursued as outlaws. Have you become friendly with any of the women you are with? Could you give my regards to Elisabeth?

She did not dare refer to her as the queen, and she doubted Isabella would understand the message she was trying to convey. She could only hope that her friend allowed the queen to read the letter.

I am isolated now and I should like any news that you could possibly send. We have no war news now, no news of friends or family, making these times even more difficult. I can only pray for us all.

Your dear friend,
Margaret Comyn

"To whom are you writing?"

Margaret leapt up, knocking over the ink, but fortunately, she did not damage the letter. She stared in shock at William.

Ten days had passed since Sir Guy had left Castle Fyne. William had been improving on a daily basis, but this was the first time he had walked any distance, much less on his own. "How did you get downstairs?" she cried.

He smiled. "As one usually does." He was leaning on a cane. "I am much better, Meg." His eyes were bright. "In a few more days, I will be well enough to go home. Well?"

She had no intention of lying to her brother. "I am writing to Isabella."

His smile vanished. "She is a damned harlot—the damned enemy!"

By now, William knew that she and Isabella had left Balvenie in the middle of the night and that they had been at Bruce's coronation—and that Isabella had participated in the ceremony. He had heard the gossip about her affair with Bruce, too.

He was a Comyn first, and in an instant, his affection for her had turned to animosity. "How can you write to her?" he asked, rather coldly.

"She remains my friend," Margaret said.

His stare hardened and he limped over to the table.

"Will you now read my privy correspondences?" she asked.

He jerked to look at her. "I suppose not. I am your older brother, Meg, and I could forbid you from writing to her. We both know that neither Buchan nor Sir Guy would allow it."

"I am not a lackey to be bullied about," she said tartly. Then she softened. "Will. Poor Isabella. She has ruined her life. I am her friend. She needs me!"

He sighed. "She is a fool as well as a strumpet."

"Will!"

"It's the truth." Then his stare became searching. "Is that the only letter you are writing?"

"I already wrote Buchan." She had written their uncle the day Sir Guy had left—and not just to defend Isabella. She had asked him if she could return to Balvenie with William. Remaining at Castle Fyne, awaiting—and dreading—Sir Guy's return, was impossible. And once there, she would reveal that she could no longer marry Sir Guy—and perhaps, she might even reveal why.

And once at Balvenie, she would be somewhat free of Sir Guy—she would not be his prisoner—and she would be so much closer to the war...and to Alexander.

Buchan had not yet replied. But she had heard rumors of the war. Bruce was in the north, causing havoc. He had attacked Dundee, and then gone on to besiege a series of castles near Banff. He was taking hostages, holding up merchants and demanding excessive ransoms—mostly to finance his war.

And one of her uncles was a victim. The Earl of Strathearn had refused to levy men for him. Bruce and Atholl had thus captured him.

HER BROTHER WAS now studying her. "There is one subject that has not arisen since I have become well," he finally said.

She froze in alarm. He had not asked her about Alexander, not a single time, and she had thought he had not remembered their conversation, as he had been so ill when they had spoken.

Now, she had the uncanny feeling he was about to raise the very subject. "Do you really wish to converse now, at midnight?"

He came forward, sitting down awkwardly on the bench by the table. "Yes, I do, as I have been in bed far too much these past weeks. You know, Meg, I have not been able to decide if I dreamed this very strange conversation I keep recalling."

He did remember, she thought grimly. Margaret sat back down, picked up the vellum and blew carefully on it.

He caught her wrist. "Why do you hate and fear Sir Guy? What happened?"

Though she was relieved he was not asking about Alexander, that ill feeling instantly returned. Since Sir Guy had left, she had refused to think about that violent encounter. She refused to do so now. "You don't like him, either, and you never have. He is English. It is that simple."

His smile was self-deprecating. "But we need him now. We need the damned English now. We must defeat Bruce."

Why? She wanted to ask. Would Robert Bruce be such a terrible king? But she refrained. For she knew his answer. Bruce hated the Comyn family. His gain would be their reversal.

"Did you tell me that you were in love?" William asked seriously. "Did I really have such a conversation with you?"

So he recalled it, after all. She wished she could lie to him and deny it. But she could not; Margaret nodded.

He began shaking his head. "MacDonald? Our blood enemy?"

"Our aunt Juliana married Alexander's brother," Margaret said.

He was dismayed. "You are not Juliana! He rides with Bruce!"

"I know. Do you think I wanted to fall in love with him?" She reached out and took his hand, gripping it tightly. "He attacked my castle. He took it from me. He held me prisoner. Of course I did not want to fall in love with him!" Margaret cried.

Her brother simply stared.

"He is a great warrior, William, and a courageous and honorable man."

His eyes were wide. "You truly are in love."

She nodded, then felt herself flushing. "I came here because I was afraid you would die. But I am in danger, Will. I am in danger from Sir Guy, if he ever learns the truth."

William blanched. "You have slept with him."

She nodded. "I love him and we were lovers."

A terrible expression filled his face. "You betrayed Sir Guy, Meg—and you have betrayed Buchan!"

"I never meant to be disloyal. I am a Comyn woman. I am proud of it! I fought my feelings, I truly did."

"Maybe Sir Guy will never know," William began. "You could deceive him."

Margaret stood up slowly. "Others know."

Will also stood, forgetting to use his cane. "What?"

She wet her lips. "Isabella knows. Some of his men know. Atholl knows."

Will's expression was ghastly. "Then the whole land will know!"

"I am afraid," she finally said, and it was a long overdue confession.

William grimaced, composing himself. "What do you intend?" He caught the edge of the table to balance himself. "You cannot remain here. When Sir Guy finds out you have been unfaithful, he will hurt you—or kill you."

Margaret stared. "I asked Buchan if I could go to Balvenie with you—but I want to return to Alexander."

William was disbelieving. "You would leave us."

"No. Not entirely. I am a Comyn—I will always be your sister."

His eyes had become moist: "And when you marry him? You will marry him?"

"If he will have me...but I will still be your sister!"

"No. You will be his wife, and we will be at war," her brother said. "But I will help you—God help me."

CHAPTER SEVENTEEN

Early May, 1306, Kildrummy Castle, Scotland

WIDE-EYED, MARGARET stared up the hill at the great stronghold of Kildrummy Castle. It dominated the horizon with its huge round towers and imposing curtain walls, and was reputed to be impregnable, enough so that King Edward had stayed there in the past. Because its stout walls could not be breached, the queen and her women had been sent there.

Margaret had never been to the fortress. Staring at it now, she inhaled. Images flashed in her mind, of a lifetime spent in loyalty and duty to her family.

But because she could not marry Sir Guy—because she wanted a future with Alexander—this, then, was her choice.

She was a Comyn, yet she must now beg the queen to admit her to her court. Once the queen accepted her amongst her women, there would be no going back. Her uncle would never forgive her for her reversal of allegiance—for her treachery.

Her trepidation was vast. For now she had to face her greatest fear—she was worthless without her dowry. She had lost all of her value as a bride when Sir Guy had taken Castle Fyne. She believed Alexander cared about her. But did he care enough to marry her without her lands?

No one married without gain. No one married for love.

She was seeking admission to the queen's court, hoping that Alexander wanted her still; she was forsaking her family now, with no guarantee that any future union awaited her.

She was afraid and she had to admit it.

Abruptly, her brother reached over from his mount beside her, and he squeezed her hand. "I dare not linger, Meg."

She was jerked back to the reality of that moment. They were about to part company, perhaps for a very long time. The war would be between them now, with them on opposing sides as William had so feared last February. She dared not contemplate the possibility that they might never see one another again. "I cannot thank you enough for taking me to Kildrummy," she whispered. And he was right—it was dangerous for him to linger with her on the hillside, in view of the great stronghold.

Will was stoic. "Buchan will be furious when he hears of it."

But they had already discussed the ramifications of her defying both Buchan and Sir Guy—with William's help. They had discussed the fact that she was betraying the Comyn family in such a manner, that she could never go back. But their actions paled in significance to the consequences she would surely suffer if she were to remain with the family.

Buchan had ordered her to return to Balvenie with Will. Margaret suspected that he had heard of her misbehavior from Sir Guy. But Will now supported her. He feared for her life, should Sir Guy ever learn of her affair with Alexander.

Together, they had made this terrible decision—she would attempt to join the queen and her women, in the hopes of marrying Alexander and attaining the future she deserved.

Meanwhile, William would claim that he meant to take her to Balvenie, and that she had stolen off in the night, just before their arrival there. Kildrummy was a short day's ride south of her uncle's seat. He would also deny the rumors, as if she were innocent, in case Alexander had changed his mind about marriage. Still, neither one believed that if he had changed his mind, she would ever be welcome home.

Her heart hurt her terribly now. Margaret did not want to release Will's hand. "I love you so," she whispered. "Please, stay out of harm's way. Please, stay safe."

"I will do my best, but you must promise me to obey your husband, for he will surely keep *you* safe." Will's tone was brisk, and she knew it was to mask his emotions. "And if he doesn't marry you, I may kill him myself."

"You will do no such thing—because I love him. I will try to send word," Margaret said, choking up. "Oh, Will. I will miss you so much! I miss you even now!"

He leaned over his horse to hug her briefly. "You have made your choice, we all have. Now, our fate is up to God. God bless you, Meg. God keep you safe." He released her hand and turned his mount abruptly, nodding at the dozen knights riding with them.

Margaret choked on a sob, incapable of movement as her brother and their escort galloped down the hill. She watched them until they had vanished beyond the curve of land.

And suddenly, she was entirely alone, as never before.

Tears blinded her. Had she just given up everyone and everything dear to her, with the exception of Alexander?

When she did not even know if he would take her back and offer marriage again?

She had never felt so fragile, so powerless. Surely, if a wind blew up, she would be knocked over.

She heard a bird chirping above her. The sound was bright and merry. She glanced up, wiping her eyes with her fingertips, and saw, through the leafy green top of the nearby oak tree, a bright blue sky, and a pair of hawks wheeling above. For a moment, she watched the pair as they soared through the sky. Undeniably, it was a bright, beautiful May afternoon. The hawks flew so freely, and she watched them until they had disappeared from her sight.

Her tears dried up. She blinked and gathered up her reins and her courage. She could do this. She must do this.

She nudged her mare slowly forward. The gatehouse was as formidable as the rest of the stronghold. Two towers guarded the entrance, larger, higher round towers at the corners of the front walls. She trotted steadily closer, the watch now having spotted her, until she halted her mare a stone's throw from the closed front gate. Margaret looked up at the two men who stood on the edge of one watchtower, staring down at her. Clearly, they were not alarmed by a single female rider.

"Who goes there?" one shouted.

"It is Lady Margaret Comyn, a friend of the Countess of Buchan and Fife." Margaret watched the men conferring, and then she watched one disappear from her view, obviously to ask a superior if she should be let in. Perhaps ten minutes later dozens of archers appeared on the walls, while two riders galloped out to her.

The first rider became recognizable. Clad in a shirt of mail, he wore no helmet, and his hair gleamed almost black in the sun. "Lady Margaret!" Sir Neil cried, grinning.

She could barely believe it was Sir Neil—her Sir Neil! "Sir Neil!" She was thrilled. "But, you ride with Alexander! What are you doing here?"

His blue eyes twinkled as he rode up to her, taking one of her reins. "The Wolf left me behind, lady—to guard the Countess of Fife."

Margaret's heart lurched hard. Alexander knew she cared about Isabella—and he had left one of his men behind to look after her. She knew he had done so for her sake, not Isabella's.

"I am so pleased to see you," she said as they trotted over the lowered drawbridge and through the entryway of the gatehouse.

"And I am pleased to see you! But Sir Guy let you go?" Sir Neil was puzzled. "And why have you come to the queen?"

"Sir Guy did not let me go. He wished for me to remain at Castle Fyne. I have disobeyed him directly," Margaret said. "I have come to attend Isabella, if I will be allowed to do so."

Sir Neil stared in surprise at her.

But he did not know she had no intention now of ever marrying Sir Guy, and that she would not suffer the consequences of her defiance. But it was not the time to discuss such matters with him now. Instead, she plucked his mail sleeve. "How is Alexander?"

Sir Neil smiled with pride. "He has brought a great many keeps to their knees, my lady, often without lifting a sword. He has been far to the north, where Bruce has spent most of this past month."

There had been rumors of Alexander's actions since she had returned to Castle Fyne, including rumors of his taking a great many smaller keeps without even a battle, his mere appearance frightening the enemy into surrender, but she was pleased now to hear the news firsthand. Otherwise, she had not heard from him, but she had not expected to. She had wanted to write to him, but William had advised her against it. He had feared her missive might be intercepted, and that Sir Guy would be alerted to her plans.

"Now they march southward," Sir Neil was adding. "Bruce will not give up on Strathearn."

Margaret thought of the Earl of Strathearn, her uncle by marriage, whom she had never met, and her aunt, whom she had met but twice in her lifetime. Their lands were under siege and Strathearn had been captured. She should be concerned, and she imagined Buchan was furiously aiding them in their defenses, but she was not. "Is the earl still Bruce's prisoner?"

"I believe so, but his men are holding out, and Bruce wishes for the castle to fall." Sir Neil grinned. Then he sobered, as if realizing the family connection. "I am sorry, my lady. I keep forgetting—we are on opposite sides of the war."

"Perhaps not," she said. Then, "How is Isabella?" She had not received a response to her letter from her, and she wondered if the queen had prevented the correspondence, or even denied her receipt of her letter in the first place.

She became alarmed when Sir Neil took his time answering; they were now walking their mounts through the great cobbled stone courtyard. "I worry for her, my lady."

"Has anything transpired that I should know of?"

He hesitated. "In April, the women were in Aberdeen. Bruce spent a week there with them."

Margaret felt her heart lurch with dismay. Did they carry on still?

"There are rumors," Sir Neil said. He now shrugged. "I am certain you will hear them. It is said that the queen caught them together." He blushed, not looking directly at her.

Margaret hoped desperately that was not the case. "Has the queen dismissed her from her court?"

"Bruce has ordered her to remain with the queen and her women. The queen could not remove her from Kildrummy if she wished it."

They had reached the great front doors of the hall, and had halted their horses. Sir Neil dismounted, and came over to help her do the same. She looked down at him. "What else bothers you, Sir Neil?"

He smiled ruefully. "Am I so obvious? Now everyone says she pines for Bruce. My lady, she writes him almost daily—and she asks me to send those letters to him!"

Margaret allowed him to help her off of her horse. "Have you done so?"

He flushed again. "I am to obey her, my lady. Of course I have sent the missives to the king. But I believe the queen knows she is writing to him—it is unwise."

It was very unwise, Margaret thought grimly. Everything Isabella did was unwise. "I am so glad you have been here to help her through this time. And now, you are here to help me."

"I want nothing more," he said fervently. And then he got down on one knee, head bowed. "My lady, I have sworn my fealty to the mighty Wolf, but remain devoted to you, always."

She almost cried. Then she had a thought. "Sir Neil, if you can get letters to Bruce, could you get a missive to Alexander?"

He looked up at her. "Of course."

Margaret's excitement abated. Now she must consider what she wished to say—and how she would say it.

MARGARET FOLLOWED SIR NEIL through the castle. A huge hall was ahead, its great wood doors fully open. The stone floors within were covered with beautiful rugs, and the high ceiling was raftered. Two large hearths blazed. Tapestries covered both walls.

As she approached she could see the queen within, surrounded by some twenty ladies-in-waiting. Elisabeth sat in their midst in a huge, thronelike chair. A parchment in her hand, she was resplendent in a dark red gown with puffed sleeves and gold trim. Garnets and rubies circled her throat and were dangling from her ears. Her reddish hair was pulled tightly back beneath a gold circlet, but she did not appear severe. She appeared elegant and regal—she appeared every bit a queen.

Her ladies sat and stood around her, one playing a flute, others sewing, a few in conversation with her. Most of the ladies in attendance were about the queen's age, two were quite older. Some wore Highland garb—simple leines with plaid mantles—others, finer French gowns. Margaret instantly saw Marjorie Strathbogie, the Earl of Atholl's wife.

She sat with the queen, as did Christina Seton and Mary Campbell, the king's sisters.

They had reached the threshold of the great room, where guards barred their way. Margaret looked past Sir Neil, her gaze on Marjorie. The other woman had seen her as well, and quickly smiled at her.

Her heart thudded. Could Atholl be a spy for Aymer de Valence? Should she share her suspicions with Queen Elisabeth? What if she was wrong?

She had always liked Marjorie, who was a pleasant, good-natured and pretty woman. Marjorie had always welcomed her into her home, and had been eager to chat when visiting Bain or Balvenie. But then, Margaret had always liked her husband, and he had, possibly, betrayed his dear friend, her uncle Buchan.

Either he was a traitor to King Edward, or he was a traitor to King Robert. But he was a traitor all the same.

Margaret realized that the great room had become silent. Queen Elisabeth had seen her and was staring. So was everyone else.

And now, Margaret espied Isabella, standing far behind the other ladies, almost against the wall. She was beaming—the only woman in the room who was pleased to see her. Margaret almost expected her to wave.

"Your Majesty," Sir Neil said, bowing low. "Lady Margaret Comyn seeks an audience."

For a moment, the queen no longer appeared regal—she appeared bitter. And as they stared at one another, Margaret recalled her odd remark after Bruce's coronation. She had accused her husband of playing a children's game of pretend, of playing at being a king.

Margaret bent on one knee. "My lady...Your Majesty," she said.

"Rise, Lady Margaret."

Margaret stood. The queen gestured and everyone stepped away from her, except for Marjorie, Mary and Christina, who remained seated with her. She waved at Margaret. "Your presence here is a surprise."

Margaret came forward. "I have fled Castle Fyne, Your Majesty, with my brother's help. I was hoping to join you and your women here."

Her blue eyes were cool. "Really? And why would I allow a Comyn in my court?"

Margaret hesitated. "I have fled Sir Guy, Your Majesty. I cannot marry him so I am seeking sanctuary here."

"Really? You cannot marry him, or you will not do so?"

She felt her cheeks heat. "I cannot and I will not, Your Majesty."

"So you give up your great castle, just like that?" The queen was disbelieving.

"I am hoping that Alexander, who has sought my hand, will take Castle Fyne back."

Surprised and titillated murmurs sounded.

The queen's eyes widened. Then she demanded, "Speak forthrightly, Lady Margaret. Have you chosen to defy your family? Have you chosen MacDonald over Buchan? Do you support my husband now?"

Margaret wet her dry lips. "Yes, Your Majesty," she answered. "I have chosen Alexander and I now support Robert Bruce."

Shock rippled through the room. Everyone began speaking at once.

"Quiet!" the queen exclaimed. "And I am to believe you?"

"She is a spy," Christina Seton said sharply. "Sir Guy and the Earl of Buchan have sent her here to spy upon us. Perhaps she has been in Alexander's bed for the sole purpose of spying!"

Margaret gasped. "I am not a spy!"

The queen stood up. She was actually a tiny woman, no taller or heavier than Margaret, but her stature was immense. "All of Scotland speaks so highly of you, Lady Margaret. You are a legend in your own right, the great lady of Castle Fyne, a tiny woman brave enough to defy a mighty Wolf, a lady who would die of loyalty for her family. Are those legends not the truth?"

"I have been loyal and devoted my entire life. It is my nature to be loyal," she said.

"Then you must have been sent here to spy," the queen said.

She was going to become a prisoner of the queen, Margaret thought wildly. "I have not been sent to spy, Your Majesty. I have had to make a terrible choice!"

"And you chose to betray Buchan?" Queen Elisabeth was incredulous and mocking.

Margaret trembled. "Could I have a privy word, Your Majesty?"

A moment passed before the queen nodded. Everyone left the room, except for Marjorie, Mary and Christina. "They will not betray us," the queen said flatly.

Margaret did not wish to speak openly in front of Marjorie, in case her husband was a spy for her uncle and King Edward. "I meant to obey my uncle. I meant to go forth in marriage to Sir Guy. It is why I refused Alexander, not once, but two times."

"Go on," the queen said, her red brows raised.

She bit her lip. "I do not want to sound foolish. But I have been influenced by my parents—their marriage was arranged, but they respected one another, and they even loved one another greatly."

The queen was amused. "Will you now tell me you seek love in marriage—with the handsome Wolf of Lochaber?"

She knew she blushed. "I seek a future with someone I trust and respect, Your Majesty. As it happens, I care greatly for him, as well."

Marjorie said softly, "She does not have a deceptive nature."

Margaret started, then faced Elisabeth. "Your Majesty, may I try to prove my sincerity to you?"

Her gaze narrowed. "Please do."

"I sent a letter to Isabella. Did she receive it?"

"She did."

"I was hoping she would share its contents with you. I was trying to warn you that you and your court are in danger."

The queen sat back down and folded her hands in her lap. "I read the missive, Lady Margaret. Was that a warning?"

"Yes, it was." She glanced at Christina, who stared coldly at her. "Aymer de Valence has been ordered by King Edward to capture you, Your Majesty. Sir Guy seeks the command."

Christina leaned over to the queen and whispered in her ear. The queen said, "We know all of this, Lady Margaret. What else do you know?"

Margaret hesitated. "Aymer has spies amongst Bruce's closest friends." She did not look at Marjorie now.

Christina looked surprised, while the queen remained impassive. "How do you know this?" Bruce's other sister, Mary Campbell, demanded.

"Sir Guy told me," Margaret said.

Christina turned to Elisabeth. "We must warn Rob."

Queen Elisabeth nodded. Then she said decisively, "There is one way you may prove your new loyalties once and for all. Will you get down on your knees and swear your fealty to me and King Robert?"

Margaret trembled. But she lifted her chin and said, "Your Majesty, I will swear my fealty to you and Robert Bruce."

MARGARET MADE HER way back to the hall, having left only to use a privy chamber, aware of one of the queen's guards carefully following her. She was now in attendance on the queen, but she was not trusted yet. She would swear fealty to her new liege after the mass on Sunday. Margaret did not think that she would be trusted even then.

She turned a corner in the corridor and was seized by both shoulders. "I am so happy you are here!" Isabella cried.

After the harrowing interview, Margaret had taken a seat behind Marjorie and Christina, and she had remained quiet for the rest of the afternoon. What she had really wished to do was retire, in both exhaustion and relief, but she knew better than to ask for permission to leave the queen. She also knew better than to openly seek out Isabella, which would only garner more disapproval from her new liege.

Now, Isabella embraced her wildly. Margaret smiled, hugging her in return; she had missed her dear friend. "How are you?" she asked.

Isabella's smile vanished, tears filling her eyes. "Margaret! I am in grave jeopardy!"

Margaret glanced around, but, except for the single guard, they were alone. "Can we speak freely?" she asked. "Were you given permission to leave the queen?"

"I do not need permission, as they know I am not a spy. I pray to God you are not here on some terrible mission."

"I am not," she said firmly, alarmed, because if Isabella was suspicious of her, then the queen and her ladies would be even more so. "I spoke the truth when I said that I had left Sir Guy, Isabella. I am defying him and Buchan."

"I am glad. Come with me," she said urgently.

Margaret did not think that a good idea. "Isabella,"

she began, but Isabella pulled her toward the stairs. "I believe I need the queen's permission to leave the hall!"

"She gave you her permission," Isabella said with a scathing glance. Clearly, she despised Elisabeth. She hurried down the next corridor, pulling Margaret with her. She pushed open the door of a small bedchamber. "I sleep here, with three other ladies," she said. "We must make certain that you and I share a chamber."

Margaret thought that unlikely, considering that the queen did not like Isabella and did not trust Margaret. Then Isabella seized her in a crushing embrace.

Margaret took one look at her unhappy face and put her arm around her. Isabella cried, "I am so glad you are here now! It is terrible being here with the queen, she hates me!"

"Of course she despises you. You are sleeping with her husband. You must end your affair."

"I cannot. I love him!"

"Isabella! You must think clearly! No good can come of loving Robert Bruce. You are making an enemy of your own queen—when you must remain with her, for safety's sake. And you know that what you are doing is wrong," Margaret said more gently.

She burst into tears. "He hasn't answered my letters."

Margaret was relieved. Had Bruce lost interest? How she hoped so!

Isabella now gave her a strange, teary look, walked to the farthest bed, and began to reach under the mattress. She straightened, holding a parchment. "But I am not safe, Margaret," she said, her tone filled with tension.

Margaret was alarmed. Before she could ask if those letters were from Bruce, Isabella said, "He hates me, Margaret." Her hand trembled as she extended the roll.

Margaret inhaled, filled with dread. "Is that from Buchan?"

She nodded, starkly white. "He has damned me to hell. He has called me a bitch and a whore." Tears sparkled. "He has even threatened me, should we ever meet again."

Margaret's mind raced frantically. Of course Buchan was furious with her.

She was grim as she took the parchment and quickly read her uncle's bitter words. He had disowned his wife. He would not accept a treacherous bitch and an adulterous whore as his spouse, and he wished that she would rot in hell for all eternity.

"Pray Isabella," he then wrote, "that the day does not come where we come face-to-face. For if ever that day comes, you will be treated like the treacherous whore that you are. I will strip you of your clothes, parade you through the streets in shackles, and hang you from the closest gallows, where your body shall rot for all time."

Margaret trembled. Would her uncle really punish Isabella in such a vicious manner?

"I am not safe," Isabella whispered. "He means his every word."

"He is angry. Understandably so. But we must hope his anger will pass. Why do you keep this?"

"I want Rob to see it."

"Bruce is king, Isabella. He has no time for these intrigues."

"I have given up everything for him."

Margaret went to her and put her arm around her, when she heard a noise at the door. Both women turned instantly, Margaret hoping it was her guard. But Christina Seton stood there.

"Elisabeth wishes to know why the two of you have run off, perhaps to conspire against her?" Christina said coldly to Margaret. Then she turned her attention on Isabella, and her entire demeanor softened. "Isabella, you know better. You cannot simply vanish from the queen's hall, even if you wish a privy moment with your friend."

Margaret realized that Christina had some affection for Isabella, and that she was protecting her from the folly of her impulsive nature. She was relieved, and she thought she understood—Christina undoubtedly felt gratitude for Isabella's help in crowning her brother.

"She would not allow me a moment with Margaret if I asked," Isabella said petulantly, sounding much younger than she was. "She will not allow me anything, other than to stand alone in a corner." She turned to Margaret. "She has made her women dislike me. She has made certain I am an outcast in her hall."

"You are not an outcast." Christina was firm. "I am your friend, as are a great many of the ladies, but we must respect the queen. If you will carry on with Rob, openly, then you must suffer the queen's anger." Then she looked up at Margaret. "If you are luring her into your intrigues, do not. She has enough on her plate."

"I have no intrigues," Margaret said. But she was pleased that Christina Seton was attempting to guide Isabella into some sensibility of action. "If you are taking care of her, I am thankful."

Christina shrugged. "If you have truly turned your back on the Earl of Buchan and King Edward, then we will have nothing to divide us."

"Then we have nothing to divide us," Margaret said.

For one more moment Christina stared, and then she smiled at Isabella. "We must return to the hall. It is time for supper."

Isabella turned and replaced the roll of vellum beneath her bed.

Margaret tensed as she did so, reminded of the disturbing contents of the letter. As she met Christina's gaze, she knew that the other woman was also concerned about Isabella's fate.

Margaret shivered, suddenly chilled. Hadn't she always had a terrible and dreadful feeling about Isabella's fate, should she aid Bruce as he seized the crown? Now, she forced aside the graphic image of Isabella, naked and being hanged from a noose.

A RIDER WAS approaching, and the ladies attending Queen Elisabeth began to speak excitedly amongst themselves. Margaret felt her own heart leap in the same excitement. Their only ties to the outside world were the occasional passing merchant or wandering friar and gossip from the villagers outside Kildrummy. A lone rider, coming directly at a gallop, must be a messenger.

As usual, the ladies and the queen were in the great hall. It was midafternoon, and an uneventful week had passed since Margaret had arrived. The days were long, with little of substance to do—at Castle Fyne and even at Balvenie, she had had a household to look after. The women read, sewed, sang, danced and several played musical instruments. Mostly, there was a great deal of conversation, filled with speculation, fear and trepidation, as they longed for news of the war.

Queen Elisabeth, seated once more upon her throne-like chair, was now whispering privately with Bruce's two sisters, her expression severe. Margaret had observed her for an entire week, and Elisabeth de Burgh was an aloof and mostly unhappy woman. She kept Marjorie, Mary and Christina with her constantly; they were her confidantes and favorites.

Margaret sat on a bench near the wall with Isabella, a

habit she had taken to. The other women avoided Bruce's mistress in public, fearing Elisabeth's disapproval and dismissal. The queen mostly ignored her, but when she did give her attention, it was in a disdainful and angry manner. Other than Christina and herself, Isabella had no friends. Margaret felt sorry for her, but Isabella had brought this circumstance down upon herself.

And Margaret found herself in a similar situation as her friend. She had made her vows to the queen after the last mass, yet the other ladies did not quite trust her. Still, she had chosen to go to Queen Elisabeth, and she refused to allow herself to become an outcast like Isabella. She had deliberately taken the time to become acquainted with the other ladies, attempting to be helpful when she could, determined to always be pleasing.

And then there was Marjorie. They had not had a single privy conversation, which was odd, although they spoke in passing. Margaret wondered if Marjorie was avoiding her or attempting to please the queen.

Booted footsteps sounded outside the hall, urgently approaching. Margaret smiled at Isabella, who was pale. "Maybe it is news from Bruce," the countess whispered.

Margaret hoped it was war news. She hoped it was a message from the king himself. And she also hoped there was a letter from Alexander.

She had written him the day she had arrived at court. It had been a difficult letter to write, as she did not know what his feelings for her were. She had told him that she had left Sir Guy and of her flight from Castle Fyne; she hoped he was well and safe. She had wanted to write so much more! But she had had to be careful and circumspect. Sir Neil had taken the letter and dispatched it the very next day.

She trembled as a disheveled and muddy Highlander

strode into the room with Sir Neil and Bruce's young brother, Sir Nigel. Instantly, all the ladies fell silent. The Highlander paused before Queen Elisabeth, dropping respectfully onto one knee.

Sir Nigel Bruce was as tall as his brother, his dark blond hair almost brown, with a slight copper cast. He had been given the responsibility of keeping the queen and her women safe since Bruce had taken the crown. He said, "Rob has sent us missives." He handed the queen a parchment as the rider stood, still holding another rolled-up vellum.

Margaret's heart lurched hard. Was that vellum for her?

The queen nodded at him, then untied her parchment and unrolled it. Everyone stared at her as she read the missive. She finally looked up at her audience. "King Robert is well. The war goes well."

Relieved murmurs sounded.

"We are to remain here, where no army can assail us," she continued. Her voice was strong and deep.

And when she did not say anything else, Christina said, "That is all?"

The queen smiled tightly at her.

There was more, Margaret thought, now turning to stare at Sir Nigel. As she did, the queen also looked at him. "What news do you have?"

"Details, Elisabeth, details of this war." Clearly he was not about to discuss his missive with her, or at least not openly.

The queen stood up. "I need a privy word," she announced, "with Lady Comyn and Lady Isabella."

Margaret stiffened, her dismay at not having received a communication from Alexander instantly turning to trepidation. Why did the queen wish to speak with them?

Immediately, Sir Nigel stepped back, allowing the twenty or so women to file past him. Margaret turned her gaze upon Sir Neil. He gave her a reassuring smile, but it was false and her tension increased.

The queen gestured at her and Isabella.

Margaret walked over, holding Isabella's hand. "Your Majesty, I am becoming frightened."

"You should be." She was tart, the hall now empty except for the queen, her confidantes, the two knights and Margaret and Isabella. "The Earl of Buchan demands his wife's return. He also demands your return, Lady Margaret."

Her heart slammed. If she was sent back to Buchan, she would be punished, and after that, she did not know what her fate would be. "Was there no word from Alexander?" she whispered.

Sir Nigel turned to her. He was almost as commanding as his older brother, and even more masculine in good looks. But his regard was reserved. "Sir Neil does nothing without my approval, my lady. The missive you sent is, perhaps, reaching the Wolf now. It is far too soon to expect a reply."

Disappointment flooded her.

"However, he has surely heard that you have fled Castle Fyne and that you have cast your commitments to Sir Guy aside."

Of course he had, she thought. If her uncle was demanding her release, then Alexander knew she was with the queen. She dared to look at Elisabeth now. If the queen sent her to her uncle, she was doomed. "May I speak, Your Majesty?"

Elisabeth stared, her gaze narrowed. "Please do."

"I am begging you to consider how I risked everything to come to your court, and that I have sworn fealty to you and King Robert. I cannot return to Buchan. Nor can Isabella."

The queen sent a scathing glance toward Isabella, one which was dismissive. She then looked seriously at Margaret. "I cannot send Isabella away. She has my husband's protection for as long as she shall live."

Margaret glanced at Isabella, who was as pale as a ghost. On this point, she was relieved.

"Please don't send Margaret back to him," Isabella whispered in fear.

"I did not give you permission to speak," the queen said with controlled anger. She turned to Margaret again. "I shall have to take some time to decide what to do with you."

Margaret felt fear stab through her. She did not speak now.

"But thus far, you have behaved in a manner that is both pleasing and pleasant. My ladies all seem to like you, even though you are a Comyn. You seem kind and sincere. But I do not trust you yet."

Margaret glanced with worry at Sir Neil. He was grim.

Elisabeth faced the knights. "Nigel? Did Robert decide what we should do with Lady Comyn?"

"Bruce has ordered that Lady Comyn stay here, Elisabeth, with you and your women, until he does decide."

There was a respite, Margaret thought, shaking in sudden relief. But for how long?

Bruce had wanted her to marry Alexander. Had he changed his mind?

She no longer had Castle Fyne, she was no longer a prized bride. He would want one of his best commanders to marry another heiress, one who brought him other strategic strongholds.

Nigel had stepped closer to the queen, who was waving Margaret and Isabella away. They hurried across the hall, Sir Neil falling into step with them. At the closed doors they paused, Margaret facing Sir Neil. Instantly, he took both of her hands. "I will not let you go back," he said.

Margaret looked past him, where a whispered conversation was taking place, but she had been forgotten, and she knew they were not discussing her. "You may not have a choice," she said, strained. "Remember, you serve Alexander now, Sir Neil."

"I will always protect you."

Their gazes met. "I must hear from Alexander," she said. And as she spoke, she knew she was a fool. He would not want to marry her now. Politics—and war—demanded a different course. But she thought—and hoped—she could still ask him for his protection.

If he cared, he would not allow her to be handed over to her uncle.

THE DAYS PASSED with agonizing slowness, turning into weeks. As summer settled over the land, Margaret waited for a response to the letter she had written to Alexander, but none came. She began to lose faith in her dream of marriage to him.

But there was war news—a great deal of it. Bruce continued to besiege Strathearn, who had escaped, at Kenmore, with a huge force, the Earl of Lennox and Atholl at his side, as were his most trusted men—Sir Christopher Seton, his sister Mary's husband, Neil Campbell and Alexander. Margaret wondered if the battle for Kenmore was so great that Alexander had never even received her missive. She was afraid to hope.

It became difficult to maintain a pleasant humor. Isabella wished to know what was wrong. Marjorie began to send her questioning looks. So did Christina.

It was the first day of June when the queen even summoned her to demand, "What has happened to cause such unhappiness, Lady Margaret? When you first came here, you smiled all of the time. You made my ladies smile. Now you appear to be mourning."

Margaret had managed to answer, somehow. She was worried about her uncle, her brother, and she was worried about Alexander.

The news continued. King Edward had forfeited most of the rebels' lands. And Bruce was infuriated. Kenmore fell. He turned his armies upon a series of smaller strongholds in Aberdeenshire.

But Atholl's lands had remained intact. Margaret's suspicions about the earl's loyalties remained. Why hadn't he been deprived of his lands? Did King Edward hope to win Atholl back to his side, if he was, indeed, truly a rebel now?

The great armies of King Edward remained on the march, attacking the rebels where they could. Bishop Wishart surrendered after a fierce battle at Cupar at Castle Fife, with Aymer de Valence and his great army drawing inexorably closer to Perth.

The court had become nervous. From Perth, Aymer could send an army north to Kildrummy, and attempt to besiege them. No matter how impregnable Kildrummy was, Bruce was too busy to come to their aid. And even more ominous, their supplies were low at Kildrummy. Their cellars were less than half full. A siege could now succeed—they would simply be starved to death.

The women waited to be reassured that Aymer de Valence had been turned back. But no such word came.

One early evening, Margaret sat in her bed in her

chamber, which she shared with Christina and Marjorie, not with Isabella. A small writing tray was on her lap, a quill in her hand, the inkwell on the floor. She knew she must not beg, she knew she must have dignity and pride. Yet she was compelled to write to Alexander another time. At the very least, she could ask after his welfare.

But now, she felt as if she were pursuing him—it was not a good feeling at all.

"Have you secluded yourself? It is time to dine," Marjorie said from the threshold of their chamber. As always, her voice was gentle and kind.

They were on friendly terms, in spite of Margaret's concern. But a tension was between them, one that had not existed before the war. Margaret slowly removed the tray with the vellum from her lap and laid it on the bed. "I have no appetite, Marjorie."

"You should eat, Margaret, while we still have food to put upon the table."

Margaret studied her. "You received a letter from Atholl the other day."

"Yes, I did, and I thank God he is well," Marjorie said with sudden fervor. "I miss him terribly." She now came inside and sat down on the other bed, facing Margaret.

Margaret looked at her knees, which she now drew to her chest. She did not question Marjorie's love for her husband, but Marjorie had written him, and he had replied, never mind the war.

"You miss Alexander," Marjorie said softly. It was not a question.

Margaret flushed, deciding to be honest—even if Marjorie was married to a spy. "Yes, I do."

"He still hasn't written you?"

Margaret bit her lip and shrugged, the gesture indicating that he had not.

"I asked about him," Marjorie said, stunning her. She smiled a little. "He is well, Margaret."

"Why would you ask about Alexander?"

"Because we are friends…because I am determined to guard our friendship."

Margaret stared. Images flashed, of that long-ago night at the peel of Strathbogie, when she had been interviewed by Buchan's allies, when her uncle and Atholl and the entire company had sworn vengeance against Robert Bruce. "I hope we are friends," she said carefully.

"What do you really wish to say?" Marjorie asked as carefully.

"Your husband was allied with my uncle, Marjorie. They were friends for years. Yet now, he rides with Bruce. Now, he fights my uncle."

"Does that make you angry?"

"It makes me wonder," Margaret said. Her pulse raced. "Did you approve, when your husband chose to go over to Bruce?"

Marjorie did not speak for a moment, her gaze unwavering. "I know you think he is treacherous—and not to be trusted." She did not speak with rancor, and she stood up. "He is not a spy, Margaret."

Margaret slid to her feet, too, filled with tension. "I never made any such accusation."

"But you have been thinking it. Even though you changed your loyalties, and there are some who think you are a spy. It is the reason our friendship has been so strained."

"So we will speak openly now?"

"I think it is best."

"I haven't known what to think…. He was a loyal ally and a friend of Buchan's for a great many years."

Marjorie said slowly, "We hate the English. We always have. It was unnatural, becoming allied with King Edward."

Marjorie did hate the English, of that, Margaret had no doubt. And, until the past year, when King Edward had forced a truce upon the land, Atholl had been fighting the English—as had her uncle, Buchan. They had all despised the English and King Edward, until so recently.

"It wasn't easy," Marjorie said tersely, "having supper with your uncle and Ingram and the others that night. We had already gone over to Bruce."

Margaret wanted to believe her. "I hated betraying my uncle, too. And now, I am here at the queen of Scotland's court, while my brother and my uncle ride with King Edward, making war upon us."

Marjorie came to her and hesitantly took her hand. "And you thought you would become Alexander's wife."

The aching inside her chest intensified. "He will not marry me now. My dowry is gone. I thought he would still have some affection, that he would protect me in these dangerous times, but I must be sensible now. If he wished to do so, he would have sent some message by now."

"I am sorry. I thought you would marry him, too. But maybe you should not give up all hope. This war will end one day. The Wolf could attack Castle Fyne then, or Bruce might let him do so sooner."

Margaret did not want to be enslaved by hope. If Alexander cared for her, he would have signaled it. "I have given up my family in a time of war. I have changed my politics."

"Do you wish you had not done so?"

"I worry I have done it for nothing."

"Alexander is a fool if he has decided to let you go! I am very sorry, Margaret, that you are so alone, but we will keep you safe, John and I." Her stare was determined.

Margaret trembled, disbelieving. "You would do such a thing? When I have had such grave doubts about you?"

"We have known each other for most of our lives, and John has known you since you were a small child. Yes, we would do such a thing."

Margaret hesitated, for her suspicions about John had been allayed—but they had not been vanquished. But still, the two women hugged.

Marjorie pulled away first. "It was good, to speak openly," she said. "And at least we have restored our friendship."

Margaret smiled. As long as Atholl was not a spy, they had restored their friendship. But there was still a chance Marjorie could not be trusted. "I am glad we spoke as we did."

Marjorie took her hand and they went down to dine.

THE DEVASTATING NEWS came within days: Aymer de Valence had occupied the great city of Perth.

The enemy was within striking distance of Kildrummy Castle.

"Why does he leave us here?" Isabella asked, ashen.

Margaret took her hand. There was hardly any conversation in the hall that morning. How could there be? Ever since they had heard that de Valence's great army was in Perth, an army of thousands upon thousands of well-trained soldiers and knights, the court had become stricken. And the queen was not present. She was behind closed doors with Sir Nigel, his other foremost knights, Marjorie and Bruce's sisters. Clearly a great discussion was afoot.

The court was going to have to flee, Margaret thought

uneasily. They could not remain there, with so few stores left, awaiting an attack from de Valence.

She had little doubt that Sir Guy remained one of Aymer's commanders. Just as she felt certain he was chafing to be let loose upon Kildrummy—upon her.

"You are so quiet!" Isabella accused. "Can you not at least pretend to be confident of our fates?"

Margaret trembled, a scant instant from screaming at her. Instead, she said calmly, "It is time to grow up. We are in grave danger and I have no desire to pretend otherwise. There are fifty knights here to defend us. Aymer de Valence has an army of six thousand men. His knights are the best in the land. And—" she paused, now perspiring "—Sir Guy is with him. I am certain. And if we are captured, he will seek me out."

Isabella gasped. "I am so thoughtless!" She embraced her, hard. "God, he will punish you for leaving him. But perhaps he doesn't know you had an affair with Alexander?"

Margaret closed her eyes. Perhaps Alexander's having left her would save her from Sir Guy's rage in the end. But she did not think so.

Suddenly the doors to the hall burst open, as if rammed by a siege engine. Several women screamed. Sir Neil ran inside, followed by five of his men. He was ashen.

Margaret lifted her skirts and began running to him. "What has happened?"

He had been racing toward the doors at the room's other end, beyond which were the queen and Sir Nigel. He reversed course and ran directly to her, seizing her by both arms. "Bruce's army has been massacred!"

Margaret felt the room tilt wildly. "What?"

"There has been a terrible massacre at Methven," Sir Neil was shouting.

And in that moment, all she could think of was, had Alexander survived?

The women began crying out, shouting questions, someone even screaming that Bruce was dead! Margaret looked into Sir Neil's panicked eyes as the doors behind them opened. She heard the queen, the women, and Sir Nigel racing to them.

"What has happened?" Christina cried. "Is Rob dead?"

"The king lives!" Sir Neil shouted over the pandemonium. He appeared ready to weep. "But he was ambushed at Methven and there, his army was slaughtered like sleeping sheep!"

Margaret could not breathe as Sir Neil released her, panting in distress. Sir Nigel took his arm. "Calm yourself and tell me what has happened."

Sir Neil nodded, a tear now sliding down his face. "Bruce arrived at Perth and rode directly to the city gates, where he challenged Aymer de Valence. He demanded that Aymer either come out and fight or surrender. De Valence said it was too late to go to battle then, but they would begin the fight the next morning."

Sir Nigel nodded grimly. The queen was stiff and unmoving, as were her ladies. No one in the hall was moving—the tension and fear were too great.

Sir Neil swiped at the single tear upon his face. "Bruce retired his army to Methven for the night. Some of his men were sent to forage for fodder, others told to cook, others had disarmed and were sleeping. And then the English army descended upon them."

Christina choked. Mary put her arm around her, as ashen.

"They were ambushed, and a terrible melee ensued," Sir Neil said. "They were mostly asleep, mostly unarmed, and outnumbered. Bruce was unhorsed three times! Sir Christopher saved him from capture." He looked at Christina briefly. Then he turned to Sir Nigel. "A massacre ensued."

Sir Nigel was as white as everyone else. "But the king survived?"

"Atholl, your brother Edward and Neil Campbell managed to defend him. They escaped into the forest."

"Oh, my God," Christina said. "What of the others?"

"Most were murdered. A few were captured in the field—but Sir Christopher escaped."

Christina began to cry. Mary held her tight, upright. She was crying, too. Marjorie was white.

"What of Alexander?" Margaret whispered.

Sir Neil whirled. "I do not know if he was captured, if he escaped or if he is one of the dead."

Margaret began to shake so badly, she knew she might collapse. Isabella took her hand.

Sir Nigel was so stricken, his nose was red. "Are you telling us that Bruce's entire army was slaughtered? That over four thousand men are dead?"

"Perhaps a hundred men escaped into the forests."

Margaret staggered blindly away. It was over—and Alexander could be dead.

Her fists clenched. But hadn't she known that Robert Bruce could not go up against England and win? Yet he had dragged Alexander into the damned war, and now Bruce lived, but she did not know if Alexander did!

"There is more, Sir Nigel," Sir Neil said hoarsely.

How could there be more? Margaret turned back to them and saw that the queen, who was so stoic all of the time, was as stricken as everyone else. Elisabeth was fighting the same tears of horror and anguish as everyone else.

"King Edward has issued a royal proclamation." Sir Neil cleared his throat. "Every wife and every sister, every daughter amongst us, is as guilty of treason as we are."

Gasps sounded.

"They must be hunted down," he continued, now sounding shaken as he glanced at Margaret, "but the punishment will not be hanging."

The queen cried out. Marjorie and Christina seized her, to keep her from collapsing. Margaret gasped, "How will King Edward punish us?"

"By royal decree, any man may now rob, rape and murder you."

CHAPTER EIGHTEEN

A TERRIFIC NOISE awoke her.

Margaret was suddenly awake. It took her a moment to realize where she was. Since the news of the massacre at Methven, the sleeping arrangements had changed. She had been invited to share the queen's chamber—as had Isabella. For she had risen in the queen's esteem. As for Isabella, she suspected that the queen had been instructed by her husband to keep her close.

It was the middle of the night. She was instantly aware of the commotion below the royal bedchamber. Margaret froze, her heart pounding with fright. She could hear men shouting and racing into the great room.

"Are we being attacked?" Isabella cried, seizing Margaret's hand in their shared pallet.

Someone held a taper aloft. Margaret glanced across the space between her bed and the closest adjacent one. Christina held the candle high, Mary beside her. Their gazes were wide with fright.

And Elisabeth, terribly ashen, was on her feet, Marjorie helping her don a warm mantle. Marjorie's movements, which were usually gentle, were rushed.

Margaret's mind raced frantically. Was Aymer de Valence attacking?

She heard a great many voices raised in urgent conversation. What she did not hear was the ring of swords, or the cries of soldiers in battle. It was clear the others heard the same and were realizing that they were not being attacked.

A sharp, urgent banging sounded upon the queen's doors. Elisabeth cried out loudly, "Enter."

The doors burst open and Sir Nigel stood there. "You must come below, Elisabeth," he said quickly.

But she was already crossing the room, Christina and Mary with her. They vanished into the hall outside with Sir Nigel.

Margaret quickly got up, lighting another taper. Isabella also slid from the bed. Marjorie joined them and they exchanged glances. "Who could it be—in the middle of the night?" Isabella whispered.

"I don't know." Margaret took up a plaid and draped it about her shoulders. She could not imagine who had come to rouse the queen at midnight, nor did she think the news good. She hurried out with the two women, everyone silent. The hall outside the chamber was brightly illuminated.

She led the way, hurrying down the stairs. The conversation in the great hall was now muted. When she reached its threshold, she faltered.

And then her heart exploded.

His back was to her, but Alexander stood with the queen.

Alexander was at Kildrummy; Alexander was alive!

Tears arose, blurring her vision. Isabella seized her hand. "He lives," she whispered.

Margaret nodded, speechless and beyond relief. *Alexander lived.*

But Alexander spoke rapidly and urgently. The queen listened attentively, her expression grim. Bruce's sisters stood with her, as did Sir Nigel and Sir Neil. Another man she did not recognize was also with them, but he resembled Bruce and she imagined he was another one of his brothers. Everyone was frighteningly grim.

Her relief and joy were short-lived. Why had he come? She stared at the women in their nightclothes, the men armed with sword and dagger. Alexander and the other nobleman had come from the war—they had come from the forests, where they had been hiding since Methven.

"What news could he be bringing?" Isabella whispered. "The queen looks frightened!"

Elisabeth did look frightened, Margaret thought. And in another moment or two, Alexander would see her. Her relief and excitement changed instantly. She had not seen him in three months, and he had never answered her letter.

She no longer feared the news he was bringing. Instead, trepidation assailed her. What would happen when he turned around to face her?

"What are you going to do?" Isabella whispered in her ear.

She could not even look at her friend. And she did not know what she would do—or what she should do.

The queen was now talking to him, and then Sir Nigel was saying something. As Bruce's brother spoke, Alexander turned and glanced at her.

She stiffened as their gazes met.

He did not smile at her. For an instant he simply stared, his expression impossible to read. Then the queen spoke to him and he turned his attention back to her.

"I don't know what I will do," Margaret finally said to Isabella. And anguish began—anguish she must not allow to arise.

"I wonder why he is here. Maybe he has come for you," she said.

Margaret finally glanced at her. "He is here on the king's business, Isabella."

Isabella's eyes popped and she jerked hard on Margaret's sleeve.

Margaret turned. Alexander was striding toward her.

She froze. She no longer saw the queen and her women, who were having a sharp discussion with the three men. She was no longer aware of Isabella. As he approached, it felt as if her entire future was hanging from a thread.

Alexander paused before her. "Lady Margaret," he said politely.

Dismay warred with hope. "Alexander," she whispered.

His gaze slipped over her. "I was pleased when I learned that ye had fled Castle Fyne."

She somehow nodded, when she wanted to blurt out so much, all at once. "You are well," she managed to respond.

"I am as well as a man can be in these times," he said.

"I am so sorry. The news has been so terrible," she whispered, referring to the massacre of Methven.

His eyes flickered. "Many good men died. Other good men were captured. But the king lives."

"And you are alive," she said.

"Did ye doubt it?"

"When we received the news, no one knew if you had survived, escaped, been captured." Moisture began to arise in her eyes.

"I am not so easy to capture or kill."

She blinked furiously, suddenly recalling the vow he had made to her—that if she was waiting for him, he would always return from war. She wondered if he recalled it.

"I was also pleased to learn that William survived," he said.

He was being so careful now—so polite—as if they had never been lovers. "William was badly hurt—had I not tended him, he probably would have died."

He nodded, studying her. "Then I am glad ye went to him." He hesitated, glancing briefly at the queen and her circle. "I am glad ye are well, Margaret."

Her heart skidded as their gazes met and locked.

"We have matters to discuss, but now is not the time. We leave immediately, as soon as the sun comes up."

Alarm began. "Where are we going? What has happened?"

"Yer no longer safe here at Kildrummy, not since King Edward declared the women outlaws. Bruce wants the queen and her women with him."

"But he hides in the forest!"

"He is now at Aberdeen, and I am to take ye there."

Would they be better off—and safer—if with Bruce? His small army was surely greater than the handful of knights now guarding them at Kildrummy. She looked up fearfully and found Alexander staring far too closely.

"No woman should have to run and hide like an outlaw." Anger darkened his eyes. "Gather up yer belongings. Dawn comes swiftly." He turned to go.

She seized his arm, surprising them both. Touching him brought back so many memories, which should, perhaps, be illicit now. "Did you receive my letter, Alexander?" The moment she had spoken, she wished she had not.

"Aye." His gaze seemed wary now. "I meant to respond, but these three months have been difficult."

She released him. He had not found the time to write

a line or two in reply? She did not believe it. And hadn't she already known that his lack of a reply *was* the reply?

He nodded at her, turned and strode back to the queen and her closest advisors. Margaret stared after him.

Everything had changed. They were no longer lovers—it felt instead as if they had become strangers. She blinked back more tears.

"Thank God Bruce has sent for us," Isabella whispered.

Margaret had forgotten her presence. Now, the other woman put her arm around her. And for that, Margaret was grateful.

THE FIRST THING Margaret saw was Bruce's red-and-yellow banner waving high in the sunny blue sky above his tent.

It was a bit after noon. Bruce had made camp just outside the city's walls, and Margaret was surprised to see that his army was larger than she had expected after what she had heard about the massacre at Methven. Tents covered the grassy slopes surrounding the city. Their warhorses grazed freely among sheep and cows. The city gates were open, and men and women were coming and going freely. The scene seemed pleasant and almost gay.

But there was nothing pleasant about the mighty Robert Bruce being reduced to a king in hiding, she thought grimly.

The queen's cavalcade slowed as it approached the camp, the queen riding at the forefront with Bruce's two brothers, Sir Nigel and Sir Edward—the man she had not recognized that night alongside Alexander. Christina, Mary and Marjorie were behind her, several dozen knights alongside and behind the group.

Alexander rode a bit ahead of her. He had continually changed his position, sometimes going to the front ranks to speak with Sir Nigel and Sir Edward, at other times dropping back to ride with the rear guard. She felt certain, knowing him as she did, that he had scouts positioned along their route to make certain they could pass safely through the countryside.

He had ridden past her once. They had simply gazed at one another. The moment had felt significant, when all they had done was exchange stares.

Sir Nigel was helping the queen dismount. Bruce came striding out of his tent, and as he did, his men began to cheer. "King Robert! King Robert!"

Along the city walls, the cheering was taken up by the men and women watching the camp. "King Robert of Scotland!"

Isabella had been riding alongside her, and Margaret glanced at her. "So he remains beloved, at least here in the north."

Isabella did not answer and Margaret took a closer look at her set face. She was not happy.

She turned back to Bruce and saw him embracing Elisabeth, the way a husband hugs his wife after a long period of separation. Elisabeth actually smiled at him, and touched his cheek, a simple caress.

Margaret glanced back at Isabella, who appeared furious. "She is his wife," Margaret stressed.

Isabella wisely did not answer, but her color was high.

Suddenly a woman began crying out. "John! John!"

Margaret saw Marjorie running across the camp. Atholl was rushing toward her from the other side of the camp, his arms open.

She watched them embrace. Atholl held her, hard, for a long time, and then they kissed as if they were lovers, not man and wife.

Feeling so happy for them, she no longer believed Atholl a spy for King Edward. His life had been at risk at Methven. He would have fled to the English ranks during the massacre, had he been their agent.

As she watched them hugging one another, Margaret realized she was being closely watched, as well.

Alexander was staring at her. She felt her cheeks flame. Did he know that she yearned to be embraced in just such a manner?

He rode his warhorse over to her. "Two tents have been made for the women." He slid from his horse, handing the reins to a young Highland lad, and approached, reaching up for her.

Her heart continued to race. He was going to realize that he still affected her in a great many ways. Margaret let him help her dismount, and then he turned to aid Isabella. He gestured to them both to follow. Margaret fell silently into step behind him with Isabella, who clearly was reluctant. Margaret knew she wished to veer away and attempt to see Bruce. She so hoped Isabella would behave sensibly now.

She gazed at Alexander's broad shoulders, at his unruly dark hair. She hated the awkwardness between them. Inhaling, she said, "Do you know how long we will be here?"

He turned and paused, allowing her to fall into step with him. They walked past a large cook fire and several tents. Young boys were playing with a stick and a ball of rope. "No, I dinna ken. But Bruce plans to send the women to the Orkney Islands."

Margaret gasped. She had no wish to live in the Orkney Islands!

Her dismay must have shown, because he said, "He needs to keep the queen safe, Lady Margaret. His sister

Isabel is the Dowager Queen of Norway. He has already sent emissaries ahead."

Margaret's head began to ache. She wished to remain behind—the Orkney Islands were so far away from Alexander.

He said, "That tent is for ye and six other ladies."

She did not look at it. "Will I be forced to go to the Orkney Islands?"

"Where else could ye go? 'Tis no secret that ye have joined Queen Elisabeth, defying Buchan. All of Scotland knows ye refused to marry Sir Guy when ye ran from Castle Fyne."

He was right. If the queen went, taking her ladies with her, she would have to go with them. She had nowhere else to go. "I am afraid, Alexander."

"I ken. Margaret…" He stopped.

"What? If you have something to say, please, say it!" she cried.

"I have so many questions," he said sharply. "And even now, I dinna like it when yer afraid."

What did that mean? She knew she must stop being emotional. But she wanted to cry—and rush into his arms—and demand her own answers. "I will answer all your questions—you must merely ask them," she managed to answer.

He took her arm and guided her away from the tent, toward the outskirts of the camp. Margaret realized Isabella had already wandered away from them. She did not look back to see where she was, as she could guess. "I do not like this awkwardness," she said. "How can we have become strangers?"

He glanced at her as they approached a pair of majestic fir trees. "It has been three months since we last spoke."

"I wrote you a letter. You did not reply." She cringed at hearing her own desperation!

"I dinna ken what yer asking me, Margaret," he said abruptly.

"You were fond of me. You once wished to marry me. Is there another woman you wish to wed—one with a real dowry?" She could not look away from him now.

"No. We're at war," he said, quite unnecessarily.

"Bruce wanted us wed, once. Has he changed his mind?"

He stared for a moment. "Castle Fyne remains my ambition."

What did that mean? And he hadn't answered her question.

"And what of ye, Margaret? Have ye decided to fall in love with someone—Sir Neil, perhaps?"

There is only one man I love, she thought, but she was surprised that he would ask her such a thing. "No," she said.

He flushed. Then, "If ye dinna love someone else, then why did ye write me such a letter?"

"I am uncertain of your meaning, Alexander."

"Ye wrote me as if we were strangers! I hardly believed ye wrote it."

She inhaled, struck by his words. "Is that why you did not write me back?"

"The lady who wrote me was not the same woman I held in my arms," he said with finality.

She began shaking her head. "Should I have written to you, proclaiming my eternal love? Begging you to return my affections when you left me so angrily? I am a proud woman, Alexander. Without my dowry, I have no value as a bride and we both know it. Most men would have lost interest in taking me to wife once Sir Guy conquered Castle Fyne. You are not most men, yet surely, you wish a bride with lands."

"Is that what ye wished to ask me—if I cared still? If I still wanted ye as a bride?"

"Yes."

His eyes widened. A long moment ensued, and he said slowly, "And do ye love me—eternally?"

She trembled. "I do love you, Alexander. Of course I do."

A fierce look covered his face. "I have missed ye, Margaret."

And before she could utter another word, Alexander crushed her in his arms, his mouth upon hers. Margaret held on to him, as tightly as she could, kissing him back. They stood that way for a very long time.

And when the kiss had ended, he looked down at her. "I will come to ye tonight."

"I HAD FORGOTTEN," Alexander said, "how beautiful ye truly are."

Margaret lay in his arms, their naked bodies entwined. He had said he would come to her in the middle of the night, but it was later that afternoon, and they were in Alexander's tent. He shared it with several other men, but he had obviously instructed them to give them an hour of privacy.

She had missed him so much. "I did not forget how handsome you are," she said teasingly. Then she sobered. "I have been so afraid for you."

"I have worried about you, as well." He shifted so they could look at one another more easily. "I have heard that yer uncle has disavowed his wife—and that he is furious with ye, too."

"He has threatened Isabella. I pray they never see one another again."

"Ye were so loyal to yer family fer so long. Ye were so loyal to Buchan. What happened at Castle Fyne?"

Her tension spiraled. She felt ill in the pit of her belly. She had not thought about Sir Guy's attempt to rape her in months—she had deliberately buried the memory. Now, images tried to emerge within her mind, along with grotesque tactile sensations, of being brutally gripped and violently kissed, and she remembered how fear had clawed at her.

"Did Sir Guy hurt ye?" Alexander asked.

She pushed away from him and sat up, unable to breathe. She did not want to look at Alexander now—she did not want to have this conversation. But their gazes met.

"Why won't ye answer?"

She inhaled, shaking. "He wanted to consummate the marriage—I refused."

"What happened—exactly?"

She pulled away. "A messenger came, interrupting us. I was fortunate."

Alexander also sat up, the covers falling to his waist. "Did he try to rape ye, Margaret?"

She met his gaze, and somehow she nodded.

Alexander did not move, except for his chest, which slowly rose and fell. "I am going to kill him."

Margaret whispered, "It is over, Alexander." But it did not feel over, not at all.

"It is over when he is dead." He pulled her unyielding body close. "I was not there to protect ye, Margaret. What he tried to do will haunt me till I die."

She felt tears of grief arising.

He stroked her hair for a moment. "If the queen and

her women are captured before they reach the Orkney Islands, they will suffer a terrible fate. And ye could be captured with them."

She stiffened, aware that what he said was true, but wondering at his declaration.

If she was ever captured, Sir Guy might come for her. He might demand she be handed over to him certainly wanting some kind of revenge for her actions. "If I am captured, I might be handed over to Sir Guy."

"If yer captured, ye will shout to anyone who listens that yer Buchan's niece."

"Everyone knows I fled Sir Guy—and I swore fealty to Bruce."

"Ye will deny ever paying homage to King Robert. And yer still Buchan's niece—the most powerful Comyn lord alive." He clearly saw her surprise and misgivings. "I have not changed my mind about our marriage, Margaret. But I will never marry ye while the king's proclamation against the women stands. I will never marry ye if doing so puts yer life at risk. Ye have some protection now, being Buchan's ward and niece, if everyone believes yer still loyal to him."

She was shaken. "I don't know if Buchan will try to save my life. Sir Guy might even let me hang."

"Sir Guy will seek to marry ye—for the sake of Castle Fyne, for the sake of his alliance with Buchan."

Could that be true? "I cannot marry him," she said tersely.

"If yer captured, ye might have no choice—and it is a better choice than death." He was sharp. "If we marry now, ye'll be hanged as a traitor the moment yer captured—for ye'll be the Wolf of Lochaber's wife."

He had no doubt, she saw that, and he was so much

worldlier than she was, especially when it came to matters of war and politics.

"And you, Alexander?" she whispered. "Who will save you, if you are ever captured?"

"I live by the sword, Margaret. One day I will die a warrior's death."

She wondered if he considered being hanged—or drawn and quartered—for the crime of treason a warrior's death. And Bruce's army had been reduced to a few hundred men. The English army numbered thousands. "Will Bruce ever give up? Does he truly believe he can somehow defeat King Edward? If he loses this war, he will be hanged—and his allies will hang, too!"

"Bruce will never surrender—he is Scotland's king." He gave her a hard look. "I am not afraid to die, Margaret, but I also intend to live. And Bruce intends to raise a new army with my brother's support. He will hide from the English until we are strong again, until we can fight back. I doubt we will see more fighting until next spring. Sometimes a battle is lost, Margaret, before the war is won."

She shivered. This war would last for years, she thought in dismay, and when it ended, so many would be dead. Alexander somehow believed the cause was not lost. If only she could believe that, too.

He suddenly pulled her close. "We may have a few days or a few weeks here. I dinna wish to argue. I wish to hold ye—while I can."

SUMMER HAD SETTLED over northern Scotland in all her glory.

Each day brought blue skies filled with puffy white clouds and bright sunshine. Birds sang merrily from treetops, hawks soared above the encampment, Bruce's men repaired their weaponry, played mock war games, fished and hunted, and wenched amongst the village women.

It was as if the war for Scotland did not exist.

Margaret resolved to cherish every moment of the strange respite they were being given, well aware that at any time, Bruce's emissaries would return from Norway, and she and the queen's court would be sent to the Orkney Islands. They had so much leisure time now. Alexander took her swimming, taught her to use a bow with better accuracy, gifted her with a small dagger, and took her for long rides in the forest, where they made love to the sound of scurrying squirrels and merry blue jays. At night they retired to their respective tents, he with the men, she with the women. And as pleasant as the summer was, everyone knew it was only a matter of time before they must flee King Edward's armies again.

Margaret dreaded the impending separation, but did not speak of it.

For the first time since arriving at Aberdeen, the skies were gray, threatening a summer storm. Alexander had indicated they would take their usual afternoon ride, and she hurried through the camp to meet him. As she turned past one tent at the end of the camp, the forest a short distance ahead, she came face-to-face with Marjorie and Atholl.

The earl had his arm around his wife's waist, and clearly, they had come from a tryst of their own in the forest. Margaret smiled at the couple. "Have you seen Alexander?"

"No, we have not," Atholl answered. "It is going to rain, Margaret, and I wouldn't go into the forest if I were you."

She happened to agree, so she joined them as they started back into the encampment. At that moment, a deer leapt out of the forest, directly in front of them, and then it streaked away across the road.

Atholl seized his wife's arm just as thundering hoof-beats could be heard. He then grabbed Margaret, pulling both women back off of the deer path, as a rider galloped out of the woods.

He raced past them, a man in Highland garb, his horse covered in foam and sweat.

For one moment, they just stood there, watching as the rider galloped his mount into the camp at a break-neck speed.

"News," Atholl said, and he began to run.

Margaret and Marjorie ran after him, Margaret's mind racing. A messenger had come. The summer was over. The war had come.

They ran hard through the outskirts of the camp, which was oddly vacant—everyone had rushed toward Bruce's tent to find out what tidings the rider was bringing. Margaret thought her lungs would burst. She prayed the news held some tiny seed of hope.

Finally they could see Robert Bruce standing with the rider, who remained astride his blowing mount. Most of the court had gathered in a circle around the king and the messenger, including the queen, Bruce's brothers and sisters, his closest nobles, Isabella and Alexander.

Margaret and Marjorie slowed to a staggering walk, clutching one another for support, breathing too hard to speak. But neither took her gaze from Bruce and his entourage.

The rider finally ceased his diatribe and slid from his horse. Bruce simply stood there, stiff with tension, unmoving.

"Oh, God," Margaret finally whispered, still out of breath. The news was as bad as she had expected.

Alexander suddenly saw her. They rushed to one another. "What is it? What has happened?" she cried.

He caught her by her shoulders. "Aymer de Valence is in the north—he knows where we are and is two days' march from us."

"How is that possible?" Was Sir Guy with him? Of course he was!

"Some of our scouts were captured, tortured and hanged."

Margaret stared into his eyes and saw how worried Alexander was. "What will happen now? What will we do?"

"I dinna ken. But we must plan and we must do so swiftly."

He had hardly finished speaking when a woman's scream rent the afternoon. It was a scream of protest and anguish, a wail unlike any other. Margaret's gaze flew past Alexander.

Christina Seton was on her knees before Robert Bruce, screaming in protest and sorrow. Bruce dropped down to his knees and pulled her into his arms. She screamed again, pummeling him repeatedly.

Margaret felt tears flood her eyes as she gazed up at Alexander. He put his arm around her. "Sir Christopher was captured and hanged."

SHE HAD LEARNED to hate the forest.

Margaret sat her mare in single file now, as Bruce's court and his army traversed a narrow ravine in Dalry. The king and his soldiers led the cavalcade at a walk, the queen and her women following. Behind them were more knights, and behind them, the foot soldiers. There were no wagons, no supply carts. They had fled Aberdeen with what could be carried by hand, or upon one's back.

The morning was shockingly silent. No birds chirped

from the pines on the slopes of the gully, no squirrels raced through the trees. No one spoke—it was not allowed. The only sounds being made were the steady clip-clop of their horses' hooves, the jangle of their bridles, the creak of their saddles.

She had come to hate the silence, too—she feared it.

Had the enemy finally caught up to them, and was it lying in wait, around the next bend? Or was it Bruce's own men and women who had chased the wildlife away?

She had lost count of the days that they had been traveling through the forest. She had lost count of the nights. She slept in Alexander's arms, but sleep had become impossible. Beneath the open stars, they listened for the same sounds of pursuit among each and every sound of the night, when the forest came alive. Brush whispered, leaves sighed, owls hooted, wolves howled…. At night, it would be almost impossible to discern an enemy that was stalking them.

For how long could they go on this way?

Bruce believed he could elude the English and find sanctuary in Argyll—upon MacDonald lands. They were in Argyll now. But they were not on lands belonging to the king of the isles—they were on MacDougall lands.

Margaret did not want to think about Alexander Mac-Dougall of Argyll, her mother's brother, now. But she did. He had never responded to her single plea for aid last February, after Alexander had besieged Castle Fyne. He was at war with Bruce and he was at war with Alexander. She could not wait till they had crossed his lands.

Her glance wandered to Christina, who remained deeply in grief. She rode with her head bowed, which she never lifted, her entire body hunched over. From time to time, she wept. Christina was so anguished that she had not spoken more than a syllable since they had left Aberdeen.

Margaret knew she would be as inconsolable, should anything happen to Alexander. But maybe there was hope. Maybe they would somehow arrive safely at a Mac-Donald stronghold....

Suddenly, Highland war cries rent the day.

Margaret halted her horse as arrows whizzed from the treetops above the ravine, as soldiers leapt down from the trees and rocks above them, as knights began charging down the precarious sides of the gulch. In front of her, a horse screamed, struck by an arrow, and collapsed. She realized in horror that Marjorie was astride it! But before she could cry out, battles began between Bruce's men and the attackers, up and down the column, throughout the ravine. Screams sounded, both the screams of horses and men. In horror, she saw several of their knights falling from their mounts, slain by Aymer's archers.

In panic, she prepared to flee, except the ravine was narrow—and there was nowhere to flee to!

A man seized her, pulling her from her mount. Terror gave way to relief when she slid into Alexander's arms.

He dragged her across the ravine, through the fighting men, the wheeling horses, the bodies already strewn about, and shoved her into a crevice between several boulders. "Marjorie!" she cried.

"Stay here," he ordered, and then he whirled and ran into the melee.

Margaret watched him swiftly engage an English knight, exchange blows and expertly knock the man's sword from him. He pulled the knight from his horse and thrust his sword into his enemy's chest. He then leapt astride the English charger and turned to face his next opponent, sword raised. He moved with such practiced grace and speed it seemed a blur.

Frantically, Margaret looked for Marjorie. Hundreds of men filled the ravine, most on foot, although a dozen knights were close to where she hid, including Alexander. Everyone was engaged in life-and-death combat.

Finally she saw Marjorie, on foot, hunched over, trying to run through the warring men.

"Marjorie!" Margaret screamed. But she knew she could not be heard, not when everyone was screaming, when arrows were whizzing, when horses were neighing....

Margaret glanced for Alexander, but he was far down the ravine, still astride, and slaying those in his path. She ran from the boulders.

She leapt over a body and saw Marjorie being seized by an English knight, one on foot. "Marjorie!"

Her friend was struggling frantically. Margaret hadn't realized she clenched her dagger until that moment. With a howl, she leapt up and thrust the knife as hard as she possibly could into a spot on the base of the knight's neck, beneath the mail of his helmet. He released Marjorie, howling. Margaret seized her hand and both women ran, Margaret leading the way.

She jammed Marjorie into the crevice. She was about to slip into the space as well, when suddenly her skin prickled.

Margaret whirled, pressing her back against the boulder, as Marjorie cried, "Margaret!"

A huge gray destrier faced her, blowing hard, pawing the earth. An English knight was mounted upon it, his visor down, and he was staring at her.

And Margaret could not move. She knew who it was before he lifted his visor.

"Treacherous bitch," Sir Guy said. He withdrew his word from its sheath in a hiss, while smiling coldly at her.

He had no honor—he meant to kill her. Margaret had no doubt.

In that moment, she became paralyzed. She could not look away. His gray eyes burned with hatred. And he was walking his mount forward....

Margaret pressed her spine into the rock, wondering if she could somehow wriggle backward into the space there, knowing that if she turned to escape into the crevice, he would use his sword to cleave her back.

"How long have you been MacDonald's whore?" he demanded, crowding her against the rocks.

She could feel the horse's breath blowing upon her face; she could smell its breath. She did not dare answer.

"Tell me, whore!" he shouted.

"I love him!" she shouted back.

Sir Guy drove the destrier forward. Margaret screamed as the animal, having nowhere to go except over her, reared in protest. She saw its deadly hooves above her....

"A Donald!" Alexander roared.

Margaret covered her head with her arms as Sir Guy's horse came down a mere inch away from her, and she heard their swords ring wildly. She looked up and saw Alexander and Sir Guy braced sword to sword against one another, each man's face filled with vicious fury.

"Margaret!" Marjorie begged her to hide in the rocks.

Margaret ignored her, as the men exchanged enraged and violent blows. Both men were skilled. Both men were determined. Both men meant to kill the other.

And then Sir Guy's sword danced off of Alexander's arm, dripping blood. She cringed in dread. But Alexander parried so hard now, it was as if he hadn't been wounded. A series of terrible blows were exchanged before both men moved their horses a few steps backward. Alexander was panting—so was Sir Guy. Neither man ever looked away from the other.

In unison, they both leapt to the ground, swords raised. Their horses raced away. Alexander and Sir Guy began circling one another. Alexander's smile was cruel and menacing. Sir Guy's smile was as vicious.

And they both struck at once.

Blow after blow was dealt and parried. Margaret could not stand it, when suddenly Sir Guy's sword went flying from his hand.

Sir Guy froze, his expression one of fear.

Alexander smiled ruthlessly, in triumph, as he raised his sword and brought it ruthlessly down....

Margaret closed her eyes, but she heard the terrible sound of the blade driving through a human body. And she heard Sir Guy scream.

There was another horrific sound, followed by a thump. A moment later Alexander closed his hands upon her shoulders. "It is over, dinna look."

She opened her eyes, meeting his burning blue gaze—careful not to look past him, where she knew Sir Guy lay dead, his body probably decapitated. Margaret somehow nodded, trembling, in shock.

Sir Guy was dead. She could not believe it.

And then she realized that the battle was also over. She looked in the opposite direction from where Sir Guy lay. The ravine there was littered with the bodies and corpses of dying and dead horses and men. She sank against Alexander in relief, and for another brief moment, he held her.

The queen. Isabella.

Margaret looked wildly down the ravine, and finally saw Sir Nigel with Queen Elisabeth, both on foot, and both, apparently, unhurt. She now remarked Isabella, Sir Neil, Christina Seton, and then she saw Robert Bruce. He was astride his mighty warhorse, giving orders to his men.

Tears blinded her. Those dear to her had survived this battle, but for how long?

Alexander put his arm around her again. "We must tend to the wounded," he said. "And if ye can, we could use yer help."

Margaret gathered up her composure and nodded. "Of course."

CHAPTER NINETEEN

MARGARET SAT WITH Isabella, arm in arm, in exhaustion. They had gathered up the wounded and fled the ravine. In a more defensible area, they had paused and Margaret had spent the afternoon with the other women taking care of their wounded.

Margaret leaned tiredly against Isabella, her cheek upon the other woman's shoulder. The camp was spread out before them. The wounded lay in one area; the women had gathered near them while the able had gone to forage for their supper. The horses grazed. "I am too tired to move."

"I am afraid," Isabella whispered.

Margaret took her hand. "We're all afraid."

She was so tired that she did not want to think. But she had to contemplate the future. Bruce had lost hundreds more men. His army had been reduced to almost nothing. His men were exhausted. The horses were exhausted. They had no supplies, no food. Now what would they do?

She had heard bits and pieces of their conversations all afternoon. Sir Guy had not led the attack. It had been devised and commanded by Argyll's son—John the Lame. They remained on MacDougall lands. Everyone expected to be attacked a second time.

Bruce was considering a different path of flight, into the lands of his close ally, the Earl of Lennox. But Lennox had not been seen nor heard from since Methven....

She saw Alexander walking slowly toward her. He was so tired. She saw it not just by his pace, which was more sluggish than usual, but in the set of his broad shoulders.

Nevertheless, he smiled at her. "Can we speak?"

"Of course." He put his arm on her shoulder and guided her aside. "What will we do now?"

He smiled again and tilted up her chin. "Bruce has decided to send the women back to Kildrummy. They're not safe here, and he needs to travel swiftly now, in order to hide from those who seek to hunt him down and kill him."

Margaret trembled in dismay. Kildrummy was now safe? Since when? "I do not want to return to Kildrummy," she began.

He held up his hand, silencing her. "Bruce is sending the horses with the women. It will be too hard to find grazing for them."

Margaret had thought the situation very dire before. Now, he meant to hide in the forests with his remaining men, on foot! "They will not move as swiftly on foot."

"They will move swiftly if they do not wear mail."

She inhaled. They would abandon their armor. "So they will flee with but sword and dagger?"

He nodded.

She was suddenly furious. If an English army found them, they would be destroyed. A man on foot could not fight a man on horseback. No one would survive such an encounter. "God, and you will flee with them?"

"No. He sends me back to Kintyre to warn Angus of what has happened—to beg him for his aid and for refuge."

He was leaving Bruce and his decimated army—she was relieved!

"I want ye with me, Margaret."

She took a deep breath, but before she could speak, he said, "Kildrummy has never been under siege. But I fear for the queen and her women with Aymer in control of so much of the north. I could be captured, Margaret," he warned. "If yer with me, ye'd be captured, too."

She nodded tearfully. "I don't care. I will come with you, Alexander."

They stared at one another for a long time. "I'll tell Bruce."

Dunaverty Castle—late August, 1306

"I AM EAGER to acquaint ye with my brother," Alexander said, smiling.

She could not believe they had reached the great Mac-Donald stronghold. Margaret walked beside Alexander, his arm around her. She had been exhausted, for they had ridden long and hard for the past four days, only pausing to rest for a few hours at night.

Just a short while ago they had been at sea in a vessel borrowed from a fisherman, crossing the Firth of Clyde. The seas had been choppy, with a strong breeze filling the single sail, and they had swiftly approached Kintyre. Margaret had been seated in the bow of the tiny vessel, clinging to its side. When Dunaverty had come into view, a bulky castle perched high above the sea upon great cliffs, her exhaustion had vanished. It had been immediately replaced with excitement and awe.

They had escaped the mainland. They had left the war behind.

Finally, they were safe.

And maybe, just maybe, this was a new beginning....

They were strolling through the castle's large outdoor courtyard, now. Margaret smiled up at Alexander; he smiled back.

He thinks this is a beginning, too, she thought.

The MacDonald flag with its dark field and red dragon flew proudly from one high tower, whipping in the wind. Highlanders stood above them on the ramparts. And then she heard the sound of Alexander's name, and she slowed and turned, as did Alexander. Highland soldiers had come to the edge of the ramparts to look down upon them.

"Alexander!" they called. "The mighty Wolf returns!"

Chills swept over her; tears filled her eyes. These men were his kin, and they worshipped him.

His name was being echoed amongst them again and again. And a refrain began, one that turned into a chant.

"Alexander! The mighty Wolf is home! The mighty Wolf returns! Long live the mighty Wolf of Clan Donald!"

His grasp on her shoulders tightened. He leaned closer. "Welcome to Dunaverty, Margaret."

She looked up at him, overcome with relief. She reached for and squeezed his hand. "They love you," she whispered.

He smiled at her, a twinkle in his eyes—one she had never before seen. "And soon, they will love ye just as much," he said. "Come."

She stiffened, even as he propelled her inside the great hall of the castle. For his meaning was clear. Soon, she would be his wife, the lady MacDonald.

She thought of her mother, Mary MacDougall. Somehow, she knew Mary would be happy for her, and that she would be pleased.

Margaret's attention was diverted. The great room had high-beamed ceilings, and two massive stone hearths.

Otherwise it was sparsely furnished, with one table, benches and a few chairs. Rushes were upon the floors, banners hanging from the high rafters. Fires blazed. And a tall, dark-haired man was at the far end of the room.

Even without the MacDonald plaid worn about his broad shoulders, Margaret would have recognized him instantly. He looked so much like Alexander—no one could doubt that they were brothers.

Margaret thought him in his early thirties. He was taller than most men, with broad shoulders, and arms sculpted from the years he had spent wielding swords and axes. His dark hair was shoulder-length. His eyes were sky-blue. He was an attractive man, one resonating power and command.

Angus Og, lord of the isles, approached. He was beaming.

Alexander hurried forward, smiling, as well. Both men embraced, the hug filled with warmth and feeling. Then Angus withdrew, clasping his brother's shoulder. "I dinna expect ye. What news?"

Alexander sobered. "None of it is good, Angus. Bruce hides in the forests. He has been defeated twice this summer, at Methven and Dalry. At Methven, there was treachery and a massacre—he lost most of his army. John the Lame and Sir Guy de Valence ambushed us at Dalry. Sir Guy is dead."

Angus was grim. "News of Methven reached us a few weeks ago. But not of Dalry. Where is Bruce now? What men does he have left?"

"I left Bruce in Argyll, not far from Dalry. He has few men, no horses and his women have been returned to Kildrummy Castle, with few knights to guard them and no stores."

"Is it true that Aymer has six thousand men?"

"Aye, and he holds a great many castles once taken by Bruce. He continues to hold Perth."

"And Bruce?" Angus pressed.

"Bruce thinks to pass to the west of Loch Lommond and then onto the lands of Lennox. But we dinna ken if Lennox survived Methven. He has sent Neil Campbell ahead to procure ships. If he can cross into Campbell territory, he will need the vessels to cross to Dunaverty."

Angus stared at Alexander, his expression impassive and impossible to read.

"I have been sent ahead to ask ye fer yer help," Alexander said.

"Bruce is Scotland's rightful king. I promised him my support long ago. He will have it now, in his darkest hour." And as if the conversation were concluded, his gaze veered to Margaret briefly. He seemed surprised, and he took a second glance at her, before returning his attention to Alexander.

Alexander nodded with hard satisfaction. "It is up to Bruce then—and to Lennox if he lives, and to Campbell. But I have been instructed to begin to raise a new army for him."

Angus's smile was knowing. "He has many here in the isles who will support him. We'll sit later and discuss it." He now turned and faced Margaret. "Introduce me to yer lady, Alexander."

Alexander smiled. "Brother, there is nothing I wish to do more. She is Lady Margaret Comyn."

Angus Og approached. "The Lady of Loch Fyne."

Margaret had tensed. She and Alexander now planned to marry, and she wanted his brother's approval. But she was a MacDougall by birth—she was the blood enemy of his entire clan. "My lord," she said. "I am Lady Margaret

Comyn. I pray it does not distress you that I am here, imposing upon your hospitality now in our time of need."

He seemed amused as he studied her. "I ken who ye be, Lady Margaret. I heard the tale long ago of how bravely ye tried to fight off my brother."

Margaret hoped that was praise. "At the time, he was the enemy, and there was no other choice."

"How old are ye?"

"I will soon be eighteen."

"Most women yer age would not have tried to defend a castle with but a handful of men."

Alexander said, "She is not most women. She is uncommon."

Angus glanced at him with a smile. "Uncommonly brave, uncommonly beautiful. I can see why ye keep her. Ye remind me of yer aunt, Lady Margaret."

Margaret was surprised.

"Ye look very much like Juliana. She is another Mac-Dougall who is brave and beautiful—who dared to love one of my brothers."

Margaret wasn't sure how to respond.

Angus said, "Do ye love my little brother?"

"Yes." She bit her lip. "I love him greatly…I hope that pleases you."

He studied her. "It would please me to know that ye have truly forsaken yer MacDougall loyalties."

Of course he cared mostly about her loyalty to the clan he hated more than anything and anyone. "I will always be loyal to Will—my only remaining brother. I will always be loyal to my mother and my father, God bless them, for they are dead. But—" she looked at Alexander, and tears arose "—I love Alexander. I never meant to love him, but it came to pass. When I fled the Englishman I was meant to wed, I knew I was giving up my every ancient loyalty. I am loyal to Alexander, my lord. For now and forever."

Alexander slid his arm around her. "I have asked her to marry me—many times, actually. She has only recently agreed."

Angus's stare remained upon her and it was thoughtful. "The last time a MacDougall married a MacDonald, ancient loyalties were tested and torn asunder. It isn't easy to love the enemy."

"I know," Margaret whispered.

"But Juliana never wavered—my older brother never wavered—and ye remind me of her." He walked to Alexander and laid his hand upon his shoulder. "If ye love her as our brother loves Juliana, she will be fortunate, indeed."

Margaret trembled, holding back tears. They had just been given Angus Og's blessing.

He smiled at them then, and suddenly turned and exited the hall, leaving them very much alone.

Alexander reached out. Margaret gave him her hand.

"Will ye marry me now?"

Speechless, her heart thundering, she nodded.

He laughed and swept her into his embrace. His forehead against hers, he said thickly, "Now I can tell ye how I never thought to see this day."

"Me neither," she answered.

He lifted her into his arms. Margaret gasped in surprise as he carried her from the hall. "Alexander!"

"Ye said yes," he teased, striding up a narrow stairwell and hunching over to do so.

"It isn't noon!" she protested, clinging to his shoulders.

"So? I happen to ken well that ye like sex in the morning better than at night!"

She could not believe he would speak so openly, and she felt her cheeks flame. Fortunately, they were alone as he reached the landing and strode down the corridor. And she had no desire to protest.

The tradition of handfasting was as old as time. She had agreed to the union. As soon as they made love and consummated it, they would be man and wife.

He kicked open a door and she saw a dark bedchamber, but knew it was Alexander's. An old, rusted shield hung on one wall, and a coat of mail, worn and in need of repair, cloaked a straw replica of a man. Instinctively, she knew the shield and armor had belonged to his father, the last lord of the isles, Angus Mor.

He kicked the door closed and laid her down on the bed, coming down on top of her. She met his dark, intense stare.

"Will ye marry me now?"

"Yes."

His gaze did not waver. "Will ye be as loyal to me as Juliana is to my brother?"

"Yes."

"Till the death?" His tone was now thick.

She could not speak then, so she nodded, then managed, "Yes." Then, "I will love you for all time, Alexander. And you? Will you be loyal to me—will you love me—for all time?"

"Yes." He leaned low and covered her mouth with his.

Margaret had never loved him more. She reached for his face and held him, letting him kiss her deeply. When he finally ended the kiss, she realized she was crying.

He brushed her tears away with his fingers, then untied her girdle, tossing it aside.

Margaret had become breathless. Desire had risen up, hot and hard, joining the impossible surge of love.

He removed her surcote and cote together, lifted her chemise, and then settled his hard thighs between her legs. He thrust deep, watching her, and Margaret did not move. Pleasure took her breath away. So did love.

He said, "We're man and wife now."

A FEW WEEKS later, Bruce arrived at Dunaverty Castle.

The news of his arrival swept the castle. Margaret was putting away clothing that had recently been washed when she heard a young maid running past her chamber, crying out to her as she did so. Bruce had come! Dropping the pile of tunics, Margaret ran after the maid.

They charged up to the ramparts, which were filled with men and women, everyone hanging over the walls. "Bruce!" a man shouted.

"The Bruce!" another cried.

"King Robert Bruce!" men and women cheered.

Margaret reached the edge of the crenellations and hung over them breathlessly. It was a brisk autumn day, the seas beyond the beach choppy with white foam, the sky above bright and blue, clouds racing across it. She saw six galleons beached below, and then she saw Bruce striding up the last of the road leading to Dunaverty's front gates.

Three dozen men were behind him. Everyone carried their swords, but nothing else. Bruce was thin and gaunt, as were his men—frighteningly so. And many of the men were barefoot. Their hair was long, she now realized, their clothing in tatters. She was shocked.

When she and Alexander had left Bruce at Dalry, they had not been so lean, and he had had no more than twenty men. Tears filled her eyes. She could not imagine what had happened as they had tried to flee the mainland of Scotland to Kintyre.

But the cheers did not abate. Bruce had not changed otherwise. His head was high, his shoulders square. He did not look like a man who had suffered defeat after defeat. He smiled, holding up his hand. The crescendo increased. The crowd roared its approval.

When Bruce had disappeared from view into the entry tower, Margaret returned to the keep. She hurried inside, intent on getting down to the hall, for she wished to learn what had happened.

Bruce stood with Alexander and Angus before one hearth, the rest of his men already being given wine. Margaret slowed her pace as she approached.

The king saw her. He smiled. "Lady MacDonald. Congratulations. You have made a fortunate choice."

Margaret bowed her head. "Your Majesty." Then she met his piercing blue stare. The moment she did, she saw the resolve in his eyes—the strength in his demeanor.

Robert Bruce had been defeated, but nothing had changed. He was Scotland's king.

He turned back to Angus and Alexander. As she listened, she learned about how he and his men had been reduced to surviving upon roots, berries and small game. With winter approaching, it had been terribly cold, causing everyone to suffer. They had found shelter in caves.

They had been able to avoid a dangerous journey through MacDougall lands at Loch Lommond, by finding a sunken boat to carry them across the loch, in stages. By now, they were near starvation. Bruce divided his men into two hunting parties, as they were desperate for venison. And by sheer good fortune, the sound of their hunting horns was heard by the Earl of Lennox, who was also out hunting that day. A wonderful reunion ensued, as each man had thought the other to be dead.

Bruce and his men then joined Lennox at his camp,

as he was in hiding, as well. There, they managed to eat and drink, and then go on to meet Neil Campbell, who had been sent ahead after Dalry and who had two galleys waiting for them.

Bruce now paused, handing his cup to a passing maid for more wine. Angus clasped his shoulder. "But ye live. The king of Scotland lives."

"Was there ever doubt?" Bruce asked with his usual arrogance. "There can be no delay. I am sending my brother to Ireland to raise men from my estates there, and I will visit my brother's wife, Christiana of the Isles, as she will also give me men."

Margaret heard them discussing an invasion of Scotland in the following spring. She was in disbelief. Bruce's army had been reduced to a handful of starving knights. Yet he intended to invade Scotland and rejoin the war against King Edward in a matter of months! Aghast, she left the men.

But as she went upstairs, she began to think of how Bruce had thus far stolen Scotland's crown, and survived attack after attack by the mightiest army in the land. His ambition knew no bounds. If anyone could raise a mighty army now, it was Robert Bruce.

She was alone in their bedchamber, needlepoint in her hand, when Alexander came in many hours later. He smiled at her. "How can ye see to sew now?" Only two tapers were burning, while a small fire crackled in the hearth.

She set the embroidery down. Her heart had filled with warmth the moment Alexander had entered the chamber. How she loved him, for better or for worse. "Will Bruce be able to raise another army—one strong enough to fight King Edward?"

"Can ye doubt it?" Alexander came to her and took

her into his arms. "I ken ye hate war." He kissed her temple. "But ye married a warrior, Margaret. Do ye have regrets?"

She turned and put her arms around him. "I will never regret loving you or becoming your wife." For a moment, she simply pressed her face to his chest. Then she looked up. "I am glad Bruce lives, Alexander." And she meant it.

"Yer becoming a MacDonald, Margaret," he warned, with a gentle smile.

"I hope so," she said.

ALEXANDER WAS THE one to bring her the letter from her brother. It was a crisp October day, the skies bland and gray, the seas dark, the waves high. "Ye have a letter, Margaret, from William," he said, smiling.

His smile seemed odd but she ignored it, thrilled to have a missive from her brother. She had written to him shortly after her marriage, telling him that she was now Alexander's wife. She had written a lengthy and similar letter to Buchan. She did not know if her uncle would ever reply, but she was ecstatic to hear from her brother.

She eagerly read his every word. "He is at Balvenie now," she reported to Alexander. She read on and looked up. "He is enjoying days spent hunting and fishing." She read more. "He does not mention Buchan's reaction to my letter!"

Alexander sat down next to her. "Is there more?" he asked quietly.

She suddenly realized that his eyes were dark, his expression grim—something dire had happened. She picked up the parchment and read the final two paragraphs, her insides curdling. "Kildrummy has fallen."

"Aye," he said.

In horror, she reread what William had written.

"'Sir Nigel and Sir Neil valiantly defended Kildrummy Castle, but it fell on the tenth of September,'" she read. "'There was treachery from within the castle, Margaret, otherwise, perhaps they might have triumphed over Aymer.'"

He then changed the topic, inquiring about her well-being, and ended by saying that there was word in Scotland that Bruce would return, and he expected a resumption of the war in the spring.

Margaret was horrified, and she stared at Alexander, mistakenly crumpling the page in her hand, she held it so tightly.

"The women were not there, Margaret."

She choked in relief. "How is that possible?"

"They never went to Kildrummy. Sir Neil and Sir Nigel were left behind to defend the castle, while the women fled north with Atholl."

Kildrummy had been besieged, but the queen, Isabella and the other women had not been there. For that, she was thankful. But there was no relief. "Sir Neil? Sir Nigel?"

Alexander hesitated.

They were dead, she thought, suddenly faint.

"They were caught and hanged. Margaret, dinna ask me for the details." He put his arms around her.

She wanted to weep and scream. Her beautiful Sir Neil had been hanged. And Sir Nigel, Bruce's handsome, courageous brother, had been hanged with him!

"This is war, Margaret. Men die in war."

She pulled back and looked up at Alexander, sick with anguish, but furious, too. "If there is more bad news, you must tell me. Now! Is the queen hidden safely? Is Isabella?"

He studied her for a moment, and then he slipped away.

"Alexander!" she screamed, already knowing his answer.

He paced past her and closed the shutters. "It is truly cold in here."

"What happened to them!"

He slowly faced her. "They sought sanctuary at St. Duthac. They were all captured, Margaret. They are King Edward's prisoners."

Tears flooded her eyes. "What will he do to them?" she managed to ask.

"I dinna ken."

"Liar."

"Margaret!"

"Tell me the truth!" she cried. "Do you think I haven't heard how vengeful King Edward has been? I know what he did to Sir Christopher, he was drawn and quartered, Alexander, after he was hanged! What did they do to Sir Neil? To Sir Nigel?" she screamed.

He pulled her into his embrace. "I willna tell ye."

"I will find out, anyway!"

"Let it rest, Margaret," he said.

She wept against his chest then. Alexander held her and stroked her hair. And when she had spent a tiny portion of her grief, she looked up. "Where is Isabella? Marjorie? Christina?"

"They were being held at Aberdeen. I dinna ken where they are now."

She swiped away her tears. "I want to see them. I want to see Isabella."

"No. I willna allow it."

As they stared at one another, Margaret realized her demand had been impossible. She and Alexander would be captured if she went to visit her friends.

Her mind raced. Buchan would visit Isabella. Wouldn't he?

"I must see my uncle, Alexander."

His eyes widened. "Fer what cause?" Then comprehension covered his face. "So ye can beg him to spare Isabella his wrath? Ye canna do so, Margaret!"

"I must beg him to show her mercy! Buchan is an ally of King Edward. If he wants his wife back, King Edward will surely agree! Please! I must convince my uncle to take Isabella back! She will be better off if he is the one to punish her! God only knows what her fate will be otherwise!"

Alexander shook his head, resigned. "I must be mad—to agree to such madness."

Kilmory Knap Chapel, Loch Sween—November, 1306

ALEXANDER AND HIS men had gone into the small stone chapel where Margaret was to meet her uncle. In spite of the promises that had been made, he wished to make certain that they would not suffer an ambush. After all, the chapel was on MacSween land, and they were allied with the MacDougalls—they had taken up arms against Bruce.

But the meeting had been arranged by Alasdair Og and his wife, Juliana. Everyone had agreed that Juliana would be able to best bring both sides together, as she was a MacDougall by birth, and married to a MacDonald.

For Buchan, such a meeting posed little danger. Although Alasdair Og had managed, through his wife, to obtain the promise of safe passage for them, they were in the midst of the enemy's territory. Alexander trusted no one. Neither did Margaret.

She shivered, although fur-clad, astride her mount as

she waited outside the chapel. It was a frigidly cold day. Snow covered the ground, weighed down the evergreens, and capped the mountain peaks. The loch was as dark as iron as it swept out to the sound.

Alexander came outside, a fur swinging from his broad shoulders. Margaret breathed hard as he strode to her.

He was not happy; his mouth was downturned. "They're within—waiting fer ye."

Tension filled her, so much so, she could barely breathe. Somehow she nodded.

Alexander came forward to help her slide down from her mount. "Ye dinna have to meet him, Margaret. 'Tis not too late to turn back."

"I am not turning back," she said. If she could, she hoped to be forgiven by her uncle for falling in love with Alexander. For months, she had yearned to explain to him what had happened and how it had happened. But her needs were mostly irrelevant now.

She had one real ambition—to save Isabella.

Alexander guided her forward and they walked along the snow-covered stone path to the chapel's door. Alexander swung it open for her, but then he made her wait so he could enter first. Margaret only followed when he turned and indicated that it was safe for her to do so.

Margaret stepped inside the century-old stone church. She saw the group of men standing at the end of the knave, which included William and her uncle.

Buchan looked at her, his eyes dark with anger. She cringed.

William ran up the knave, toward her. "Meg!"

Her tension vanished. She could not believe how much he had grown since she had last seen him! He had seemed more of a boy then, but suddenly, she was faced with a grown man. "Will!"

She leapt into his arms and he hugged her, hard, rocking her as he did so. Then he stepped back and stared, amazed. "How beautiful you are!"

She smiled. "You look so well, too. I am happy, Will." And then she saw him glance at Alexander and she watched the two men whom she loved most in this world exchange long looks. There was a great deal of relief. She understood that both men had come to terms with one another—for her sake.

She glanced at her uncle now. He was so angry with her. Trembling, sick with dread, she slowly walked to him. "Uncle John."

He was breathing hard. "Ye betrayed me."

"I did not mean to fall in love with him."

"Love? Love has *nothing* to do with marriage!" Buchan said harshly.

"Uncle, I love you, I always have and I always will—but I fell in love with Alexander. I did not mean to. I fought my every emotion."

"You fought your emotion? You married him."

"I had to choose."

"There was no choice to make!" her uncle cried. "I made the choice for you!"

She brushed aside incipient tears. "Is it too much to ask for your forgiveness?"

"You turned your back on us all, on your mother, your father, on your brother, on me!" Buchan said. His nose was red and moisture glistened upon his eyes. "I will never forgive you, Margaret. I disowned you the day you fled Sir Guy—and swore your fealty to Bruce."

She inhaled, trembling. "I so wish for your forgive-

432		A ROSE IN THE STORM

ness, but so be it. Just know, Uncle, that I am in grief
over losing you."

He made a harsh, dismissive sound. "Is this why you
have asked for a meeting? To seek my forgiveness? If so,
you have wasted my time."

"I had to see you, I had to explain and I had to try
to persuade you to forgive me. But there is more." She
paused.

He slowly smiled at her, but it was unpleasant and
cold, as if he knew what would come next. "Of course."

"Uncle, I wish to talk to you about Isabella."

"Do not bring up her name!"

"Please, forgive Isabella. She is young and foolish, impulsive and reckless. She did not know what they wanted
of her—and she did not think it through. Bruce took advantage of her—a young, naive woman. And had she not
helped him, he would have forced her."

He snarled, "She is a whore."

"She was used by an older, powerful and clever man!
You loved her! I know—I saw it, time and again! How
can you stop loving her now?"

"I stopped loving her long ago."

Margaret believed him. But she had never thought
their marriage salvageable. She only wanted to save Isabella's life. "This is her time of need. How can you refuse
to aid her? I understand why you will not take her back
as your wife, even if, in God's eyes, she will always be
your wife. But do you want to see her hanged? Just aid
her, Uncle, just help her escape the king's rage, help her
avoid execution."

He was shaking, but he smiled tightly now. "King
Edward is not having her executed. How fortunate for
Isabella."

Margaret froze. His smile was so savage that she feared whatever punishment had already been meted out.

"King Edward has ordered her *caged*."

"Caged?" Had she misheard?

"She is in a cage at Berwick! She has been caged like an animal, and she has been displayed so anyone, everyone, can see her, taunt her, insult her, condemn her for the treacherous bitch she is! And she will stay in that cage until she dies!"

Margaret stared, stunned.

"God damn her to hell. And God damn you, Margaret," he choked. "I trusted you!"

"I am sorry," she managed to say. As they stared at one another, both of them in tears, for an instant she thought he was going to come to her and forgive her after all. But then he whirled and strode through a back door and out of the chapel.

William rushed to her. "I love you," he said.

She could not speak now and she nodded.

"And I am happy for you!" With that, he turned and hurried after the Earl of Buchan.

Margaret did not move. Alexander put his arm around her. She looked up at him. "I am truly a MacDonald now."

"Aye."

Castle Fyne, Scotland—January, 1307

MARGARET PAUSED ON the threshold of the bedchamber that had belonged to her parents, holding her slightly protruding belly in both hands. She looked down at her tummy and smiled warmly at her unborn child. "We are home, little one," she whispered. "Welcome."

There was so much disbelief—and so much relief. Castle Fyne was hers again. They were home.

As she stood there, she could hear Alexander in the great room below with his two brothers. He had been planning his attack upon Castle Fyne ever since she had met her uncle and Will at the MacSween chapel. A January siege had been devised. The entire plan was to retake Castle Fyne, fortify it, and then Alexander could join Bruce.

Bruce had been forced to flee Dunaverty after all, as the English pursued him there, and he had hidden upon Rathlin Island. But he continued to solicit support amongst a great many clans, including those in the western islands. Promises of men and arms had begun to come to fruition. Bruce had sent a small army to raid the castle upon Arran, as it was being supplied by the English. The raid had been a success, and now Bruce was gathering up several armies, a great many ships, preparing to launch an attack upon the mainland.

As for the attack on Castle Fyne, it had been swift. With Sir Guy now dead, a great many of his men had simply fled the battle. His remaining men had not been eager to defend the stronghold. The keep had fallen to the MacDonald brothers in a single day.

Margaret knew she had no right to the happiness she felt then. But her pregnancy had changed everything. Even with the war looming, she had never been as happy, and she had never loved Alexander more. She wandered to the chamber's open window and stared down at the loch. Patches of ice floated upon the nearfrozen waters. Snow-clad trees covered the shores.

She thought of her mother, her heart lurching. How pleased Mary MacDougall would be—Margaret had no doubt. She had loved her husband, and she had given her daughter Castle Fyne. Now Margaret was following in her mother's footsteps, loving Alexander, and being able to one day bequeath her daughter with the same gift.

It was foolish, but she almost felt her gentle presence, as if she were close by, smiling at her.

She could still hear the men below in animated conversation—the three brothers were warriors, and they were relishing their victory. Cups of wine were being raised. Boasts were being made, jests were being told. Food was demanded.

And she recalled the first time she had ever seen Alexander, below the castle walls, when he had come to demand her surrender. She smiled. He had been a proud and great warrior then, he remained a proud and great warrior now, and he was her husband.

How frightened she had been. How the past year had changed their lives. How fortunate she was, that they had both survived the first months of Bruce's war.

She sobered, thinking of Christina Seton—and then of Marjorie. Atholl had been captured with the queen and her women—he was in London, awaiting trial. No one believed he would survive; the trial was meant to be a spectacle. She prayed for him and the women daily.

She prayed for Isabella.

How she wished she could visit her. How she wished she could send her a letter. But she could not. All Margaret could do was send her prayers and love.

A soft knock outside the open tower door interrupted her thoughts. Margaret turned, warmth rushing through her.

Juliana MacDougall stood there. And she looked so very much like her mother, there was no doubt that they were sisters. She was a slim, beautiful woman with red-brown hair and bright blue eyes. They had met when

Alasdair Og and she had come to Kintyre. They had become friends instantly. Juliana understood what it was like to love one's enemy, and to choose that love over family.

She came into the room. "What a wonderful day this is. Mary would be so proud of you."

Margaret clasped her hand. "I thought I felt her here, a moment ago. Silly, isn't it?"

"You don't believe in ghosts?" Juliana smiled.

Of course she did. It was a Scottish tradition. "Thank you for your help—yours and Alasdair's."

"We were pleased to help you meet Buchan, and even more pleased to help young Alexander take Castle Fyne."

"I am so glad I have a new friend," Margaret said impulsively.

Juliana took her hand. "When it is time for the birthing, send for me. I wish to be here."

Margaret nodded, too moved to speak.

Rapid footsteps sounded, booted spurs clinging. Margaret felt her heart skip and she turned. Alexander came striding into the room, appearing very satisfied.

He smiled at Juliana. "My brother is asking for ye, Lady Juliana. He wants ye to join him at our table. He says he hasn't seen in ye in two entire days!" Alexander laughed.

Margaret thrilled at the sound, as it was so rare.

"Men," Juliana said to Margaret with mock exasperation. "Just remember to always be at your husband's beck and call, and your marriage will be fine." Juliana kissed her cheek, patted Alexander on the arm and left.

Margaret went into his strong arms. "Thank you."

He raised his brows as if he had no idea of what she spoke. "Fer what, pray tell?"

"For taking Castle Fyne back for us—for our daughter."

His eyes widened. "Do ye carry a girl?"

"I don't know…but I do know that one day we will have a daughter, and Castle Fyne will be her dowry, just as it was mine."

"And what of our sons?"

"You will have to win more lands," she said, at once teasing and also meaning it.

He smiled at her. "I will manage that, Margaret, if it is yer wish."

She clasped his face in her hands. "I am so fortunate."

"I am the one with good fortune," he said.

And then they both turned to admire the majesty of the Highland day in the midst of a snow-filled winter.

The loch below gleamed as brightly as a diamond. Dark and lush, green forests covered the land. Snowy mountain caps jutted into the sky. Eagles soared.

They held hands and Margaret whispered, "It is so beautiful—so quiet, so peaceful."

"Aye."

She knew he was thinking that the respite from Bruce's war for Scotland's independence was almost over. "We must enjoy these next few days and weeks," she said.

He pulled her close. "Dinna be afraid."

She looked up at him. "I'm not."

She thought about how brave and bold Robert Bruce was—how great his ambition. He had stolen a crown, he had gone to war against the mightiest army in the land, he had survived massacres and defeats, and now he returned to fight for Scotland another time.

And Alexander would be at his side. He was a warrior in his heart and in his soul. She had known it before she ever loved him, just as she had known it when they married. She could not imagine him differently. In times of war, he would go to battle; in times of peace, like these, he would be at her side.

How she hoped King Robert defeated the English, and quickly, so a real and lasting peace might befall Scotland.

She was beginning to believe that he would succeed.

She realized the nature of her thoughts and she smiled. "I am such a MacDonald now."

"Good." He smiled back at her.

Bruce would return, because he was Scotland's rightful king. He would fight to free the country from England's yoke. And if God willed it, he would triumph, with Alexander at his side.

While she would be at Castle Fyne, caring for their newborn child.

And now, she would leave politics and wars to the men. She had had enough of wartime intrigues, enough to last a lifetime.

* * * * *

Dear Readers,

When my publisher asked me if I would like to write a series of romance novels set in the Highlands, my immediate reaction was yes—if the period could be medieval. And as I began to dig into the era, I never imagined that such a huge, epic story like *A Rose in the Storm* would result. There is nothing that inspires me as much as an innocent heroine swept up in historical events beyond her control, and in this case, the war for Scotland's throne.

This novel is a work of fiction. However, I have tried to portray historical events and historical figures as accurately as possible. But this period in Scotland's history is filled with conflicting accounts and huge gaps in information, leaving me to pick and choose what I want to write, and where I wish to fill in the blanks. It is also a period of myriad and ever changing politics and alliances. I have done my best to sort through what must seem to be terribly confusing characters and events. Any errors in fact are mine.

For the sake of the story, I have deliberately taken a few liberties.

Margaret Comyn is a fictional character, but the great Comyn family, both the earls of Buchan and Badenoch, are not. The Comyn family came to power in the north and south of Scotland in the thirteenth century, and their power increased when their relation, John Balliol, became king in 1292. Likewise, the great Clan Dougall also became preeminent under King John. Alexander of Argyll was married to a Comyn, making for a powerful alliance between the Comyn family and Clan Dougall.

The Comyns and MacDougalls fought against the English in Scotland's Wars for Independence until the very day that Bruce murdered Red John Comyn, Lord of Badenoch, in a church in Dumfries. On that day, old alliances were broken, and new ones formed. On that day, both Comyn and MacDougall took to the field against Robert Bruce, in support of King Edward.

Margaret could have existed. History in this time period is not kind to women. It is usual to find a family tree where the sons' names are listed, but the daughters are unnamed—although their husbands might be named. Often the birth of a female was not even recorded.

Her father, Master William, was supposed to have received the bishopric of St. Andrews, and was disappointed when he did not. I have discovered nothing else about him. But that is the beauty of this time period— sometimes, historical details abound; more often, they do not. And then the lucky author—me—gets to fill in the gaps.

Alexander MacDougall of Argyll did have two sisters, Mary and Juliana. When I first "invented" Margaret, I gave her a MacDougall mother: Mary MacDougall, a completely fictional character. Imagine my surprise when I learned that Alexander of Argyll really had a sister named Mary, and therefore, he was really Margaret's uncle (another invention of mine). However, in history, Mary was married to three other men; it is pure poetic license on my part to have had her married to William. Unless, of course, she was married a fourth time....

Alexander MacDonald, the Wolf of Lochaber, is also a fictional character. I based the legend of the Wolf of Lochaber very loosely upon a different legend. In the late fourteenth century, the notorious Wolf of Badenoch was excommunicated for choosing his mistress over his wife, and in revenge, he burned a cathedral to the ground—

along with a nearby town. It was unforgettable, and so Alexander, the Wolf of Lochaber, was born.

But he could have existed, as well. Angus Mor had two sons, Alexander "Alasdair" Og and Angus Og, as I have described. The enmity between Clan Donald and Clan Dougall was a blood feud. Yet Alexander Og did marry Juliana MacDougall, sometime before 1292. It is not clear why, or how the union came to be. Some historians believe that Alexander Og died in 1299 in the Massacre of Clan Donald. Others believe that he died in 1308, when he was captured while fighting against Bruce—having taken his wife's family's side in the war. If he did die in 1299, then no one quite knows who the other Alexander MacDonald was in 1308, or where he came from.

In 1309, Bruce wreaked his vengeance upon the Comyn family in the north of Scotland, ending their power for all time. A deliberate misrepresentation on my part was the battle led by John the Lame of Argyll against Robert Bruce and his men in the late summer of 1306, when Bruce and his army were in hiding after the massacre at Methven. There were two battles, not one. After the first successful attack, Bruce sent the women to a castle on a nearby loch for safety, and then there was the second, as devastating, attack. He then sent the women and his warhorses back to Kildrummy as I have described, while he made his way across Scotland and to Dunaverty.

Sir Guy is also a fictional character, Guy being a family name (Aymer had an uncle of that name). But the mighty and oh-so-impressive Aymer de Valence—who was King Edward's military commander in Scotland, and the following year, became Earl of Pembroke—was not.

And finally, there is Isabella, both the Countess of Buchan and the Countess of Fife.

Poor Isabella. She did ride away in the middle of the night to attend Bruce's coronation, and stand in for her brother, the Earl of Fife. One can only assume that her husband, the Earl of Buchan, was enraged. Gossip held at the time that she and Bruce were lovers. And her fate was to be captured with the other women at St. Duthac, and imprisoned in a cage for four years. She was moved to a friary, perhaps because she remained an important prisoner, at which point, her fate remains unknown.

I have always been fascinated by the struggle of women to find courage and strength in bygone times of great adversity, when all power was reserved to men, when women were either chattel or pawns, and merely wives and mothers. I hope you have enjoyed Margaret's story of struggle, challenge and survival—and yes, of love.

Sincerely,
Brenda Joyce